NO STRANGERS HERE

Books by Carlene O'Connor

Irish Village Mysteries

MURDER IN AN IRISH VILLAGE

MURDER AT AN IRISH WEDDING

MURDER IN AN IRISH CHURCHYARD

MURDER IN AN IRISH PUB

MURDER IN AN IRISH COTTAGE

MURDER AT AN IRISH CHRISTMAS

MURDER IN AN IRISH BOOKSHOP

MURDER ON AN IRISH FARM

CHRISTMAS COCOA MURDER
(with Maddie Day and Alex Erickson)

CHRISTMAS SCARF MURDER
(with Maddie Day and Peggy Ehrhart)

A Home to Ireland Mystery

MURDER IN GALWAY

MURDER IN CONNEMARA

A County Kerry Mystery

NO STRANGERS HERE

Published by Kensington Publishing Corp.

A County Kerry Mystery

NO STRANGERS HERE

USA Today Bestselling Author

CARLENE O'CONNOR

KENSINGTON
PUBLISHING CORP.

www.kensingtonbooks.com

KENSINGTON BOOKS are published by

Kensington Publishing Corp.
119 West 40th Street
New York, NY 10018

Copyright © 2022 by Mary Carter

Library of Congress Card Catalogue Number: 2022939861

ISBN: 978-1-4967-3752-6
First Kensington Hardcover Edition: November 2022

ISBN: 978-1-4967-3754-0 (e-book)

10 9 8 7 6 5 4 3 2 1

Printed in the United States of America

First, this book is dedicated to my parents. My mother, Pat Carter, who could have been a mystery writer herself, and was instrumental in listening to plot point after plot point as I worked through the story, offering advice and encouragement. Next, to my late father, Carl Carter. Forever in our hearts. I love you, Dad. I hope you are soaring like an eagle.

I also need to give a nod to Fungie the Dolphin. I didn't get to meet you, but you brought joy to so many and are missed. This book is also dedicated to veterinarians for all the work you do despite the many hardships the profession brings. And last, to the people of Dingle. Let me tell my readers, this is a work of fiction, and none of the murderous bits are based on the lovely people who live there.

There are no strangers here; Only friends you haven't yet met.

—William Butler Yeats

CHAPTER 1

*D*OWNTOWN DINGLE WAS COMING BACK FROM THE DEAD TO CELE-brate Saoirse Griffin's thirteenth birthday. Bang on time. She planted herself alongside the Fungie the Dolphin statue, *the* primo spot to witness the sun's demise. The fiery star plunged into the Atlantic, unleashing a triple crown of red, orange, and purple onto the skies. A mishmash of boats winked from the harbor, and a string of white lights dangled above Strand Street like a row of blazing candles. Make a wish. *Lá breithlá shona duit. Happy birthday* to her. *Ser-sha, ser-sha, watcha searching for?* Lads at school liked to sing that while grabbing their dirty trousers and crooning they got what she was searching for "right here." They hoped it would make her cry, but she liked it. Not the grabby bits, but the searching part. She *was* a searcher. A spy. She was going to have the best birthday of all birthdays of anyone who had ever lived. *Period.* If only she had someone to party with. Not a bother; all spies were lonely. It took guts to conquer this world alone, and Saoirse wasn't going to waste a single minute crying over it. *Dry your eyes,* her mammy always said. *Now.*

She placed the palm of her hand on the dolphin's bronze head, wishing it was slick and gray, wishing Fungie was still with them, wondering if he was out there all alone, chirping into the depths of the ocean, fighting his way back to her. Fungie had been the town dolphin for more than thirty years. Saoirse couldn't imagine ever being that old. Her mam said he had gone off to die, that it was nature's way. Nature could stuff it. She wanted him back.

After a gloomy spring, when folks either wrestled with brellies twisting in the wind, or darted in and out of the colorful shops, pubs, and restaurants, cloaked in hooded raincoats, a warm start to June was breathing life back into her harbor town. Strand Street teemed with revelers and mourners. A dance for old people was being held at one end of the street, and a wake for a dead mammy at the other. Irish music spilled out from the pubs competing with the one-man-band-slash-puppeteer camped in front of the statue. He was a scraggly bearded man manipulating a harmonica, drum, banjo, cymbal, and three slack-jawed puppets. With their pale wooden faces, frozen eyes, and gaping red mouths, they looked like miniature corpses being forced to hop up and down just to entertain the living. She knew how they felt. Controlled. Unhappy. Forgotten. Like the dead people who got embalmed so living people could drape over their caskets and wax on about how beautiful they looked now that they were dead. Saoirse would never understand adults. She still couldn't decide what she wanted to happen to her body when she died and sometimes it kept her up late into the night. She wondered if the dead mammy was going to be embalmed or sunburned.

Soon, tourists encircled the puppet-man, euro clutched in their foolish hands. It would do no good to try and nick any of his tips. She'd done that once and he was faster than he looked. He had chased her all the way down to the harbor, forcing her to drop ten euro even though she had only taken five, just so she could get away. Angry bruises had sported on the back of her arm where he'd grabbed her, and they took forever to fade away. *Eejit.* She turned her head, feasting her eyes in the other direction. Finally, Saoirse was going to have a birthday party, and who cared if no one else knew it. She was happy out pretending all the fuss was just for her. She was officially a teenager.

She would prove her mammy wrong; thirteen was *not* an unlucky number and celebrating it wasn't "asking for trouble." They were better off, her mother said, celebrating it next weekend when she was thirteen and one week. But next weekend wasn't her birthday. It was now. Tonight. A Saturday to boot. And even if it was asking for trouble, she'd pick that over another night watching *Mrs. Brown's*

Boys and eating beans straight out of the can. *Gross.* Saoirse had nicked a full bottle of Irish Cream, which she'd then left at their door with a bow, and she didn't even have to sneak out of the house. An hour later, her mammy was flat-out on the sofa, snoring as the telly prattled on, the empty bottle tipped sideways on the floor.

She lingered at the end of the street, surveying her options, and there were three. Option One: Cross the street to the harbor and pick a boat. So many choices! Not just dirty old trawlers, where fishermen left crumpled bills and half-smoked fags lying about in heaps, but sailboats, and speedboats, and the odd fancy one, like the medium-sized white one she'd been keeping her eye on: *Dreamscape.*

Some of them kept their hatches locked stingy-tight, but there were always a few that yawned opened at her touch. Saoirse was a strong swimmer, and a mad climber. Should she start with the boats, or leave them for the end? Tonight was also the first Saturday in June which meant Option Two: The old people would be dancing. It was so easy to slip a hand into their suit pockets as they shuffled around to trad music, leaving their treasures behind on ring-marked tables. And today, the trifecta. There was Option Three: The dead mammy's fundraiser.

Cancer had taken her "way too young" and they were collecting money for the three children and husband she'd left behind. No one had held a fundraiser when Saoirse's father had been carted off to jail and charged with a "domestic"—and Saoirse wasn't quite sure what that even meant. Why didn't they just say it was for getting drunk and being mean? He really was mean when he was drunk. Would jail make him nicer? Doubtful. Because right now, things were worse than when he was around. Now they had no money and her mam was sad all the time. Like all the time. And nobody gave a fart about it. How was that fair? Their house had been egged three nights in a row. Maybe Saoirse all by herself wasn't worth it; maybe she was supposed to scrub up and put on a dress, or maybe she needed cute brothers and sisters. Or maybe her mammy needed to get cancer, or maybe people only cared about you if you were dead.

After agonizing over her choices, she had finally come to a decision. It was her birthday; she would hit them all, starting with the dance and ending on the fancy white boat. Think of all the prezzies she'd collect! Maybe she'd even spend the night on the boat, letting the waves rock her to sleep. She'd keep nicking things until her purple backpack was stuffed. No one would notice her. No one ever did. The head-shrinker she'd been forced to see after Detective Byrne had nearly killed her father with his fists, leaving him in a bloody heap in their garden, taught her that adversity could be an adversary. You could take a negative and make it positive. She was an invisible girl who nicked things.

Coins from pockets and cubbyholes, lipstick from handbags and bathroom cabinets, fags from tabletops—she could make one sweep through a pub after happy hour, and by the time she'd reached the back door, her pockets would be overflowing. Drunk people were such eejits, although now that she was thirteen, she was determined she was going to have her first taste of drink. She was a troublemaker, like her da.

But after the bullies, after those taunts, she'd turned it around just like the head-doctor taught her. *Ser-sha, ser-sha, watcha searching for?* Tonight she was searching for birthday presents. She wondered if that detective was here, somewhere in the crowd. Was he shaking his hips or comforting motherless children at the wake? He'd probably forgotten all about her. She was supposed to call him Mr. Byrne now; he was no longer a detective because of nearly killing her father. Maybe if he knew it was her birthday, he would have thrown a party for her. She had a feeling he wouldn't approve of her shenanigans, but who cared? He was no longer a detective. If he didn't follow the law, why should she?

She was about to slip into the pub where the gray-hairs danced, when she stole another glance at *Dreamscape*. A person was exiting the fancy white boat, dressed all in black with a hat. Was it another street performer? Or someone famous? Was he so famous he didn't want to be recognized? Imagine if she nicked something off a celebrity. That would be a dream come true. She decided the mysterious figure was a man, although it was hard to tell, the coat was so baggy. His hands were shoved in his pockets, and face down so all she could see was the top of his dark cap. He was striding away from the boat now, headed for Strand Street. This was her chance. He was wearing mourning clothing; no doubt his destination was the wake. He'd probably be away from the boat for hours. She hurried across the street to the harbor, keeping her eyes trained on the man in black as they switched sides, craning her head and watching him until he disappeared into the crowd. *Dreamscape.* What a perfect name. Sneaking onto this fancy boat was going to be a birthday dream come true.

CHAPTER 2

*T*HE DEAD MAN WORE A DESIGNER SUIT TO THE BEACH. HE WAS found along Slea Head Drive, at the base of a small cliff, on Clogher Strand. There he was, early on a Sunday morning in June, reposed against a craggy boulder in his fancy navy suit, starched white shirt, and vibrant green tie. Next to his body, two words had been formed using sixty-nine gleaming black stones: LAST DANCE. The stones popped against the pale sand. It wasn't a whisper; it was a shout. His legs were straight out in front of him, his hands rested palms-up on his thighs, and his sky-blue eyes were open, forever staring out to sea. The only visible sign of distress was the white foam pooling at the corners of his gaped mouth. The lines fanning out across his face, and wisps of silver hair clinging to a mostly bald head betrayed his advanced age. A card with a black background peeked out of the dead man's suit pocket. Detective Inspector Cormac O'Brien maneuvered around the cordon they'd placed around the body to get a closer look.

A red-faced Devil sporting a lascivious grin stared back. "Would you look at this?" He turned to Detective Sergeant Neely, but her face was buried in her iPad, and her honey-colored hair, whipped around by the wind, obscured her eyes. He was the new sheriff in town, as they said in the black-and-white films he loved to watch, and, despite being by-the-book polite, the rest of the team seemed on a mission to wall him out. Swallowing his frustration and resisting the urge to yank the electronic yoke from her hands and chuck it into the sea, Cormac turned back to the strange card. He was dying to pluck it out of the dead man's pocket, but Cormac could not touch the body or any of the tantalizing evidence. The state pathologist had been notified, and a local coroner, deputy state pathologist, and technical unit were on the way. Once it was officially declared a crime scene and processed for evidence, they would transport the body to Kerry General Hospital and, fingers and toes crossed, the postmortem would begin in the morning. They already had an identification on their victim, for this was Dingle, County Kerry, Ireland, and the man was a local.

Cormac once again turned to Sergeant Neely, the only member of the Dingle Gardaí he'd allowed to remain with him on the small curved beach. Although she was no doubt used to being the one in charge, she was giving Cormac room, letting him do his thing. Not that she had much choice, but Cormac was grateful she wasn't sending out any territorial vibes, or Cormac would be forced to pull rank. The guards back in Killarney sometimes called Cormac "Napoleon" behind his back, and he didn't need that business starting up here. The rest of the guards were gathered in the car park, along the road, and perched atop the cliff.

"I want to go over it again."

This time D.S. Neely heard him, and her head popped up. She was somewhere in her sixties if he had to guess, but she was well-preserved with a lean, strong body. "Right, so." If she was sick and tired of repeating herself, she had the decency not to show it. Repetition helped Cormac think. "Johnny O'Reilly, sixty-nine years of age, wealthy racehorse owner. The O'Reillys have a massive estate and horse barns just outside of town. Ever hear of Ruby?" D.S. Neely was looking at Cormac as if the answer should be a resounding yes.

"Ruby slippers?" he quipped.

Neely frowned. "What's that now?"

"Click my heels three times?" He attempted a smile. "No place like home?"

Neely shook her head, a look of exasperation stamped on her face. "She was a beauty of a racehorse, so she was. Ruby was the O'Reillys' pride and joy. Their first million-pound-purse winner."

Cormac tried to feign interest. It was obvious the sergeant expected him to be impressed. "Her sire was named Last Dance."

Now she had his attention. "Is that so?" He glanced at the message written in stone and waited for her to offer more. She did not. "Let me guess. Another million-euro-purse-winner?"

She shook her head. "You really don't know?" The tone of her voice was clear. He was an eejit.

He threw open his arms. "Indulge me."

"The poor thing was struck dead in a road accident before he could even run his first race." She paused. "It was all over the news, like." Her eyes traveled over him as if assessing his worth. "But I suppose you were just a lad in short trousers."

"What else?" He smiled and tried to sound chipper, which just elicited another frown. He'd been warned about the locals. Friendly, if you kept your distance. She returned to her electronic notes. "In town, Johnny was known for his other proclivities." She cleared her throat. "Namely dancing and women."

"I thought he was a married man."

A look flickered across her face, as if she'd just tasted something foul. "He's married, alright. Róisín O'Reilly." She leaned in. "She'll strike the fear of God into ya, so she will."

Cormac would get to the widow later. He couldn't stop staring at those stones. *Last Dance.* Was it just a euphemism or did it refer to this dead horse? "How long ago was this road accident?"

She lifted her head as she silently counted. "Has to be well over twenty-five years ago. Maybe longer?"

In this case, a cigar was just a cigar and Last Dance just meant *last dance.* "How well do you know this fisherman?"

"Finbar? I've known him all me life."

They turned their gaze to the cliff where puffs of cigarette smoke hovered over Finbar Malone's head before dissipating in the crisp air. He looked the part of an old fisherman, with a grizzled white beard and seafaring attire. A tall and sturdy man to boot. You had to be tough to make the ocean your mistress. He'd been the one to find the body, and Cormac found his initial statement odd. He said he'd stopped here to have a smoke in peace before going home to the missus. When he spotted the body, he clambered to the nearest cottage to request a call out to the guards, and this was the odd part—"*Because I don't own a mobile phone.*"

As if sensing he was being watched, Finbar looked down and met Cormac's eyes straight on. The waves had picked up, lapping farther up the shoreline. "A working fisherman without a mobile phone?" *That dog don't hunt.* The fisherman was lying. But why would he lie about a mobile phone?

"Perhaps he meant he didn't have it with him," Neely said. "Or maybe it wasn't charged."

"But that's not what he said, is it?"

Neely directed her gaze to Finbar Malone. "Finbar Malone is harmless." She paused. "*Sir,*" she added emphatically.

Cormac didn't need the "sir" routine. He didn't even want to be called Inspector or D.I. O'Brien. He'd rather everyone just call him Cormac, or Mac, and go about their business. Hell, even *Napoleon* was better than *sir.* But with this high-profile case, he was going to need all the clout he could get. His gaze returned to the fisherman. He didn't know why, but he was lying. Regardless, Cormac was grateful that the burly man hadn't trampled all over Cormac's murder scene in his clunky boots. His thoughts returned to Finbar's first words when Cormac had arrived on scene. *Shock of me life, I'm telling ye. On the beach in a suit? Dead as a doornail. I wasn't expecting that, now.*

What had he been expecting?

Cormac had been a member of An Garda Síochána going on nineteen years now, and an inspector for three. Stationed out of Killarney, he was an outsider in this close-knit Dingle community. This was his first murder probe, and given the victim was one of the "elite," he was going to have multiple sets of eyes on him, a collective hot breath on his neck. There would be no room for error.

Too treacherous to swim, this tucked-away beach was a popular spot for social media photos. Dramatic waves, a curved white beach abutting a rocky cliff, a patchwork of green and brown mountains rising up to the sky—it was Insta-worthy, as the kids said. Cormac, at thirty-nine, felt too old to be in the Insta-anything crowd, and too young to be with the old-timers. But right now, planted in front of this fascinating scene, he felt he was at the beginning of what could be the murder inquiry of the century. Certainly of his life-time. Cormac was having trouble reconciling the jaw-dropping scenery with the bizarre scene in front of him. The stones fasci-nated him. Every one of them had been coated with a clear gloss and was nearly identical in size. "Sixty-nine stones."

"You counted them?" From the tone of her voice such a thing would have never occurred to Neely.

"I did. And yer man here was sixty-nine years of age."

"Isn't that something," Sergeant Neely said, but she looked at Cormac as she said it.

The stones had not all been sourced from this beach, at least not at the last minute. Finding ones nearly identical in size would have taken a tremendous amount of time and effort. And then their killer had painted them, ensuring that when the sun kissed them, they would sparkle.

The gloss was a small clue, but it was at least a thread to pull on. Even cunning killers were human. And humans were gloriously im-perfect. Painted stones and a posed body ruled out suicide, some-thing he'd already heard guards begin to utter under their breath. No way was this an elaborate suicide. Although . . . if one were to choose an absolutely gorgeous place to die, it didn't get much bet-ter than this. Mountains and cliffs that drew one's eyes up to the skies, Slea Head Drive curving through, and the great Atlantic roar-ing below. If God was an artist, then the Dingle Peninsula was his masterpiece. But why pose the body here? Did this exact location have significance to the killer?

"The waves are advancing," Neely said in alarm, pointing. Her yellow visibility vest flapped in the wind, distracting Cormac, mak-ing him think of the poet Seamus Heaney and how he'd once de-scribed the weather in Dingle as "loud." It took Cormac a moment to see what had agitated Neely. Frothy waves licked at the soles of the dead man's leather shoes. "Shit. See if we can get some kind of plastic barrier," he said. "Something to toss over them."

"I mentioned that ages ago," Neely said under her breath as she hurried back toward the car park, holding her iPad aloft and care-fully following the shoreline. *Had she?* He'd been lost in thought, no doubt. His ability to shut everything else out while concentrating was both a blessing and a curse. He supposed there was no getting through this investigation without ruffling some feathers. He'd been trying his hardest to bond with them, but they were going to have to meet him halfway. He was here to solve a murder, not make friends, although truth be told, he was a friendly sort by nature. His mam always said he could talk the hind leg off a horse. Cormac stared into the dead man's lifeless blue eyes. He had a feeling he'd be seeing them in his dreams the rest of his life.

"Who did this to you?" Above, a helicopter whirred, and Cormac could feel the *thwack thwack thwack* in his chest. Out on the sea the Irish Coast Guard churned, directing boats away from the inlet. A buzz of excitement hung in the air, mingling with cigarette smoke and that distinct ocean tang. Seagulls screeched above, as if they too were glued to the drama. Despite the wind, it was a bright morning, blue sky smiling down at them, but ominous clouds hung in the periphery like actors gearing up for a dramatic entrance. Sergeant Neely returned, clutching a clear plastic cover with gloved hands. She and Cormac tucked it over the dead man's shoes and around the sides of his legs. Alongside the body, a rocky finger extended from the cliff, and something black and small flapped in the wind. Cormac leaned in. "There's a piece of black fabric caught on the rock," he said.

"Clothing?" she asked.

"No." He removed a pair of tweezers from his pocket. "Evidence bag?"

She reached into the plastic bin they'd set up on the shoreline and handed him one. He lifted the piece of fabric and examined it up close. "It's not a rubbish bag. It looks like some kind of a tarp." He hesitated. "Like a body bag."

"A body bag?"

His eyes traveled over the body. "Could be he was brought here in a body bag." Did their killer work for law enforcement? The morgue?

"Based on this?" Neely jiggled the evidence bag as he dropped the shard into it. She drew it close and stared at it. "Bit of a stretch, don't ya think?"

"It would explain how he was brought up to the beach in a boat, and yet he's not wet," Cormac said. Apart from his shoes, the dead man was dry as a bone.

"Perhaps he's just had time to dry," she said. "The wind alone could have done the trick."

"Inspector," a guard on the other side of beach yelled. "We have footprints."

Sticking to the shoreline, Cormac and D.S. Neely crossed to the base of the hill. There, on the incline, small indentations could be seen ascending the muddy hill. "Jesus," Neely said. "It's a young one."

"Maybe a kid found the body first," the guard said. "Scrambled away out of fear."

Cormac examined the prints. "They're only going up."

The guard frowned. "What?"

"If a kid found the body, we would see prints going both ways." He gestured as he spoke. "The prints are only going up."

"Then where did the kid come from?" the guard asked.

"A boat," Cormac said. All heads turned to the waves pounding the shore as they pondered this. "Let's cordon this hillside off so the technical team can get impressions." The guard nodded. "Check for more prints, and any signs of disturbances at the top of the hill."

"Right away." The guard scrambled back up and soon the rest were efficiently conducting a search. "We have more," the guard yelled back. "The kid at least made it to the top of the hill."

"I want impressions of all of them," Cormac said.

"What are you doing?" Neely said. "You can see that this is a suicide, can you not?"

"Suicide?" he said. "No." He understood why she wanted to label it thus. A suicide would mean this case was closed. Nothing to fear. Dingle was a place for Irish music, a pint or twelve, and the best seafood chowder in the country. A place for water sports and boating. Quaint and colorful little shops. Murphy's Ice Cream. An outdoor museum of ancient architecture. Ferries to the Blasket Islands. Wine imported from Spain. Downtown even had a small, yet he had to admit, charming aquarium. Fish didn't set off his allergies; he could do fish. Irish was spoken everywhere you turned, and every sign included the Irish translation. This was the Gaeltacht region, the Wild Atlantic Way, the thirty-mile-long Dingle Peninsula. *Ryan's Daughter . . . Wasn't that filmed here? Yes, that's right, bragging rights.* It was bad enough that Fungie the Dolphin had disappeared. Murder wasn't anywhere in the tourist brochures.

Cormac headed back along the shoreline and Neely followed. They stopped when they reached their original spot near the body. "Make the argument for suicide."

Neely pointed out the vial and syringe they'd found lying on the sand near his hip. Although they couldn't touch it, they had zeroed in on the vial with a camera lens and read the label: RELEASE. The department iPad had informed them it was a euthanasia medication used by veterinarians. "He owned a lot of horses and employed a lot of vets," she said. "He could have easily gotten ahold of the medication and syringe." Next, she gestured to the cryptic message in stone. "He also left a note."

"Does he mean 'Last Dance' as in 'Goodbye, cruel world'?"

"He could be paying homage to his horse too."

"Why would a wealthy dancing man take his own life in such an extravagant way?" Cormac asked. "Had he ever threatened suicide before?"

Neely took a step forward. "He was stepping out on the wife. My guess? She threatened divorce. He wouldn't have wanted all that publicity. He was a man of means. This is an elaborate way to go, I'll give you that, but it's suicide."

"He had access to the medication and syringe and left a note," Cormac repeated. "What else?" If she was going to insist this was suicide, which it was not, she was going to have to give him cold, hard facts.

She glanced around the beach. "There's no evidence that another person was here."

"There's no evidence that *he* was here either."

Her frown deepened. "Inspector?"

"Besides ours—do you see any tracks in the sand?"

Her mouth twitched as she took in the beach. "Not a single one."

"Indeed." He loathed that they had walked on the crime scene. They were suited up with gloves and booties and had carefully walked along the water's edge, but he could still see their partial prints marring what had been a pristine stretch of beach. A killer's canvas. "Any signs of a body being dragged?"

She shook her head. "It's as if he just materialized on the beach."

"You think he walked sixteen point six kilometers in the dark with sixty-nine polished stones in his pocket?" He'd clocked the distance from Strand Street in Dingle, where O'Reilly had attended a local dance, to this spot via Slea Head Drive. It was 16.6 kilometers. This man did not walk to his death. "Kills himself yet makes sure not to leave a single footprint on the beach?"

In lieu of an answer, Neely crossed herself. Was he making headway?

"Look at those shoes." Cormac pointed, and she looked. Not a scuff mark or clump of dirt to be seen. "These are the soles of a man who wanted the world to carry him."

"That was Johnny O'Reilly, alright," she said. "Unless he was dancing."

"He didn't do much dancing last night, unless someone brought him a change of shoes." The smooth beach reminded him of the allegorical poem, "Footprints in the Sand." Where your man complains that through all his many troubles God had abandoned him for there were only one set of footprints in the sand. But God is quick to correct him. Cormac's mind raced to the last line: *It was then that I carried you.* He looked again at Johnny O'Reilly. *Who carried you?* Cormac took a moment to study the craggy boulder serving as Johnny's headrest. *Nature's La-Z-Boy.* The long rocky finger extended from the base and disappeared into the ocean. Cormac tilted his head back to have a gawp at the cliff hanging above them. "If this was suicide, why didn't he just jump off the cliff and disappear into the ocean?"

"If it was murder, why didn't the killer just toss him into the ocean?" Neely responded.

"Touché." *Because then we would miss the show.* "Our killer came up by boat. O'Reilly here was in a body bag. He dragged him up this rocky finger, and lucky for us he did."

"Lucky?"

"The body bag ripped."

"Right." Not that Cormac was holding on to much hope that the small piece of ripped bag would lead them to the killer, but it did suggest mistakes had been made. He pointed this out to Neely. "Mistakes?" Neely still sounded guarded, but he had moved the needle just a little, he could tell.

"Mistakes like ripped fabric and failing to notice a young stowaway."

"It would have to be a small boat to maneuver up to this inlet," Neely said.

Cormac nodded. "I think a larger boat was waiting out in the ocean. I think the killer used a life raft, some kind of smaller boat, to bring the body in close. And I think the boat had a stowaway. I'm guessing a young lad."

Neely whistled. "You think the stowaway made a swim for it?"

Cormac nodded. "While our killer was staging the scene. It probably saved his life."

Neely said something in Irish and crossed herself once again. Cormac, rusty on his Irish, did not ask for a translation. He thought of his mam and granny, constantly working their rosary beads until blisters formed on the tips of their soft fingers. At the time he thought they were actually communicating directly with God, sending out distress signals in a Morse code of their own making. "We're definitely looking at a murder scene," Cormac said. "And this clever killer came to play."

CHAPTER 3

*C*ORMAC O'BRIEN STRETCHED AS HE LOOKED OUT AT THE FORMIDA-
ble ocean, wondering if he was the only one who felt overwhelmed
by its mass and power. *You're nothing, human. You'll be long gone, and
I'll still be raging.* He glanced at his watch. Half-eleven on a Sunday
morning. Last known sighting of their victim Saturday night 10:45 P.M.
They were hot on the trail, so to speak, and it excited Cormac more
than he was going to admit, at least to the locals. "Do you do the
crosswords?" he asked Neely.

"No, sir."

"Sudoku, word scramble, crosswords. Keeps the brain sharp."

"Yes, Inspector."

She had no more interest in going over the message. He was having a hard time believing it was a suicide note, but a nod to a dead
horse from a quarter of a century ago? That didn't seem likely either. She cleared her throat. "Something on your mind?"

"We need to schedule a media briefing," Neely said. "We can't
do that until the family is notified. And if we don't notify them immediately—they're going to hear from someone else." The look on
her face conveyed her point. She might as well have said it. *And
that, Detective Inspector O'Brien, would be a total fuck-up.*

"You're right, you're right." The helicopter alone was like a beacon that a drama was unfolding. "I'll do it now." He took a step; her
hand shot out to stop him.

"It might be better to send a familiar face." She pointed to herself as if it wasn't clear whose face she was on about. "I'd be happy to do it for you."

Cormac wanted to push back, but if he was going to get anything done around here, he needed to show that he was a team player. "I appreciate it." He reached into his pocket then handed her his calling card. "Extend my condolences, let them know I'm at the scene, and I'll meet with them as soon as I can."

"I will, so."

"Emphasize that they will not be able to access the murder scene. But assure them we are going to do everything we can."

"Absolutely." She was interrupted by a phone call. "D.S. Neely. Yes. Yes, that's right. *Release.*" She made eye contact with Cormac. "Are you joking me?" From the tone of her voice, this was something big. "Isn't that something. Hang on to that report, I've got the inspector right here." Cormac made a move to take the call, but she'd already hung up. "You might be right," she said. "Maybe this was murder."

She was going to string him along, torture him. "Talk to me."

"Lad at the station thought there was something familiar about Release." She pointed to the vial. Cormac nodded his understanding. "He did some digging and turns out a vial of Release was reported stolen two weeks ago from a local veterinarian clinic."

"Interesting," Cormac said. Neely's face was a portrait of a woman keeping a juicy secret. "And?" he prompted.

"The vet is Dr. Eamon Wilde. His wife is Maeve Wilde. She was the one 'dancing' last night with Johnny O'Reilly. Remember how I said Mr. O'Reilly was stepping out? It's rumored that Maeve Wilde is the one he's been dancing with, alright. Dancing in the sheets," she added, in case he was as dense as he apparently looked.

Cormac nodded, torn between Neely coming around to this being a murder probe, and preferring not to speculate based on gossip. "That is something," he said. Was Dr. Eamon Wilde, this cuckolded vet, their creative killer? Or was it Maeve, a possible home-wrecker, and one of the last people to see their victim alive? "Let's put them at the top of the list." They would be conducting house-to-house interviews immediately.

"The Wildes and the O'Reillys have a complicated history," she said. "O'Reilly's been overworking vets for years. One could hardly blame them if it all got to be too much."

"You were going to meet with the family," Cormac said.

"Right, right."

"Not a word about this vet, or his wife."

She gave him the side-eye. "They'll hear it from someone," she said. "This is Dingle." Before he could reply, she was hurrying back to the car park. She'd be getting her steps in today, and Cormac wondered briefly if she had one of those gadgets that counted them. He turned back to Johnny O'Reilly's body. Given his pristine state, it wasn't hard to imagine him alive, going about his Saturday night. People were creatures of habit. And someone had altered Mr. O'Reilly's creaturely habits last evening. One didn't just disappear from a dance like Cinderella at the stroke of midnight. Someone must have seen something.

"Detective Inspector?" A garda was scrambling down the hill and nearly came close to stepping on the beach before reeling himself in. "The O'Reillys are here."

Cormac's head shot up. "Here? Now?"

"Here," the garda confirmed. "Now."

Cormac stuck to the shoreline as he hurried over to the guard. Together they climbed the hill to the car park. He glanced up toward the blockade, where he could make out a vehicle, something sleek and silver. Shit. The warning had come too late. Detective Sergeant Neely was already halfway up the hill. "Radio the guards at the blockade. Tell the family I'll be there in a moment."

Finbar Malone's boots and cigarette butts had been bagged as evidence, and he'd been cleared to leave. Cormac watched the truck rattle toward the barricade, kicking up a cloud of dust. Somewhere nearby a dog barked. Cormac's thoughts returned to the local veterinarian. His nose was itching already. He was allergic to all creatures great and small. He was going to need his allergy meds, and a new inhaler. It was always something. Then again, in this job Cormac was constantly reminded that no matter how bad he had it, there was always some poor bastard who had it worse. He turned to his team.

"C'mere to me. This local vet and his wife. Someone paint me a picture."

"They have a bit of an unconventional family," a guard answered. He was in his early thirties, thin and pale.

Unconventional. That certainly matched his murder scene. "Go on."

"Maeve Wilde lives in a caravan on the property in the summer months. Eamon is rumored to sleep in the flat above his clinic," the guard continued.

"The secret to a happy marriage. Live far apart and don't speak to each other." Cormac grinned and a few guards laughed politely. As if he knew. "Do they have children?"

"They have a grown son and daughter. The son, Donnecha, is a bit of a hothead. He's a known drug user, been picked up a few times for being a public nuisance."

Was an addict smart enough to stage such an elaborate scene? Cormac didn't think so, but he had to leave room for all possibilities. "He lives in Dingle?"

"Aye. In the summer he's a caretaker for one of the O'Reilly yachts at the harbor."

Cormac's ears perked up. "What size yacht are we talking?"

"I suppose you'd call it a small yacht. But compared to the trawlers and sailboats, it's an upgrade."

Boom. There it was. A small yacht with a lifeboat or rowboat that could have made it up to the boulder with a body. "Does this Donnecha Wilde have a kid?"

"No, sir. Not that I'm aware."

"I want guards to secure the harbor and search that yacht pronto. I want that yacht cordoned off—it could be our original crime scene. I want guards talking to every single person at the harbor, check with the harbormaster and coast guard and see what activity they logged last night—any boats coming and going from that harbor. I want to know who was there last night and if they saw anyone near that yacht—especially a kid. Kill the lights and sirens. I don't want anyone at the harbor to know we're coming."

Guards around him came to life, nodded, and hurried to their squad cars. The activity was going to alarm the family at the barricade, but he couldn't worry about that now.

"There's also a matter of the Wilde daughter," a guard who remained behind said. "You'll probably recognize the name."

He highly doubted it. "Why's that?"

"Dr. Dimpna Wilde."

He felt a jolt. "Out of Dublin? Niall Flor's widow?"

Heads nodded. He knew who she was, alright. Her picture had been on the front page of nearly every Irish newspaper for an entire year. Her husband had been one of three men wrapped up in a retirement investment scheme. Hundreds of wealthy Dubliners had lost their life savings. Niall Flor had hung himself in his carport before they could arrest him. Dr. Dimpna Wilde swore that she and her son had no knowledge of his activities. The Irish government had swooped in and taken most of their assets, and people were both enthralled and divided on the prominent veterinarian. She was a striking figure despite her diminutive size. Pale blond hair nearly the color of bones, and eyes like mint-chocolate-chip ice cream. Neither here nor there, but it was his favorite flavor. *Dimp the Imp,* one tabloid had called her. Another likened her a cross between a fairy and a miniature Viking. After months of watching the nauseating coverage, he'd found himself on Team Dimpna, wanting to believe she wasn't privy to the scandal. He felt a squeeze of pity for the additional drama that was headed her way. *When it rains, it pours.* Especially in Ireland.

Who'd a thunk it? His nose twitched again. Fecking allergies. He faced his team. "I'm going to greet the family, and then—would someone kindly point the way to the nearest chemist?"

CHAPTER 4

*D*R. DIMPNA WILDE SPAYED AN ORANGE-AND-WHITE TABBY, SURGICALLY removed undigested biscuits wrapped in a child's dirty sock from the insides of an overweight bulldog, then vaccinated an African Parrot who called her a "cheeky bitch." When the vet tech turned away, covering a laugh, Dimpna stuck her tongue out at the parrot. She was dying for a cup of tea and a biscuit (minus the dirty sock), but today was not going to be her day. Her next client was a wiggling black Labrador puppy who hadn't chosen his friends wisely. She stitched him up, grateful he'd already been in for his rabies shots, then gave him an injection to ease the stings. A course of antibiotics and he would be right as rain. He looked up at her adoringly, his brown eyes practically mooing with love. She rubbed his puppy head, then laid a finger on his wet nose. "Don't let the bastards get you down." As her assistant started the closing paperwork, she returned to the waiting room with the foul-mouthed parrot and handed it to a rotund older woman who grudgingly looked up from her crossword.

"Cheeky bitch," the parrot said in a loud and cheerful voice, drawing both laughs and glares from people in the waiting room.

"I thought that's what she said," Dimpna said. "Excellent pronunciation." A sheepdog with a bandage wrapped around its left ear lunged on its leash.

"Settle," Dimpna said to the sheepdog in a stern voice, and it lowered its belly to the floor, hiding its eyes. "Good boy."

The older woman lowered her crossword. "I'm so sorry. Me daughter taught her that, and now she won't quit repeating it. I think she does it just to get on me nerves." The woman leaned close to the bird, her nose within biting distance. "Bad girl, Fancy Pants. Bad, bad girl."

"You should probably back off a little—" Dimpna started to say, but it was too late. Fancy Pants clamped her strong beak down on the tip of the woman's nose. The woman screeched. Dimpna carefully extricated bird from woman and her assistant hurried over to help her place Fancy Pants back in her cage.

"Cheeky bitch!" the woman screamed.

"Your daughter taught him. Is that it, now?" Dimpna couldn't help but ask.

The woman held her nose and had the decency to look ashamed. "Perhaps I say it now and again when I'm provoked."

"When an animal is in a stressful environment, I'd advise you not to get that close."

"Yes, Doctor." The woman stood, her crossword falling to the floor as she rushed for the checkout, now in a hurry to get away from the attention.

Dimpna bent down, picked up the crossword, her eyes scanning it. "Prodigal son," she said, then set the newspaper on the counter.

The woman frowned. "Pardon?"

"Wayward one in a parable. Seven down." Dimpna nudged the crossword closer, hopefully making it clear that she didn't allow her clients, human or animal, to dirty her reception floors. "Prodigal son."

The woman wrinkled her nose. "Thank you."

"Not a bother." People thought Dimpna was in the animal business. She wasn't. She was in the people business. She turned to update the Lab's owner, a fresh-faced young blonde overcome with tears. "Stargazer is going to be fine, luv. I gave him something for the pain and I'll be sending you home with antibiotics. I'll need him back in a week to remove the stitches. My assistant will have him out to you shortly."

"He's not going to die?"

"He'll live to see many more days. I'd suggest no more doggie play dates unless you know the other dogs well." Owners were always trying to shove random dogs together, a tendency just as dangerous in animals as it was in humans. Dimpna's phone buzzed in her pocket. Her personal phone. She glanced at the screen. She didn't recognize the number. She silenced it.

"I'm so grateful, like." The blonde clasped her hands in prayer. "When I came in, I nearly thought you were the vet's daughter. Until you turned around, like."

Although many of Dimpna's clients were regulars, this was Dublin, and fresh faces appeared all the time. Technically, she was the daughter of a vet, thus "the vet's daughter," but there was no need to add to the confusion. "I'm a grown woman," Dimpna said. To be fair, she was wearing her white-blond hair in pigtails today. She didn't need stray hairs falling across her face while she worked. When she wasn't in her vet scrubs, Dimpna also liked to wear flowery dresses and colorful wellies. She had a closet full of both, and she wasn't afraid to get either of them dirty. The good thing about being teased her entire life for being "the spitting image of a fairy" was that she could do whatever the hell she wanted and people thought it was cute. Dimpna was cute sometimes. Other times not so much, at least not on the inside, but that didn't stop her from using it to her advantage. The girl laughed a little too loud, and Dimpna threw a look to her receptionist.

"I'll take care of you over here," the receptionist said. "Dr. Wilde, the hamster is next, then the turtle." Dimpna glanced at the waiting room, prompting the owners of the turtle and the hamster to raise them into the air, like offerings to the gods.

"Please keep your darlings in their carriers while you wait," Dimpna scolded. "We don't want any little critters making an escape and getting into worse shape." Over the years, she'd seen it all. More furry creatures had flung themselves at these walls trying to escape than she could count.

Dimpna had just accepted the hamster, forgoing the carrier since the animal was already wiggling in her hands, when the door flew open and a terrified man barged in. He saw her and shoved an upside-down vase in her direction. The vase was vibrating. Underneath it, two white feet frantically pedaled.

"Doc, me rabbit is stuck and I've tried everything."

"I see that," Dimpna said. "Now you see why magicians choose the top hat." She handed the hamster to her vet tech who had sidled up, and reached for the vase. Yep. It was going to be one of those days. "Would someone check if we have Kerrygold Irish Butter in the fridge?"

"For your lunch?" the receptionist asked, her mouth agape. Dimpna rarely took lunch.

"For the rabbit, luv. If that doesn't work, try saying 'Abracadabra' and waving your hands about, willy-nilly." A vet tech grinned and headed for the kitchen. Dimpna's phone buzzed in her pocket again. *Go away.*

"Dr. Wilde." Her assistant was at her side, taking the stuck rabbit out of her hands, and then everything happened at once. The receptionist, phone-to-ear, gasped. Dimpna's phone buzzed once more. The door opened and four members of An Garda Síochána stepped in, and all of the focus in the room snapped to their blue uniforms and caps with gold shields. Her first thought was that they had an emergency dealing with an animal, but another part of her pulsed with dread.

The tallest guard stepped forward, and that's when she realized what was happening. She recognized the tall one. It had been six months since she'd seen him, and a year since life as she knew it had turned into a nightmare. A year since her late husband was swept up in a pyramid scheme, a year since he'd taken his own life without leaving them so much as a note, a year of defending her and her son's name, and a year of the courts deciding what else they were going to take from them. They'd seized the house in Clontarf, emptied nearly all their bank accounts, and most of all, they'd dragged their heretofore stellar reputations through the mud. It had only been a month since the last brick had come through the clinic windows.

"What now?" she asked. *Cheer up,* her da used to say. *Things will get worse . . .* "What now?"

He looked down at the paper in his hand. "I'm sorry, Dr. Wilde. There was a bill due and given it's not been paid, I'm afraid there's a lien on the clinic."

Behind her, the receptionist gasped again. Dimpna closed her eyes briefly. This too shall pass. . . . "I see." She took the notice. EVICTION. Closure. They had seventy-two hours. She knew this day would come. She hadn't been able to get loans. She'd been in a bit of denial, tossing notices into the bin and covering them up with chocolate wrappers and wine-and-tear-stained napkins. "Do I get to finish the day before closing me shop or do you want all these animals to suffer too?"

His face remained passive; he was just doing his job and no doubt he'd seen worse. "Seventy-two hours."

"Took four of ye to say that, did it?" She regretted the comment immediately. None of this was their fault. It wasn't hers either, apart from marrying a man who allowed himself to get sucked into the dark side. "I understand, Garda. Message delivered." That was the best she could do. There were nods all around and then they were gone. Dimpna's phone buzzed yet again, making her jump. Perhaps she was just desperate for a distraction, but this time she answered.

CHAPTER 5

*F*OR A MOMENT DIMPNA HEARD NOTHING ON THE OTHER END OF THE phone but heavy breathing. Her thumb hovered over the end button and she was just about to depress it when a male voice spoke.

"Dimp?"

"Who is this?" Only folks from home called her that.

"It's Paul Byrne."

Paul Byrne. Lost love. Not the one that got away but the one that stayed. She hadn't spoken to him in twenty-seven years. His voice was familiar and comforting, like a warm blanket she'd shoved in the back of a press for twenty-some years. "I really can't talk now," Dimpna said. "We're in a bit of a heap." Just say it. *I'm in a bit of a heap.* Scratch that. This involved her loyal employees too. Dimpna would do everything she could to make sure they were okay. If she sold the business to a colleague, she'd stipulate that her staff must stay on. Dimpna had to cover one ear to hear over the receptionist's sobs. "Is everything okay?" she asked, stepping outside and onto the footpath. She could have sworn that no more than twenty minutes had passed since the start of her shift at half-seven, yet the scene before her was the typical Dublin lunch crowd. She could smell last night's ale, and bleach from the pubs mixed with yeasty breads and coffee from the bakeries. Workers and shoppers vied for space on the footpath, a cacophony of handbags, man bags, and shopping bags. A busker sang slightly off-tune on the corner. She waited for Paul's answer, knowing whatever this was, everything wasn't okay. Everyone knew bad things came in threes.

"Johnny O'Reilly is dead."

"You're kidding me." O'Reilly's face appeared in front of her, uninvited and uncomfortably close. *Dead.* "What happened?"

"It's a murder inquiry."

"Murder? My God. Who did it? Was it Herself?" Róisín O'Reilly. Such a gorgeous name. *Rosheen.* Little Rose. Not in this case. This Róisín was all thorns. The most twisted branch in the O'Reilly family tree. Another thought struck her. "Was it Sean?" Her thoughts shifted to her son, Ben. Niall had arguably been a good father figure to Ben, but the scandal had uprooted everything, erasing those happy memories, like wiping a chalkboard clean, reducing them to faint, illegible streaks. Shortly after the scandal, Ben had disappeared on her for eight months, adding to her agony. When he'd finally resurfaced, he'd been distant and harsh. There was no easy way to process trauma—the scandal and the spotlight it put them under would have been enough to break the average person, but then there was Niall's suicide. Ben had been the one to find him.

"That's why I'm calling," she heard Paul say.

Her brain locked up. "Why? Is it Róisín or Sean?"

"I have no idea. It's an open inquiry."

"It has to be her"—although to be fair, there were probably numerous suspects. The O'Reillys were ruthless, and wherever money led, greed and envy followed. She pushed all thoughts of Sean O'Reilly out of her mind. Thinking of him as a normal man with a wife and daughter was surreal. "How did Johnny die?" Morbid question, but she had to know.

"He was found on Clogher Strand. In a suit, leaning against a boulder. Eyes open, foam at the mouth."

Bizarre. Thing like that didn't happen in Dingle. "Some kind of poison?"

There was a long pause, and for a second Dimpna thought the connection had been severed. "I wouldn't be telling you this, only someone's already let the cat out of the bag. The Gardaí are going to take major heat for it. Some detective inspector out of Killarney . . ."

Paul should be leading the case. Dimpna knew he'd been a detective. But he'd been booted from the force for beating up a man who abused his wife and kid. Paul had always been a good man. And good men didn't always get the happiness they deserved.

". . . which brings me to the last bit of news. A syringe and a vial of Release was found near the body."

"Release?" Dimpna was jolted back to the present. That didn't make sense. "Was it empty?"

"I don't have that info yet. Could it kill a human?"

She thought about it. "I suppose. But it would take fifty milliliters if not more to kill a man O'Reilly's size. They come in hundred milliliter bottles. I'd need to know how much was left in the vial that was found. But it would mean plunging multiple syringes into him. Was he tied up?" She instantly thought of all the ropes hanging around his horse barns. *Lassoed.* There they were again, her not-so-nice thoughts, taking over.

"Not that I'm aware."

Paul probably knew a lot more than he was saying. It was par for the course with him. "I can't imagine he just stood still while being injected multiple times."

"Maybe the first jab of Release took him by surprise and rendered him woozy?" Paul sounded hopeful. What was he after?

"No. Release doesn't have instant sedation effects. I suppose he could have been given a tranquilizer first."

"In your professional opinion—would a vet think of using Release to kill a person?"

"No. There are much easier ways to kill a man." A woman walking past her on the footpath stopped and gave Dimpna the side-eye. She smiled at her and waved. The woman shook her head and walked away, her pace quickening.

"Good to know. Like what?"

Dimpna knew Paul. He was a heat-seeking missile. He probably wanted this case. "Immobilon."

"What is it?"

"Etorphine and acepromazine"—

"Translate."

"We call it Monster in a Bottle."

"I'm listening."

"It used to put the fear of God in veterinarians. Five to fifteen milligrams would immobilize an African elephant. A single drop is lethal to humans." Paul emitted a low whistle.

"You got that right," Dimpna said. "That's why it's packaged with an antidote. Diprenorphine. Otherwise known as Revivon. If Revivon is administered quick enough it can reverse the effects. Anyhoo. They're both banned now."

"Impossible to get?"

Dimpna hesitated. Why was he asking? "It wouldn't be unheard of for older vets like my da to still have bottles tucked away. My father kept it in a purple vial so that it could never be mistaken for anything else. But believe me, they're all scared out of their minds to even think of taking it off the shelf."

"There's more," Paul said. She waited. "This is strictly confidential, but sure, lookit. I thought you should know."

"My lips are sealed." He had information he wasn't privy to anymore. She'd bet anything that the local guards still considered Paul a member of the team.

"A tarot card was found tucked into the pocket of his suit jacket."

"A tarot card." Her mam was a local tarot card reader in Dingle. "Which one?" It hardly mattered, but she couldn't help but ask.

"The Devil."

"Temptations," Dimpna said without thinking. Although she didn't read the cards herself, she'd watched her mammy enough to know the meanings her mother assigned to them. Some mornings before sending off Dimpna to school she'd pull a card and give her cautionary tales for the day. On "Devil Days" she'd always warned Dimpna not to fall prey to temptations. Whatever those meant to a young Dimpna . . . Her ongoing temptation had been the man whose deep soothing voice was talking to her now.

". . . and stones placed next to the body spelled out a message." There was a catch to his voice and another pause.

"What message?"

"Last Dance."

"What?" She straightened her spine. Last Dance. "Because of . . . the horse?" An image of the black colt shimmered before her, his gorgeous leg muscles reflecting the morning light. She'd been there for his first breath, cleaned the birthing fluids from his dark skin, helped him stand on trembly little legs, and felt his soft nose in the palms of her small hands. She'd understood fully in that moment why they called it the miracle of birth. There was no other word for it, no greater honor. She'd witnessed many miracles of birth since, but one never forgot their first. To this day she could feel the joy bursting within her. She'd loved him like he was a part of her. One moment he was poised to be the most promising racehorse in all of Ireland, the next he was lying dead in the road. The horror of seeing him laid out, all life in him gone just like that, had never left her. Time didn't heal grief; it just muted it in a shallow grave. But moments like this and it clawed back full force. She would have traded her life for Last Dance, she would have given her breath in exchange for his. Because she was responsible for his death. Her actions had led to his demise. She'd spent the rest of her life trying to atone, sweeping the guilt into little corners of her mind, but always knowing the dirty piles were still there, that she would never be clean. Paul had been warming up to this, trying to be kind, but she felt like he'd just punched her. "You're saying . . . What are you saying?"

"Due to the evidence at the murder scene, and mitigating circumstances, your parents are both suspects in the murder inquiry." Blunt. Truthful. He sounded like a detective now. Parents. Murder. Suspects. Downhill slide meet avalanche. The door to the clinic yawned open and her vet tech stuck her head out. "We buttered it up and the rabbit is out of the vase, no injuries."

Thank you, luv," Dimpna said.

"Kerrygold Irish Butter," the tech said with a grin. "Cracking good call."

"Good work," Dimpna said.

"But we added an 'Abracadabra' just to be safe." She waved her hands dramatically.

Dimpna laughed but the sound rang false in her ears and the feeling from the past year came boomeranging back, the one where it felt as if someone had taken an ice cream scooper and hollowed out her insides, leaving only frosted-over bits. She turned her attention back to Paul. There was so much to say but this was not the time or the place. "I have to go."

"Just one more thing. Rumor is your father isn't well," Paul said.

"What do you mean?"

"When is the last time you spoke with your parents?"

"Mostly postcards from my mam." Maeve Wilde sent Dimpna postcards once a month from places she'd never been. *Hello from Tahoe. Greetings from Sweden. Tipping away in Thailand . . .* Dimpna wasn't sure where on earth she got them all, whether friends who traveled gave them to her, or she bought them online, but she had a good stash and thoroughly enjoyed sending them out, writing cryptic little messages in sharp black ink on each one. Trying to get ahold of either of her parents on the phone usually resulted in a maddening game of phone tag.

"Your mam hasn't mentioned anything about your father's state of mind?"

"No. What's the story?" She was on high alert now.

"Maybe you should call her."

"I will. But first—tell me what's going on."

"I don't know if there's been a diagnosis—but rumor is he's forgetting things."

"I forget things all the time."

"Not like that. They say it's dementia. I'm so sorry. And your mother . . . She and Johnny . . ."

"She and Johnny what?"

"Talk is they were having an affair. Your mother might have been the last person to see Johnny O'Reilly alive."

"Why do you say that?"

"Because so far she's the last person to see Johnny O'Reilly alive."

It was delivered like a punch line, but all Dimpna felt was another punch. Clinic closing. A murder. Dementia. An affair. Parents as suspects. What happened to the rule of three? They had blown way past the Rule of Three. How was she supposed to take any of this in?

"Dr. Wilde?" Her vet tech was back. Animals couldn't wait, not even for murder inquiries.

"Thank you for ringing me." Dimpna hung up. He would understand. Why hadn't her mother rang her? Where was Donnecha?

How bad was her father's dementia? She headed inside and faced the receptionist who was still sniffling. She reached into her pocket and gave her the chocolate bar she'd been saving for a break. "Have a cup of tea and dry your eyes. I'm going to make sure you're all alright, petal." She would give her staff every last penny she had in severance. Write them glowing recommendations. She turned to the wall of clients, with their own burdens, and fears, and lovely, lovely pets with big eyes and even bigger hearts that needed endless care. Veterinarians faced one of the highest suicide rates of any profession. Dimpna was tough. But she didn't know if she had it in her to face this kind of trauma. The kind that hit too close to home. But then again, what choice did she have? She took a deep breath. Smiled. "Now. Who's next?"

CHAPTER 6

*B*Y THE TIME CORMAC ARRIVED AT THE HARBOR, ALLERGY MEDS IN TOW, he was still trying to shake his encounter with the widow. *Cold and calculating.* Róisín O'Reilly had demanded to see the body, and when that request wasn't granted, she had asked for the name of his superior, wrote it down in large block letters on the back of his calling card, then immediately name-dropped several prominent councilmen and judges before phoning a solicitor right in front of him. When she hung up, she refused his invitation to come into the station and said any interviews would be handled through the solicitor. His firm came with no less than four names, which was no surprise given everything he'd heard about their wealth and status. The son had seemed a little bit more reasonable, catching his eye and saying, "We just need a moment," but in the end, he'd followed his mother's every command. D.S. Neely was now going back and forth with the solicitor, trying to get them into the station. A briefing was scheduled with the media in less than an hour. And now this. The guards he'd sent to the harbor had found Donnecha Wilde scrubbing the O'Reilly yacht top to bottom. By the time they'd hauled him off, it was too late. If the yacht had been a crime scene, the evidence had been wiped clean.

Furious, Cormac strode along the walkway toward *Dreamscape.* The sleek white yacht with a navy blue and green stripe through the center certainly made an impression. The presence of guards had everyone on alert. Folks hurried along, avoiding eye contact altogether, or stood in fortified clumps openly staring. Cormac noted with dismay that the staring clumps were growing in size. Drama was impossible to resist. He even had three missed calls from his mam back in Killarney, no doubt wanting the details straight from the horse's mouth. He'd call her later and try to make it as exciting as possible, take her mind off her woes. He texted her care advocate to make sure everything was alright and was relieved to hear that it was. A minute later his phone dinged again. Fourth one from his mam: **Wasn't me that called. Must have been me arse.**

He chuckled and texted back: **Tell your arse I'll call it later.**

Sounds like an awful mess. Take care and God bless. His mother was dying. It was just six months ago she'd been diagnosed with MND, Motor Neuron Disease, or ALS as they called it in the States. She was already at the wheelchair and feeding-tube stage and communicating via text or text-to-speech via her iPad. He was her only child, although she had a brother and sister and a fabulous care advocate and visiting nurse. It was a cruel disease, especially for a woman who had been as active as his mam—an avid hill walker and yoga practicer. She was only sixty-five. Through it all, she'd kept her head held high and was handling each blow like a champ. Cormac wished he could say the same. His stomach was in constant knots worrying about her, and he rarely slept for more than a few hours at a time. Taking this case meant precious time away from her, but she not only understood, she had insisted he go. He'd video chat with her as soon as he could; she was the one person he could trust without reservation, and her mind was as sharp as a tack. Cormac shoved his phone back into the pocket of his blazer and arrived at the yacht.

Donnecha Wilde was bare-chested and bare-legged, standing on the dock in a pair of shorts, suds clinging to hairy, skinny legs. He seemed keen on negotiating with the guards, as if this was a traffic violation he could wriggle out of by turning on the old charm. His head shot up when Cormac appeared, with the expression of a kidnapped victim pleading with his captors to be set free. He was about Cormac's age, somewhere in his late thirties, but apart from that, the two men were chalk and cheese. Cormac could tell this was a Peter Pan man, trying desperately not to grow up. Or maybe it was his foul mood, the overwhelming smell of bleach ruining what could have been the key to solving this murder within hours. As instructed, the guards hadn't given Donnecha Wilde an explanation for hauling him off the boat midscrub, face stamped with suds and panic, leaving him to twist in the wind.

"I have rights," he said. "Since when is it illegal to clean a boat?"

Cormac stepped forward. "I'm Detective Inspector Cormac O'Brien."

Donnecha nodded, then chewed on his bottom lip. "What's the story?"

"The harbormaster saw you leaving the docks on foot at approximately four P.M. yesterday afternoon and returning early this morning."

Donnecha's head swiveled around the dock and he took in the gawpers. "Is that a crime?"

"Who operated this yacht last night? And before you answer, you can believe we're going to check every CCTV footage in the area, so I wouldn't even think about lying."

Donnecha looked Cormac in the eye. "The owner reserved it for a friend. He wanted me gone by the afternoon."

"Where did you go?"

Donnecha frowned. "I don't see how that's any of your business."

"I assure you, it's my business. Where were you?"

"I checked into the Dingle Inn."

Cormac looked to one of the other guards. They pointed in the general direction. "A quiet one. Tucked away a few streets back."

Donnecha folded his arms but didn't respond. Cormac continued. "Who gave you the instruction to leave by afternoon?"

"I already told you. The owner."

"Name?"

Donnecha looked to the other guards but once again was met with a wall of silence. He reluctantly turned back to the inspector. "Johnny O'Reilly."

"You're saying Johnny O'Reilly himself told you to vacate this boat by afternoon yesterday?"

"That's right."

"How did he contact you?"

"Text."

"Where's your phone?"

Donnecha pointed to the boat. "In the cabin. And I'd like it back."

"And when we retrieve this phone—which we will—we'll see a text to you from Johnny O'Reilly?"

"You're not from around here, are you?" It wasn't said with malice, which for some reason irked Cormac even more.

"Answer the question."

"Johnny O'Reilly doesn't communicate with someone like me directly. He has people for that. People like him have people for everything."

"And which of his people texted you?"

"Tommy Healy."

Cormac jotted down the name in an old-fashioned little notebook he kept in his pocket. "And what does Mr. Healy do for Mr. O'Reilly?"

"Are you joking me?" Donnecha laughed. Then stopped when Cormac gave him a look. "Everything. He does everything for the O'Reillys. Has for years."

He'd get the scoop from his guards later. He wanted to keep Donnecha talking. "You always use this much bleach to clean a boat?" The smell was overpowering, even mixed with the smell of fish and the deep blue sea.

"I do when some kid gets their messy shoe prints all over everything."

Cormac felt the words like a punch to the gut. He gripped his Biro so hard, he was surprised it didn't snap in two and bleed ink. "In a few minutes my men are going to take you to the Garda Station and you're going to tell me every little detail about your day yesterday—scratch that—your entire week leading up to yesterday. But right now—assuming you're not a barefaced liar, and I'm not ruling that out, you're going to tell me every detail of what you saw in and on that boat when you returned to it this morning."

Donnecha shifted his weight. "There's not much to tell. Just the footprints. Either Johnny's guest had a kid, or some kid snuck on the boat last night. There were some dirty prints—"

"Describe these prints."

"Describe them?" Donnecha's eyebrows shot up, and from the look on his face, describing things wasn't in his job description.

Cormac could feel his temper rising, even while recognizing the young man in front of him seemed genuinely caught off guard. Was it an act? "I want every detail you can remember."

Donnecha rocked back on his heels for a moment. "Faint but noticeable shoe prints. Kid-sized. Runners if I had to guess. Regular walking around type dirt I'd say."

Before the kid jumped off the boat and swam to shore. "How big were the prints?" Donnecha held out his fingers in an approximation. They lined up with the prints they found scrambling up the hillside. "What was the name of the VIP guest taking the boat out for the evening?"

"I have no idea. They don't tell me those things."

"When O'Reilly made this request, was there any mention of a kid?"

"No, sir." Donnecha was standing straighter now, as if to show he was taking the questions seriously.

"Would he have mentioned a kid?"

Donnecha shook his head. "I doubt it."

"Is there any place on the boat for a kid to hide?" Cormac asked his questions rapid-fire, giving the young man no chance to concoct or spin tall tales.

"Funny you should mention that." He paused as if waiting to see if Cormac had a response. Cormac simply stared. "There's a utility closet. That's where the cleaning supplies are kept. All the supplies were shoved to the back, and a few were knocked over."

A stowaway. Cormac tried not to let anything show on his face, but he could feel his adrenaline pumping. They had a missing kid. And that kid was in danger. "Anything else? Stray hairs, candy wrappers, anything?"

"Not that I noticed."

"Have you removed anything from the boat?"

"No." The pitch of his voice had risen. "Would you please tell me what the hell this is all about?"

"Are we going to need a pass code to unlock your phone?"

Donnecha swallowed. "You can't take my phone. Don't you need a judge's order to do that?"

"Your phone is now part of a crime scene."

"Crime scene?" His head whipped back to the boat several times. "Because of a few shoe prints?" When Cormac didn't respond, Donnecha once again looked to the other guards. "You lads know me. Tell me what's going on." When they didn't respond, he was forced to address Cormac again. "Call Mr. O'Reilly. Or Sean. Or one-armed Tommy." Sweat dripped down the side of his face.

One-armed Tommy. Cormac jotted down the nickname. "What time did you start wiping away evidence?"

"What?" His head whipped around once more. "That's not what I was doing."

Cormac pulled back. "What time did you start cleaning this boat?"

"Been at it an hour or so."

Cormac wished he could punch something. They'd missed their biggest opportunity by an hour. He gestured for the nearest guard to follow him down the dock. Garda McCann was young and thin, an earnest look stamped on his freckled face. When they were out of hearing distance Cormac leaned in. "One-armed Tommy?"

"Works for the O'Reillys. Has for years," McCann said. "Even with just the one arm he was an aspiring jockey. Was supposed to ride Last Dance to his first big win."

Last Dance. There it was again, that horse from a quarter of a century ago, rearing up from the dead. "Supposed to?"

McCann nodded. "Last Dance was killed by a trailer the night before the big race. Tommy never got on another horse again. Been the foreman for the O'Reillys ever since."

"What about this Donnecha lad?" They glanced over. Donnecha hadn't moved, but he was jittery, legs bouncing up and down. No doubt gagging for a cigarette, or twelve.

"He's alright," McCann conceded. "Bit of a hooligan, but no history of violence."

There was always a first time, but Cormac kept that to himself. "You think he's telling the truth? Gut reaction."

"Knowing Johnny O'Reilly?" McCann tilted his head toward the increasingly gray skies and pondered the question for a beat. "It rings true."

"Does he always clean with bleach?"

"I imagine O'Reilly insists on a tidy yacht." He caught himself. "Or at least he did."

"Hey," Donnecha called across the dock. "There was one other thing that was a little odd."

This got Cormac's attention. He held up his finger then turned to McCann. "I want Tommy Healy brought into the station and find out where we are with the O'Reillys' solicitor. He can only stall so long before we need to speak with his clients. And inform Sergeant Neely she'll be handling the press briefing solo."

McCann nodded and took off. Cormac returned to Donnecha. "I'm listening."

"Can I show you?" He gestured to the boat.

"We can approach, but you're not to step on it or touch anything." Not that it mattered now with everything wiped clean, but the lad was on edge and Cormac wanted to keep him that way.

Donnecha headed for the boat. He pointed to the bow. "There was a strange marking here." He then pointed to the floor of the boat. "And there. Nothing sinister, mind you. Just faint lines." He held his hand out approximately two feet. "About this long."

A makeshift ramp so the killer could slide the body bag up and over. Probably a board. "What about a black tarp?" Cormac asked. "Was there one aboard?"

Donnecha scrunched his face. "What do you mean?"

Cormac didn't want to give away anything more on that front. He needed every advantage he could get against the killer, and he certainly wasn't going to utter the words *body bag*. "Any signs of a struggle?"

"Jesus. No. Would you please tell me what's happened?" Stress was evident in his voice. "Is it the kid? O'Reilly is going to kill me." He looked to the sky where a helicopter still circled. "I wondered what that was all about," he said. He plastered his hands to the side of his face. "I'm begging you, Inspector. What's the story?"

"If O'Reilly told you to leave the boat for someone else, why would he blame you if something went amiss?" Cormac asked.

"You think O'Reilly is going to blame someone in his inner circle?" Donnecha patted the pockets of his shorts. "I need a smoke."

Cormac didn't let up. "I thought you said you don't know who took the boat out."

"I don't. But it has to be someone in his inner circle. O'Reilly only let VIPs and family take his boat out."

"Is there a lifeboat?" Cormac headed for the side of the boat. There, attached to the side was his answer. A small rowboat, just big enough for a body. He pointed to it. "Have you bleached that yet?"

"Why would I?"

Thank Christ for that. Cormac nodded to the guards. "I want this rowboat tagged for the technical team." Donnecha shifted forward and stared at the rowboat as if seeing it for the first time. Cormac swore he saw something in his expression, something akin to surprise. "Something on your mind?"

"No." His eyes flicked away.

"You sure about that?"

Donnecha stole another glance at the rowboat. "It's not tied the way I remember."

Cormac edged closer. "How do you remember it tied?"

Donnecha squinted. "Honestly I can't say for sure. You're making me nervous."

Good. Cormac handed him his notebook and a pen. "Sketch the way you think it was tied."

Donnecha thought about the request for a moment, and then shrugged. He quickly sketched out a knot—a double loop instead of the triple now holding it.

"Sign it," Cormac said when Donnecha tried to hand the notebook back.

"Are you serious?"

"As a heartache." *Or a poisoning.*

Donnecha sighed and scribbled his name. "Please," he said. "Is it the kid? Did something happen to a kid?"

Cormac relented. "Johnny O'Reilly was found dead this morning on Clogher Strand."

"What?" The shock sounded genuine, but the lad could have practiced it. "Dead?" He took another look at the boat. "Crime scene," he said to himself. His head snapped up. "You think he was killed on the boat?" His fawn-colored eyes blinked rapidly. "Where does the kid fit in?"

"You're here to answer questions, not ask them," Cormac said.

Donnecha wiped sweat off his forehead with the back of his arm. "There wasn't any blood or anything violent on board. I would have called the guards. I swear. Just messy prints. I thought the prints belonged to a lad in short trousers, but Sean has a daughter. Aisling. She's okay, right?"

Cormac came to attention. "How old is she?"

"Eight. Nine? Something like that." He scratched his head. "The prints are too big for her, right?"

Exactly what Cormac was thinking. There hadn't been a child in the car when Mrs. O'Reilly and son pulled up to the murder scene. He assumed they would have mentioned it if she was missing. He turned to a guard who had heard the entire exchange.

"On it," the guard said. Cormac nodded his thanks.

"The Dingle Inn," Cormac said. "Did you check in under your name?"

Donnecha crossed his arms over his chest. "Found dead on the beach. Like—drowned? Washed up?"

"Did you check into the Dingle Inn under your given name?"

"Because if he took the boat out and drowned—then who returned the boat—and why would you be crawling all over the harbor if it was an accidental drowning?" Donnecha may be a drug user, but he wasn't befuddled.

"I'm not asking you again," Cormac said.

"Oh my God. You think someone pushed him overboard, held him under, and then drove the boat back?"

Donnecha was fixated on drowning. Was he clueless or clever? "That's it. You're coming into the station. You're giving us the name you used to check into the Dingle Inn and I want to know who you spoke with yesterday—especially the last time you spoke with your folks."

"My folks?" Donnecha came to a standstill. "What the fuck?" He was on the precipice of a complete freak-out.

Cormac lowered his voice and stepped closer. "Listen to me. You said it yourself. I'm not from around here. But *you* are. Johnny O'Reilly dead? You wiping down this yacht with bleach? You think that looks good for you?"

Donnecha's eyes widened and he shook his head. "I didn't have anything to do with it."

"You think the O'Reillys are going to take your word for it?"

"Oh my God." He ran his hand through his hair, then gripped it as if he intended on pulling it out from the roots. "Help me. You have to help me."

"Did you check into the Dingle Inn under your name?"

He dropped his hands. "Why wouldn't I?" His left eye began to twitch.

"Were you alone?"

"Yes." The twitch deepened.

"We're going to check CCTV."

"What do you want from me? I ordered takeaway, a delivery guy came to the room. I ate fish and chips."

The twitch had Cormac's radar pinging. "Any other visitors?"

Donnecha frowned. "A mate stopped by."

"Name?"

"Is this really happening?" Donnecha's hands covered his face.

"Do I look like I'm taking the piss?"

"I'm not dragging my mate into this until I talk to a solicitor."

Cormac nodded to the closest guard. "Escort Mr. Wilde to the station for an official interview."

"Do I *need* a solicitor?" Donnecha asked, a hard edge creeping into his voice.

"I don't know. Do you?"

Donnecha glared. They stared at each other without blinking.

"Inspector?" A guard holding up his mobile interrupted the moment. Childishly, Cormac told himself he would have won. "It's Sergeant Neely." Cormac held up his finger so that the guard wouldn't blurt whatever else he had to say down the length of the dock and strode over. "We've traced the batch number off that vial of Release found near Mr. O'Reilly's body." The guard waited, his eyes dancing with bombshell news.

"And?" Cormac could no longer hide his exasperation.

"That vial came from Eamon Wilde's Mixed Animal Veterinarian Clinic."

CHAPTER 7

*A*MONG THE ITEMS DIMPNA HAD BEEN ALLOWED TO KEEP WERE HER fiddle and her green-and-white Volkswagen bus. It was gratifying that her two favorite possessions in the world (apart from her animals, who were family, not possessions) were the two things the Irish government had no desire to confiscate. Peace out. The bus she'd had nearly twenty years, a gift to herself after graduating from vet school at UCD, University College Dublin. She still had a vivid, giddy memory of inching it home, drivers laying on their horns incensed by her turtle speed, babying it every step of the way. It cocooned all her memories, hopes, adventures, and late-night animal calls. She'd made love in it, been drunk and high in it (only while camping, never while driving), and slept in it. Adventure on wheels. Her fiddle, one of many she'd owned over her lifetime of playing trad music, had been a wedding present from her parents. It was the nicest one she'd ever held, and it made beautiful music. She finished packing the bus with her earthly essentials: emergency veterinarian supplies, her favorite leather satchel that she used for home calls, clothing, treasured books, and shoeboxes filled with photos.

After sorting out the clinic transition—thankfully a colleague had agreed to pay the debts in exchange for the business, and had agreed to keep her staff—she said a tearful goodbye, including to the pudgy clinic cat, Sammy, then texted all her friends that her possessions were available at no charge, although she encouraged them to donate to animal shelters instead, and she gave the snarly landlord enough rent for the rest of her term. Neither her parents nor her brother had answered their phones, and she didn't want to leave any messages that could be misconstrued by the guards, so she'd finally stopped trying. Was there something in her family's gene sequencing that prevented them from communicating in times of crisis?

She had also rung Ben numerous times, but her son wasn't answering either. Was she this aloof at twenty-seven? Yes, he was a grown man, but she'd told him it was urgent and that he needed to call her back as soon as possible. She prayed he wouldn't hear about the body found in Dingle, but if he did, news outlets were not yet reporting a connection to her family. And Ben did not know that the victim was part of *his* family. In Dimpna's mind the O'Reillys were not a part of Ben; she'd so thoroughly excised them from his life that sometimes she forgot their blood ran through his veins. She sent one more text before starting up the bus: **Family emergency. Call me!!** If she didn't hear back soon, she'd harp on him until he answered.

Once her three-pack commandeered the back seat of the bus, they were ready to roll. She hauled herself into the driver's seat, perched on two old-fashioned phone books (which worked better than a booster seat, but she had to wear pointy boots to reach the gas and brakes and still be fit to see out the windshield), and turned to double-check on her cuddle bugs. Two out of three seemed wildly enthusiastic about their spontaneous adventure. *Road trip, excellent idea.* Spike, her black cat, so tall and regal she imagined he once belonged to Cleopatra, was curled up in the seat behind Dimpna. Pickles, a two-year-old exuberant and wicked-smart collie, sat in the middle, pink tongue hanging out, so shaggy he was going to block her rearview mirror. And Guinness, her old and overweight English bulldog, the one sourpuss about this road trip, had shoved himself as far as he could against the far window, his drooly right cheek smooshed against the glass. Knowing him, he would indulge in his favorite form of revenge: flatulence. She empathized; she had second thoughts about this trip as well. Although, if he started in on the stink bombs, he'd miss out on all the snacks she'd brought to bribe them into compliance. She cranked on upbeat dancing music and pretended it was completely normal to be leaving the rock and venturing home to the hard place.

The four-hour-and-change trip morphed into six as she indulged in potty, food, and stretch breaks. She jumped every time her phone dinged, but every message was either from colleagues trying to wheedle gossip out of her, or friends offering their support. Just before entering Dingle, the curves and peaks of the Slieve Mish Mountains appeared, then, as she drew closer, the Tralee Bay shimmered in the midday sun. She took her time driving through the village of Camp near The Dingle Way, a 168-kilometer hiking trail circumventing the peninsula. A part of her wished she was here to make the eight-day-trek, loaded up with nothing but a backpack and a dream. Camp was a cheerful village replete with a stone fort, a golden beach, tidy cottages, a historic stone church, and winding roads flanked by thick green hedges.

Spike, Guinness, and Pickles all vied for the same window, competition driving them blind to the open window on the other side of the bus. Animals made her laugh daily, and she was grateful for it. At least she'd only have to clean saliva from one window. She knew her destination by heart: a small valley to the west of Tralee, Gleann na nGealt, often called the Valley of the Mad. It was the perfect place to have a walkabout after the long drive. She took the remote lane to the designated car park and soon her pack piled out of the bus, tripping over each other to be the first out. She was dying to let her creatures run free, but this was a popular place for tourists and hikers, so she stuck to the rules and kept them on long leads, including a little harness and leash for Spike.

The weather was overcast but mild, a familiar gray mist welcoming her home. The Valley of the Mad was named for two wells where poor souls inflicted with madness once flocked to eat watercress and drink from their depths, praying to be cured. Now hollow, the wells were marked with stones, one appropriately called the Mad Stone. Thick hedgerows along the path boasted wildflowers, and in this area one could also encounter a fallen fairy tree and an old stone house falling to ruins. No matter how many times she'd been here, Dimpna had always discovered something new.

Pickles and Guinness sniffed around while Spike hissed at the audacity of being put on a leash. "Sorry, luv," Dimpna said as he yowled. "Welcome to my world." She wished the wells were still flowing and the legends were true, for she would cup her hands and drink. Instead, she imagined all the people who had once gravitated here, purportedly even kings, each with a burning desire to be cured of insanity. It was comforting and sad all rolled up in one little ball. Rumors abounded as to why these wells held so much power, including of course that they were blessed by the fairies. But in 2012 a chemical analysis detected higher traces of lithium in the water compared to nearby sources. Given she could no longer drink from the wells, Dimpna drank in the scents and sounds of home. Land of ocean, and mountains, and pints, and music, and madness. *Home.* They completed a circle, and then turned around to head back to the bus. Up ahead, a scraggly young girl peeked out from behind a small hill. Only her profile was visible: messy black hair, and the side of a purple backpack. Pickles seemed keen to pull her toward the girl, and Dimpna was inclined to let him say hello, when her mobile phone blasted out a familiar tune. *Ben.* Finally. She pivoted from the girl and answered.

"Ben?"

"Mam?"

"I can barely hear you," she said. "I don't think I have a strong connection here."

"Where are you?" He sounded impatient and put out.

"I'm almost to Dingle. Where are you?"

"Spain."

"Spain?" Without telling her? On one hand, she was poised to scold him for keeping her in the dark. On the other, she was thrilled she could continue keeping him in the dark. That tangled web Shakespeare had warned of was deeply woven into the fabric of her life.

"With my girlfriend." There was a chipper note in his voice, the delight of spilling a secret.

"This is news," Dimpna said. "What's her name?"

"Angelina."

"Where did you meet?" She was stalling, but also insanely curious. It had been a while since he'd mentioned a girl. This was perfect. He would need the distraction.

"I'll tell you everything when I see you next. What's the story?"

She wished she could regale in all the details now, savor the moment. At least he was far, far away. Relief settled in her bones. "I had to leave the clinic and Dublin," she said. "I'm going home for a bit." She paused. *Tread carefully.* "Have you been reading the news?"

"No," he said. "Why?"

"A prominent racehorse owner in Dingle is dead. Everyone is talking about it." *Murdered. And my parents are suspects. And by the way, he's your paternal grandfather.*

There was a pause. Had he heard what she said? "You said you'd never return to Dingle." His voice was tinged with accusation.

Ben had always pressed her about why she never brought him to Dingle, why they always met her parents somewhere, anywhere else but home. Dingle was one of the most popular tourist destinations in Ireland, and she often used that as an excuse. "We see enough tourists in Dublin. Let's have a break from them, shall we?" No doubt she had made mistakes. Maybe she should have told him everything about his father, and the O'Reilly side of his family, including the fact that Ben had been the opposite of a love child. Conceived during a hateful act. She'd practiced it in her head with a variety of carefully selected words. The closest she could come was a sanitized version of the ugly truth: "Your father forced himself on me. I never told him about you."

In the end, she decided against it. She couldn't imagine staining her innocent son with such an ugly truth. Even if she didn't utter the vile word *rape*, it would hover in the cracks, changing his sense of self forever. Hadn't enough damage been done? Hadn't she suffered enough? Niall had been a good surrogate father to Ben, and he'd kept her secret, but he refused to say he was Ben's biological father. "I won't do it," he said. "I won't be involved in that big of a lie." But Ben was a curious lad and he wanted answers. She told him his biological father had been a talented jockey who died from a heart defect shortly after Ben was conceived. No doubt this fictional father was based on the crush Tommy Healy had on her back then. The shy, nice jockey he'd been before Sean O'Reilly corrupted him.

"You and a jockey?" Ben said, cocking his head. "Then why am I so tall?"

Whoops. "My father is tall." That was true. Even so, she had to be careful, keep her answers vague enough that Ben couldn't poke any more holes. He'd been a stranger, she'd said, in town for only a week, for a local horse race. It was a quick, drunken shag. He was a winner, though, I remember that. *His name was Brendan. I don't remember his surname.* Tommy had had a twin brother named Brendan. Stick close to the truth; wasn't that the old, sage advice? When DNA kits came out, she'd held her breath, paralyzed with fear that Ben would want to submit one, but as he grew older, his interest in the subject waned. Now she wasn't sure what to do, what to say. As little as possible was the motto that had gotten her this far. "Your grandfather has dementia." *And the other one is stone-cold dead. Murdered . . .*

"I'm so sorry." Ben's voice finally softened. "Has this only recently started?"

"I don't know to be honest. I've only just heard about it."

"Should I come to Dingle as well?"

"No!"

"Jesus, Mam. There you go again." His hard edges were back. "What is it you're so afraid of?"

Everything. She was afraid of absolutely everything. "I just want you to enjoy your holidays. With Angelina. It will be all doctors' appointments and chaos here. Enjoy Spain. Stay as long as you'd like."

"You're sure?"

"I'm positive."

"And there's nothing else?" For a second he sounded suspicious. Had he heard something? Was he testing her? Ben was like that—he gathered information and often used it to attack. Had she mentioned it was a murder inquiry? Now she couldn't remember. Surely they were reporting *that* on the news. "This prominent man is well-known in Dingle and it's a suspicious death." She couldn't even bring herself to mention his name, as if in doing so, she was inviting trouble across her threshold.

"Suspicious?"

"It's a murder inquiry."

She heard an intake of breath. He said something to his girl-friend before returning to the phone. "Did you know him well?"

"We didn't run in the same circles, but my father did care for many of his horses." *I cared for one of them and now he's dead. And for some reason that horse's name was spelled in stones next to the dead body. And a vial of Release and a syringe were found, and the Devil card, and your granny may have been knocking boots with him.* Dingle. The land of saints and stones . . . and sinners. "I'm sure there will be a ton of gossip." That was the best she could do for now.

"Sorry—I'm getting a beep—my phone is about to die."

"No worries. Call me when you can. Say hello to Angelina, and I love you."

The connection severed. She stared at the phone. "Love you too, Mammy," she said. "Miss you." Pickles whined. Dimpna whirled around to see if he was still lunging to get to the girl, but there was no one there. "Hello?" Dimpna called out. "Young lady? Hello? Are you alright?" The wind rustled, and a gull shrieked overhead. She too had roamed all over the peninsula as a little girl; it was com-forting to see some things hadn't changed. She headed back for the bus. It was time to go home. "Come on, gang. Off we go." As they made the trek back to the car park, the crossword from the other day swam into view. *Wayward one from parables.* Prodigal son. This time the prodigal daughter had returned.

CHAPTER 8

A PULSE IN DIMPNA'S NECK THROBBED AS SHE TURNED UP THE DEAD-end road leading to her father's clinic. It was still there, coursing through her blood, that old familiar feeling of being—like it or not—where she belonged. The limestone clinic resided where the road ended and a green field began. A squad car loomed in front of the practice, delivering Dimpna an additional jolt. In front of it, a red Toyota sat perpendicular to the squad cars, positioned as if it had stopped just short of driving into the stone wall surrounding the courtyard. Two guards were leaning back against the squad car, arms folded across their chests. Pacing in front of the stone wall was a scruffy but handsome man in denims and a tan blazer. Unusual attire for a local. He was short with a mop of dark hair. It must be the inspector out of Killarney. She wondered briefly if Paul's jealousy also stemmed from the fact that this inspector was younger than him, albeit by only six or so years. She clocked the moment his attention turned to her bus pulling in, how intense and curious his gaze. An odd sensation rippled through her. It was as if he had been waiting for her. But that was ridiculous, even she didn't know she was coming. It wasn't until Dimpna drew closer that she realized why they were holding fort outside. Animals domineered the courtyard.

A goat rubbed the top of its head on the stone wall as if tunneling out an escape. A pheasant paced in circles. Two sheep, marked with purple dye, devoured the grass, lifting their heads to stare openly at the guards as they chewed. Three ducks pecked at the ground, attempting to run away from two chickens vying for the same seeds. A turtle crept down the footpath as if walking through a minefield. A hare cowered underneath a tree, nose twitching. Six dogs patrolled the stone wall, teeth bared, while a black Lab guarded the clinic door. Intermittent barks pierced the air. This was far from normal. And it didn't stop there.

Dimpna counted five cats. One, an extremely obese tabby, was draped on top of the stone wall as if it were a feather bed and not ancient limestone. Bowls of water and food littered the yard, most of them overturned, the few upright ones reduced to dribbles. They were not starving. The yard was covered in poo, not to mention heaps of feathers and fur. Horrifying. The inmates had taken over the asylum and the result was an abject squalling disaster. Dimpna had gone on animal hoarding calls that looked a lot like this. The father she knew would have never let the place get overrun. She and Donnecha used to call him The Dictator behind his back. So rigid. So exacting. And very, very orderly. She climbed out of the bus, her gut twisting with worry.

The exterior of the clinic had seen better days as well. The once-cheerful yellow paint with blue trim was chipped and fading. The wooden sign above the door hung askew: WILDE'S MIXED ANIMAL VETERINARIAN CLINIC. It screamed out for paint. The short man in the blazer tracked her every move with intense blue eyes rimmed with thick, dark eyelashes. She felt them on her as she stepped away from her bus. And although normally she wasn't at all self-conscious about her out-of-work attire of flowery dresses and her cowboy-driving-boots, today she felt X-rayed and vulnerable. Across the street, an old auto body shop that had long been abandoned, competed for worst-courtyard-ever with its hulking pieces of rusting metal. Across the field, some distance away, the top of her mother's white caravan flashed, swallowed by wildflowers and tall, reedy grass.

"This clinic is closed, lassie," one of the guards said as she approached. He wore sunglasses a size too small.

The detective, if that's who he was, folded his arms and watched.

Even through his suit jacket, she could make out his bulging arm muscles.

"That's Dr. Lassie, to you, Garda," Dimpna said. She was startled by a chuckle, and turned to find the man in the blazer thoroughly amused. He caught her gaze, covered his mouth briefly, and when he took it away the smile was gone. He had a pack of tissues sticking out of his pocket and his eyes were rimmed in red.

"Dr. Wilde." He thrust out his hand. "I'm Detective Inspector Cormac O'Brien."

"You know who I am," she said, not surprised but somewhat irked.

"I do," he said, still proffering his hand. "I've learned a lot about you and your family in the past day."

For a moment, a vain part of her was glad she had worn her hair down instead of in pigtails. She'd let her hair grow long since Niall's death. There was no reason, other than wanting things to be different, wanting to feel different. It hadn't worked. She was the same old Dimpna with the same old Dimpna-like problems. "I can't shake your hand," she said. "I've been touching dogs and cats all day. It'll only exacerbate your struggles."

He tilted his head and studied her as his hand dropped to his side. "That obvious, is it?"

"Yes." Being a vet meant you had to tell people the truth, whether folks wanted to hear it or not. Most times they didn't.

"A kindred spirit then," he said.

"How's that?"

He tapped his head. "Observational skills."

"If you say so."

He studied her for another moment, then straightened his spine. "I take it you're aware that we're conducting a murder inquiry?"

"I'm aware that you found Johnny O'Reilly deceased on Clogher Strand. How do you know he didn't take his own life?" Dimpna hadn't expected to blurt that out, but she knew firsthand you could swear up and down a person wouldn't take his own life, only to find him hanging from the rafters of your carport. Before the inspector could respond, from inside the clinic came the sound of glass shattering followed by a woman's shriek. The guards tipped forward, and the courtyard erupted with barks, flaps, and bleats. The door to the clinic flew open and a woman with red hair and vet scrubs darted out. Dimpna recognized her immediately and felt another jolt. Sheila Maguire. Her once-best friend and her father's longtime vet tech. Her long red hair still flowed with wild curls, and her statuesque figure with impressive cleavage was impossible to miss. Dimpna wondered if she had mellowed or if she was still the same rebel of a girl she'd once known. Selfish too, but Dimpna had enough of her own faults to start keeping track of others.

"Is everyone alright in there?" Detective O'Brien's voice projected across the small courtyard.

Sheila put her hands up and waved them around. "I'm alright."

"Is anyone else being held inside?"

Dimpna whirled around. "Being held inside? As in hostage?"

His eyes flicked to Dimpna, then back to Sheila. "Is anyone hurt or stuck inside?" he repeated in a tone that left little doubt her father was enemy number one and Dimpna was to keep her mouth shut.

Sheila shook her head. "It's only Dr. Wilde in there now." She finally made eye contact with Dimpna and as they stared, a slideshow of memories clicked through Dimpna's mind. Once upon a time this had been their peninsula, and they had ruled it with an endless stream of shenanigans. Girls staking claim to trails, and mountains, and white beaches, and sheer cliffs. Trekking through fields, dodging cow patties, and wielding sticks like swords. Skipping stones across the water, scouring the strands for mussels and periwinkles, slipping on stones and seaweed in hot pursuit. Fortifying themselves against parents, and siblings, and nuns, and lads. At the start of their summers they'd be bone pale, midsummer they'd be burned, but by the end they would finally be brown, the soles of their feet like tanned hides. Sheila Maguire and Dimpna Wilde against the big bad world.

Dimpna would accompany Sheila when she was forced to call into the pub to drag her father home. Sheila would accompany

Dimpna when she wanted to beg off a shift at the clinic, leveraging the soft spot Dr. Wilde had for Sheila's charm. They'd traversed every right of passage like sisters until they fell prey to that worn-out old song, that angular, pointy shape, the triangle. In the end, they'd traded their sisterly love for the promise of happily-ever-after with Paul Byrne. What eejits they'd been. Twenty-seven years later, they were practically strangers and he was still a confirmed bachelor. Yet, in the end it was Sheila who had betrayed Dimpna, not just breaking her heart, but doing so with a ruthlessness that had shocked her. So callous was her betrayal that it severed every bond their memories had so painstakingly built. Dimpna liked to think she'd grown past it, but her thudding heart and quickening pulse told a different story.

Scratches from the inside of the bus interrupted the moment. Dimpna's pack had been left out of the excitement and they were not going to stand for it. She released her three loves, feeling a strange flush of pleasure as Detective Cormac O'Brien backed away. She headed with them into the courtyard, for a messy zoo was better than being stuck inside a little bus. Spike led the way, his spine arched and tail swiping.

"I don't think that yard can take any more animals," Detective O'Brien said.

"Funny," Dimpna said. "I was just thinking it couldn't take any more guards."

He shifted his weight to the other foot as if caught off balance by her retort. "If your father doesn't come out of the clinic, we're going to have to go in after him," he said. "Will you speak with him and see if we can deal with this peacefully?"

She had no idea what *this* even was. "I will, so just give me a minute." She entered the courtyard, watching carefully not to step in a pile, made sure her animals were comfortable with their new friends, then scratched behind numerous ears before turning to Sheila. "What's the story?"

"Dimpna," Sheila said. "I can't believe it's you." Her voice sounded genuine but her eyes were all over the detective. Still all about men. Some things never changed.

"My father?" Dimpna prompted.

"He's having an outburst," Sheila said. "I had to call the guards."

"Are you alright?" Detective O'Brien shouted to Sheila. He pointed to her left eye. Dimpna hadn't noticed at first, but there it was, an angry welt just above Sheila's left eye, bright red and beginning to swell.

Dimpna edged forward, gobsmacked. "What happened?"

"Your father happened," Sheila said. "He hit me."

CHAPTER 9

"*H*E HIT YOU?" AS DIMPNA WAITED FOR SHEILA TO ANSWER, SHE prayed it wasn't true. Her father had never raised his hand to anyone in his life. *Please say no. Please say no.*

"He threw a book at me," Sheila said, patting her eye with the tips of her fingers. "Literally. I should have ducked."

Dimpna resisted the urge to ask her the title of the book. A hefty volume by the looks of it. This was hardly the time for a good reading recommendation. "I have an ice pack in the bus."

"She needs to go to hospital," Detective O'Brien said. "We need photos and we need to create a report."

Photos. A report. Against her father. "Oh my God."

"I'm sorry," Sheila said, training her good eye on Dimpna.

"I had no idea things were this bad." She should have known. She'd been too wrapped up in her own drama. Her parents were from that generation of Irish folks that never talked openly about their troubles. Even when the wolf was already inside your door. *Especially then.*

"Whatever you're thinking," Sheila said, "it's worse."

"Ma'am, is Dr. Wilde a danger to himself?" Detective O'Brien shouted across the courtyard. The goat bleated and dogs barked. His nose twitched, and then contorted as he violently sneezed five times in a row.

"God bless you" rang out from everyone but Dimpna.

"He is not a danger to anyone," she yelled back. *Was he?* What if one of her parents was the killer? Or both of them? Then again, it had been ages since her parents had done anything together, so she highly doubted they had skipped a romantic dinner for two and gone straight to co-planning a murder. *The couple that kills together . . .*

"I don't think so, Detective," Sheila said. "He's just standing in the middle of broken glass, ranting about something he can't find."

"What?" Dimpna said. "What can't he find?"

"He can't remember," Sheila said. "I'm sorry, Dimp. It's really bad."

Dimpna gestured to the packed courtyard. "I'll say."

Sheila nodded, following her gaze around to all the messy little creatures. "Poor things. It wasn't like this a few days ago. He's really gone off the rails." Sheila glanced at her watch. "I don't have time to take care of it, but I can make some calls if you'd like." It took a moment for Dimpna to realize Sheila was waiting for her to respond. Barely home and apparently she was in charge. "I finished cleaning out all the back kennels. We have room for at least twenty," Sheila said. "I can get a few folks over here to help sort them out."

"I would really appreciate it," Dimpna said. She meant it. No matter what had happened in the past, she could use all the friends she could get.

Sheila nodded. "Consider it done." Sheila offered a shy smile. She was a beautiful woman. Earthy. Exuberant. She'd never married or had children. Did she ever have a love greater than Paul? Dimpna hoped so. For her sake, she hoped so. She had also been loyal to her father. Would that remain the case? Was she friend or foe?

"Do you think you can get him to come out?" Detective O'Brien called.

"I will do me best, Detective," Dimpna said. Tears streamed down Sheila's face, darkening her freckles.

"You're really here," Sheila said, her voice thickening. "Home at last." She opened her arms for a hug.

Dimpna hesitated. She hadn't quite worked up to the hugging stage. Even if they were no longer like sisters, even if the blood they once mingled from slicing their fingers and pressing them to-gether had run dry, Sheila should have called her to tell her what was going on. Then again, her parents should have too, and Don-necha for that matter. Sheila, sensing defeat, dropped her arms. Dimpna felt someone's gaze and turned around to lock eyes with the detective. *Great.* She turned away again, let him stare.

"I suppose I should have rang you," Sheila said. "I assumed you wouldn't want to hear from me."

It was as much as her old friend would concede. "How long has my father been . . . not himself?"

"It started a few months ago, I'd say. He'd be found wandering around the streets at all hours of the night. Showing up late to the clinic. Forgetting the names of things. Then forgetting what those things were used for. Forgetting our names. Forgetting what our jobs were. Asking us the same question a dozen times within the hour. We all tried to get him to go to hospital, but he refused. We had to call all the clients and tell them we could only make house calls and they had to schedule them through Niamh."

Dimpna had heard about Niamh—the front-office manager and a bundle of positive energy according to her mam. If the courtyard looked like this, it was obvious that her father was now on his own. It takes a village, and he had shut them out. "I see." She didn't, though; she couldn't see anything. She felt like something was right in front of her, taunting her, an opaque window sealed shut.

"There's been a rapid decline the past few weeks." Sheila low-ered her voice and moved in closer. "I've seen Dr. Wilde fly into a violent rage more than once."

"Dementia-related?"

Sheila shrugged. "That's what it looks like. He gets uncontrol-lably angry." A silver BMW with a custom navy-and-green stripe slic-ing through the middle shot up the street. Dimpna's heart lurched. Was it going to plow straight into the field? Brakes screeched as it came to an abrupt stop, sending gravel flying and the guards scram-bling.

"O'Reillys," Sheila groaned. "I smell trouble."

Dimpna had an overwhelming urge to run, but her legs grew roots that burrowed into the ground. The driver and passenger door opened simultaneously, and the widow and son stepped out. Dimpna waited for the animals to erupt yet again, but oddly they stood still, fur raised and eyes trained on the newcomers. Róisín O'Reilly, tall and slim as ever, her once-dark hair now a shock of coiffed white. Her dove-gray suit, and white feathered hat and gloves, seemed more suited for a day out at the races than . . . whatever the reason for this visit was. She was nearly seventy years of age by now. It was only when Dimpna took in Sean's nearly matching gray suit and crisp white shirt with a navy and green bowtie that it dawned on her. They'd probably just come from a meeting with the parish priest to plan the funeral. An image of Johnny O'Reilly flat on his back in a coffin assaulted her, his dancing shoes pointing to the heavens, still and useless.

The back door of the vehicle opened and another man exited. He wore denims, a black long-sleeved shirt, and a white cowboy hat. His left sleeve hung loose where his arm should have been. Tommy Healy. Here it was, she was barely home, and all her enemies had crawled out of their hidey-holes. One of the last times she'd seen Tommy Healy, he'd been pretending to be dead on the floor of a horse barn. Even now she couldn't look at him without seeing his body slump to the ground, his eyes rolling back in his head as Sean O'Reilly towered behind him, strangling him with a tie. Or at least, that's what Dimpna thought. The trauma had never quite left her, even after all these years. Reality was perception, and in her experience she had witnessed a murder. If Sean O'Reilly had known it would scar her for the rest of her life, would he still have done it? She fell for it, as the old saying goes, *hook, line, and sinker.* One of his most disturbing pranks. She could still hear Tommy's raucous laughter as he sat across from her at the O'Reillys' dining table hours later, resurrected and chuffed to bits that they had pulled it off. The guards did little to hide their smirks, failing to comfort her with *Lads will be lads.* Psychopaths the pair of them.

Dimpna felt a gaze on her, as hot as a breath on her neck, and she turned her head in Sean's direction. Their eyes locked. He had slimmed down and his face showed the years. Tall, like his mam, with sand-colored hair arranged in perfect little waves, framing intense hazel eyes flecked with green. She may not have seen him in twenty-seven years, but she'd seen a constant echo of him. Ben.

The same sandy hair and hazel eyes flecked with green, but right now she even saw her son reflected in Sean's furrowed brow and clenched jaw. Were they just genetically doomed to be brooding men? He looked as if he was dying to speak but unable to make his mouth form words. The widow O'Reilly flocked to the detective as Tommy Healy stood like a statue by the car. Did he laugh at Dimpna every time he saw her? Imagine her crouching behind a horse stall in abject terror? *Lads will be lads. Lads will be lads.*

"Why hasn't Eamon Wilde been arrested?" Róisín demanded, her voice carrying across the field. She wasn't using his title. Dimpna knew that was purposeful.

"Mum," Sean said. "Let me handle this."

"You've done a stellar job so far," she said.

Sean spoke directly to Dimpna. "Evidence was found near my father's body," he said. "A syringe and a vial of euthanasia medicine."

"Release." The word fell out of Dimpna's mouth before she could stop it.

"Did he do it? Did your father put my father down like a dog?"

"I loathe that expression," Dimpna said. "We treat all in the animal kingdom with respect." She was trying hard not to sound cruel, given his father's sudden demise. But being present for the last moments of an animal's life on this earth, bearing witness to owners in the grip of raw and oh-so-vulnerable grief, hanging on to the last precious moments, as she strived to make their final journey as painless and reverent as possible . . . as her da would say— *Help them romp into that forever field . . .* it was one of the most profound and humbling experiences of her life. She could not explain to a layman how those moments embodied not only the miracle of our fragile existence, but the epiphany that love wasn't a feeling, it was a powerful force. One that did not die. Her father had never taken that awesome responsibility for granted and neither had she. That expression pushed all her buttons. "And no— my father would not have used Release to kill a man." *He'd have used the Monster in a Bottle. Immobilon.*

"Don't forget his whore of a wife," Róisín said. She shook her finger at the inspector. "A tarot card in me husband's pocket. The Devil."

Dimpna resisted the urge to tell her that the Devil simply meant *temptations.* She'd learned long ago that people believed what they wanted to believe. She watched the muscles in the inspector's jaw tighten, and she saw a pulse where there should have been a dimple. He was already losing control of the narrative. "I'd like to know where you heard that information," he said. Dimpna knew from listening to the press briefing on the radio that the tarot card had not been mentioned. Then again, this was Dingle, and The Dancing Man had been one of their own.

"It's true, isn't it?" Róisín said. "That's why you're here. Have you come to arrest him?"

Had he? Dimpna's head jerked in the direction of the inspector, awaiting his answer.

"Mrs. O'Reilly," Detective O'Brien said, "Mr. O'Reilly." Dimpna was startled. Mr. O'Reilly? Wasn't he dead? It took her a hot second to realize he was referring to Sean. "Why don't you head over to the Garda Station? I'll be there momentarily and I'd be happy to discuss our progress on the case."

"We'll stay while you arrest him," Róisín said.

"Right now we're still conducting our inquiries," the inspector said. "We'll be waiting to hear results from the state pathologist. Until then, I urge you not to believe every random bit of gossip you hear."

Róisín gestured to the derelict auto body shop. "We own this property. We have every right to stand in front of it." Technically, she was right. They owned a piece of everything in town. A piece of everyone. *Then why don't you clean it up?* was on the tip of Dimpna's tongue. *Because they wanted the Wildes to stare at rusting heaps of car parts all day long.* "We're not going anywhere until we see that murderer carted off in the back of your squad car."

Sean and Dimpna locked eyes, sending her insides sloshing. Now that Niall was dead, Sean was the only other person in the world who knew the truth of what happened that awful, awful night. The dark secret she'd so carefully walled in brick by brick. It created a morbid sense of intimacy between them. *You have a son,* she thought as they stared at each other. *I've kept him from you.* Sean gave her the faintest of nods, and to her surprise Dimpna found herself nodding back. "What about all these beasts?" Mrs. O'Reilly said, her lips curling up as she took in the animals in the courtyard. "They should also be carted off and put down."

Dimpna started forward, her mouth ready to spit. Sheila held her back. "Don't." Sheila's voice was commanding. "Don't make it worse." Dimpna forced her lips closed. There was no point attacking the widow even if every cell in her body was primed to do just that. "Get inside, see to your da." Dimpna allowed Sheila's words to sink in. Róisín O'Reilly wasn't worth it. What must it feel like to be inside that woman's skin? To be inside her hateful skin and see the world through her hateful eyes, and feel such disdain for everyone and everything? Had she killed her husband just to blame the Wildes? It sounded far-fetched unless you knew the woman. The inspector out of Killarney was out of his depths. Dimpna wouldn't be surprised if that was the exact reason he had been brought in. Everyone in this town was afraid of them. The O'Reillys got away with everything.

"Dimpna Wilde, as I live and breathe, you've finally decided to show your face," Róisín called across the courtyard.

"It's Dr. Wilde," Dimpna said. "And I am sorry for your loss." The words felt like dirty pebbles in her mouth she was forced to spit out one by one.

"It's not your pity I want. It's your father behind bars. And your mother. She's in on it too, don't you know. In fact, they should round up the lot of you." She swiveled her gaze to the inspector as if she expected him to do just that.

Sheila gently shoved Dimpna to the door. "Go."

"I assure you, you have the wrong end of the stick," Dimpna said. "My father is not a murderer. He's been loyal to this town his entire life. Who looked after your precious animals all these years?" She didn't dare utter the word *horse*. She did not want the death of Last Dance thrown in her face, even if she deserved it.

"He showed his hand!" Róisín said. "Left the poison near my husband's body." It took every ounce of energy Dimpna had not to accuse Róisín of doing the evil deed herself. "Where is that whore mother of yours?"

"That's enough," Dimpna said. She started forward again and felt Sheila's hand grip her arm.

"Like mother, like daughter," Róisín said.

"Mum!" Sean said. "Calm down."

"Are you out of your mind speaking to me like that?" Róisín said. Sean closed his eyes and took a few steps back.

"This isn't what we agreed," Sean said. "Dr. Wilde has nothing to do with this." His voice was deeper and calmer than she'd ever heard it before. Sean O'Reilly, the voice of reason? Had hell frozen over?

"Dr. Wilde has nothing to do with this?" Róisín said to her son, mocking his tone. "He murdered your father!"

"I meant this Dr. Wilde," Sean said, gesturing to Dimpna.

"Christ almighty," Róisín said. "I'm not calling her that." Róisín O'Reilly had married into money. Somehow charmed one of the richest lads in Ireland. But Róisín's hardscrabble upbringing was still tumbling inside her. A tiger pretending to be a house cat. Her stripes were showing.

Dimpna allowed Sheila to urge her toward the clinic, and she had just reached the door when Detective Inspector O'Brien called out. "Does he have a weapon?"

"A weapon?" Dimpna whirled around. "Are you joking me?"

"We know he has syringes, doesn't he?" Róisín said. "And vials of deadly poison."

"Every vet in all of Ireland has vials of Release and syringes," Dimpna said. "And you have a stockpile at your estate." The O'Reillys employed numerous vets, including her father, whom they'd taken advantage of for the past twenty-seven years. A "gentleman's deal" hashed out between fathers in the dark of the night.

"But not every vet failed to report a missing vial of Release a few weeks before my husband was murdered, now did they?" Róisín responded.

Dimpna didn't need to ask how Róisín knew about the vial of Release. The O'Reillys had eyes and ears everywhere. "Release didn't kill Johnny O'Reilly," Dimpna said. "Mark my words."

"Really?" Inspector O'Brien said. He sounded genuinely curious. "Why do you say that?"

"She's a liar," Róisín screamed. "Did you know Dimpna's husband swindled half of Dublin?"

"Mum," Sean said. "It won't do any good to start a row." He threw a look to Dimpna that seemed almost apologetic. That look would change if he knew the secret she'd been keeping from him for the past twenty-seven years. Over the years, she'd waffled on whether or not she'd done a bad thing. But this moment had wiped it clean. She'd done *exactly* the right thing. The hatred she felt toward this woman wasn't healthy, and she couldn't help the thought boomeranging through her mind: *Why wasn't it you, Róisín? Why didn't someone murder you?*

"I'm not here to start a row," Dimpna said. "I want the guilty party to be caught, no matter who he or she turns out to be." *Did she?* The question had been hovering in the periphery, blanketing her thoughts like a thick layer of morning fog. What if it was one of her parents? What would she do? Or not do? It startled her that she did not have an immediate answer.

"We are very early days in this investigation," Inspector O'Brien said. "We need an official cause of death from the state patholo-gist," he repeated.

No one even looked his way.

"Give me one good reason to believe it's not her father," Róisín said. "Just one!"

"It would have taken multiple injections of Release to kill Mr. O'Reilly," Dimpna said. "Unless there was a sign of a struggle—rope marks on his wrist—something—I can't see why your husband would just stand there while someone injected him multiple times." She left the bit out that the killer may have used a tranquilizer first; it wouldn't have helped her argument.

"He must have been taken by surprise," Róisín said. "The cow-ardly way."

"What if someone came up from behind him and plunged the syringe into his neck?" Detective O'Brien asked.

Róisín O'Reilly's gloved hand flew up to her mouth. Sean put his arm around her shoulder and tried to coax her back toward the car.

"He would have been able to fight them off," Dimpna said. "The first jab would not have delivered any immediate effects."

"Interesting," the detective said. From the way he was looking at her, she didn't know if he meant her or the statement.

"It would have required multiple syringe-fulls to induce death. Was there any Release left in the bottle?"

He squinted at her. "I'm not at liberty to say."

"If Release killed him, the vial should be empty. If it's not—then you'll either find an extra vial at the scene, or the killer took it with him, or that's not what killed Mr. O'Reilly."

"Or her," the detective said, looking straight at Dimpna.

"Excuse me?" She had no idea what he was talking about.

"You called the killer a him. I'm simply pointing out that it might be a her."

"See what you just did there?" Dimpna pointed her index finger at him and it felt good. No. It felt great. This was the best she'd felt all day.

"What?" He glanced at the animals in the courtyard as if she was going to sic them on him.

"You called the killer an 'it.' Kind of hypocritical when you were lecturing me on gender, now don't you think?"

"Fascinating," he said, studying her as if he wanted to zip her up into one of his little plastic evidence baggies.

"He's not going to get away with this," Róisín said. "We demand an arrest."

"I promise you, we are going to investigate this case thoroughly," Detective O'Brien said to the widow. "You must let me do my job."

"I'll call the council chairman," Róisín said. "We need a Dublin Superintendent on this case."

Detective Inspector Cormac O'Brien looked pained as he headed for Róisín. Dimpna had an urge to warn him not to get too close. He turned and spoke with Sean, their heads bent as they whispered. Was this detective going to be in the O'Reillys' pockets? Would there even be a thorough investigation? A minute later Sean O'Reilly ushered his mother back into the car then headed for the driver's seat. He paused before getting in, making eye contact with Dimpna once again. It lasted an uncomfortable five seconds before he got into the car. Tommy Healy waited a second, his eyes also trained on her, the corners of his mouth turned up in a sneer. It was impossible to imagine he was once such a sweet boy. What had happened? The answer was obvious: The O'Reillys had happened.

Sometimes she wondered if he knew. He lived in those barns. Despite his big prank, she blamed mostly on Sean, Tommy had liked her back then. He would have tried to stop Sean, if he had known, wouldn't he? He opened the back door, climbed in, and slammed it shut. Róisín O'Reilly lowered her window and stuck her head out. "Do something about those nasty animals or someone else will," she said. "And I'm not just talking about those pathetic creatures taking over the garden—I'm including those sinners you call your parents."

CHAPTER 10

THE MINUTE DIMPNA STEPPED INTO HER FATHER'S CLINIC, A BELL jangled and the familiar scent of disinfectant and fur enveloped her. It was just as she remembered it. The curved front reception counter with cabinets and chairs behind it, benches for clients and their fur-babies forming an *L*-shape in the waiting room, and large posters on the walls of the waiting room showcasing kittens and puppies in various stages of growth. But her favorite feature hung on the wall behind the reception desk: three large photographs of cattle, bulls, and sheep in the Irish countryside. Being the center of a murder probe and losing his memory of all the animals he'd healed and saved, or at least attempted to heal and save, over the past five decades, was not the way a seasoned veterinarian should end his reign. A bottle of cleaner and a rag sat abandoned on the counter. It looked as if Sheila had been here to help clean up, before her father's tantrum had interrupted.

Dimpna headed down the hall past the kitchenette that led to two treatment rooms, one on the left and one on the right. The third room at the end of the hall was for surgeries. The last and smallest room contained medicine and surgical equipment. It was currently padlocked. Had the guards verified the batch number on the vial yet? Was that why they were here?

Was the padlock Sheila's doing? Dimpna hardly saw her da making such a move. She gave the rest of the place a quick once-over to see if it too was as she remembered, and it was. The dark staircase that led to an upstairs flat, and a door leading to the backyard and kennel. Dimpna hoped Sheila would come through and call a few heads to sort out the animals in the courtyard, transfer them to the kennels, and care for them until they could find them all homes. She took a deep breath, turned her head to the left, and spotted her father.

He stood in the treatment room with his back to the door. It looked as if a storm had come through and swept all the contents onto the linoleum floors. Books, vials, surgical instruments, papers, a keyboard, the computer chair—even the examination table was lying on its side. The lone window in the room let in the rays of the sun, making the steel table gleam like the blade of a knife. "Da?"

Eamon Wilde whirled around, his face a distortion of confusion and rage. He stared at her for a moment, before his eyes softened, a wide grin broke out, and he threw his arms open. "Hello, Dew." The nickname filled her with nostalgia. Dimpna Eileen Wilde, or as he liked to put it—Dew. *You're like a little drop of morning dew,* he used to sing to her. He was a tall man, but otherwise father and daughter shared many features. The same pale blond hair and mint-green eyes that everyone always commented on. "How's my miniature Viking today?"

She had more nicknames than fingers. "I'm good, Da." *The Irish Times* had gotten wind of the miniature-Viking nickname (somehow) and used it in one of their headlines. The media's ability to form public opinion was terrifying. It fascinated Dimpna how one's personality was partially formed by others, like waves eroding stones in the sand. Things repeated until you took them as gospel. *You're the messy one. Why can't you be neat like your brother? You're such a runt, I bet people step on you all the time. You're a freak. You have the prettiest eyes I've ever seen in my life. It's like you aren't even human. You're from out of this world, like an angel, so why don't you start acting like it? You swallowed it whole! You'll believe anything. You're so little, I bet people don't even notice you coming and going. You could hide anywhere. You're so little, you practically disappear. You'll act like a child the rest of your life. How can you hold that fiddle? It's barely bigger than you! You can get away with anything because you're little and cute. You can get away with anything!!*

The last refrain had come from her brother, Donnecha. He was obsessed with the idea that she could get away with anything, but it wasn't true. She only got away with some things. More than he got away with, she'd grant him that. But he had way more privileges as a lad that he still didn't recognize, so they never got far rehashing their childhood. Her father's hair was even paler now; it was no longer blond, but shifting toward silver, his eyes cloudy.

She went to hug him, but he dropped his arms and stepped back as if he didn't even recognize her. Her hands suddenly felt clammy. "What on earth is going on in here?"

"When's the next patient?" He looked at his bare wrist as if consulting a watch, his index finger tapping his wrinkled skin. "Did that wolfhound get his antibiotics?"

"Everything is settled for today. Why don't you come out and have a cup of tea?"

"It's closing time, is it? Shall we skip off to the pub?" He sounded delighted and completely without sarcasm. If only things were that simple. "Da. An ambulance is on the way and there's a zoo in the courtyard. The guards are demanding we clear it."

"Did you tell them it's a veterinarian clinic?" He sounded outraged. "They should be alarmed if there *weren't* animals in the courtyard."

"We can't leave them all loose and jumbled up. To whom do they belong?"

"They're lost souls, Dew. They belong to no man."

She didn't know this man. Her father had always been measured. When he spoke, it was deliberate. Never philosophical or whimsical. She'd often thought he'd make a great professor. He had little patience for loose tongues and profanity. He did not suffer fools. Only a few supervised animals were ever allowed in the front yard at a time. Eamon Wilde ran a tight ship, and it had worked for him the better part of five decades. He, more than anyone, would recoil at the thought of her witnessing a disease that would slowly disassemble the man he had so carefully built. She had to help him however she could, but she was out of her depth. He needed a doctor. "Why don't we go outside and get a bit of fresh air?"

"I don't have time. I'm looking for something." He scanned the floor as if the answer was buried in the heap of overturned items. "It's urgent." She believed him. She could hear the scraped panic in his voice.

"I'll help you. What is it?"

"I'm close," he said. "Somewhere. Something."

Sirens wailed outside, the blare growing closer. "They're here."

"Who?" He squinted.

"Paramedics, Da."

"What happened?"

"You happened."

"What do you mean?"

"You won't calm down, you threw a book at Sheila." They were going to write a report. A paper trail of violent behavior. For the Director of Public Prosecution. They were building their case against Dr. Eamon Wilde brick by brick. They probably weren't even going to do a proper investigation. Sheila was right. This was worse than Dimpna thought. She was going to have to beg Paul Byrne to get involved.

"Hit her? I did not."

"She has a welt near her eye."

"I saw that," her father said. "She needs to be more careful."

"She said you did it."

"Me?" His shock sounded genuine.

"You threw a book at her." Dimpna scanned the room. There it was by the far wall, a thick veterinarian tome splayed on the floor. She had an urge to hide it. She couldn't do that. Could she?

"That's just an expression, Dew. I should throw the book at all of them!"

"Where's Mam?" Dimpna was suddenly furious with her mother's absence. She felt like marching over to her caravan and dragging her out by her hair.

"Sheila Maguire is a good vet tech. But she'll never become a veterinarian. Not like my daughter."

Dimpna felt a lump in her throat. Eamon Wilde had always been long on lectures but short on praise. "You taught her well."

Her father frowned. "Sheila?"

"Your daughter."

"She's in Dublin." He covered his eyes briefly with his hand. "Did I make a mistake?"

"What do you mean?"

"Sending her away."

"I'm right here, Da." The torturous thoughts returned. What if she had stayed? Told the truth about everything? *It's not fair. You get away with everything!* But not without paying a hefty toll. She was still paying it.

"She left one monster only to marry another."

"My husband wasn't a monster. He just did a monstrous thing." Niall Flor had not been a monster. Not like the ones she'd known here. "I'm okay, Da. Ben and I are okay."

"He was here," her father said. "But it wasn't a nice visit."

"Niall?" she asked, dumbfounded.

"What?" Her father was confused. It was painful to watch. A helpless feeling enveloped her.

She softened her voice. "You said 'He was here.' Who was here?"

"Ben."

"No, Da. Ben has never been here." *Never.* She'd made sure of that.

Her father looked at her as if he'd never known her a day in her life. His gaze returned to the floor. "Where did this mess come from?"

"You turned the clinic upside down." Looking for something. What could he be looking for?

"This is serious, Dew. They're going to arrest your mother for murder unless we do something." He sounded more like himself now, and held her gaze.

"I don't think it's Mam they're going to arrest."

"She's a good woman, your mother." He shook his head. "But I probably shouldn't have married her."

Great. Just what she needed. A trip down honesty lane. "Tell me about the missing vial of Release."

"Did that fat receptionist forget to order a new batch?"

The father she knew would have never called a woman fat, especially not one of his loyal employees. "We need to get you to hospital." She didn't know how to deal with him. Was she supposed to lie to him? Tell him the truth? A dose of both?

"That ginger banshee has been stealing from me. I told you not to hang around that Sheila Maguire, didn't I?"

He had. Many times. Only, he'd never called her a "ginger banshee." "Why didn't you report the theft of Release?" she said. "And if someone broke into the clinic—why didn't they steal anything else?" And although it wasn't a padlock, the meds had always been kept under lock and key. Only her father and Sheila and "the fat receptionist" would have had access. What if Sheila was the thief? What would that mean?

He waved her question away like it was a trivial matter. "Release didn't kill the bastard. You know that."

She did know that. And now he sounded like the father she knew. Was he faking this? Was he guilty of murder and faking dementia? No. He had too much pride for that. Then again, what was pride when one's freedom was at stake? "Please. Don't talk like that around the guards."

"Like what?"

"I just need you to be with me for a few minutes. The guards think you murdered Johnny O'Reilly." Did he still have that Monster in a Bottle stored somewhere in the clinic? She was too afraid to ask. A single drop of it and Johnny O'Reilly would have been dead as a doornail. No vial or syringe needed. A single drop. To her this was proof that her father had not done this. But convincing the inspector of that would be nearly impossible.

Her father stepped over silver surgical instruments, and biros, and charts on the ground, to reach her. He grabbed both her wrists and held them tight. "Family comes first, Dew. Don't forget that."

"What does that mean?" His grip was strong; she pulled her hands away.

"It's family before everything." He turned and walked out of the room, then strode down the hall with a confident gait.

She followed him. "Tell me you didn't do this."

"You're here now. I'll hold them off as long as I can, but you need to fix this." He looked around the empty reception room. "Where is everyone?"

"Fix what?"

He turned and patted her on the head. "Good girl."

"Thanks, Da. But at least next time pat my head and say Good Dr. Wilde, will ya?"

He flung the front door to the clinic open, stood in the doorway with his hands raised. "You want me? Here I am, lads. Take a good look."

Detective O'Brien, who had been leaning against his car, and might have even nodded off, jerked his head in her father's direction. "Dr. Wilde?"

"Da," she hissed.

He looked back and grinned, then stepped outside. "I don't need an ambulance." Paramedics stood at the edge of the gate eyeing the half-dozen dogs who had lined up on the other side. At the sight of her father, the dogs pivoted from the guards and raced toward him, tails wagging. When they reached his heels, they stayed in step with him, looking up at him like they were his faithful subjects and he was their king. "Good lads," she heard her father say. "Good lads."

"If you don't agree to go to hospital for evaluation then you're coming into the station with us," a guard said, stepping up.

A second squad car had pulled in. Backup had arrived. They weren't playing.

"He'll go in the ambulance," Dimpna said. She had no idea what would come out of his mouth if they put him in the back of the squad car, except that none of it would be good.

"Dr. Eamon Wilde," Detective O'Brien said. "We are going to conduct a search of the clinic. We need the courtyard cleared of all these animals."

"What we need," Eamon said, "is an ark!" He thrust his index finger up theatrically. "Who wants to build one?"

"You need formal charges and a warrant," Dimpna said to the detective, not at all confident in what she was saying.

"There's been an assault here," Detective O'Brien said. "And the batch number on the vial of Release found on Clogher Strand has been traced to this clinic." He waited to see if she had a response. It was a blow, and she struggled not to let her emotions give her away.

Empty vials were discarded in proper bins and discarded following all regulations. Who took that vial and syringe and why? And then there was the matter of the tarot card. *Framed.* Her parents were being framed for murder. Could Sheila be the killer? Did she have a connection to Johnny O'Reilly? Dimpna had been away too long; she did not have her finger on the gossip pulse. The killer had to be someone they knew, someone with a knowledge of vet meds and easy access to the clinic. Maybe her father was right. Maybe Sheila Maguire was a thief. "We're within our rights to do a search," the inspector concluded.

Dimpna stepped to the side and gestured to the front door, making sure to sweep over all the lovely, lovely creatures standing between the inspector and the front door. "Be my guest."

He shifted his weight again, his nose twitching. "You need to get those animals somewhere safe. Isn't that part of your job? To keep them safe?"

"I thoroughly intend to keep them safe. Finding the best place for them, not to mention figuring out if any of them have owners. But it isn't going to happen by the snap of my fingers. No matter how many times I wave my hands about and say 'Abracadabra.'"

Detective Inspector O'Brien took a step toward the courtyard, then veered back again. "You think he did it," he said. "That's what's going on here."

"Have formal assault charges been drawn up yet?" Dimpna kept her voice light and innocent. Sheila would not press charges. Time and distance couldn't change the fact that they were both Dingle women and they would not turn on each other. Right? She enjoyed watching the detective frown.

"It won't take long to get a warrant." He'd come impulsively, banking on her father letting him in. And given his state of mind, he may have done exactly that. She'd arrived bang on time.

"You'd best get on with it then." She should have removed the book. He had a point about the courtyard, though. She couldn't keep the animals like this for long. In the seconds she'd been inside, the feathers and waste had seemed to multiply. The smell wasn't pretty either. She'd nearly forgotten her father was still by her side until he reached out, and soon Dimpna felt his hand in hers. He'd barely hugged her her entire life, and now he wanted to hold hands? Instead, he palmed something into her hand and closed her fingers around it. It was cold and metal. A ring? It felt too big to be a woman's ring. She was terrified to look. Her heart pounded as she continued to squeeze her hand around the object. Her father strode toward the paramedics.

"Away we go, lads," he said.

"I'm coming with you." Dimpna nudged her handbag closer, unzipped the top, and dropped the object into its depths.

"No," her father said. "Clean up this mess. Then find your mother." The look he shot her was one she knew well. He meant business. Somewhere, locked inside him, the father she'd always known was within reach. Dimpna nodded, her eyes filling with tears. She bit the side of her cheek to keep them at bay. She would not let that Killarney inspector see her cry.

The paramedics helped him into the back of the ambulance. He saluted her. "I'm going on a call, Dew. You can't come with me, you're not ready." Her father waved at her from the back of the ambulance as if he was on a float in a parade.

"Don't say a word to anyone," she said. "I'll find you a good solicitor." *I'm going to do my best for you, Da. My absolute best.* The paramedics closed the ambulance doors; the sirens wailed and lights flashed as they pulled out.

"Where is your mother?" Detective Inspector O'Brien said. "I'd like to speak with her."

Dimpna's gaze turned to the caravan, and she was shocked to see a line of people snaking from the front door all the way across the green field. "What in the world?"

Detective O'Brien seemed just as perplexed. "What's the story?"

Dimpna nearly spit out that her mam was a tarot card reader when she remembered the card found in O'Reilly's suit pocket. Was he waiting to see if she'd say it? Since when did her mother have so many "clients"? *Since she was the prime suspect in a murder probe. Devil days,* Dimpna thought. *Temptations.* She shrugged. Two could play it cool. "I suppose neighbors are offering their support."

"Support?" The detective sure did a lot of frowning. The creases on his forehead backed up her assumption.

"Her husband is suffering from dementia, and the guards think the man who dedicated fifty-odd years of his life to saving animals has killed a human." Her annoyance bloomed into a slow-burning rage. He'd spent his life saying "Yes" to the residents of Dingle. Yes, I'll get up at all hours of the morning and drive out to you. Yes, I'll save your family cat, or dog, or the farm animal you depend on to put money in your pocket and food on your table. Yes, I'll test your entire herd of cattle for TB, standing on my feet in the sun or rain or both for days. Yes, I'll be there day and night during lambing season. Yes, you can pay me next Friday. Yes, you can drop off the stray you found on the side of the road. Yes, I'll work in substandard conditions to save an animal's life and not give a thought to my own. Where were these people now? Fifty years. Where was the benefit of the doubt? "My father is not a killer."

Detective O'Brien locked eyes with her. "How would you know?"

His tone was gentle but she received it like a bite. "I beg your pardon?"

"When was the last time you were home, Dr. Wilde?"

There it was. Somehow, this stranger had reached way down inside her and squeezed the muscle that was supposed to be her heart. It was pulsing now, that ever-throbbing-guilt. "Twenty-seven years," she said, barely able to bring her voice above a whisper.

"What?" He nudged closer.

"I haven't been home in twenty-seven years." Her voice was clearer now, resentment for his probing bubbling to the surface.

"Really?" he said, sounding as if that wasn't the answer he'd been expecting. Or perhaps he knew exactly how long she'd been away and he was purposefully jabbing at wounds. "Why is that?"

A beat-up lorry rumbled up and interrupted the strange moment, brakes squealing as it jerked to a stop. Detective O'Brien reached down with his right hand and used his left to barricade her behind him. "Stay back."

"For God's sake, are you reaching for a gun?"

"I said, 'Stay back.'"

"It's an old man!"

The door to the truck swung open and the old man emerged, wiping sweat from his brow. He was skinny but his arms bulged with muscles. He wore a flannel shirt, tan trousers, and a tweed cap. Dimpna knew from the look of him that he was a local farmer. "I need Dr. Wilde," he shouted.

"Which one?" Cormac O'Brien said under his breath. "This clinic is closed," he said louder.

The farmer looked past him to Dimpna. "Detective Byrne said I might find you here," he said. "You're the daughter. You're a vet too." He pronounced it like *vit.*

"Yes, sir," she said.

"I'm Val Keegan. Call me Val, Doc. You were an itty-bitty thing when I last saw ya."

"She still is," she heard Detective O'Brien say.

She tapped the inspector on his shoulder and he turned to face her. "I'm just an itty-bitty thing," she said. "What astute detective skills. You want to say more about it, get it out of your system?" He shook his head. She barreled on. "How about 'How's the weather down there?'" He moved his lips but no sound came out. "What about this one? 'I bet everyone loves you. You're so down-to-earth.'"

"That's a good one," the farmer said, flashing yellow teeth.

"Or—'You sit on that phone book so much, I bet your arse has memorized everyone's number.'" The inspector was shaking his head but she couldn't stop. "'Say what you like about Dimp the Imp. At least she doesn't look down on people!'"

Detective O'Brien held up both hands as if she was arresting him. "I truly, truly apologize, Dr. Wilde," he said. "My comment was completely out of line."

"I'd say. You're hardly a tall drink of water yourself." His cheeks blazed pink and satisfaction bloomed within her. "I'm only messing," she said. "I may be short, but I'm known for my tall tales." She laughed, politely at first, harder when she saw the look of absolute agony on the detective's face. This was the best she'd felt all day. "Ah, stop," she said. "I'd get out my fiddle and play you a tune, but I'd best see what this nice gentleman needs." She turned to the farmer. "Now."

"Hate to interrupt the jibber-jabber," the farmer said. "But I've got an emergency. Me donkey got spooked and ran through a barbed wire fence. It's wrapped all around him and the poor thing is stumbling around in pain but won't let us anywhere near him. It's wretched to watch, like. He's bleeding all over, pure panicked, like. Can you come, Doc?"

"I've got my things in the van," she said. "I'll follow you." She strode past Detective Cormac O'Brien.

He reached for her, and she instinctively recoiled. "If you don't clear the courtyard so we can search the clinic, I'm going to have to call an agency to deal with these animals."

It was Tuesday and sliding toward afternoon. If he did reach the Irish Society for Prevention of Cruelty to Animals, they'd be coming from outside of Dingle. And that was once the detective figured out the right "agency" to call. "I swear to you Sheila is already placing calls for help. And as soon as I'm back from this call, if it hasn't been done already, I will sort out these animals. In the meantime, you can see they're not in any danger, and they're certainly not threatening anyone."

His gaze traveled over the courtyard and she wondered if there was more going on than just allergies. Was he afraid? Either way, not an animal person at all. She felt a squeeze of pity as she always did for those who didn't fall madly in love with animals. She couldn't imagine a world without them. "What about your mother?" he asked. "Would she be able to sort them out?"

"Good luck with that," she called over her shoulder. "And if you have any ounce of decency, will you also tell her that her husband was just taken to hospital in an ambulance?" She whistled for her pack who would freak if she dared to take a ride in the bus without them, herded them into the VW, then hopped in and slammed the door shut before he could respond.

CHAPTER 11

*P*AUL BYRNE WAS IN THE HOME STRETCH OF HIS DAILY HIKE AROUND THE peninsula, his German shepherd, King, proudly leading the way home despite the arthritis in his hips. His loyal friend was getting old, like Paul, but he was still giving it a go. King's perseverance filled Paul with pride. Once back at his cottage he filled King's water bowl, gave the old one a treat, and poked around in his garden. Anything to keep his mind off Dimpna Wilde. She was probably here by now, and he'd taken his mobile out of his pocket to give her a bell at least a dozen times before changing his mind. Let her come to him. She had enough to deal with.

The biggest murder inquiry of a lifetime and it wasn't going to be his case. He was itching to see the murder scene, although truth be told, he saw it every time he closed his eyes. His guards were still loyal; they'd kept him in the loop. Johnny O'Reilly murdered. And Paul didn't feel the least bit sorry. He was just about to heat up his stew when he glanced out his front left window. A middle-aged woman in a tattered jumper was straining up the hill toward his front door. He stepped out, hoping whoever it was wouldn't stay long. It wasn't until she was a few feet away that he recognized her. Nancy Griffin. She must have taken a bus to get here, and that fact alone had him on high alert. Although Saoirse still came to the odd activity at the group home, he hadn't seen the mother since the night he'd almost beat her husband to death. He still didn't regret it, even though it cost him his job. He'd have enough to worry about once the man was out of jail.

"Is she here?" Nancy called out.

"Who?"

"Saoirse."

Paul shook his head. "She's never come here, Mrs. Griffin."

Nancy stopped to suck in a few breaths, her face red, either with exertion or alcohol or both. "She said she talks to you."

"She does, so. At the center." Paul volunteered with a children's group home that housed troubled children. Those without parents, those with dysfunctional parents, those who were lost and struggling. Saoirse had taken to him like a magnet, had seen him as some kind of savior, and Paul had quickly ascertained she needed to be around kids her own age. He'd tried to warm her up to the group, but it was him she came to see. And King—she had a great fondness for dogs.

"She never came home," Nancy said. Now that she was closer, he could see she didn't appear intoxicated, but looked as if she was just coming around from a bender.

He glanced at the sky. "We have a bit of daylight left," he said. "I'm sure she'll be home soon. Do you want me to call the center?"

"I already did. They haven't seen her either."

"She's been gone all day, has she?"

Nancy shook her head. "She's been gone since her birthday."

Paul felt a little jolt. He hadn't known it was her birthday. "When was that?"

"Saturday night."

His hands flexed. "Saturday?" He stepped toward her. "She's been missing since Saturday night?" The night of the murder. Nearly seventy-two hours. Forty-eight hours would have been troubling enough. The most critical window of time after a kid went missing. Slammed shut.

Nancy swallowed, then nodded. "She must have run away."

"Tell me you called the guards."

"I figured you could do that for me."

"Your child has been missing since Saturday and you haven't notified the police?" A rush of outrage threatened to bring out the worst in him. The thought of that poor girl being born to a violent man and this absent, self-indulgent, alcoholic mother—well, it was no wonder Paul stuck to animals. They were so much better than human beings.

Nancy's face contorted. "I thought she was getting back at me. I told her we'd celebrate her birthday next week. Thirteen is an unlucky number."

Paul headed inside for his mobile phone. "Does she have a phone?"

Nancy shook her head. "We can't afford one of those yokes."

Paul knew he was clenching his jaw, and he couldn't help it. They should have given her a phone. For safety. He'd have to talk to the group leaders, raise money to get them all mobile phones. That was of no use to Saoirse now. Had she simply run away? He held up his finger and grabbed his phone from his desk, then returned to the front garden as he dialed 999. "Do you have any idea where she was headed on Saturday night?"

"I told you she snuck out. But my guess is the harbor. There was a lot going on that night. She likes to people-watch."

Why hadn't she called him? He turned his back to Mrs. Griffin as he talked to the clerk who answered the phone. He quickly filled them in on the situation and then hung up. "We're going into the station," he said. "Do you remember what she was wearing Saturday night?"

She shook her head. "For the third time, she snuck out while I was napping."

Napping. That was one word for it. "Is there anything you can give us to go on? Anything at all?"

Nancy chewed on her bottom lip. "She took her purple backpack."

The wire-wrapped donkey was staggering downhill like a drunkard, braying, and kicking. Every movement caused more of the fence spikes to sink into his flesh, igniting his blind panic. Dimpna knew how he felt. If he wasn't careful, he was going to topple over. Despite being a vet, Dimpna had yet to get used to witnessing an animal in pain. It cut through her, every time. But a loud client was a fighting client, and she was grateful this one was literally still kicking. Dimpna had wire clippers given to her by the farmer and a syringe with a sedative, and the farmer trailed after her, clutching an old rope. Their only other tool was a baby-faced lad accompanying them who looked to be about fifteen years of age. This was going to require a little bit of prayer and a lot of creativity. "Don't you have some kind of a dart gun you can shoot him with?" the farmer asked, giving her the side-eye.

"Didn't realize we'd be on safari today," Dimpna said. "Give me a minute to think." If they could get the donkey uphill and into the barn, they could secure him in a stall with a harness where they could safely clip the wire from a neighboring stall. Or they could wait until he passed out from the blood and hope and pray it wasn't too late. Dimpna loathed seeing the poor thing filled to the gills with terror. "Any sheepdogs or border collies on the property?"

"Only one left and she's too old," the farmer said with a shake of his head.

"We're going to have to borrow one from somewhere. If she'd had the discipline to train him, Pickles could be an excellent herder. As it was, he was too hyper, and might startle the donkey. Why don't you make a few calls?"

"How many do you need?"

"Just one good one," Dimpna said. That was true with so many things in life.

"Malone had one show up next door. Young 'un," the lad said. "But he listens real good, like."

"Malone?" the farmer said. "He's the reason we're in this mess in the first place."

Dimpna didn't have time to decipher a neighborly feud. "Can you see if we can borrow him?" She directed this to the farmer as she wanted the lad to stay with her. He had better energy, and she trusted him more around the freaked-out donkey.

"Alright." As the farmer moved out, Dimpna directed the young lad to move downhill. Not too close but close enough that maybe the bugger would move uphill on his own. She had wire clippers with her, but the last thing she needed today was a kick to the head.

"We're going to need some treats," she said. "Carrots? Apples? Turnips?"

"We've got apples." The lad disappeared for a brief moment and came back with the treat. Dimpna nodded her thanks and tucked it in her pocket.

"What's the plan when the sheepdog arrives?" the lad asked.

Dimpna eyed the opening to the barn. If the sheepdog was able to herd the donkey toward it, that was half the battle, but he wasn't going to be as compliant as sheep, and they still needed him ensconced in a stall so they could safely move around him to clip the wire. And even if they could get close enough to inject him with a sedative, it might cause the donkey to fall, which would sink all the sharp bits into his skin. If one pierced the wrong artery, the donkey would be a goner. She needed to get on a horse and get close enough to start snipping. If she could get the donkey in a head harness with blinders, that might help. It felt like forever, but when the farmer returned, a young sheepdog was trotting after him. "I'm also going to need a horse," Dimpna said. "And a head harness with blinders."

"I'll saddle one up for you," the farmer said. "She's an old mare, but the least likely to throw you."

"Brilliant." She tested the sheepdog, pointing at the donkey. "Away to me." It looked at the donkey, then looked back at her. "Go on."

"Bye," the lad said to the sheepdog. "Bye, bye." It barked and began dancing around the donkey, still somewhat confused by the shiny silver wire encasing it. The donkey brayed and stuttered toward the barn before stopping and letting out a pitiful bray.

"Come on, luv, we want to help you." The donkey brayed again. Dimpna sighed. How many creatures did it take to rescue a stubborn donkey? Apparently, this one was going to need the whole village. Dimpna saddled the old mare, then reluctantly called for the lad to give her a lift up—there was no time to find a step stool or a bucket. He obliged without a single crack about her height. Once on the mare she headed to the field, and slowly triangulated herself between the donkey and the sheepdog. She asked the lad to move to the entrance to the barn, hoping the donkey would see him as a beacon to follow. Reluctantly, bucking and braying, step by step he was herded toward the opening of the barn. When he reached the entrance, Dimpna moved in from the side and tossed the head harness over the enraged creature. She nearly slipped off the mare, who then stomped her feet a bit, sending her sideways, as the donkey started to fight. She could hardly blame him; his poor head had been the only thing that was free of restraint.

"Relax, relax, relax," she said, partly to the donkey, partly to herself. She was still slipping off the mare and had to concentrate to right herself, all the while grappling with the harness until it was somewhat secure. A metal spike scraped along the back of her arm, and soon bright spots of blood appeared and began to run, but at least she was able to secure the donkey with blinders. It did the trick and he stood still, breath labored and nostrils flaring. "It's alright, luv, you're alright." She snuck the apple out of her pocket, and once it was near his nose and mouth, the donkey's soft lips curled up and his pink tongue came out to slurp it up, his mouth like velvet in her palm. "See? Better things are in store." Ignoring her bloody arm, and not bothering to move him into a stall, she leaned in quickly with the wire cutters, snipping away as fast as she could. The young lad was soon by her side and with gloved hands began removing the loose bits of fence. The donkey, sensing freedom, began huffing, his cheeks puffing out air. "Good lad," Dimpna said in a low and soothing voice in between snips. "Good lad."

When all the wire fencing was gone, she saw there was a fair bit of cuts on the poor creature. The farmhand tossed her a towel and she began dabbing the donkey gently.

"That was for your arm," he said.

"Oh. Right."

He tossed her another one and she wrapped it around her arm. "Thanks a million."

"Not a bother."

"We need to get him into a stall because the antiseptic is going to sting." The farmer and the lad helped guide the donkey into a stall. Dimpna shouted for the lad to bring her more apples and an empty pail. He frowned in confusion but returned with both items. "You're on apple duty," she said handing them over to him. "Once I start administering the antiseptic, keep feeding him." She turned over the bucket and stepped on it, finally able to reach over the stall. From here she administered the antiseptic and a shot for the pain. "Is he up on his tetanus shots?"

"He is, so," the farmer said. "Your father always remembers." He cleared his throat as if suddenly remembering their situation.

"That's a bright side," Dimpna said, keeping her voice chipper. The apples were gone and Dimpna was still dabbing at sore spots with the antiseptic. The donkey howled and stomped in outrage, but Dimpna spoke in a soothing tone the entire time, even humming a little until he calmed down. Finally the lad turned up some carrots. The donkey gulped them up, and life was good again.

Dimpna slipped off her boiler suit and washed up in a bucket of water and soap provided by the young farmhand. Her cuts were still bleeding although they weren't deep enough to merit stitches. She reached into her bag, removed a bandage, and tended to her arm. "You're going to have to keep the cuts clean and watch for signs of infection in the coming days."

"We will of course," the farmer said.

"Does that happen a lot?" the lad asked, pointing to the bandage.

"I'm prepared for almost anything," Dimpna said with a wink. She almost felt bad when the young man's face turned bright red. "What spooked the poor fella?" Dimpna asked with a head nod to the donkey.

"Malone's been shooting off his rifle," the farmer said. "The lad here doesn't like loud noises." He scratched the donkey behind the ear.

"What is he shooting at?"

"Gawpers have been driving by his property ever since he found Johnny O'Reilly's body. As if shooting at them is the answer. Makes me wonder if he had something to do with the whole mess." He went back to cooing at his donkey. "Isn't that right, Petal?"

"Petal?" Dimpna said. The donkey had an enormous penis. "Never heard of a jack named Petal."

"Me daughter named him when she was young," the farmer said. "I didn't have the heart to change it."

"I like it," Dimpna said. "Males can be petals too. Can't they?" She made the mistake of glancing at the young farmhand. His face turned so red, she could barely see his features. She hoped she hadn't stepped in anything other than the usual pile of poo. Her thoughts returned to the farmer's previous words. Finbar Malone. The fisherman who found the body. She'd seen his picture in the paper. He said he'd stopped at the cliff for a smoke after several days at sea. She thought of how she'd been hounded after becoming an overnight celebrity, and she couldn't blame him for wishing he could shoot off a gun. But wishing and doing were two very different things. He was going to beget more trouble.

"Will ya see this young pup home on your way out?" the farmer said. "Malone is expecting him back."

"Hopefully he has a treat ready for the good boy," Dimpna said. "Not a bother." Dimpna slipped a lead on the sheepdog just in case it decided to take off, then headed for her bus. The dog jumped in the back without prompting, tongue hanging out, excited for the adventure. Her pack all moved in to check him out and probably put him through the ringer. She ruffled his head before hopping into the driver's seat. It was after she pulled up to Finbar's small house that she spotted her handbag on the passenger seat and remembered there was a mysterious object within its depths. She opened it and stared inside. A silver ring rested on the bottom. Instinctively, she reached into her glove compartment and slipped out a pair of medical gloves. Then she picked up the item and found herself staring at a man's ring. It was silver with Celtic knots, and in the center was a giant ruby. She knew this ring. Everyone in Dingle knew the ring. It was bought in honor of his first million-euro winner, also named Ruby. There was no doubt in her mind. This was Johnny O'Reilly's flashy piece. Why on earth did her father have it? Was it possible? Was her father a killer?

The dog whined in the back seat. She turned to find her canine passenger squeezed in by Pickles, Spike, and Guinness. But the sheepdog wasn't bothered; instead, he was eyeing the ring as if he sensed the drama. She dropped the ring back in her handbag and removed the gloves before placing her index fingers over her lips. "Shhh. Not a word," she said. "Not a single whine." She reached into her glove box and fumbled around until she found a loose dog treat. The sheepdog snapped it up then pleaded with her for more. She laughed and turned her attention out the window. Finbar Malone was nowhere in sight. She exited her bus and opened the back door. She kept her pack at bay as the sheepdog bounded out, then stood looking at her, tongue hanging out. "You're home." The dog didn't move. The house was white with a blue door and matching window trim. It might have been charming in its day, but the paint was peeling off and the roof sagged to the left. But the yard was tidy, including a well-tended garden in front. A trailer was parked in the drive with a large boat lying on top, covered with canvas. This had to be the right place.

"Hello?" she called, heading along the drive. The dog stayed at her heels. Finbar must have trained him well, or perhaps it was the missus. Fishermen spent days, weeks, months out at sea; she doubted he was home often enough to spend much time working with the dog. As they drew nearer to the house, she heard what sounded like a shovel hitting dirt. "Hello?" The noise stopped abruptly and before she'd taken another step, Finbar Malone, thick gloves on his hands, came barreling toward her, nearly knocking her down. He was tall with a messy white beard, his head covered in a tweed cap. His face was like a treasure map to nowhere, lines fanning out in all directions. He was broad and big and towered over her. It wasn't a pretty sight given he was missing half his teeth; the other half were yellow and brown. The sheepdog jumped up and placed his paws on Finbar's chest.

"Down." The dog obeyed but began dancing around him. Was he herding him? This suddenly didn't seem like a love relationship between dog and fisherman.

Finbar removed his gloves. His right hand was red and swollen.

She pointed at it. "What happened?"

His eyes flicked over his hand as he flexed it. "You think that's bad. You should see the wall." His steely eyes met hers. "Did you get the donkey sorted?"

"We did." She glanced around to see if a hunting rifle was visible, but when she nudged forward, there was nothing to see but a partially dug hole. "Thanks to your doggo, here. He's a good worker," she said.

Finbar shook his head as if he disagreed. "He just showed up at me door a few weeks ago. Would you be interested in taking him back to the clinic?"

Apparently he knew exactly who she was, and they were considered an animal shelter now. If Finbar was telling the truth, some family was missing this dog. They may even have his records at the clinic. "Only if you're not going to look after him." Finbar Malone had a hard look about him. No doubt being tossed around on the ocean day after day took its toll. "Are you sure you don't want a companion?" Dimpna teased. She wanted to see if humor would crack his tough exterior.

"Me wife is enough for me."

Dimpna glanced at the dog, who seemed more than ready to hit the road. "What's the name?"

"Me wife or the dog?"

Dimpna laughed. Finbar did not. "The dog."

"Dunno."

If he hadn't named him, he didn't deserve him. Only home a few hours and she was already breaking her three-pet rule. But if this man was shooting off rifles and being hounded by gawpers, the dog would be better off with her. But what if no one stepped forward to claim him? It was possible the farmer next door would take him, but Dimpna liked the young sheepdog, and there was already a zoo to contend with back at the clinic—what was one more? She turned to head back to the bus when the sheepdog tugged in the opposite direction, and she dropped the lead. The dog took off like a shot, heading directly for the hole. When Dimpna took a step toward the dog, Finbar Malone planted himself directly in front of her. There was no doubt; he didn't want her to pass him.

He towered over her, his scraggly beard hanging above her head. These were the times that being short irked her the most. Then again, she was in a prime position to tug on his beard, drag him down to the ground. She indulged in the fantasy for a few seconds before taking a step back.

"Everything alright?" Dimpna asked.

He nodded. "I'm afraid you caught me."

"Caught you?"

He stepped aside and gestured to the hole. "Dead rabbit." The sheepdog was lying next to the hole, his large head dipped all the way inside.

"I'm so sorry," she said. "A pet?"

He scrunched his face as if trying to comprehend the meaning of the word. "Wild rabbit."

"A wild rabbit."

"That's what I said."

She stared at the spot, then for some reason tried to memorize it. A silver birch tree behind it to the left, a broken-down chair to the right. She couldn't pinpoint why, but she had the distinct feeling the fisherman was lying. The sheepdog's body was now farther inside, as if he intended on joining the poor rabbit.

"Git," Finbar said, shaking his fist. "Git." The dog, jaw clamped tight, jerked out of the hole, then shot past Dimpna toward the bus, lead trailing after him. When he reached the back door of the VW he sat and waited. He was no fool; this was not his home.

"You might want to ease up on the rifle," Dimpna said to Finbar. "You're frightening all the neighboring creatures."

"Funny," Finbar said. "I thought it was your father giving everyone around here a fright."

Anger coursed through her. *He's a pro. Fishing. Don't take the bait.* "Don't believe everything you hear." But even as her words rang in the air, the image of the ruby ring hovered above it. She had no idea what she was supposed to do about it and wished to hell she didn't have to make the decision. She jumped back into the bus and slammed the door, then looked back at the dog. Something black fell from its jaw and hit the floor. "What did you do?"

She leaned closer. It was a mobile phone. She had to get out of her seat and crawl in the back. When she reached for it, the dog growled, baring teeth. Then the good boy lay down on top of the phone as if he was a bird protecting an egg. *Mine.* Spike, Guinness, and Pickles turned their heads toward her en masse, wondering if the newcomer was going to get away with that. "I don't have time to wrestle a sheepdog." Dimpna returned to her seat and looked out the window, wondering whether or not to offer the dog a bribe, or wait until she got home. Finbar was shoveling again. The rhythmic sound of the blade hitting the dirt filled her ears. Had he been burying his mobile phone? Or had he simply dropped it when he leaned over to drop in the dead rabbit? No. Pun intended, that didn't ring true. The sheepdog had definitely snatched the phone from the hole. Had there been a rabbit in there, even a dead one, that's what the dog would have swiped instead.

Finbar Malone had lied. He'd been standing in his backyard burying a mobile phone. Didn't he know you could just remove the SIM card? Or toss if off the side of your trawler and into the ocean? She wasn't sure what he was thinking, but you didn't have to be a detective to know that burying a phone was odd behavior. Perhaps turning in the ruby ring to Detective O'Brien would go down a little easier if she also handed in a mobile phone buried by the very man who had discovered the body. If there was nothing incriminating on the phone, then the detective could simply return it to Mr. Malone. The fisherman had also been shooting off guns, so couldn't one also surmise that he had a tendency toward violence? Did he have any prior dealings with the O'Reillys? Was there some kind of personal connection between the fisherman and The Dancing Man? Dimpna felt someone's gaze, and looked up to find Finbar Malone leaning on his shovel, glaring at her. She felt frozen with indecision. Return the phone. Give the phone to Detective O'Brien. Return the phone. Finbar suddenly lifted his shovel and lined it up as if it were a shotgun, aiming it at Dimpna. He pretended to take a shot. Give the phone to Detective O'Brien.

CHAPTER 12

*C*ORMAC HAD NO PROBLEM CLEARING THE LINE OF FOLKS FROM MAEVE Wilde's caravan. He simply flashed his badge and they scattered. Technically Cormac was supposed to be accompanied by D.S. Neely on any interviews, but besides dealing with the media, she'd been tasked with tracking down their missing stowaway. Given this child might have witnessed a murder, speed was of the essence. At least that was one detail of this case that hadn't yet leaked. And there was recent progress. He'd received a text from Neely that a local woman had just come in to report a runaway. Saoirse Griffin.

Congrats, another guard had texted him. **It's a girl.** He told Neely to keep him posted. He took a minute to marvel at the caravan. Propped up on four cement blocks sinking into the ground, it had probably seen better days. But there was a quirky charm to it that appealed to him and made him curious about the woman inside. Blue velvet curtains obscured the small windows, and above the door wind chimes pealed. The field was in full bloom. Purple loosestrife, bluebells, and cowslips vied for space with clumps of jagged rocks. An orange variety whose name escaped him, blazed in the distance. Don McLean sang in his ear about Vincent. *Flaming flowers that brightly blaze* . . . He wondered what a starry, starry night would look like in this field, and he imagined it overhead, and oddly Dimpna Wilde was by his side. *Focus.* Besides, he'd rather see the stars from Inch Beach. *Alone.* He was investigating a murder for Christ's sake. He'd have to keep his lusty meanderings in check or he'd be booted off the case. Cormac was just about to knock when the door flew open and an attractive older woman stood framed in the doorway staring down at him.

She was taller than her daughter but still a short woman. She had dark hair piled into a bun and brown eyes so dark they were almost black. Her hand rested on the side of the door frame and he took in her nails, painted a shiny pink. She wore a matching pink scarf around her neck, and she was sporting two-inch black heels. In a caravan. In a field. He instantly liked her, a fact that equally raised his guard. She reminded him of an aging movie star; he could easily picture her with one of those elongated cigarette holders draped over a chaise lounge. His own mam flickered into his thoughts—pink slippers clinging to her shriveled feet, a feeding tube down her throat, her vocal cords destroyed—and he felt a squeeze of envy. It was an impotent feeling, not being able to ease his mam's suffering let alone change her cruel fate. Even being here in Dingle meant he was taking precious time away from her. At least she was excited that he was leading this case, and he video chatted with her every single day, regaling her with as many details as he could. Damn the rules, she wasn't chin-wagging to anyone, and they always made sure the nurse was out of earshot. It wasn't lost on him that Dimpna Wilde was dealing with a father whose body was fit but mind was failing, whereas his mam's mind was sharp but her body was falling to bits. So much of life was a roll of the dice. Maybe that's why he was even more determined to catch this killer, bring a little justice back to the world. Maeve Wilde tracked the people as they retreated across the field.

"I'm sure they'll be back," he said.

"Ah, they will, so." She still didn't look happy about it. He couldn't blame her, but he had a job to do.

"Detective Inspector Cormac O'Brien. You must be Mrs. Wilde?"

"Guilty," she said. "But only of being Mrs. Wilde. Not guilty of anything else. Will that do?" She went to shut the door, and he had to haul arse up to the caravan door.

He held his hand up to stop her. "We're conducting house-to-house inquiries and I'm afraid it's your turn in the hot seat."

She patted the back of her head, as if her hair wasn't quite right for a police inquiry. "You're going to interrupt everyone in the middle of their work. Is that what you're telling me?" She had a flirtatious tone, quite the opposite of the brusque treatment he'd experienced from the daughter. He held up the Devil card he'd slipped into a clear evidence baggie. It was just for show. The one found tucked into O'Reilly's pocket was being sent to headquarters. He was grateful they'd tracked down the same deck, although it took them an entire day. One of the guards finally found it in some kind of mystical shop in Galway. The fingerprints results would come back sooner than the autopsy results, but he wasn't holding his breath. The killer would have worn gloves. The scene was too deliberate to be tricked up by a rookie mistake. Everyone knew the first rule of Murder 101 was: *Wear gloves.* Unless, of course, Eamon Wilde turned out to be both wickedly clever and memory-impaired enough to make monumental mistakes. It wasn't out of the realm of possibility. Dementia. It was one of Cormac's biggest fears. Without his memories who would he be?

"Do I have to ask you inside?" Maeve asked.

He really wanted to say yes. He definitely wanted to check out her caravan. "Based on the evidence I have, I could get a warrant to search this caravan. I haven't done that yet, so no. You don't have to ask me inside. But house-to-house inquiries are commonplace, and it saves you a trip to the Dingle Garda Station. If you don't invite me in, I'm probably going to think you have something to hide, and you'll definitely have to come to my place of work to see me."

Maeve pondered this. "You could schedule a tarot card reading. I would let you inside then."

"We don't pay for our inquiries," Cormac said. "Most folks are happy to help bring a killer to justice." *Especially if she was sleeping with the victim.* "I understand you had a close relationship with Mr. O'Reilly. I'm sure you'd be happy to help in our efforts to find the person responsible."

Maeve stood back and gestured for him to come in. It was a cramped space, but it was clean. To the right was a small kitchen with a built-in-table; To the left, the bed was partially hidden by a blue velvet curtain. This type of caravan was meant to hook up to a vehicle and be driven to a beach. There were most likely permit violations she was breaking by living in it in this location, but he wasn't here to nab her for that, although he could always keep the threat of it in his back pocket. He gestured to the table. "Shall we?"

"Would you like a cup of tea?" She gestured to the counter where a box of Barry's Tea and a biscuit tin sat.

He really wanted a cup of coffee. He scanned the counter and didn't see a coffeemaker or French press. He didn't do instant. "I'm grand, thanks."

They sat down. Maeve removed a deck of tarot cards from the table and slipped them into a velvet bag. Beneath them was a small black mat covered with a gold Celtic cross. She folded it neatly and placed it and the bag in the press. It was chock-full of velvet bags in a variety of colors stacked one on top of another. She returned to the table where she sat across from him. He gestured to the press. "Are those all your tarot decks?"

"Gold star, Inspector," she said. "No wonder you rose in the ranks despite looking so fresh-faced and handsome."

She was cheeky. He liked that. He imagined his mam healthy and chipper, imagined her and Maeve Wilde becoming friends, dancing, gossiping, playing hands of Twenty-five, living out their golden years with comfort and joy. "How many decks do you have?"

"Hundreds."

"Hundreds?" He was glad he'd refused tea; he would have choked on it.

"I don't keep them all here. Most of them are back at the house."

"Where is your house?"

"It's outa ways." She fluttered her hand like no one really cared where her home was. Cormac already knew the address; it was a terraced house on Goat Street, a short drive from the clinic. "I like camping here in the summer."

"Who is occupying your house right now?" He already knew that too. It was a good way to experience what subjects looked and sounded like when they were telling the truth. It made it much easier to catch them in barefaced lies.

"No one, but Eamon and I will be moving back in."

"Why is that?"

"I saw the ambulance. My husband is in hospital. I'm presuming he'll have to go back to the house. He can no longer practice veterinarian medicine."

"And you'll go with him?"

"I'm his wife."

If she saw the ambulance, why wasn't she already at hospital? Could she have killed O'Reilly and framed her husband? He wanted to ask about the rumors that they'd been living apart for a decade, but that probably wouldn't help the conversation flow. Cormac slid the tarot card across the table. "Do you recognize this?"

A flicker of fear flashed in her eyes. "Temptations."

"Pardon?"

"The Devil card warns the client not to be distracted by temptations."

He hadn't been asking as to the meaning of the card, but now he was interested. "What kind of temptations?"

"Whatever plagues the client." Her eyes met his and she stared at him as if she was trying to suss him out.

"It doesn't mean—the actual Devil? Hellfire and brimstone? Evil?"

She shook her head vehemently. "Not at all. Not to me."

"Not to you? Isn't there a standard meaning, like?"

"No. Tarot reading is an art. It's up to the individual reader to ascertain their meanings."

"Interesting."

She smiled, a patient smile, as if he was a child trying to grasp a new concept. "For example, if I was reading for you, Detective Inspector O'Brien. What are your temptations?"

Women. Whiskey. Music. Bizarre murder scenes. Miniature Vikings with eyes the color of mint-chocolate-chip ice cream. "Are you a fortune-teller or a therapist?" He tried to make it sound like a joke, but he was downright uncomfortable with this topic. He wasn't into horoscopes, or anything woo-woo. He had enough trouble wrestling with reality.

"I am whatever my clients need me to be."

"You call them clients?"

"What shall I call them, Detective O'Brien?" She folded her arms and sat up straight.

She was attractive and intelligent. Colored her hair. Not too much makeup—not like he imagined a fortune-teller to look. Nothing woo-woo about the place. "I didn't mean to offend you." He didn't care whether he offended her or not, but he wanted to see if the statement would soften her.

"You didn't."

He settled back against the booth and waited to see if the silence would prompt her to talk. No luck. "And what do most of your clients need you to be?"

"A light that shines through the darkness."

There she goes. Now she sounded a little woo-woo. He nudged the card closer. "Does this tarot card belong to one of your decks?"

Maeve pursed her lips. She unfolded her arms and touched the plastic bag that held the card with the tip of her finger. "Not that exact card."

"How could you possibly know that?"

"I'm psychic." He frowned. She startled him with a loud laugh.

She tapped the card again before withdrawing her hand. "That card is brand-new. Do I have the same deck? Yes, I do. At the house. However, my deck is not brand-new and that's how I know this is not my card."

He'd only glimpsed a portion of the card found on O'Reilly, but once his effects were turned in, he'd be sure to check its condition. "Can I see your matching deck?"

"Are you saying you want me to drive to my house right now and collect it for you?"

He sighed. She was somewhat maddening. Definitely shrewd. "Are you missing any cards from that deck?"

"I'd have to look and see."

"As far as you're currently aware, are you missing any cards from that deck?"

"The last time I used that deck it was complete."

"What is the definition of complete?"

"All seventy-eight cards were accounted for. Twenty-two major arcana cards and fifty-six minor arcana." *Whatever that meant.* "Do you know the history of the tarot, Detective?"

He shrugged. "It originated in the fifteenth century in Italy. Mostly it was used as a parlor game."

"My, you've done your homework." She nodded approvingly.

"What can I say? I like to read." He picked up the evidence bag and jiggled it. "When is the last time this card was in your possession?"

"Whoever said it's ever been out of my possession?"

She'd hadn't broken her composure. Not once. She was definitely smart enough to stage their murder scene. He had a feeling her husband was too. Was he faking his dementia? Did this couple pair up to murder their victim? "When is the last time you used this deck?"

"I used this deck around Christmas. Then again in January. In February I switched to a brighter deck. We all needed a little spring."

"You have a deck for every season?"

"I have multiple decks per season."

"Why do you think our killer placed this particular card in our victim's pocket?" He'd never intended for that detail to leak out—he thought for sure he'd sworn Finbar Malone to secrecy before letting him go—because every single guard insisted they'd kept their mouths shut. There was another, even more disturbing explanation. What if the killer had been the one to leak the details to the press?

"I think the killer chose that card to place in O'Reilly's pocket because he was calling Johnny the Devil," Maeve said. "And that means—I am not the killer." She folded her arms and smiled.

"Because to a professional like you this card means temptations, not the literal Devil."

"Correct." She held his gaze.

He leaned in. "Why would anyone call Johnny O'Reilly the Devil?"

She shrugged. "Where there's money, there's trouble."

"Have you heard wind of any trouble?"

"Certainly not. I was only his once-in-a-while dance partner." She pursed her lips. "He had partnerships with rich businessmen. I don't know how many racehorses he owns with others, but I believe it's quite a few. You'll definitely have to speak with all of them. Maybe someone felt cheated?"

"Why do you think someone wrote 'Last Dance' next to his body with stones?"

"I haven't the faintest idea." A twitch formed in the corner of her lips.

"Didn't he once have an aspiring racehorse named Last Dance?"

Another flicker of *something* crossed her face. Something in the vicinity of panic. He'd struck a nerve. "He did," she said. "That story had a very sad ending."

"Do you think someone is referring to that horse?"

"I'd be happy to consult my cards. Otherwise I haven't the faintest idea."

"What was the exact nature of your relationship with the victim?"

She glanced out the caravan window before answering. "He was a neighbor in the sense that all Dingle townsfolk are neighbors. That said, there's no mystery that the O'Reillys run in a different circle."

"What circle is that?" *Dante's Inferno* came to mind, but Cormac kept that to himself.

"The elite. Private clubs. Private schools. A sprawling estate. The racing circle of Who's Who." She leaned forward. "High society, Inspector. The kind of people who look down on regular folks like you and me."

He wasn't going to confirm his opinion of the elite. "But you did have dealings with the O'Reillys, did you not?"

She nodded. "My husband has been one of their primary veterinarians for years."

"And . . . you had been seeing Mr. O'Reilly socially, had you not?"

"Johnny O'Reilly was a good dancing partner. I liked riding in his fancy cars and dancing with him. That's all we did together, Detective."

"How long have you been dancing partners?"

She crossed her arms over her chest. "Going on six months. I needed something to keep my mind off the news."

Dimpna's late husband. He wasn't going to touch that topic. Not unless and until he thought there was a connection. And he didn't have proof of an affair, so he let that go for now and gestured to the press. "You keep tarot card decks in velvet bags in there?"

"Yes. As I stated, I also keep some at home."

"Let's say the card in Johnny's pocket turns out to be your tarot card. And let's assume you are not the killer."

"That is easy to assume because I am not the killer. Nor is my husband."

He ignored the bit about the husband for now. "How do you suppose someone got a hold of it?"

"I do readings all the time."

"You opened that press and I saw nothing but velvet bags."

"Your point?"

"Do you leave your clients alone for hours at a time?"

"No."

"Out of all those decks stacked up, did the killer simply grab a random deck and get lucky?"

"Get lucky?" She fixed her gaze on him. He stared back. "I don't understand what you mean. Every single deck has a Devil card; it doesn't matter what deck the person chose."

"Right." He'd been on a different track, the fact that this Devil card really stood out when placed in O'Reilly's shirt pocket. The horns were on fire too. It really made a statement. He had no idea if every Devil card in any tarot deck would have the same look and effect. But he did know the killer had meticulously painted the murder scene, right down to his or her choice of tarot cards. "How many cards did you say are in a tarot deck?"

"Seventy-eight."

Sixty-nine stones. Seventy-eight cards. There didn't seem to be a connection, but Cormac liked number puzzles. "Let me see if I have this straight. You have hundreds of decks. In each deck there are seventy-eight cards. How many of them are the Devil?"

"Just one."

"Out of seventy-eight cards just one."

"You like repetition. Does it help you think?"

He frowned. She was interrupting his flow. "Please answer the question."

"Yes, Detective. Out of seventy-eight cards just one is the Devil."

"And clients are left alone under what circumstances?"

"It doesn't happen often but—in between clients I need to use the restroom, make tea, and there may have been one or two instances where I had to step outside the caravan to place a phone call."

"Roughly how long might a client be alone?"

"Five, ten minutes at the longest."

"How would a person have time to shuffle through multiple decks, seventy-eight cards, to find this one particular Devil card?"

"There you go again. How do you know they wanted that one particular card?"

She nailed him there. He was giving away too much information. "My question still stands."

"You're asking me to explain something I cannot. I truly wish I knew when I used this particular deck last and where, and who else was present, but I certainly wasn't expecting to be recounting it to a detective inspector one day, and I'm afraid I can't help you any further." She stood.

"I see." He didn't make a move to get up.

"Would you like a reading?"

"No." He grinned. "I like my secrets."

"It seems any detective worth his salt would want to know whether or not I'm as good as they say."

"Is that the word around Dingle, then?"

"You should find out for yourself."

She was distracting him. "I am going to ask you to locate that deck for me. How long will you need to do that?"

"I could do it in a few days. Does that suit?"

"As long as you don't forget." Now that she'd already noticed how shiny and new the card in the evidence bag was compared to hers, he would pay attention that she didn't replace her Devil card with a brand-new one as well.

"I won't forget. But if someone has my Devil card, there's a chance they took the entire deck. Or perhaps I left it at one of the readings."

Had he been too obvious that this was a serious piece of evidence, and now she was going to try and pretend the entire deck was gone? He needed absolute proof—admission—that this was her tarot card. Otherwise it would be no good in court.

"Are we finished?" she asked.

"I want to hear your account of that evening. Take me through getting ready for the dance, the dance, and the rest of your evening after the dance. I want to know every detail up until the very next time you saw your husband. Everything about Johnny O'Reilly that evening, right down to his green tie."

"Green tie?" she said, turning to the small cooker and putting the kettle on. "He wasn't wearing a green tie. Johnny O'Reilly wouldn't be caught dead in a tie." Maeve gasped at her choice of words and slapped her hand over her mouth. When she removed it, she stared at him. "*Was* he caught dead in a tie?"

Cormac felt a jolt. "Why are you so certain he didn't like ties?"

"Everyone who knew Johnny O'Reilly knew he loathed ties." She bit her bottom lip and looked away.

"That's . . . odd . . ." He was trying not to show his emotions. "Why didn't he like ties?"

"Why does one like or dislike anything?"

"Do you remember exactly what Mr. O'Reilly was wearing that evening?"

"Navy suit, white shirt, black polished shoes—they looked Italian and expensive, and a green bow tie."

Everything else was a match. Except for the tie. Unless the pathologist found a bow tie in one of his pockets, there had been no sign of a bow tie at the scene. Another piece of the puzzle, only he had no idea where it fit.

Cormac's mobile buzzed with a text: **Griffin girl last seen Saturday night near the harbor—she may indeed be our stowaway!** Cormac stood. "I have to go. But first—is there any way that you're mistaken?"

"About the necktie?" He nodded. She shook her head and pointed a finger at him. "I swear to ya. He wasn't wearing one. If you found him in one—somebody else put it on him and he was already dead."

CHAPTER 13

MAEVE WILDE WATCHED THE DETECTIVE INSPECTOR MAKE HIS WAY across the field to his red Toyota. There was a presence to him that was intoxicating. Short, but handsome and intense. Intelligent. And on a mission. If only they'd met under more pleasant circumstances. He didn't believe in her gift—he'd made that quite clear— but Maeve was no stranger to cynics. She'd even managed to open a few minds in her lifetime of doing readings. She would do a card spread later to see what else she could glean about him. No wedding ring, but perhaps he was the type who didn't wear it. There was a sadness lurking in him, a brooding element that her daughter would no doubt find irresistible. When the car finally started off and showed its taillights, she grabbed her mobile phone and locked the caravan door. She'd put him off for now, but he was plucky and he would be back. The tarot card had been a grave mistake. What had she been thinking? If only Eamon had his wits about him, he'd know what to do. She could try to buy a new deck and find a way to make the card look worn, but she'd be leaving a trail of damning evidence. Receipts. CCTV footage of her going into a shop. A witness statement from the shop clerk. If she tried to buy the deck online, there would be an electronic trail. Nothing one did with technology these days was safe. Including sending a text. What if the guards confiscated one of their phones? She brought the number up and typed: **The inspector was here, asking about the Devil card . . .** She did not hit send. Too risky. She erased the text. She hurried to the drawer in her kitchenette, slid it open, and rifled through her pile of blank postcards. She chose one from Disney World, a lovely castle with fireworks raining down. She grabbed a biro and turned it over. *No.* Her handwriting would be recognizable, and what if someone told him about her proclivity to send postcards? She slipped it into her handbag as she mulled it over. She'd have to use the computer and printer in the clinic. Did printers leave fingerprints?

She was at a sudden loss. She had to do something, and that was the safest bet. Type the letter on the computer, erase history, print it out, and pray. At least there were no staff there to poke their noses in her business. She could use a computer and printer somewhere else, but unless she drove out of town, *that* could be evidence. How aggravating! And she was due at hospital; there was no time to dillydally. Dimpna would have to reopen the clinic soon, but now it was empty and the best in a sea of bad options. She'd type and print the note, figure out a clever way to deliver it, and then go to hospital. She grabbed her handbag and keys and headed across the field to the clinic.

When Dimpna returned to the clinic with her pack, including her new pal the sheepdog (whom she'd decided to name E.T. given his infatuation with Finbar's mobile phone), the animals were still all jumbled up in the courtyard and there was a postcard from Disney World tacked to the clinic door. The front featured colorful fireworks raining down on a fairy-tale castle. Dimpna turned it over: *At hospital. No need to visit. I will bring your father home. Please do not sleep in your vehicle. Sleep in the caravan, or your father's room. God bless.*

"She lives in a caravan and she's putting down my bus," Dimpna said. The animals in the courtyard turned and looked at her, some enthralled, others clearly disinterested. "I only slept in it when I was young," she said to E.T. He stuck his tongue out and panted. "Hungry?" None of them turned down the offer for food. She set about watering and feeding all of the gorgeous creatures, and then checked the status of the back kennel. To her relief, Sheila was right. Someone had been keeping it up; there were twenty large kennels and they were clean. What the animals really needed were walks and cuddles, but it was getting dark now and Dimpna was knackered. So much for Sheila calling in for help.

Dimpna kenneled as many creatures as they had room for, and only left the ones in the courtyard who were used to sleeping outside—but even the ducks and turtle seemed content to be in the kennel area. But there were a few holdouts—the goat and sheep, and a few stubborn cats, most of whom were already on the prowl. It was not wise to allow dogs to wander around at night, but there was one stubborn black Lab who refused to move, and clearly had no intention of ever leaving the yard. She set a dog bed for him next to the door and he happily slumped into it. Before she even stepped away, the old Lab was snoring. She smiled, taking a moment to enjoy the deep rumbles—the sound of dogs snoring was one of the best sounds on earth next to rain falling on a tin roof.

Dimpna took her now-four-pack into the clinic and flipped on the light. The low mechanical hum was comforting too, and she was thrilled her pack was with her; it was creepy to be here at night by herself. Tonight she would sleep in the flat upstairs, praying her father was still a tidy man and had extra sheets for the bed. Finding a place to live would have to be a priority. She didn't have much savings left, but she didn't need anything fancy. Then again, she was going to be accompanied by three dogs and a cat, never an easy feat as a renter. Maybe she would be out in the kennel. But this was Dingle; there had to be a farmer somewhere who had a place to let. She could even do it in exchange for veterinarian services. And then there was a matter of all the other animals her father had recently collected. The sheep with the purple markings should be easy—their color markings would correspond with a Kerry farmer. But the others would be more challenging. If they could not find the owners, they were going to have to arrange a local adoption day. She had a feeling folks had taken advantage of her father's condition, seeing as he suddenly allowed all these strays to pile up. It infuriated her.

It was common for people to drop off strays at veterinarians, especially sick, injured, and those with behavioral problems, leaving the burden of life and death to them. Dimpna had a soft heart, but the harsh reality was that she couldn't save them all. Veterinarians had to have boundaries. If every cent went into saving the animals nobody else wanted, they wouldn't be able to feed and clothe themselves. Their overhead costs included expensive equipment, vet techs, receptionists, assistants, lab work—it was never-ending. There was a misconception that vets were rich. Most of them were just keeping afloat. Part of her training had been accepting this reality. That didn't stop her heart from bleeding.

She set up pet beds in the waiting room of the clinic and was relieved that her darlings seemed as knackered as she was, for they didn't put up a fuss. E.T. settled near the clinic door with a satisfied sigh. She wondered if he would dream of herding sheep. Spike ignored his little bed and leapt onto a waiting room chair where he curled up into a tight purring ball. Guinness was already snoring, legs splayed out froglike behind him, and Pickles was flat on his back, all four paws up in the air, tongue hanging out and to the side. She loved them more than she could express, and was eternally grateful that the one soft spot in life was the joy of animals. She couldn't understand how not everyone felt that way, and she pitied those who didn't. Even all the horrors that veterinarians had to put up with, for her the good still outweighed the bad.

It was only as she turned to go upstairs that she realized there was waste to clean up in the courtyard. She nearly cried in exasperation and for a second her mind began trying to talk herself out of doing it. Couldn't she put it off until tomorrow? What was a little poo on top of everything else? But she was already in motion, so she grabbed a large plastic bag from the back room and a little scooper and returned to the courtyard. She flicked on the outside light and began her task. Twenty somewhat-disgusting minutes later she had it sorted.

She threw the giant bag of poop in the rubbish bins just beyond the stone wall of the courtyard. She felt a sensation wash over her, as if she wasn't alone. She looked toward the abandoned auto body shop. It took her several seconds to realize there was a man standing across the street watching her. He was so still, she wondered if it was some kind of hallucination. But her body was on high alert, and on a gut level she knew this was no mirage. With only the dim light above the clinic to cut through the darkness, she couldn't make out his features. Half of him was swallowed up, making him look more shadow than man. But man he was. Her skin continued to prickle. The old Lab was awake and at the gate, his low growl filtering into the air. If this man had a weapon, he could hurt the dog. "Stay," she said. She didn't have her mobile phone on her. Why wasn't the person making a move—either toward or away from her? "What do you want?" The figure shifted his head, looking around as if checking to see if anyone could come to her rescue. Just then she realized she did have a weapon of sorts; she had just thrown it into the rubbish bin.

She ran over, opened the lid, and grabbed the hefty bag of dog poop. Luckily, as a veterinarian, she was no longer squeamish. Once you stuck your hand up enough cow arses, a bag of poop was child's play. She twirled the bag over her head. She saw the figure hesitate, then step left and then right, as if not sure what in the world she was doing. She let the bag go and it sailed across the road. The figure started to move, but the bag clipped him somewhere on the face. She heard a soft thud as it made contact, and a second as it hit the ground.

"Fuck!"

She didn't recognize the voice, but it was definitely a man's. Had she made a terrible mistake by enraging him? Slowly she backed up toward the door. She didn't want to turn her back on him and show fear by running. Man was an animal too and animals who spied on people in the dark were no doubt excited by fear. But this man didn't come after her. He turned and disappeared around the back of the derelict building.

"Come on, pal," she said to the Lab. This time she planned on running. She turned to hurry inside but had only taken a few steps when something shiny flashed in the grass. She bent down and retrieved what appeared to be a child's necklace. Gold letters spelled out the name: AISLING.

Although it was a common Irish name, there was only one young lassie in Dingle that she personally knew with this name. Aisling O'Reilly. Sean's daughter. She was eight years of age. From the photos Dimpna had glimpsed online, she had her father's sandy curls and his prominent cheekbones. She was cute as a button, always smiling. It was hard for Dimpna to believe that Sean was a good father, but all evidence pointed in that direction. Guilt assaulted her. Ben had an adorable sister. One he would never get to know.

She cupped the necklace in her hand as she hurried back inside the clinic, wondering when the lassie had lost it and what had brought them into the clinic. She locked the door behind her and set the necklace on the counter. The Wildes usually went out to the O'Reillys' estate to care for their animals, not the other way around. *Half sister. Say it. Aisling is Ben's half sister.* Was she a horrible person for shielding that side of his family from him? No. Aisling was innocent, but the rest of the O'Reillys were corrupt. Fruit rotting on a tree. Dimpna wouldn't be surprised if it was a suicide and Johnny O'Reilly's last selfish act was to cast Dimpna's parents as murderers. What on earth had her mother been doing cavorting with him of all people? It didn't make any sense.

Should she tell the guards that a strange man had been standing across from the clinic watching her? Given there was a murderer loose, it seemed prudent. She reached in her pocket and found the calling card the detective had given her. It was going on half-nine; at least it wasn't the middle of the night.

He answered on the first ring. "Detective O'Brien."

"Sorry to bother you. This is Dimpna Wilde."

"Dr. Wilde. Is everything alright?"

"I debated on whether or not I should ring. I was taking rubbish to the bin and there was someone standing in front of the abandoned auto body shop across the way. He was dressed in dark clothing and I couldn't see his face clearly. He was just standing there, staring at me."

"Where are you now?"

"I'm inside the clinic. I hit him with a bag of dog poo. He ran away and I'm fine. I just figured it was best to call."

"You hit him with what, now?"

She explained how she had just cleaned out the courtyard and had then used the bag as a projectile. "I was bang on, so I was. Clipped his cheek, I believe."

She heard a soft chuckle before he cleared his throat. "The creeper smells like shite. Is that what you're telling me, now?"

"That's exactly right." Dimpna found herself grinning. "Just follow the smell."

"You did the right thing. Your doors are locked?"

"My doors are locked and my dogs are with me. The other animals are safely kenneled except for one old Labrador, a few cats, two sheep, and a goat."

There was a pause and then he chuckled. "I guess that's an improvement. I'm going to send a squad car to the area."

"Thank you." Should she mention the ruby ring? Finbar's mobile phone? Was that Finbar she'd seen standing there in the dark? She hadn't made out a beard, but she also couldn't swear to it that the stranger didn't have one. Had Finbar realized the phone was gone and he'd come back to collect it? "There are a few other things I should tell you," she said. The phone was still in the bus. She'd forgotten about it as soon as she'd pulled up to the clinic. What if there was incriminating evidence on it? And the ruby ring. Wouldn't she be an accomplice if she didn't mention it? "You said a squad car is coming round?"

"They're on their way."

"Can you have them stop at the clinic? I have a few items that you'll probably want to look at—but is there any way we could talk about them another time?" She was so exhausted, she was almost delirious. Was it only this morning she'd left Dublin?

"That depends on what they are." Realizing she had no choice, she relayed the incident with Finbar Malone and the mobile phone first, and then backtracked to the ring her father had palmed into her hand. "Put that phone in some kind of plastic bag if you have one. Use gloves when handling it, please. A guard will collect it within the hour. Have you touched it with your hands?"

"No, but it's been in E.T.'s mouth. It's in the back of my VW bus right now."

"E.T.?"

"Sorry. That's what I named my new pal the sheepdog."

There was a pause and then laughter filled her ears. "Phone home."

"Exactly." Satisfaction spread through her that he got it right away.

"Are the doors to your bus locked?"

"Probably not." She heard him curse. "It's parked right in front

and the outside lights are illuminating it clearly. I highly doubt anyone has been near it. But if you like I can go and get the phone
now. I'm pretty sure the creeper is long gone."

"Wait for the guards to arrive. They'll help you collect it."

"What about the ring?" She tensed as she waited for him to accuse her of being an accomplice to murder.

"Hang on to it. I have no need for it at the moment."

Was he messing with her? She'd nearly forgotten he wasn't a
local. "Are you sure? Because there is only one man I know of who
owned a ruby ring."

"Keep it in a plastic bag, but hang on to it for now. I'd come myself but we have our hands full with a missing girl."

Something prickled in the back of her mind—the scraggly
young girl peeking out from a small hill in the Valley of the Mad.
Was it really just this morning? "Missing girl?"

"Saoirse Griffin, thirteen years of age."

"Do you have a photo?"

"I just got one from the mother. Why?"

"I saw a girl this morning in Camp where I stopped with my
pack."

"I'll text it to you."

She heard her phone ding. She put him on speaker and opened
the photo. She stared at the picture of the angry but pretty girl.
She knew that face. "Does she have a purple backpack?"

"Yes, she does. By God, she does."

"I saw her this morning," she said. "In the Valley of the Mad."

CHAPTER 14

AT THIS HOUR OF THE NIGHT, DIMPNA MADE GOOD TIME GETTING TO the Valley of the Mad. Her muscle memory kicked in, and she was delighted to discover she remembered nearly every curve in the roads. By the time she arrived at the car park in Camp, squad cars and search volunteers were clogging the lot, but she managed to squeeze in. She and Pickles hopped out of the bus, and still wearing gloves, she handed Finbar's mobile phone off to a waiting guard. Why didn't they want the ring? She couldn't worry about it now. She guided Pickles to where the search group was huddled. She'd never been here at night; the usually familiar surroundings had morphed in the dark, the terrain lit up in patches by the beam of torches. It was a cold night, and hard to imagine a young girl out here all alone. Inspector O'Brien instinctively backed away when his light swiveled over Pickles. "Kids likes Pickles," Dimpna said. "And he's an excellent tracker."

"Good idea." He removed an inhaler and breathed in.

"There's a doctor in town who can help," she said. "His pills would be better than the general ones at the chemist."

"I'll keep that in mind."

"Dimp?" She turned at the sound of a man calling her name, and whirled around to find Paul Byrne standing behind her. Still ruggedly handsome. Salt-and-pepper hair, stubble, strong face, deep brown eyes. He was tall, but he never made Dimpna feel small. He stared at her for a long while before embracing her, lifting her off her feet. He set her down and they parted. Dimpna had hoped for more of a formal reunion, and seeing him stirred up a chunk of adolescent longing, and oddly, a stray guilty thought about the inspector, wondering if he was watching them. She scolded herself; they were here to find a missing girl. If she hadn't been so preoccupied this morning, trying to suss out what Ben knew, maybe she would have realized that the poor thing had been in distress. Given Dimpna used to run wild and dirty around the peninsula, it hadn't set off any alarms.

"What are you doing here?" She hoped he wouldn't take it the wrong way.

"I know Saoirse," he said. "She likes to hang out at the group home." She nodded, not surprised. Paul had always been the type to take care of others. She was glad that hadn't changed. A few seconds later she remembered the man he'd beat up, the one that had cost him his job. *Griffin.* No wonder Paul was here; she'd heard he'd been watching out for the mother and daughter ever since he'd sent the father to prison. The good deed had cost him his job as a detective sergeant.

Dimpna led them to the general area near the hedgerows and small hill where she had seen Saoirse. When they neared the spot, Pickles, most likely picking up on their adrenaline, strained on the leash. "Do you have anything with her smell?" she asked. The mother nodded and handed Dimpna a jumper. She let Pickles sniff it but kept him on the leash. He went for a nearby tree, sniffing around the base.

"It's so dark," Nancy Griffin moaned. "Where's my baby?" She began to call her name, her voice echoing in the shadows. Pickles suddenly faced forward, lunging toward a long grassy road in front of them.

"He's leaning in this direction." Dimpna pointed. "At the end of that boreen, there's a derelict house," Dimpna said. "The glass has long left the windows, and it's possible she could have crawled in. If she's still here, that would be the warmest and safest place."

Paul cut in before the inspector could speak. "Lead the way."

They worked their way across the long grassy boreen, torches swinging from left to right.

"Saoirse," her mother called out. "Baby. Are you here?"

"We're here to help," Inspector O'Brien called out. "You're safe now."

A sob escaped Nancy Griffin. "My baby. My baby." Calls for the girl rang out as they picked up speed toward the remains of the old stone house. Finally the road ended in a ford, and their torches illuminated an old stone wall. The guards held everyone back as they stepped around the water and made the first sweep along the perimeter. The door was boarded up tight but they found the nearest window, and as Dimpna had recalled, there was a gaping hole in lieu of glass. Pickles barked. The window was a few meters off the ground, but if she was given a lift, Dimpna knew she could squeeze through.

"Detective Inspector?"

He was at her side in a jiffy. "Find something?"

"If you could give me a hand through this window?"

He swiveled his torch around the old stone frame. "Are you sure?"

"Unless you're volunteering, I don't see an alternative."

He whistled for a guard to shine the torch at the window and laced his fingers together. Dimpna stepped into his palms and hoisted herself up. The stone was bone-cold, and the smell of mold and earth was pungent. She landed hard on the other side but kept her balance. "Torch," she said. A torch was handed through.

"Are you alright?"

"I'm fine." She shone the torch through the dark crevices, taking small steps and shallow breaths. Something caught her attention just ahead. A lump. *Please God, no.* She swiveled the torch. A backpack. Purple. Dimpna sagged with relief. "Saoirse?" Her voice echoed off the damp stone.

"Anything?" the detective called from outside.

"A purple backpack," Dimpna called back.

"Saoirse. Saoirse." The mother cried out. "I'm sorry, baby," Nancy said. "Thirteen is the luckiest number of all. We'll have a proper party, love. I swear on me own grave."

Dimpna wished she hadn't just heard the word *grave.* Please let this lassie be alive. Water dripped from somewhere inside. "Saoirse?"

Dimpna called. "I saw you earlier. I was with my dogs. I've got Pickles here now. He's just outside. Pickles is very friendly. Do you like dogs?"

Silence. And then, there it was, faint but audible. The sound of a young girl speaking in a singsong voice. "I'll never tell, I'll never tell, I'll never tell." The sound echoed off the walls. Dimpna aimed her torch. There, rocking back and forth on the ground, was the young girl she'd seen earlier. "I'll never tell, I'll never tell, I'll never tell."

Dimpna's stomach lurched. "She's here," she called out. "Saoirse." Dimpna slowly advanced on the girl. "We've got you. You're safe."

The girl did not turn her head. She continued to rock. "I'll never tell, I'll never tell, I'll never tell."

"Is she hurt?" the detective called out.

"She's alive. That's all I can say right now." The sounds of cheers and sobbing rose from outside. "Do you hear that?" Dimpna said. "A lot of people are here. Looking for you."

The singing ceased. "For me?" A small voice croaked out.

Dimpna didn't want to advance too quickly so she shone the torch on her face, hoping she didn't look too creepy. "Yes. Are you hurt?"

Outside, Pickles barked excitedly. "That's your dog?"

"Yes. His name is Pickles. He came to look for you too."

"Are they here to take me to jail?"

"No, sweetie. We're here to take you home."

"Mammy is going to be browned off."

"She's just outside, and she's not browned off at all. You're in no trouble, do you hear me? Paul Byrne is here too." Dimpna heard a loud sniff, and then another. Her heart broke open. "Sweetie," she said. "Can I give you a cuddle?"

Sobs broke from the girl. "Yes."

Dimpna covered the space between them and took the girl into her arms. "You must be freezing." She wore only a thin shirt and denims. Dimpna rubbed her arms, trying to warm her up. "There's a blanket, water, and chocolate out there, just for you. Can you walk?"

"Do you promise I'm not in trouble?"

"I promise. I swear it. You are loved." Another sniff, then a nod. "Can you walk?"

"Yes." Dimpna helped her up, and keeping her arms around her, they headed for the window. Dimpna lifted the backpack on the way.

"I don't want that," the girl said suddenly.

"I'll take it," Dimpna said. "It's alright, luv."

"I'll never tell," she said. "I *won't*."

"Don't you worry your head. All you need to do is come outside with me, and all those people out there are going to help you, petal."

They reached the window, and just as Dimpna was set to help the girl up and out, Saoirse was already clambering up and over herself. She heard more cheers and called out to the inspector. "Sending her backpack through," Dimpna said. "For some reason she doesn't want to touch it."

"Ready," the detective said. Dimpna hoisted it through the window. "What about you?"

"If she can do it, I can do it," Dimpna said. She placed her hands outside the sill and pulled herself up. Given she needed strength to make up for her size, Dimpna was an avid weight lifter. Mostly dumbbells, but they did the trick. She pulled herself halfway through, and suddenly the detective's arms were around her waist as he pulled her the rest of the way out. He set her down immediately, but for a few seconds his hands remained encircling her waist. He dropped them suddenly, as if embarrassed.

"Well played," he said. "We wouldn't have found her without you."

"Thank you, Inspector, but it's Pickles you should be thanking."

"I'll have to do that from a distance," he said. "Allergies."

"Right, so."

"Saoirse, say something," Nancy Griffin was saying to her daughter, her tone too harsh for Dimpna's liking. "Say something."

"I'll never tell, I'll never tell, I'll never tell."

Nancy threw a desperate look to the inspector and Dimpna. "What's wrong with her?" she said. "Is she brain-damaged?"

"It's trauma," Dimpna said. "Speak kindly to her." Dimpna approached the girl. "You're going to be alright, luv."

"I'll never tell, I'll never tell, I'll never tell."

"Stop saying that!" her mother screamed.

"Mrs. Griffin." The inspector's voice was stern. "Why don't you come with me for a minute." He turned around to hand Dimpna the backpack when his torch caught words written across it. In thick black marker four words screamed out: YOU TELL, YOU DIE.

Her mother broke away from the inspector and edged in. "What does that say? What does that say?" She read the words, then gasped. "You won't tell," Nancy said. "Will you?" Saoirse violently shook her head. "That's right. You won't say a word."

Paul approached, his hands full with a blanket, and a bar of chocolate. "You must be cold and starving. We have a blanket, a bottle of water here, and a chocolate bar. Just until we can get you a proper supper. Would you like that?" There was a pause and then Saoirse nodded. Paul moved in and wrapped a blanket around her. When he held out the water and chocolate bar, she snatched them with both hands.

"Saoirse," her mother said. "Why didn't you come home?"

"Not now," the inspector said. Saoirse was gulping the water down and wiping her mouth with the back of her hand.

"Are you hurt?" Paul asked.

She shook her head, then ripped open the candy bar.

"Good. That's good."

The inspector eyed the backpack. When he reached for it, Saoirse lunged and yanked it out of his way. "Alright," he said. He pointed to the menacing words. "Did you write that yourself?" A pause and then she shook her head. "Do you know who wrote it?"

She took a bite of candy bar, chewing as she stared at him. Then she shook her head.

"You don't have to say anything now," Paul said. "There's plenty of time. We need to get you to hospital, make sure everything is okay."

"Can't it wait until morning?" Nancy Griffin pleaded. "It's late. I want to take her home."

"Home," Saoirse said. "No hospital."

The inspector stood and gently pulled the mother away again. "She has to go to hospital. She's dehydrated and needs to be checked out." He paused. "An ambulance is on the way."

Paul approached Saoirse. "I'll go with you to hospital," he said. She shook her head. "I bet they give you ice cream."

"Ice cream?" She tilted her head, considering it.

"Loads of ice cream," Paul said. "And I bet the kids at the group home will all make you cards, and even throw a birthday party for you."

She took another bite. "Not my birthday." Dirty tears smeared her face.

"You get a Mulligan," Paul said. "Know what that means?" She shook her head. "A do-over."

Saoirse pointed to Pickles who was sniffing her shoes. "Can he come?"

Dimpna joined in. "I'm afraid they won't let him at hospital, but he can come to your birthday party. He can even wear a funny hat."

She squinted for a moment, and then shrugged her compliance.

"Good," the inspector said, gently taking the backpack once more. "That sounds like a very special party for a special lassie." They began the trek back down the grassy road toward the car park.

"I can't afford a party," Nancy said.

"You won't have to," Paul said. "The center will take care of it."

"But I don't have cancer," Saoirse squeaked.

Dimpna felt a squeeze of sadness. She was glad Paul was a beacon to the girl. She needed one. Or a hundred.

"You don't need cancer to have a party," Paul said. "You deserve it just because of what an amazing girl you are." Dimpna wanted to pick her up and take her home, and found her own eyes welling. If this girl was the stowaway she'd been hearing about, she couldn't imagine what she'd been through. You had to be a strong and capable swimmer to make it in the waters by Clogher Strand. In the dark, no less. She could have easily drowned. And the message on the backpack meant that the killer had seen her. Spared her life, but not before threatening her, traumatizing her. Dimpna knew full well the power of trauma to hold someone captive. Her own trauma had erected an impenetrable wall of silence around her, sealed by terror and shame. A single violent act could result in a lifetime of a victim re-traumatizing themselves, keeping everything bottled in tight.

Sirens sounded in the distance. Saoirse let out a shriek and grabbed on to her mother. "Nothing to be afraid of," the inspector said. "Your mam will ride with you."

They fell silent the rest of the walk. By the time they reached the ambulance, Saoirse Griffin climbed into it without a fuss. The inspector was now handling the backpack with gloves. He held it in one hand and gave Nancy Griffin his calling card with the other.

"I'll need to speak with her as soon as the doctor allows it," he said. "I know she's been through an ordeal, but the sooner we find out who did this, the safer she'll be."

Nancy took the card. "She's not going to say a word," she said. "I won't have my daughter in danger." Dimpna watched the inspector hold his tongue.

"We'll keep you both safe," he said, as Nancy Griffin crawled into the back of the ambulance. "We'll work it out." The doors shut and the ambulance pulled away, lights and sirens sounding. Hopefully, Saoirse would find it exciting; she'd already had enough trauma for a lifetime. D.I. O'Brien watched the ambulance retreat, then turned to Dimpna. "Did you hand Finbar Malone's mobile phone to the guards?"

"I did. First thing."

"Phone?" Paul said. He sounded alarmed, and if Dimpna was reading it correctly, somewhat jealous.

"Official business," O'Brien said before Dimpna could answer. "That's all we can say." He met Dimpna's eyes, staring at her until she nodded. "You and your dog did good," he said. "Hope he gets a treat."

"He certainly will," Dimpna said. "I'm relieved we found her."

"She's in no shape to be interrogated this evening," Paul said.

The inspector held up the backpack. "She saw our killer," he said. "She's in danger."

Paul continued speaking. "We need guards posted at their house twenty-four-seven. She cannot be allowed to wander off on her own."

"We could bring the mother up on neglect charges," the inspector said.

"Christ," Paul said. "That will only make things worse. She's already had her father taken away. I'll have a word with the mother. This won't happen again."

"I know you have a relationship with the girl, and I've heard a lot about you at the station, Detective Sergeant," the inspector said. "I'm more than happy to work with you."

"I'm no longer a detective sergeant." Paul was being surly. Was it jealousy?

"You are, in my book," the inspector said. "And as I stated, I welcome your assistance. In fact, I'll need it. It's obvious the lassie trusts you, and she may be our only chance of finding this killer."

"Whatever I can do to help, Inspector," Paul said. His jaw was set. This was difficult for him.

The inspector nodded and then headed for a red Toyota.

Dimpna headed for her bus, Pickles on her heels. Paul grabbed her arm. He let go, just before Dimpna could tell him it hurt. "What's this about a phone?"

"It's been a long day," Dimpna said. "I need to get some sleep."

"Still keeping secrets," Paul said. "I guess some things never change."

"You're one to talk!" She hadn't meant to engage, but she was so tired, her filters were all gone.

"What secrets have I kept from you?"

She shut her mouth. He was right. It was all in the past anyway. "I found a lost phone. That's all."

"I doubt that's all." He moved in closer. "Did I hear him say it belonged to Finbar Malone?"

"He doesn't want me talking about it."

"He also said he needed my help."

"Then why don't you ask him?" She was tired and hadn't expected a grilling. Especially not from Paul.

"Listen," he said, lowering his voice and moving in closer. "You know I'm on your side."

"I have a side?"

"Come on, Dimp."

"Come on, what?"

"We're talking about Johnny O'Reilly here. Róisín and Sean are determined to see someone in your family—probably all of you—go down for this."

She exhaled, and nodded. "I'm aware."

He placed his hand on her arm. "You can trust me."

She let out a snort. She couldn't help it. She had trusted him once. He'd broken her heart. They hadn't spoken in twenty-seven years. She didn't know him at all. "It's nothing that concerns you."

"Are you ever going to forgive me?" There was pain in his voice. She couldn't take it on. She had no room for it.

"I no longer *need* to forgive you. We were completely different people then. It's in the past."

"We're the same people. At least I am. There hasn't been a day go by that I haven't wished you well."

"And I you," Dimpna said, feeling her hard edges softening. "But right now, all I want is to sink into bed." She took a few steps away from him.

"I don't trust that inspector. You shouldn't either."

"My parents are subjects of his inquiry. I don't think it's a good idea to get on his bad side."

"Don't let him charm you. He's not your friend."

"What on earth are you getting at?" She knew him. He was holding something back.

He brought his hand up to rub his chin, and for a flicker of a second she wondered if he was the man she saw staring at her from the auto body shop

"Have you spoken with Donnecha?" he asked.

Dimpna hadn't expected him to mention her brother. *What now?* "Not yet. Why?"

"He was being held at the station." He looked back to make sure the inspector wasn't in earshot. "I don't know if he's still there."

"Why was he there?" And why didn't he call? Was it too much to ask that one member of her family behave like a normal person?

"The morning after the murder he was wiping down O'Reilly's yacht with a bottle of bleach."

Dimpna realized she was shaking her head and willed herself to stop it. "What are you on about?"

"He's a caretaker for one of O'Reilly's boats. A small yacht. The inspector thinks that particular boat was used by the killer to transport the body to the beach."

Was it true? Was this why Donnecha hadn't answered any of her texts? She'd been so angry with him for avoiding her. "What did Donnecha say?"

"Now you don't mind sharing information?"

"This is my brother we're talking about."

Paul sighed, then nodded. "He said he wasn't on the boat that evening. He said that O'Reilly told him a VIP guest was going to use it."

"If he wasn't on the boat . . . did he say where he was?"

"The Dingle Inn."

Why had he not come to the clinic? Their father needed them. "What on earth was he doing at the Dingle Inn?" Paul looked away. "Paul?"

"I don't want to gossip."

"It's too late."

"He's been running around with some lad the past few months."

Dimpna sighed. A bad influence, no doubt. Was he back on drugs? "He's not answering my texts." She pulled out her mobile and stared at it as if willing it to ring.

"Where is your father?"

"Hospital."

Paul nodded. "I heard there was an incident with Sheila."

Which meant he also knew her father had been taken to hospital. Why was he asking her questions he already knew the answers to? What was he digging at? "I don't know why you're interrogating me—you seem to know more than I do."

Paul shook his head. "I'm trying to help."

"I just can't believe this is happening. I can't even wrap my head around the fact that someone murdered Johnny O'Reilly." She glanced at her bus. Paul's Jeep was parked directly behind it, yet he had arrived before her. Had he moved his jeep once she arrived? Had he deliberately blocked her in?

"How long will you be staying in Dingle?" Paul asked.

"Until my parents are no longer suspects in a murder inquiry." Was he trying to get rid of her? She let Pickles into the back of the bus, then stood by the driver's side door. "Good night, Paul."

"How is Ben?" Paul asked.

It was odd, hearing her son's name coming from Paul. "He's grand. He has a new girlfriend and they're in Spain."

"Doesn't he want to be here to support his grandparents?"

She chewed on her bottom lip. "I don't want him here. He's had enough to deal with." So did she, for that matter. At least the girl had been found alive.

"We should talk," Paul said. "Soon."

"I need you to move your Jeep."

Paul nodded and stood by his vehicle. "Last Dance," Paul said. "We need to talk about Last Dance."

Dimpna quickly opened the door to the bus, climbed in, and shut the door, waving at him through the window with a pasted-on smile. He stared at her for a beat before getting into his Jeep and pulling away. She waited, counting the seconds after he left. There it was again, paranoia taking hold of her. Paul was a decent man. A little intense, but decent. But she'd been honest with him. They were different people now. It was a relief, knowing he no longer had the power to pluck her heart strings. Even if that meant she'd outgrown the romantic girl that once roamed the streets of Dingle. She was now a jaded middle-aged veterinarian. And she wouldn't have it any other way. She started the engine, trying to ignore the pulsing guilt she felt whenever she thought about that beautiful dead horse. Paul had been a good detective. And if he wanted to talk about Last Dance, it could only mean one thing. The message in stone. It wasn't a euphemism. It had something to do with the past. Which meant the killer was no stranger. The killer was one of them.

CHAPTER 15

BY THE TIME DIMPNA WAS BACK IN THE CLINIC, HER TIRED MIND WAS spinning through her worries. And although as a vet she was used to all-nighters, it wasn't until a wave of dizziness hit, did she realize she hadn't eaten since breakfast. She headed to the back kitchen in search of something to quell her hunger. There she found only biscuits and tea. She grabbed the pack of biscuits and climbed the stairs to her father's upstairs flat.

She flicked on the light at the top of the stairs, illuminating the large open space. To the left there was a bed, a small leather sofa with two chairs, and a coffee table. On the right wall sat an ancient entertainment center with a telly, and the center of the room was commandeered by her father's large mahogany desk. Behind it loomed two floor-to-ceiling bookshelves bulging with large tomes. Books were stacked to the ceiling. Dimpna felt the familiar rumble of excitement that occurred whenever she feasted on her father's books.

History, veterinarian medicine, biographies, classic literature, travel books, and his guilty pleasure—spy novels. His true heart shone through his books, each one a reflection of his cornucopia of interests. She was thrilled to see he had added a little kitchenette tucked into the corner, and she nearly cried with joy to discover the mini fridge stocked with ham, cheese, and brown sauce. On the counter a decanter of whiskey gleamed. She poured a small dose and made a generous sandwich, then situated herself at her fa-

ther's desk. The surface held another stack of books—biology, veterinarian manuals, industry newsletters. Next to it lay a magnifying
glass and a highlighter. It was a familiar memory of him, leaning
over a book, furiously highlighting sections late into the night. She
used to love sitting and spinning in his desk chair, opening
anatomy books, marveling over the body parts of cows, and dogs,
and horses, and cats. It was a fascinating world to her, the world of
blood and bones, and organs and muscle. She'd not only spent her
childhood naming and coloring the various body parts and their
functions, she'd memorized enough gory details to horrify teach-
ers and delight classmates.

A jar of biros and a letter opener were the only other contents
on top of the desk. Her sandwich and whiskey went down easy, but
soon she was drowsier than ever. Mostly out of childhood habit,
Dimpna placed her hand on the middle desk drawer that her father had always kept locked. She used to conjure up all the secret
things she was convinced he kept in there. Mainly, given some of
the history books on his shelf, she'd imagined her father was a spy,
and the drawer held foreign money, and passports, and pens that
doubled as poison darts. To her shock, the usually locked drawer
slid open. A plain folder with a yellow sticky note on top stared out
at her. Two words blared from the sticky note in red biro: LAST
DANCE.

"Oh my God." This time, when Dimpna talked out loud, there
were no animals nearby to make her feel less crazy. She stared at
the words, her eyes blurring, her heart tap-dancing. She opened
the folder. The first item was an old newspaper article. The headline screamed out at her:

Colt Bolts!

Local veterinarian's daughter releases million-pound thoroughbred from stall and it races to its death . . .

Her stomach seized, and she regretted the sandwich. She turned
the article over. The next item in the folder was a photograph. It
took her a moment to realize she was looking at the trailer that hit
Last Dance, skewed sideways on the road. In front of it, the body of

her beloved horse on the asphalt, blood pooling around him. A low moan came from Dimpna as she flipped the photo over. A sentence was scrawled on the back in black ink:

Forget everything you think you know . . .

What in the world? It wasn't her father's handwriting. What did it mean? Was someone making a cruel jab at her father's dementia? How long had this been stuffed in her father's drawer? Only someone who had been a witness to that evening could have taken this photo. Those weren't the days when everyone ported around phones with fancy cameras. Someone just happened to be there with a camera? Who? A journalist? She'd tortured herself with every article that had come out after the tragedy, and she had never seen this grisly photo. It would have been newspaper gold. The coverage at the time reminded her very much of the media that swarmed them after Niall's scandal and suicide. But there was a crucial difference. The first time she had blood on her hands. Last Dance's blood. *Horse killer.*

She'd tortured herself all these years. Thousands of hours of therapy hadn't helped. She could not forgive herself. Whoever took that photo had been there that night. The O'Reilly barn employed a good deal of characters. Breeders. Trainers. Farmhands. Veterinarians. Had Tommy Healy been there? She'd been so drunk, there was so much she couldn't remember about that night.

Paul was right. They needed to meet sooner than later.

There was one more item in the folder, another newspaper article. This one was a feature on Tommy Healy. The photo showed him sitting proudly on top of a horse in jockey attire—wearing the same colors as any other O'Reilly jockey—navy blue, white, and green. Another attention-grabbing headline: ONE-ARMED JOCKEY SET TO RIDE LAST DANCE TO VICTORY . . . In the background his twin lurked, a scowl stamped on his face. *Brendan.* Sibling rivalry exemplified in one shot. What were the odds that the brother with only one arm was the one destined to shoot to fame? Dimpna had only met Brendan a handful of times. He'd taken off before the big race. Perhaps he had been consumed with jealousy. Or maybe he was better at reading the room. Maybe he knew the O'Reillys were nothing but trouble. Were most siblings doomed to jealous rivalry?

Her brother, Donnecha, had wanted nothing to do with the veterinarian business. Brendan Healy did not want to become a jockey, yet maybe he resented the attention his brother was garnering. Why was this photo here? *Forget everything you think you know . . .*

Clumsily worded, but hardly the point. What did she think she knew? Was someone pointing the finger at Tommy? Tommy had been inconsolable after Last Dance died. So inconsolable, he never rode a horse again. Did he blame Dimpna for that? And Brendan Healy couldn't have anything to do with this, could he? He'd left for America and had never returned. Surely he'd put Dingle far behind him. She tucked the folder back into her father's middle drawer, got into bed, and stared at the ceiling. *Forget everything you think you know . . .* Would her father remember receiving the items in the folder? Did he know what they meant? Was there any truth to them? As she closed her eyes, a terrifying thought emerged. What if someone had been deliberately planting stories in her father's head, winding him up to commit murder?

The next morning Dimpna took the dogs for a walk in one massive heap. Spike, never a cat to be left out, followed at a safe distance. She took them across the road and around the auto body shop. She was curious if she could find any trace of the man who had been watching her. The dogs sniffed around, but Dimpna did not see anything helpful. She'd already picked up the bag of poo she'd thrown at the man, and although there was plenty of litter on the ground, she would have no way of knowing if any bit of discarded rubbish belonged to the creeper. After walking through the fields and streets for nearly an hour, she and the dogs, and Spike, returned to the clinic where she once again made sure everyone was safely ensconced in a kennel or happy out in the fenced yard, showered with water, treats, and kisses.

She settled into the reception desk and called her father's former front-of-the-house manager, Niamh. When she reached her voice mail, Dimpna introduced herself and left a message asking if she'd be willing to stop by the clinic for a chat. Dimpna intended on closing the clinic. But first she needed to re-home all these creatures. In the interim, she would need help feeding and walking them. And, she had to admit, she was curious to get Niamh's take on everything that had been going on here lately, especially when it came to her father. She was impressed with Niamh's record-keeping—not that her father would have it any other way—and just as she was admiring the manager's work, the front door opened, jangling the bell, and a young woman appeared. A yellow flower winked from thick brown hair, and a wide grin took over her face. "How ya," she called. "I got your message and came straightaway."

"You must be Niamh," Dimpna said, rising. She was already infected by her grin. Niamh could have been considered full-figured, but Dimpna tried not to label anyone's bodies, especially fellow women. Dimpna had her share of people commenting on her size. And even though they often thought it was cute—"You're so little, aren't ya? I could stick ya in my pocket!"—it was all so cringe-worthy. How nice would it be if humans just stopped focusing on such trivial matters? Animals came in all shapes and sizes and so did people. Every coin had a flip side. Being little was cute until someone was locked out of the house and Dimpna was the only one who could fit through the doggie flap in the door.

"Dr. Wilde," Niamh said, approaching and clasping Dimpna's hands in hers as she pumped them up and down. "It is such an honor to meet you."

"You, as well," Dimpna said, liking her immediately.

Niamh dropped her hands and peered at her shyly. "I have always wondered what you were like, you know, based on the other Dr. Wilde." She punctuated the thought with a nervous laugh.

"We're very different."

"He's definitely taller, so." Another laugh erupted, a throaty sound that warmed the room. "I feel like I know you, and Ben."

Dimpna felt everything come to a halt. "Ben?"

"That's your son, right?"

"Yes." She frowned. "But he isn't close with his grandparents."

Niamh made a face. "That's hard to believe. Dr. Wilde is over the moon about him."

"He is?"

"Absolutely. Talks about the pair of ye all the time." Dimpna didn't know what to say. It had to be the dementia. Her father hadn't seen Ben in years. Their visits over his lifetime had been sporadic at best. She didn't want to say that to this lovely young woman. Just the mention of him made her long for her son. She'd received another text from him this morning. They were having a wonderful time in Roses, and next planned on going to France. He asked after his grandfather's health, but otherwise did not mention canceling his trip. At least that crisis was averted for now. "I wanted to compliment you on your record-keeping," Dimpna said.

"Thanks a million. If you're going to do something, do it right, me granny always said."

"Wise words. If you have the time, I have a million questions. I can pay you." There wasn't much money left, but Dimpna was desperate for her help.

"We'll sort all that out," Niamh said. "I'm yours for the day. Shall I put the kettle on first?"

"Lovely." Dimpna nearly cried with relief that finally someone was willing to help her. Niamh set about making tea, and soon returned to the reception area with two cups and a tin of biscuits. They sat behind the receptionist's counter, in front of the computer monitor, taking a few minutes to sip tea and chat. Once the pleasantries were behind them Dimpna began with her most pressing question.

"Would you mind telling me when you first noticed that Dr. Wilde wasn't quite himself?"

"I can go through my personal records if you like." Niamh gestured to the computer monitor on the left.

"Your personal records?"

"I kept a diary of sorts. Everything that happened at work."

"Wow. Yes. Brilliant." Dimpna gestured for Niamh to pull up and take the reins. She watched her efficiently click through the screens on the computer.

"I had to give some of my records to the guards."

"Oh?" Dimpna felt her heartbeat tick up. "When was this?"

"When Miss Maguire reported the bottle of Release missing, the next day we were swarmed with guards."

Miss Maguire. Dimpna nearly laughed. She still thought of

Sheila as a rebellious teenager. "Did they have paperwork from the courts?"

"Paperwork?"

"A warrant," Dimpna said. "For our records."

Niamh swallowed. "I didn't even think to ask. It was before the murder, so I didn't think there was any reason not to turn over my records."

Dimpna felt her pulse pick up. "Of course, luv." Dimpna's parents needed the advice of a solicitor.

"I asked did they want my records," Niamh continued. "They said yes, and that was it. But I made a photocopy of them first."

"Fantastic." It wasn't fantastic that she offered—but it was fantastic she made a copy, and Dimpna couldn't afford to alienate everyone. "I think from now on we'll get the advice of a solicitor."

"Do you want the name of Dr. Wilde's solicitor?"

It was a relief, someone who knew what needed to be done. "Yes, please."

"He handles any problems at the clinic. He may not be the right person if Dr. Wilde needs . . . other legal help . . . but it's a start." Niamh rifled through a contact list on the computer, then jotted something down on a sticky note and handed Dimpna the name and number of the solicitor.

"You're fantastic." Dimpna took a deep breath. "I'm also wondering if you can pull the records for all calls my father had in the past two months?"

"Two months?" Niamh chewed on her lips as she clicked through the screen.

"If my father was having lapses in memory, I have to make sure that all his patients received the right care."

"That makes sense." Niamh tapped her lips with her index finger. "It's going to take a few days, but I can put it into a readable report."

"I'll pay for your time." How? How was she going to pay for her time? Or anything else? Her parents were going to need their savings for their legal fees. Just the thought of their retirement being suctioned out to defend themselves against murder charges was enough to make Dimpna want to make it a whiskey morning. "Otherwise, if it's beyond two months but there are any highly alarming or unusual cases . . ."

"I'll make sure to flag anything I think you should see." Niamh was smart. She understood the direction Dimpna was traveling and hopped in for the ride. Adrenaline surged through her. She was going to do everything in her power to clear her parents' names. She'd been so helpless throughout the entire Niall ordeal, stumbling in the dark as one revelation after another rained down. She'd been even more helpless when Ben disappeared. That was the most gut-wrenching time of all. Battered by worry, tormented by his silence. Was he alive? Dead? Gone forever? Thankfully he'd returned, although it had been a torturous eight months. But this was different. This time she didn't just have to be a victim; she could take the wheel and right the ship. "Do you have any idea who may have taken that vial of Release?"

Niamh shook her head. "Only myself, Miss Maguire, and your father had keys to the meds. However . . ."

"Yes?"

"Dr. Wilde kept forgetting where he put his key. The dates are in my journal. It's one of the first things I noticed."

"Meaning someone might have actually taken his key?"

"I can't say for sure, but I constantly found it lying on the counter." Her eyes flicked to the counter. Dimpna watched her take in Aisling's gold necklace. She'd forgotten all about it. Niamh seemed mesmerized by it.

"I found it in the courtyard," Dimpna said.

"The little darling will be thrilled to get it back. I can take it if you like?"

Dimpna felt her heart squeeze. "I didn't realize any O'Reillys came into the clinic."

"Just the missus—Helen O'Reilly—and Aisling. A wee dote she is."

"She . . . has a pet?"

"Aye. A golden retriever puppy. A birthday gift from her da."

More evidence that Sean was a doting father. It was dawning on Dimpna that the rumors she'd been hearing might be true. Maybe Sean O'Reilly had outgrown his bullying ways. Perhaps fatherhood had changed him. That didn't mean he was ever going to know he had a son. "Did you mention the key situation to the guards?"

"I haven't been formally questioned. I hear the guards are making house-to-house inquiries, so I expect a visit from them soon."

"Hadn't the clinic already been closed down by the time they found O'Reilly's body? Because of my father's memory lapses?"

Niamh nodded. "But the guards were here after the bottle of Release was reported missing."

"When was that again?"

"About a fortnight before the murder."

"What did my father say about the missing vial?"

"He accused Sheila of stealing it. In front of everyone, like." Dimpna could only imagine how that went down. "I can't imagine what you're going through," Niamh continued. "For the record—even with his memory problems—there's no way Dr. Wilde could have murdered anyone."

"Thank you," Dimpna said, afraid she was going to cry. It was such a relief to finally hear someone say it. "I agree. But I'm curious. What makes you say that?"

"The Dr. Wilde I knew regularly got out of bed at half-two in the morning to birth baby cows, sheep, horses. He'd finish one, then get a message about another, and off he'd go without a single complaint. Don't even get me started on lambing season. He basically lived in his vehicle. A man who dedicates his entire life to saving lives? That's not a killer."

"Exactly." Dimpna slouched in her chair. "If only the rest of Dingle saw it that way."

Niamh held a finger up, stood, and disappeared down the hall. When she returned, she was struggling under a large cardboard box. She thunked it on the counter and opened it. Dimpna stood and peered into the box. It was stuffed to the gills with thank-you cards, handwritten letters, dried roses, and photos. Hundreds, maybe thousands, of photos of lovely, lovely pets. "Dingle knows exactly who your father is," Niamh said. "Here's your proof."

"Thank you," Dimpna said. "I'm going to take this up to my father's study later. Maybe make a collage for when he gets home."

"Say the word if you need help," Niamh said.

"You've been a big help already."

"Do you want me to tell you about the last time I saw Mr. O'Reilly?"

Dimpna's antenna twitched. "I do."

"I was planning on telling the guards, but like I said, they haven't asked me. I doubt they've even looked at my records."

"Please." The pair sank back into their seats.

"It was a month ago." Niamh brought up an online calendar, running a sunflower-yellow painted fingernail down the row of white boxes. "Here." She tapped the date. "I had a dental appointment in the morning and told Dr. Wilde I'd need the morning off." She tilted her head and stared at the date. "Maybe that should have been my first inkling that something was wrong."

"Why is that?"

"He said, 'Not a bother.' "

"And that was . . . unusual?"

Niamh nodded. "Normally he'd get a bit flustered when any of us had a day off, and he'd insist on going over the back-up plan. He'd want me to call in a replacement—even if it was for a few hours. He really didn't like being out here in the reception area."

"I can see that." Despite the box of thank-you cards, her father had always been better with animals than humans, especially as he grew older.

"That's when things got strange. Instead of asking for a replacement, he asked me to cancel all his appointments that morning."

This got Dimpna's attention. In her entire life, her father had never canceled an appointment. "Did he say why?"

"He did not. However . . . I got the feeling he was waiting for someone."

A shiver trilled through Dimpna. "What made you think that?"

"He stood out here, in the reception area, constantly looking out the window and checking his watch. He definitely wanted me out of here—as if he was worried about me and this visitor crossing paths."

"A client?"

"I don't think so. I know all the clients; this was someone he didn't want me to know about. And he seemed very . . . intent. That's the word for it."

"Did you ask him about it?"

"Of course. He said, 'It's none of your goddamn business.' "

"I see."

"He'd never cursed in front of me before."

"I know. He isn't the type." As hard as it was to hear, it was helpful, like the doctor said, to pinpoint the changes.

"At the time I didn't know what to make of it other than he was either really looking forward to this visit—or really dreading it."

"Go on, so."

Niamh swallowed. "I know who he was meeting."

A pulse of dread began to throb in Dimpna's neck. "Who?" It was barely a whisper.

Niamh lowered her head. "I haven't told anyone else this, I swear."

"I believe you."

"It was none other than Johnny O'Reilly himself."

CHAPTER 16

*I*T WAS NONE OTHER THAN *JOHNNY O'REILLY HIMSELF.* DIMPNA WANTED Niamh to take it back. She waited for the young woman to laugh, even smile, anything to indicate Niamh was messing with her. "Johnny O'Reilly," Dimpna said slowly. "Came here? To the clinic?"

Niamh nodded. "It turns out my appointment was canceled. Since Dr. Wilde seemed intent on privacy, I did my messages before returning to work. Apparently I didn't stall long enough. A black BMW was parked in front of the clinic."

"Couldn't it have been someone else?"

Niamh shook her head. "I saw him. Mr. O'Reilly was hurrying out the front door. He nearly knocked me over on his way out."

"My God."

"He was flying it. Jumped into his car and screeched out."

Dimpna just could not process it. "Had Johnny O'Reilly ever come to the clinic before?"

"Not once."

"Did you ask my father about the visit?"

A look of horror came over Niamh's pretty face as she shook her head. "I wouldn't dare."

Dimpna suddenly thought of the ruby ring. What if O'Reilly had dropped it during this visit? Or planted it? No. That didn't make sense. Detective O'Brien was in no hurry to get his hands on the ruby ring her father had slipped her. The only explanation she could think of was that Johnny O'Reilly's ruby ring *wasn't* missing. Was there a second one? To whom did it belong? Was it Sean's?

"What happened after you passed Mr. O'Reilly in the court-yard?"

"All the lights were off. I found Dr. Wilde standing in the exam room in the dark."

An echo of how Dimpna had recently found him . . . Was he recreating that moment? Why on earth had they needed a secret meeting? How could Dimpna find out when one of the men was dead and the other was having problems with his memory? Had Johnny O'Reilly said something to upset her father? And even more worrying . . . What did her father decide to do about it? "That's odd," Dimpna finally said.

"I didn't know what to say," Niamh said. "He didn't notice me there. He . . ."

The way Niamh dropped the sentence made it obvious she was debating whether or not to say the rest. Dimpna wasn't sure she wanted to hear this, but if she wanted to help her parents she had no choice. "Yes?"

"He was sobbing."

Sobbing. She'd only seen him shed a tear once. Not when she told him she was pregnant. Not when she told him who got her pregnant, and not when he found out she'd been accused of killing Last Dance. But she did see him cry once. When he saw Ben for the first time. When he held him in his arms and counted all his tiny fingers and tiny toes. Her father had locked eyes with her, tears streaming down his face. *You can never tell him,* he said. *Not ever.* And he still didn't know that Dimpna had been raped. She'd let him think she'd been a foolish girl. All these years later, she wanted to talk to the younger her, explain that it wasn't her fault, tell her that one day women would start telling the truth, and put the blame where it belonged—on the perpetrator. But that night she blamed herself. The worst night of her life bookended by Sheila and Paul making love, then the death of that beautiful horse—one she loved like he was her own. She'd told herself she'd deserved all of it, everything that happened, and even that wasn't enough to pay for her sins. But even without knowing the ugly truth about what Sean had done, her father had hated the O'Reillys. He'd worked too close to their animals—he knew what they were like. Profit came before everything. Horses were a means to an end, a commodity to be used.

Why on earth had he been meeting with Johnny O'Reilly? She needed answers. "Can you gather all the records for the O'Reillys?"

Niamh nodded. "They're our largest account. Including upcoming appointments."

"Upcoming?"

"If you're taking over, that is?"

"No, I'm going to close the clinic—"

Just then the front door flew open, jangling the bell. An elderly couple struggled in, the woman cradling something in a blanket. "Doc, Doc," she cried. "She's dying. Our baby is dying." The woman wore an orange hat and matching lipstick. Dimpna hurried over to see a skinny white cat. She had black socks on all four paws as well as the tips of her ears. She was emaciated, but Dimpna could tell she was probably a gorgeous cat. But right now she was struggling to breathe; her chest was rattling, her eyes rolling back in her head.

"Is she diabetic?" Dimpna asked, gently prying the struggling cat out of the woman's arms.

"Not that I'm aware," the woman said. "She's not been eating and didn't go to the bathroom at all yesterday."

Yesterday. And they were just bringing her in today. Dimpna refrained from reprimanding them. Piling guilt on top of them would not help any of them in this moment. If the cat died, they would regret that decision the rest of their lives.

"She's lost so much weight," the old man said. "She likes to follow me around the farm in the mornings. She's a regular little helper. She'll even go into the pasture with the bull. But a few days ago, she just stopped. Wouldn't move past the hearth. We haven't done anything different, not a thing."

"Please save her," the woman begged. "Our Misty is our baby."

"This is Mr. and Mrs. Collins," Niamh said.

Dimpna knew the name. Although the land belonged to the O'Reillys, the auto body shop across the street was a business owned by a Mr. Collins. Apparently, this Mr. Collins. She'd only met him a few times when she was young. "They just celebrated their fiftieth wedding anniversary," Niamh said.

"Hello, Mr. and Mrs. Collins," Dimpna said. "Congratulations."

"We've met you before, but it was a lifetime ago, and you wouldn't recognize me now," Mr. Collins said. "But my wife, she hasn't changed a bit, now has she?" He managed a wink.

"As lovely as ever," Dimpna agreed, watching the old woman blush and smile shyly.

She touched the top of her hat as if making sure it was still there. "He might look old, but he's still the same cheeky lad I married."

"I'm sorry to see you again under these circumstances," Dimpna said. They nodded, eager to move on from the pleasantries. "We're no longer open for business here," Dimpna said, knowing it didn't matter. This cat needed treatment right away.

"O'Connell is swamped since you've closed down. There's no one else."

"Let's see what we have here." She was going to need help. She turned to Niamh. "I know it's not your job, luv, but will you assist me in the treatment room? I'll walk you through it."

"Of course," Niamh said.

"How old is she?" Dimpna asked the owners.

"She's only eight years old, but Misty is our pride and joy," Mrs. Collins said as fat tears ran down her cheeks. "I know everyone must say this about their pets. But she's more like a person. She's so smart. She makes us laugh every day. Doesn't she, dear?"

Mr. Collins nodded. "She's fierce brave. And the sweetest thing too. She's good company, so she is. I don't know what we'd do without her."

"We're going to need fluids," Dimpna said.

"I know how to set up an IV drip," Niamh said.

"Fair play to ya."

Mr. Collins continued to talk as Dimpna and Niamh headed to the treatment room. "She loves life, Doc, she's never in a bad mood, not snooty at all like some cats. She's more like a dog, really. She likes to play fetch. She even comes when we call her."

"Please have a seat in the waiting room," Dimpna said. "I'm going to do everything I can for Misty."

"Should I ring Sheila?" Niamh asked, her brow creased with worry.

"I don't think there's time, luv. Just do everything I say."

Niamh nodded and hurried to the treatment room, with Dimpna carrying Misty. Once in the room they set the cat down on the table. Her breath consisted of short gasps, and she couldn't lift her up her wee head. Niamh already had tears in her eyes. "Mrs. Collins adores this cat," she said. "They celebrate her birthday every year. They even bring us treats on the special day."

"Those aren't the fluids I need help with," Dimpna said, pointing to Niamh's tears. "Mourning always come later. Do you understand?"

"Yes," Niamh said, sucking in her breath and wiping her face. "I'll get the fluids." She hurried out of the room. Dimpna found the levers to lower the table substantially. Niamh wouldn't technically be assisting so she didn't have to compromise on the height. Back in Dublin she had a nice set of step stools, but here she was at a disadvantage. Once the table was lowered as far as it would go, Dimpna still needed to find something to stand on. She ended up grabbing a few large volumes of veterinarian medicine off the shelves. At least they did the trick, putting her at the right level to work on the cat.

Dimpna gently looked in the cat's mouth. Its gums were sickly pale. She listened to the cat's heart, not surprised to hear it beat an abnormal rhythm. Dimpna donned her gloves and inserted a finger into the cat's rectum. She did not feel any lumps, and there was no internal bleeding, but a disgusting amount of worms writhed on her glove. Intestinal parasites explained the weight loss and lack of appetite, and could be treated, but it was possible they were too late. She switched to a new pair of gloves and gently moved her fingers over the cat's stomach, and discovered no obvious masses or lumps. She repeated the procedure around the cat's neck and head. No lumps.

Niamh returned with the fluids. "This is going to require an IV, blood work, and X-rays," Dinpna said. Niamh nodded, biting her lip.

"They're retired," she said. "They barely get by."

Dimpna nodded. She understood too well what that meant. It meant she now had to go out into the waiting room and break it to that sweet old couple that not only was she probably not going to be able to save Misty, but just attempting to do so was going to require extensive tests and cost loads of money. Niamh followed her to the waiting room and announced she was going to make them a cup of tea. Dimpna sat down and gently broke the news. "Have you not kept up with routine vaccinations and deworming?" she asked as gently as possible. There was nothing worse than a client learning those vital lessons too late.

"We have, we have," Mrs. Collins said. "Your father saw him just last month and said she was all sorted."

"He sent you home with heartworm pills?"

The woman frowned. "No. I told you. He said she was all sorted."

That wasn't how it worked. He should have sent them home with pills. Had he even administered one to Misty a month ago? Dimpna made an effort not to show any obvious reaction. How many other animals had her father put at risk? She had to carefully comb through the records from the past few months. It wasn't just about lawsuits, but the well-being of the animals. If only someone had copped on earlier that he wasn't himself. If only Dimpna had been here.

"Do everything you can," Mr. Collins said, leaning over to dab a tear rolling down his wife's cheek.

"How would we pay for all that now?" Mrs. Collins said, anguish pouring out of her voice.

"Would she make it?" Mr. Collins said. "If you do all those tests and whatnot, can you save her?"

"I can't promise that," Dimpna said. "I'd put the chances of saving her at forty percent. But unfortunately, that's only if I get started with some fluids and treatment immediately."

"Do it," Mr. Collins said. "What are you waiting for?"

"I need your permission before I start on any costly tests," Dimpna said. She always gave it straight no matter how knotted up she felt on the inside; she always remained calm and gave it straight.

"We can't pay," Mrs. Collins cried. "We can't pay."

Dimpna couldn't take it. She couldn't afford to cover it either, but there was enough bad karma in Dingle right now. And her father might be the reason the cat had missed her heartworm pills. She had to at least try. "Let me start with some fluids, and see where we go," she said. "If there's no improvement, then we'll discuss the options." Dimpna hurried back to the treatment room and prepared a catheter. She quickly slipped it into a vein in the front leg, sending up a little prayer as the fluids made their way into the cat's system. She drew the bloods, then collected a stool sample. Next, she gave Misty antibiotics and medications to help settle the cat's stressed little body. When Niamh returned, they hooked Misty up to an electrocardiogram monitor. Dimpna cringed as it pulsed out abnormal heartbeats. "This doesn't look good," Dimpna said quietly. Misty looked even worse now, its poor head limp, a low moaning emanating from its belly. The monitor beeped; the poor thing's heart rate was plummeting. Dimpna started chest compressions immediately. "I need a tube," she said. "C'mere to me, Misty. You're not going anywhere today. Did you hear me? Now."

Niamh was efficient and at least knew where everything was. She handed her a tube that Dimpna slipped into Misty's trachea, administering oxygen and beginning artificial respiration once more. The heart rate dropped further. "Come on, Misty. Come on, girl," Dimpna said. "You're loved. You've got nine lives. Did no one ever tell you that?" The monitor steadied but did not improve. "We go again," Dimpna said. "From the top." Fluids. Compression. Oxygen. Epinephrine through the tube. Misty was slipping away, leaving this world, and there was nothing more Dimpna could do. The monitor flattened into a straight line. Dimpna removed the tube and stopped the fluids. "Wrap her in the blanket," Dimpna said. "Give her a last cuddle. I'll break it to the Collinses."

"Oh," she heard Niamh say. "Poor, poor, thing." Niamh wasn't used to it yet. At the front desk she was slightly removed from all the trauma in the examination room.

Dimpna gave her shoulder a squeeze. "We did everything we could. You repeat that to yourself as many times as you need to, luv. We did everything we could." Niamh sniffled and nodded as she cradled and rocked the cat. Dimpna headed for the waiting room, the familiar ache of defeat thrumming through her, hollowing her out. She'd told Niamh the truth; they'd done everything they could. If only that was any consolation. Back in the waiting room, Dimpna knelt by the couple who burst into tears before she could even speak. "Thank you, Doc, thank you," Mrs. Collins said. "You tried. We know you tried." It was one of the most staggering and touching things Dimpna had experienced over and over again as a vet. People, in their most agonizing moments, stopping to comfort *her*. Clients, who'd been put through the ringer watching their beloved pets take their last breath, would return to Dimpna's clinic with offerings of love. Wine, and flowers, and chocolates, and sweet little photos of their pets in better times. Grief not only brought out the worst in people, it brought out the best. She was reminded of that now as Mrs. Collins stroked Dimpna's head. "It's alright, Dr. Wilde, it's alright."

"Dimpna?" Niamh appeared at the end of the hall, her voice pinched.

"Just a minute." The old couple had their arms around Dimpna; they were having a moment.

"Can you come back here for a minute?" Niamh said a little louder.

"Just give us a moment—"

"Misty came back!"

The couple dropped their arms and Dimpna shot up. "What?"

"She's alive!"

Dimpna hurried after Niamh into the treatment room, Mr. and Mrs. Collins at their heels. Misty was sitting up on the exam table, eyes open and alert. She meowed when she spotted the Collinses. Dimpna stared, gobsmacked. Clips from the EKG hung off her like she was a science experiment. She let out another pitiful meow, but it was the most beautiful sound Dimpna had ever heard. She was breathing on her own.

"You lied to us!" Mr. Collins said, sounding furious. "You made us think she was dead!" He balled up his fist. "What kind of person does that?"

"I swear to ye," Niamh said. "I thought Misty was dead, too. She fooled both of us. But Dr. Wilde did everything, and I mean *everything* in her power, to save her, in lightning speed. Only looks like Misty here needed a minute to catch up. Didn't you, luv? Dr. Wilde is the only reason she's alert and looking at us like we're a bunch of blubbering eejits!"

Mr. Collins's mouth dropped open. He released his fist. "I'm sorry, I'm sorry," he said, wiping a tear off his face with the back of his hand. "Thank you, Doc. Thank you, thank you, thank you."

"We're forever grateful," Mrs. Collins said.

"I think this is as close to a miracle as I've ever witnessed," Dimpna said. "She really does have nine lives."

"That's who she is, don't you know. She does everything on her timetable, so she does," Mrs. Collins said, clasping her hands together. "You saved her. I don't care what they say about you or your father. You saved our Misty!"

"We're not quite in the clear yet," Dimpna said, making a concerted effort to ignore Mrs. Collins's last statement. "I want to keep Misty here overnight," Dimpna said. "She'll need extensive deworming, and I'm obligated to warn you, given the amount of time she was flatlined, she may have some brain damage."

"She looks like our Misty to me," Mr. Collins said. Misty was now enthusiastically licking herself. She took a few wobbly steps forward.

"Those are the medications making her woozy," Dimpna said. She massaged the cat's little head. "You're going to need a long catnap after this."

"We owe you," Mr. Collins said. "I'll think of some way to pay you."

Dimpna held up her finger; she wanted to check the cat against the monitors. She hooked Misty back up to the EKG. Perfect heartbeat. Next, she checked her oxygen. Perfect saturation. Dimpna let out a laugh. "I think this cat must have a few angels watching over her," Dimpna said. "But she's definitely used up one of those nine lives."

"There's only one angel here today," Mrs. Collins said, taking Dimpna's hand. "I'm going to tell everyone you're a miracle worker."

"I think you'd better make that two angels," Dimpna said, throwing a grateful look to Niamh. "Turns out she's one hell of a cat cuddler." Niamh laughed, her cheeks filling with a rosy glow.

"I tell you one thing I can do for you," Mr. Collin said. "I couldn't help but notice you have some strays in your courtyard."

"We've had an influx lately," Dimpna said. "What did you have in mind?"

"It needs cleaning up, but I could let you use my auto body shop across the way. If you can pay to have all the old paint cans and whatnot disposed of properly, and have any scraps or tools hauled away to the junkyard, she's all yours. It could serve as an extra kennel and yard for your creatures."

"That is a very generous offer, Mr. Collins. If I say yes—and I'm only thinking about it at this stage—I'd like to eventually start paying you rent. It might just take a while."

"Here." Mr. Collins removed a fat set of keys from his pocket and took one off the ring. "Have a poke around and when we come back to collect Misty you can let us know what you think."

CHAPTER 17

"**Y**OU HAVE TO KEEP THIS CLINIC OPEN," NIAMH SAID TO DIMPNA. IT had only been an hour since the Collinses left and they were still feeling the buzz of Misty coming back to life. "Dingle needs you."

"I don't know." But even as she said it, Dimpna had a sudden urge for the work. Misty was an outlier; the cat should have been dead. But she wasn't. And Dimpna had learned that you couldn't just wallow in the bad, you had to actively embrace the good. And if she was being honest, she needed the work. The routine. The hyperfocus. The quirky pets and their equally, if not more, quirky humans. Not to mention the money. She couldn't afford to take care of all these animals herself. And she couldn't let harm come to them.

Niamh's eyes lit up as she leaned in. "You would go a lot of places, talk to a lot of people. I hear a lot of things too. People come in. They can't help but gossip."

"That is true," Dimpna said. Maybe she could get answers. Answers like why her father had secretly met with Johnny O'Reilly. They wouldn't be found unless she had access to the O'Reilly estate. Would Tommy Healy speak with her? If anyone knew about this meeting between Johnny and her father, it would either be Tommy or Sean. She would need a legitimate reason to be near them.

"Not to mention the obvious," Niamh said, interrupting Dimpna's mental maze.

"What's that?"

"The animals need you. We couldn't even fill all the requests when we were open full-time. Unless of course, you don't need the money."

She was smart, Niamh. Whether she was trying to preserve her own job, or honestly wanted to help, the answer was obvious. Dimpna would do better if she kept busy. Her parents needed her. Correction—they needed *them*. Both of their children. Where the hell was her brother? She was going to have to find him even if she had to personally search every single boat at the harbor. "Do you think clients will accept me as the new vet?"

"Absolutely," Niamh said.

Not all of them. There was plenty of sexism in the field. Male and female farmers who would still specifically request male vets only. Add in Dimpna's size, and she had to make triple the effort to prove herself. People doubted her around horses, and cattle, and bulls. Seeing their sheer size next to Dimpna's made others fearful. Until they saw her work. She did have to make accommodations, but she made them. She'd had close calls, but so had all vets that worked with animals. It was a little easier in Dublin, in a small animal clinic. Owners thought it was adorable watching little Dimpna with their kitties and puppies, and rabbits, and hamsters, and once a chinchilla, but at 3:00 A.M. when a large cow was calving, its baby trying to come out feetfirst, the looks on farmers' faces when she showed up was akin to characters in a horror film when they realize the psychopath they thought was dead is not only still alive, he's standing in front of them with a bloody cleaver. Sometimes, Dimpna actually enjoyed those expressions of horror, because they often changed to wonderment by the time she was done. Dimpna was strong, and she'd developed techniques in which she could use her size to her advantage but still accomplish difficult tasks around enormous animals. It was possible they even relaxed more around her due to her size. Either way, she made it work, and she excelled at her job. Just like her father had excelled for close to five decades. She was not going to let him down. The clinic would not close and he would not go down as a murderer.

Did that apply even if he really was?

She ignored the nonsense tumbling around her brain. She had to focus. She needed to add a second vet to the clinic. Someone fresh out of school, hungry for his or her first placement. And if she was going to be anywhere near the O'Reilly barns, her assistant should be tall and male. Like it or not, that was the only way Róisín O'Reilly would even consider keeping them on as their vet. *Send a male vet.* Róisín O'Reilly may be the grieving widow, but the Wildes had all their veterinarian records, knew every racehorse in those barns, and had been providing care at no cost for the past twenty-seven years. What a price they had paid to prevent the O'Reillys from pressing charges against Dimpna for releasing Last Dance and agreeing to keep quiet about her pregnancy. Not that Johnny O'Reilly had any interest in claiming his grandson. Quite the opposite. As far as Dimpna knew, Johnny hadn't even told his wife. God forbid their bloodlines mix. If she was going to start snooping around their barns, she needed to keep the agreement in place, and she needed to add a male vet to the team.

Dimpna turned to Niamh. "We'll open in three days." Niamh grinned and pretended to clap her hands. "And once we're on our feet again, you're getting a raise."

Niamh held her hands together in praying position, gave a little bow of thanks, then straightened her spine and pulled her seat closer to the reception desk. "I have résumés if you want me to schedule interviews for vet techs and assistants."

Dimpna nodded. "Let's start with a second vet and a vet tech." They'd need more but it was a start. "Do you think Sheila would come back?" Dimpna had no intention of bringing Sheila back— she didn't trust her—but she wanted Niamh's impression.

Niamh's face went still. "She might."

"I sense hesitation."

"It's nothing I can put my finger on."

"I'd like to hear what you're thinking."

"I don't know if this clinic is a priority to Sheila."

"Okay."

"I'm not accusing her of anything but . . ."

"Yes?"

"I can't point to anything specific. It's just . . . she doesn't always seem to like it here." Niamh leaned in. "Maybe it's her new boy-friend. Makes her want to dash out of work as fast as she can. Be-fore all this murder business, she slipped out early more times than I can count."

Dimpna felt the irresistible pull of needing to know. "Who's her new boyfriend?" *Was it Paul? Please, don't be Paul.*

"That's just the thing. She wouldn't say a thing about her new love. I thought of us as a little family here. I guess she didn't. She started dressing up and slipping out late and coming back to work with a big grin on her face. She's riding someone, I'd bet the farm." Niamh grinned, then shrugged. "I just don't know if she wants to work here anymore."

Was it true? Was Sheila in a relationship? Wasn't Dimpna too old to feel jealous? How was it possible that being back here stripped away all those years in between and suddenly she was thinking and feeling like a teenager again? Dimpna hadn't made love in a long time. Even before Niall took his own life, he'd been distant, and she'd been overwhelmed with work. It was nearly impossible to admit, but she hadn't had sex in well over a year. *And counting.* There had been one last time with Niall, months before the news broke. Had she known it was going to be the last time, maybe she would have made more of an effort. There was nothing remarkable about their last time. Just a day when they'd found themselves going to bed at the same time and turning to each other in the dark. Pleasant, but quick.

There were times she thought she may never be with a man again. She wasn't getting any younger. She'd secretly wondered if seeing Paul again would awaken her desires. Instead, she found herself thinking of the inspector. There was something about him, a charisma, an intensity that beckoned her. He seemed lost, and so was she. The intense way he studied her was something she hadn't experienced in a long time. Or perhaps it was just a thing she did—fall for inappropriate men. But sleeping with the inspector investi-gating her parents for murder was not just foolish, it would be dangerous. Now was not the time to indulge in fantasy. There was something about the mention of Sheila that brought back all her old insecurities and petty jealousies. "My father did throw a book at her face and accuse her of being a thief," Dimpna said. "I can see how that would be a deal-breaker."

"Shall I line up interviews?"

"Yes. And if we eventually open a facility across the street, we'll need workers to help clear it out. But one thing at a time. I want to get the other vet first."

"On it," Niamh said.

"And could you start calling clients to see if they're willing to book? That will give us an idea of whether or not we can pull this off."

"I'll start now."

"Good woman." She chewed her lip. "I'm wondering if you shouldn't give Sheila a courtesy call? Offer her her position back. I have a feeling she'd turn it down—but I don't want to stab anyone in the back." *Like she did me. So many times.*

"I'll do that," Niamh said. "But I believe she's working with O'Connell now."

Dimpna nodded. It made sense that Sheila would go to the other vet in town. "Let me know what she says." Dimpna stepped into the courtyard. The skies were gray and starting to spit. She called her father's solicitor. He told her he had already spoken to her mam and had recommended another solicitor, one that dealt with criminal matters. He hung up before she could even say good-bye. At least her mam was on top of things. Dimpna called her next. Her mother picked up right away. "I'm waiting to speak with his doctor, luv. Hopefully we're going home today."

"Should I join you?"

"Not at all. You can visit your father when we're back at the house."

"I'll see you at the house later then," Dimpna said. "Have you heard from Donnecha?"

"You know your brother," her mam said. And then she hung up. Did her mother know that Donnecha had been taken into the station? That he had been cleaning the boat that the inspector believed had been used in the murder? Dimpna sighed, then dialed Donnecha's number. The voice mail picked up and told her it was full. She sent a text: **Call ASAP. Emergency!** She went back inside, wondering when she was going to have time to check out the auto body shop. The reception desk was empty. Dimpna came around to log onto her email, but when she did, she caught sight of a notebook near the monitors. It was open, the handwriting neat and elegant. It must belong to Niamh. She sat in the chair and glanced at it again. One line stuck out; this one was not neat and orderly, nor was it in the same blue ink. This was one in red, the letters large and slashed as if the writer had gone over and over and over it obsessively. Dimpna stared at the message, wondering what on earth it was all about: I HATE HIM.

CHAPTER 18

*T*HE DINGLE GARDA STATION ON BRIDGE STREET WAS HOUSED IN A lovely stone building that had tried on various paint schemes over the years but was currently on the blue end of the gray spectrum. Cormac studied the walls of his small makeshift office, annoyed at smudges mocking him. This had previously been a storage room, evident by the pile of cardboard boxes shoved to one side. He was the first to admit he could be a bit neurotic. Stacks of books needed to line up just so. Biros couldn't roll willy-nilly on a desk; they needed to be placed in a holder, ink facing down. Wet marks on restaurant tables drove him mental, to the point where he couldn't even focus on conversation until they were all dabbed up. Daily life was a struggle to accept nagging imperfections. He'd certainly tried. Meditation, meds, a few reluctant sessions with therapists. No drink. More drink. No drink. Moderate drink. More sleep, less sleep, no sleep, more sleep. Eat your veggies—that's what you need. Vitamins. That's the trick. He'd even tried fecking yoga. Only two things had ever eased the chaos in his mind: playing the squeeze-box and working a case. And this case did not disappoint. He hadn't been this hyped up in ages. But the theatrics Paul Byrne had played at Nancy Griffin's house this morning still burned in his mind, and he'd been replaying them like a film, trying to suss out the man's angle. Cormac had been thrilled when the young girl was released from hospital with a clean bill of health. And he'd been as accommodating as he could, going out to the house instead of having her come into the station. It was bad

enough they'd all been jammed into the table in that tiny depress-
ing kitchen—dishes piled in the sink, every surface loaded with
clutter, open food containers, the smell of cigarettes and alcohol
choking the air. He had a sinking feeling this wasn't due to the fact
that her daughter had been missing, that this was how the place
had always looked. He'd started sneezing, and then when that was
finally under control, he'd gotten absolutely nothing out of the
girl, and it was all Paul Byrne's fault. First, Byrne kept delaying the
questioning, insisting he let her eat her breakfast in peace, and
then when Cormac gently started his questioning—"Tell me about
the night of your birthday"—Paul Byrne cut in.

"You don't have to answer any of his questions," he said. "You
can ask for a solicitor."

The girl looked to her mother. "We can't afford a solicitor,"
Nancy Griffin said.

"We can find one who'll represent her pro bono," Paul said.
"This case is on everyone's radar. There's no use mucking it up."

"There's no need for a solicitor," Cormac said. "Saoirse, I
promise. You're not in trouble for anything you did that evening. I
don't care if you nicked things. I don't care if you trespassed on a
yacht."

Saoirse looked to Paul. "Snuck onto a boat," Paul translated with
a pointed look at Cormac.

Cormac nodded and did his best imitation of a smile. "I just
need to know what happened." She looked at him with big eyes.
She'd seen something that night—someone—and he needed to
know what it was. It had been a mistake allowing the ex-detective to
accompany them, and he saw it clearly now. Paul Byrne had set him
up. What was he so afraid of? "Did you sneak onto the big white
boat in the harbor? *Dreamscape?*"

She nodded. "I saw someone come off it. He was dressed in
mourning clothes so I thought I had time."

"Mourning clothes . . . You mean he was wearing dark clothing?"

She nodded. "It could have been a girl, to be honest. I couldn't
see a face. Just a black hat, black gloves, and a long black coat."

She was a bright girl. "That's very good, Saoirse. Very smart. Do
you have any idea who this man or woman was?"

Paul leaned in again. "If you don't know something, it's okay to tell him you don't know. He doesn't want you to make anything up."

Cormac felt his jaw clench and he threw a look to D.S. Neely.

"Detective," she said, "why don't we get a spot of fresh air?"

Ex-detective, Cormac bit back, "That's a good idea." He stared at Byrne until the man finally stood up. "It's okay if there's anything you don't want to answer," Byrne said again. "Save your energy for planning your party." He grinned at Cormac. "It's this weekend. Consider yourself invited."

"I think I'll join you for that fresh air," Cormac said, pushing back his chair. "We'll be right back."

Out in the front yard, which was also cluttered and dirty, Cormac didn't hold back. "I'm trying to catch a killer and she may be our only witness. What the hell do you think you're doing?"

Paul Byrne squared off with him. "You're making a big mistake. Putting her directly in the killer's crosshairs."

Cormac didn't need to be schooled in how to do his job. "We'll put protection on her."

Byrne shook his head as if that was exactly the wrong answer. "For how long? A day or two? What happens after that?"

"If she tells us who did this we'll go and arrest the person and then we won't have to worry about it, will we?" Was it possible Paul Byrne was involved in this somehow? Was that the real reason he didn't want the girl to talk?

"I know you're under immense pressure," Paul said. "But you need to stop and think."

"Forget what I said about needing your help," Cormac said. "You're going to step aside and let me do my job."

D.S. Neely put her hand on Cormac's arm. "Why don't you go back in? We'll stay out here and have a chat."

"Don't come back in," Cormac said to Paul. "And if I catch you interfering with this case in any way, I'll bring you in. Won't even think twice about it."

He headed back in, determined to find out what the girl knew. She was no longer at the table. "She needs her rest," her mother said. "We'll have to do this another time."

*   *   *

Cormac brought his thoughts back to the present. Saoirse was scheduled to come into the station this afternoon. He had his doubts about whether or not her mother would bring her in. It had been a huge blow not being able to speak to her last night or this morning. It had already been days since the murder, and eyewitness accounts often changed as time passed. Then again, she had been exhausted. He'd insisted that she be taken to the doctor this morning, and only if she was given the clear be brought into the station. That way, Paul Byrne couldn't accuse him of not looking after the girl. Besides the figure dressed all in black, she had to have seen something given the writing on her backpack. *You Tell, You Die.* Cormac wanted to strangle the bastard who wrote that with his bare hands. Sparing a child's life just to torture her? Scars that would last the rest of her life, even if she dealt with it properly, which she probably wouldn't. And should Cormac add Paul Byrne to his list of suspects?

His behavior was beyond the pale. Either he was so filled with jealousy that he wasn't on the case, and trying to sabotage Cormac, or he was hiding something sinister. Cormac had a feeling that there had once been something romantic between Paul Byrne and Dimpna Wilde. He'd watched their interactions and he was sure of it. He was also highly aware that he was thinking about her a little too much. No matter how unique and interesting she was, he was here on an official capacity. Besides, the only time she seemed interested in him at all was when she was poking at him. She seemed downright pleased every time she clocked his frustrations. She was an enigma. Not to mention the tension he'd felt between her and Sean O'Reilly. What was that all about? There was no time to stew over it; he had to get through today's briefing.

One thing was for sure. This station was still loyal to Paul Byrne, and they weren't quite sure what to make of *him.* His team was polite and they were hard workers, but they were a long way from warm and fuzzy. He'd still walk into a room previously filled with laughter and nattering only to have it come to a screeching halt when he entered. He'd tried going out for pints with the crew, but all that resulted was a massive pain in his head the next day, and a bin full of empty Lucozade bottles and headache tablets. The house-to-house inquiries were ongoing. He had a pile of interview questionnaires on his desk to read through. He planned on doing the O'Reilly interviews personally, but the family solicitor was still giving him the runaround. He'd finally nailed an appointment for tomorrow afternoon with the widow and her son. Was this only Wednesday? *Happy Hump Day.* What a world. Johnny O'Reilly's funeral would be held on Friday. At least he had made *some* progress and he was eager to share it with the rest of his team at the upcoming briefing. He was clicking through his presentation on his laptop when a figure materialized in the doorway. Superintendent McGraw. All the way from Dublin. *Christ.* The man was likely feeling the heat from above and he was here to beam it down on Cormac, inferno-style.

CHAPTER 19

"SUPERINTENDENT MCGRAW," CORMAC SAID, SCRAMBLING TO HIS feet and feigning as much positivity as he could. "I didn't know you were coming."

"I hear you're updating the team on your progress today," McGraw said. "I thought I'd see for myself." Great. Now he was going to learn firsthand that Cormac had been blocked from interviewing his sole eyewitness by an ex-detective. He should have never let Byrne accompany him.

"Right you are. It's nearly time," Cormac said. "We're making good progress."

"That's not what I hear." McGraw was average in most ways—average height, average looking at sixty-something, and average receding hairline. He was a jovial man if you were a rank above him, a "team player" as long as he was team leader, and a man who did not tolerate criticism.

"Glad you're here then. You'll see. They're preparing the briefing room as we speak." Cormac's eyes flicked to the full bin of Lucozade. Why hadn't the cleaning staff cleared it last night? He glanced at his watch. "We have about thirty minutes until showtime." There had been progress on the case; maybe it was a good thing he was here. And if he couldn't get the ex-detective on a leash, maybe McGraw could.

McGraw pulled out a chair, but he was eyeballing the one Cormac was sitting in.

"Would you prefer this chair?" Cormac asked with forced enthusiasm.

"It would be easier, if you don't mind."

Cormac was dumbfounded. "Not a bother." He rose from his chair, and the two made for awkward dance partners as they maneuvered around the pile of boxes to switch places. Cormac sat in the chair facing McGraw, his adrenaline now coursing as the superintendent began examining the desk as if he was going to dust it for fingerprints. "Coffee?" McGraw said with a raised eyebrow.

Cormac turned to the doorway, praying he'd catch a garda walking by so he could shout out a coffee order. He'd actually never asked any of them for such a favor, hoping it would make him one of the team. Seconds ticked by before he realized he was going to be fetching it himself. "Absolutely. Wouldn't mind one myself."

"Light and sweet," McGraw said.

"Pardon?"

"That's how I like my coffee. And my women." McGraw, a married man with three children, let out a loud laugh.

Cormac managed a weak smile. "Back in two shakes," he said, heading out the door for the coffee while imagining pouring an entire scalding pot directly over McGraw's head. Coffee would be set up for the meeting, and McGraw knew that full well. Instead, he wanted Cormac to wait on him. He returned minutes later with two coffees and a tin of biscuits, trying to erase the image of the smug grins from nearby guards who had witnessed his trek to and from the kitchenette. Cormac leaned against the wall and the pair chatted about the latest football match, and by the time their mugs were empty, a garda poked her head in to let them know the room was set up. Cormac and McGraw headed over, the smell of microwave popcorn and disinfectant in the air. Upon entering the large room, Cormac was relieved to see everything looked professional. Guards had taken their seats in chairs facing the front, and large screen and projector were ready to go. D.S. Neely took a seat up front, while McGraw lurked in the back. *Showtime.* Cormac had to make it sound good. He took a moment to connect his laptop to the projector and pulled down the large screen.

"Need popcorn back here," someone yelled out. Soon a bag was airborne, sailing over heads, until someone leapt up to catch it. Laughter filled the room. McGraw scowled in the back. Cormac asked for the lights to be dimmed. The first slide read TOXICOLOGY. Underneath it was a bottle of Release and a syringe. He'd used Photoshop to circle the vial with red marker. Cormac cleared his throat.

"This is the vial of the euthanasia medication found at our murder scene. Release. If you look closely, you'll see that it is half-full. Or half-empty depending on where you fall on the optimist/pessimist spectrum." The laughter wasn't nearly as loud as the one for popcorn, but he at least got a few chuckles. "Toxicology reports are expected to take another six weeks." A groan went around the room. Was is because of the wait or was it him? "But I had a brief call with the deputy state pathologist and we do know a few things. The injection mark on O'Reilly's neck suggests we will find the ingredients of Release present in the body. What I want to know is— was it enough to kill him? One hundred milliliters is the dose we've calculated that would have been needed to induce death. As you can see, only fifty milliliters are gone from this vial. Either there's a vial somewhere on that beach that we missed, or Release is not what killed him." The back of his neck felt hot from repeating Dimpna Wilde nearly verbatim, but the pathologist had backed up her assertions. "Due to the injection mark found on his neck the state pathologist has concluded this was a homicide. Given there is going to be a long wait for toxicology, she's releasing the body to the family." He scanned the room; no one had any follow-up questions. "We'll have a presence at the funeral. There's a good chance our killer will make an appearance."

"And what?" McGraw said. "Wave his hands about and announce he's the killer?" More laughter.

"Probably not until the wake," Cormac said. "After a few jars." Heads swiveled as if everyone was waiting to see whether or not it was okay to laugh. When McGraw finally chuckled, they joined in. Cormac flicked to the next slide. Guards shifted in their seats and made jokes under their breath as the smiling Devil was up next. "We've sent the tarot card found in O'Reilly's suit pocket to the

Technical Bureau for fingerprints, although I'm not counting on gleaning anything from that angle."

"Does the card belong to Maeve Wilde?" McGraw piped up.

"I'm assuming it does."

"Assuming?" The superintendent shook his head. "Tell me you've interviewed her?"

Cormac nodded. "I brought a duplicate of the tarot card to show Mrs. Wilde. Turns out she has hundreds of decks. She couldn't produce the card, said it was her winter deck, and she's going to check the family home."

"Winter deck?" D.S. Neely said with a laugh. "What a load of bollocks."

"She also suggested someone might have nicked the card off her, without her knowledge." He waited for more comments but the peanut gallery kept mum. "According to Mrs. Wilde, the meaning of this card is not about the actual Devil, it's about *temptations.*"

"And you fell for that?" McGraw again. He wasn't here to listen. He was here to humiliate.

"Our killer deliberately placed every single item at the murder scene. He or she is telling a story. I'm not drawing any conclusions at this point, Superintendent, I'm simply laying out the facts."

"On with it then, Holmes," McGraw said, enjoying another round of laughter. Cormac flicked to the next slide, gleaming black stones shouting LAST DANCE.

"We had a quick answer on this one. These stones are all common to the Dingle area beaches—sandstones if you hadn't already guessed—but they were coated with a black gloss. Once again we're waiting for a definitive report from the Technical Bureau, but I was given a heads-up that they believe it's automotive paint." The next slide showed an abandoned auto body shop. McGraw sat up straight. Cormac felt a flush of satisfaction go through him. "This abandoned auto body shop is located across from the Wildes' Clinic."

"Hoo-boy," McGraw said. "Now we're sucking diesel."

They probably wanted the Wildes for this. It disgusted Cormac how blatant they all were. His instincts were screaming that they

were being set up. He had a feeling the O'Reillys were working behind the scenes, getting all their little soldiers in line against the
declining veterinarian. Cormac hated piling on, but he also had to
follow the facts wherever they led. "The shop has been closed down
for five years now, and the owner—a Mr. Collins—hasn't returned
our calls to enter the building."

"Have you put in for a warrant?" McGraw asked.

Cormac shook his head. "Not enough evidence for a judge's warrant, and we're still waiting on one to enter the Wildes' Clinic despite having traced the batch number to it."

"Are you joking me?"

"Eamon Wilde is having medical issues and despite a recent
nine-nine-nine call from a previous employee, Sheila Maguire, for
a dust-up that occurred, she's not pressing charges. The DPP
knows this is going to be a high-profile case. I'm assuming that's
the reason for the abundance of caution."

"It's too late," McGraw said. "Whatever evidence they had in that
clinic is long gone. I bet the miniature daughter has been cleaning
up. Or should I say cleaning down?"

Cormac clenched his fists and waited while hearty laughter
bounced about the room. At least Detective Sergeant Neely wasn't
one of them. "To be frank, Superintendent McGraw, I find that
kind of language belittling and unnecessary," Cormac said.

McGraw sat up. "Excuse me?"

"She's a whip-smart doctor and highly admired. I find digs at her
height to be beneath us."

McGraw's head bobbed as if in agreement. He then gave Cormac the once-over. "I can see why you sympathize." More laughter.

"Touché." He could only grin, show he wasn't bothered. Had he
given McGraw leverage by defending Dimpna Wilde? He could not
lose this case. Cormac turned back to his presentation. "The land
the auto body resides on is owned by the O'Reillys. We've directed
several requests to the family, including permission to enter the
shop without the warrant, but so far their solicitors are throwing up
roadblocks to every request." Cormac flicked to the next slide. It
was the best photo he'd found so far of the esteemed colt Last

Dance. He was standing tall in front a large white barn, the sun shining down on him. All muscles and beauty. Even a layman like Cormac could tell there was something special about the horse.

"What is this?" McGraw sounded annoyed.

"Meet Last Dance," Cormac said. "I believe our painted stones refer to this racehorse."

"Based on what?" McGraw again.

"Do you know how automotive paint differs from other types of paint?"

McGraw folded his arms across his chest. "Enlighten me."

"It's lighter," Cormac said. "For speed." He tapped the picture of the racehorse. "Speed."

"Are you joking me?" McGraw said. "Isn't that a bit of a stretch?"

Murmurs went around the room. "We all remember that horse," D.S. Neely said. "Those of us out of nappies, that is. He was going to be the crown jewel of Dingle."

"You really think the killer painted the stones with automotive gloss on purpose? A nod to speed, and thus to this racehorse?" McGraw sounded outraged.

"I do," Cormac said. "I very much do." His mam did as well, but Cormac wasn't going to dare reveal that. The discovery had excited him to no end, and they'd discussed it late into the night. Cormac was developing a fascination for this killer. This was no ordinary man. Or woman.

He heard a soft curse from McGraw. In the super's opinion, Cormac was probably going woo-woo. But the truth was the truth. He flicked to the next slide, newspaper articles covering the death of Last Dance, and then more covering Tommy Healy, the one-armed jockey who was supposed to ride him to glory. "Tommy Healy was an aspiring—or should I say rising—jockey back in the day. He and his twin, Brendan Healy, had been abandoned by their parents. They were taken in and sponsored by the O'Reillys. The brother, Brendan—born with both arms—had no interest in horse racing and left for America before his twin's big race. But once Last Dance was killed, Tommy Healy never rode a horse again. He's remained with the O'Reillys all these years."

"You're telling me he's been their right-hand man?" McGraw

asked. The biggest laugh yet. It was common knowledge that humor helped with the horrific side of murder. But coming from McGraw, it didn't feel like stress-reduction humor. Just a pathetic man trying to get a laugh. But if Cormac came down too hard on it, then he'd lose respect. He couldn't afford to alienate his team. Diversity lectures would have to wait for another time. Cormac paused so they could take in a photo of a much younger Tommy Healy in his jockey attire. "Notice the colors. Navy blue, white, and green." He clicked to a photo of O'Reilly dead on the beach. "Navy blue, white, and green," he said.

"I wouldn't call that a mystery," D.S. Neely said. "Anyone in the O'Reilly racing world would have been in those colors."

"Correct," Cormac said. "Our victim lived and breathed horse racing. Yet another tic mark in the column that says Last Dance refers to that colt." It was the perfect segue to the next slide: COLT BOLTS TO ITS DEATH. The article had a photo of a younger Dimpna Wilde on one side and the beautiful colt on the other. They leaned in to read the lead: *Local veterinarian's daughter releases million-euro horse from paddock. The finish line is deadly and the prize heavenly . . .*

"Jaysus," Neely said. "I remember that one."

"Morbid and poetic," Cormac said. "I'm trying to trace down the journalist. Jack O'Shea."

"You'll be following a ghost then," Neely said. "O'Shea died two years ago."

Cormac cursed himself. He should have spoken with the detective sergeant before presenting. They'd both been stretched thin.

"Are we looking at Dimpna Wilde as a suspect?" D.S. Neely said. "Wasn't she in Dublin at the time of the murder?"

"Better call her Dr. Wilde," McGraw said. "This one is a bit sensitive."

"You know, it probably is best to call her Dr. Wilde," Neely said. "Can't be easy to get that title, and she deserves it. You're so right, *Superintendent* McGraw."

It was sorted. Cormac was going to buy Neely dinner. "It's been confirmed Dr. Dimpna Wilde was in Dublin at the time of the murder," Cormac continued. "But if someone is setting up the Wildes to take the fall, we're looking at the angle that it has something to do with this past incident."

"Twenty-seven years later?" A garda spoke up. "Like Superintendent McGraw said, 'Isn't that a bit of a stretch?'"

"Perhaps," Cormac said. "The entire scene could be a red herring. A killer hoping we'll do exactly what we're doing now. Chasing our tails." He waited, enjoying the feel of having everyone's attention. "Our job here is to get inside this killer's head. I know we don't encounter many murders in Ireland, thanks be to God. The murders we do have are often easily solved. A domestic situation. A drunken fight that gets out of hand. A greed-kill. Drugs. Money. This doesn't fit neatly into any of those boxes. Money, of course, is an angle we're pursuing. Winning purses, side bets, insurance. There's a lot to dig into. What we do know is that this killer is extremely intelligent. I think he or she is playing a game. And before we come to any conclusions about the evidence, we need to look at everything from every angle. It's our only chance of solving this crime."

"I hear you found the little stowaway," McGraw said. "What's the word from her?"

"The mother has requested a solicitor, and given they can't afford one, we're waiting on a government appointee. I've asked if they would voluntarily come in today, but to be honest, I don't expect them to show." Cormac paused. "The girl is traumatized. I believe she saw the killer." He flicked to a slide of her backpack with the message. They all stared at it. *You Tell, You Die.*

"Why didn't you interview her when you found her?" McGraw demanded.

"Believe me, I tried. Paul Byrne was present, and he convinced the mother they needed a solicitor."

"He's only looking out for her well-being," D.S. Neely said. *Interesting.* Was she protecting Byrne?

"You need to find out what she knows," McGraw said. "Hell, this case might be over by now if you'd done that."

"Believe me, questioning her is my top priority," Cormac said.

"She has a reputation of lying," Neely said. "I'm not accusing her of anything, but I don't think we can count on her to solve this case."

McGraw folded his arms across his chest. "Is that all?"

Cormac nodded to Neely to take over. She swapped places with Cormac. "The morning we found the body we also encountered Donnecha Wilde. He was on O'Reilly's boat, *Dreamscape,* cleaning it with bleach."

"Has he been arrested?" McGraw stood. "That sounds like a killer to me."

"He's been a caretaker of the yacht for a few years now," Neely said. "He was told a VIP guest of the O'Reillys would be using the boat that evening. We have him on CCTV entering the Dingle Inn just like he said at around half-six. He leaves again a few hours later, then returns with take-away. We've tracked all that on CCTV as well. He's not seen leaving again until Sunday morning, and is picked up at the harbor, heading for the boat."

"He gave us some valuable clues," Cormac said. "The kid's footprints and a few odd lines on the boat that I believe were from a makeshift ramp the killer used to slide the body up and onto the rowboat. Donnecha Wilde also sketched out how he thought the rowboat was tied, with a double knot—and when the boat was returned, it was secured with a triple. The Technical Bureau has the rowboat, but so far, nothing of evidentiary value has been found."

"Sounds like a whole lot of nothing," McGraw said. "Unless you plan on lining up our suspects and asking them to tie their shoes."

"It's early days yet, Superintendent," Cormac said. What he really wanted to do was punch him in his smug mouth. He knew lives were at stake and everyone wanted the killer caught *yesterday,* but in truth they'd made a ton of progress in a very short amount of time. Cormac didn't need outright praise, but he didn't need the sneers either. "I'm waiting to interview the widow and son. And to be frank, I find it suspicious that they keep throwing up roadblocks."

"Haven't they been alibied?" McGraw said. His tone belied his wish that the widow and son be left alone. *Money.*

"Róisín O'Reilly was confirmed to be at the O'Grady wake well past midnight. Sean said he and the wife and daughter were on a weekend getaway to Doolin."

"Said?" McGraw said. "Have you followed up on it?"

When Cormac didn't speak, Neely jumped in. "We have their car on CCTV several points along the way, and the owner of the inn confirmed they checked in at half-eight on Friday evening."

McGraw looked to Cormac. "I'd say that's an airtight alibi. What bit your tongue?"

"CCTV shows a man in his car," Cormac said. "It's impossible to verify that it's him."

"You think he let someone else drive his fancy car?" Once again Cormac didn't reply. "You think the wife is lying?"

"Wives lie for their husbands all the time."

"And the owner of the inn?"

Cormac tilted his head. "He didn't have CCTV cameras pointed at the customers. We only have an image of the back of his head and his word for it that the man who checked in was Sean O'Reilly."

McGraw crossed his arms. "Have any witnesses come forward to say that they drove Sean O'Reilly's wife and daughter to Doolin in their car?"

"No."

"There you have it," McGraw said. "I call that an airtight alibi. Let's focus our resources elsewhere."

"There's still the matter of the widow," Cormac said.

"Wasn't she in a pub full of people for a wake?"

"She was," Neely said. "Deborah O'Grady." Neely crossed herself.

"Are they all covering for the widow?" McGraw asked.

"The dance was being held just down the street. It was massively crowded. I'd be extremely suspicious of anyone who had eyes on her all night." It would have been possible for her to slip out in the midst of a drunken crowd. Make her way down the street to the husband. Perhaps she saw him dancing with Maeve Wilde, and jealousy bloomed. . . . *No.* This was premeditated. Staged. Not an impulsive kill. That didn't eliminate Róisín O'Reilly as a suspect, but he had to be careful about the narrative. If she slipped out of the wake and lured her husband away from the dance, it had all been carefully planned. He became aware of Neely staring at him. "You have more?"

She nodded. "We've heard from numerous witnesses that the

night of the murder Tommy Healy got into an altercation with someone at the wake. Healy has a reputation as a scrapper. Fights a bit dirty. We've heard he's been known to pull a knife."

"Did he pull a knife that evening?" Cormac asked.

"According to several witnesses he flashed it," Neely said.

At least McGraw was paying attention. "Do we know what the fight was about?" he asked.

"Not yet," Neely said. "We have his interview scheduled this week with both Healy and the publican." She glanced back at McGraw before directing her attention to Cormac. "The O'Reillys have asked that we give them and their employees a bit of room while they organize the funeral. It's going to be a massive public event."

"Stonewalling," someone in the room piped up.

"Perhaps," Cormac said. "But a large public event can be a blessing in disguise for us. Gives us a chance to mingle with a number of our suspects."

"Do we know anything else about this altercation with Mr. Healy?" McGraw asked.

"Rumor is it was with a dock worker," Neely said. "We're still chasing down the details."

"The Devil is in the details," someone quipped. "Or is that temptations?"

Neely sat down and Cormac returned to the front of the room. He'd saved the best few bits for last. He advanced the screen to a photo of Finbar's mobile phone "As most of you know, the fisherman who found the body lied to us. Made a point of saying he didn't own a mobile phone. On Monday, two days after we found the body, Dimpna Wilde was called out to an animal emergency. It happened to be Finbar's neighbor. Apparently they needed use of a sheepdog that had shown up on Finbar's property, and when she went to return the dog, she interrupted Finbar in the middle of burying something. The dog snatched this mobile phone out of the hole he had been digging."

"Good boy," someone quipped. "We should hire him."

"Careful, he might replace you," McGraw said. "Detective Inspector Sheepdog to the rescue."

Cormac laughed along with them to prove he was a good sport, but stopped short of barking. "We've got hackers trying to get into the phone now."

"Have you questioned him?" McGraw asked.

"He doesn't even know we have it," Cormac said. "I'm waiting to see what we find on the phone before we bring him into the station."

"You could have saved us a lot of time and just listed all the things we're waiting on," McGraw said. "I barely have anything to report back. Headquarters isn't going to be pleased."

"There is this," Cormac said. He advanced the slides to a close-up of the necktie. He then clicked through the next five slides, all photographs of Johnny O'Reilly wearing a bowtie. "It's been widely reported that O'Reilly loathed ties. You've just seen years' worth of photos showing him in bowties. I believe the necktie was placed on O'Reilly *after* he died. It suggests a killer who wanted to humiliate our victim. Someone who knew Johnny O'Reilly's past intimately. The state pathologist is releasing the personal effects to the station within a few days. Tracing this tie is going to be a top priority." He paused. "Any questions?"

"What about this shite about the vet having Swiss cheese for brains?" McGraw asked.

McGraw was needling Cormac. He'd dared to correct his bullying language earlier, and the message was clear. *Do it again. See what happens.* "He was taken to hospital. I believe they're releasing him today, but we'll have to see what the doctor has to say about an interview."

McGraw wasn't finished. "What about this affair the wife was supposed to be having with our man?"

"She denies it."

"Have any witnesses come forward about it?"

"Not so far. To sum up, we're still conducting interviews, combing through CCTV footage, and waiting for evidentiary reports."

McGraw stood. "You've got six weeks, Inspector. And don't make me report back that you aren't thoroughly investigating the Wildes." He strode for the exit.

"I am," Cormac said. "I've even got a pair of eyes on the inside."

McGraw stopped. Turned. "What do you mean?"

"Someone who's going to be hanging around the clinic."

"I thought that clinic was closed."

"It won't be for long. Dr. Dimpna Wilde will be reopening it."

"Did she tell you that?" McGraw asked.

"No, sir."

"Then how the hell do you know?"

Cormac smiled. This was a question he could definitively answer. "Because I've met her," he said. "Have you?"

CHAPTER 20

SHEILA MAGUIRE AND A CLUMP OF TOURISTS STOOD IN FRONT OF THE ancient stone chapel, the Gallarus Oratory. Yesterday's sun had given away to a heavy layer of gray clouds, casting a moody glow around them, but it suited her just fine. Dingle's weather seemed to follow the patterns of the ocean, constantly shifting, keeping them on their toes. The oratory, otherwise known as "The Church of the Place of the Foreigners," was an ancient piece of architecture constructed of perfectly cut red sandstone most likely sourced from the nearby cliffs. It was the only known existing structure of its kind, and Sheila loved her volunteer work as a tour guide. Although she was only able to do it once a week, it was a welcome distraction to her hectic life as a vet tech. O'Connell's clinic was jammed ever since Dr. Wilde stopped practicing. She'd barely had any time for the tours, and she'd missed them. The Dingle Peninsula had been gifted with a plethora of ancient monuments, and the oratory was one of her favorites. She gave her talk with ease, her only difficulty speaking over the wind that had kicked up. "Notice the shape of the structure," she continued. "Doesn't it resemble an upturned boat?" She waited for a reaction, head nods, and murmurs as they took in the sloping walls, the corbel vaulting, and an interior of approximately 4.8 by 3 meters, which she sometimes remembered to translate to feet for American tourists. Given several were in front of her now, she added the translation—the interior was approximately 16 by 10.

It was dim inside with only one round window opposite the doorway. Although numerous historians had theorized over its exact origins, antiquarian Charles Smith pointed out that there was no historical information available prior to 1756. Archaeologist Peter Harbison posited the oratory was built around the twelfth century, pointing out the fact that the east window's rounded top was composed of a pair of carved stones as opposed to a true arch. Whether it was a rocky headland, a shelter for foreigners, a church, or a funeral chapel of a prominent family from long ago, it was, indisputably, *cool*. And just one of the many ancient monuments adorning the Dingle Peninsula. Sheila had never wanted to live anywhere else. She always ended her tour here; best to leave them with a bang. "That concludes our tour for the day. Do we have any burning questions?" Given her speeches were jammed full of facts, satisfying the most inquisitive ones in the crowds, she waited for the usual questions: What restaurants and pubs did she recommend? Did Murphy's really have the best ice cream, and what did she think happened to Fungie the Dolphin? This time, the questions were different. She should have been prepared.

"How close are we to the dead body?" a teenage boy in the front said, using dirty fingers to brush back his thick fringe.

They were 9.4 kilometers from Clogher Stand, but she wasn't going to play this game. "There's no body anymore, nothing for you to worry about. Let the police take care of that."

"I heard a crazy vet killed him," another head in the crowd called out. For a second, Sheila wondered if they knew. Not just knew that she once worked for the "crazy vet," but knew everything about her, knew that she had been hefting around a rotting sack of guilt, and that she was nearly ready to crack. She'd thought doing this tour would take her mind off the horror that was now her life. How idiotic. Why hadn't she anticipated this? Why hadn't she called in sick?

"Are there any questions about any of the monuments we've seen today?"

"The stones found by the body . . . were they red sandstone too?"

"And the Devil! Is Dr. Wilde the Devil? Did he abuse horses?"

The kids became more animated than she'd ever seen them. She was going to have to shut this down quickly.

"Yeah, he's probably killed a bunch of other animals, too. For practice, like," another kid in the crowd said. Why weren't the adults stepping in? Didn't they see how flustered she was?

"Hey," she yelled, bringing the rumblings to a screeching halt. "I worked for Dr. Eamon Wilde for the past twenty years, and he's not crazy, and he's certainly not the Devil. He saved and treated thousands of sick animals over his lifetime. And he happens to be suffering from a very serious disease."

"Is that what made him crazy?"

"No one has been charged with a crime. I'm not here to talk about that, and I'm afraid that's all the time we have for today." Finally, parents stepped in, and although their mouths continued to move, Sheila headed out. She had only taken a few steps away from the oratory when the bodies in front of her parted and she spotted Donnecha Wilde lurking in the background.

She knew he'd be coming, but she'd been avoiding him. It had been stupid, letting him of all people drag her into this mess. And it was over—it was totally and completely over—and all she wanted to do was keep her head down. She had been praying every day, trying to atone. Finbar Malone had turned out a bit smarter than she'd counted on, and the murder had brought with it a glaring spotlight—one she could not afford to have shining on her. She'd been avoiding Dimpna as well. Despite only a brief run-in with her at the clinic, just knowing she was back had Sheila on edge. Part of her wanted to embrace her dear friend, reminisce with drinks over good times, return to the semblance of the girls they were, "blood sisters" by choice. But Dimpna was still holding on to grudges; she'd seen it in her eyes. And the tension when the O'Reillys pulled up. Off. The. Charts. Sheila nearly felt sorry for her old friend. But if she was being honest—she wanted her to go away. Dimpna brought out all her insecurities—especially about Paul. Sheila and Paul should have been married with kids by now. When she thought of all the years she'd wasted just waiting for him to get over Dimpna Wilde. It made her ill. And of course, he never had gotten over her. Sheila had wasted most of her life on that man.

And even though she respected Eamon Wilde, and she certainly felt sorry for him, if the O'Reillys were focused on him, maybe they would never look at her. And disease or no disease, she couldn't

forget that the man she'd been loyal to for over a decade had accused her of stealing the vial of Release. When it came to a murder
charge, it was every man for himself. Had Finbar gotten rid of his
mobile phone as instructed? Was he the one who sent her the
note? It was still in her pocket. She kept it on her as if keeping her
enemy close would somehow keep her safe. *I know what you did.*

Was it Maeve Wilde? What if she could pick up on things? What
if she knew way too much? Would she write an anonymous note?

Donnecha stayed in the background until the tour was finished
and the children and their minders all piled into buses and cars
and headed off. He looked wired and way too thin. The guards had
taken him in for cleaning the boat with bleach. He better have kept
his gob shut.

"I have another tour in an hour," Sheila said. "And I need to eat."

"Then we'll eat," Donnecha said. "But I can't keep avoiding my
sister forever."

"Then don't. Your sister is not my problem." That was a lie.
Dimpna Wilde had always been one of Sheila Maguire's problems,
hadn't she?

Donnecha shifted his weight multiple times, eyes darting around
them. "We have to get our stories straight," he said, his voice coming out like a needy whine.

Sheila's phone rang, startling them. It was O'Connell. He said
he'd only call if it was an emergency. At least the work kept her
mind occupied, kept her from becoming a basket case like Donnecha, kept her from thinking about what they did. "Sorry," she
said. "Unless you want to pay my bills, our chat is going to have to
wait."

"What do I tell Dimpna?"

He sounded desperate. She couldn't handle another needy creature. He's the one who dragged her into this, not the other way
around. "I don't care," she said. "Tell her anything. Anything but
the truth."

CHAPTER 21

"C'MERE TO ME. IT'S DOWN HERE. YOU'RE NOT GOING TO BELIEVE this." Sean O'Reilly was right. Whatever it was, Dimpna was not going to believe it. Not this time. He'd already fooled her a dozen times. C'mere to me, c'mere to me, c'mere to me. It was always something gross or scary. Mostly dead animals. And not just peacefully dead, but mutilated-dead. Blood and guts, and intestines-spilling-out-dead. Maggots, and flies, and buzzards circling-overhead-dead. As if he spent his days picking up roadkill to hide in different spots just to torment Dimnpa. What he didn't realize was that it was Donnecha who was squeamish about death, not her. She had not only seen the insides of animals, she'd carefully drawn and colored them from all the books in her da's study. She'd seen dead animals in the clinic. Her father had even let her watch a few surgeries. And it fascinated her. She wasn't squeamish. It made her sad, but she wasn't afraid of death.

And once they were dead, there was nothing she could do. Her father's advice had stuck with her. *Focus your energy on the ones you can help, Dew.* And so it came to be that after many failed attempts trying to freak her out with the dead, Sean O'Reilly turned to the living. He'd been planting a seed about the new lads at the estate, twins, the Healy brothers. It was easy to tell them apart because one was missing an arm. He was actually the nice one. But the one with both arms hated animals. He said there was a litter of kittens at his home and Brendan was threatening to toss them into a sack and drown them in the ocean. The mere mention of it made her imagine it over and over until she was physically ill. Dimpna had begged Sean to tell the guards.

When he wouldn't, she decided she had to sneak over to the estate and see for herself when her father was busy with cattle, checking them for TB. It was a long procedure of pricking them, waiting for results, and checking them again. It was going to take up his entire week. It was now or never—she had to find out if Sean was telling the truth, she had to make sure the kittens were safe. She took a bus, and then walked to the O'Reilly estate. She snuck up the long drive and into the barns. They had three big racing barns just for horses and a fourth for sheep, and a few cows. She checked every nook and cranny of those barns, slipping in and out, and hiding behind hay bales, stalls, and equipment whenever farmhands or jockeys were present. She was an excellent hider. She didn't hear any kittens. She didn't even see a mama cat. She thought that would be the last of it, that Sean would be forced to admit he was a big fat liar. She'd followed him again today, determined to make him do just that. Make him admit there were no kittens, no sack, and no fully-armed lad bent on murdering them. Now here he was, standing in front of her, not at all surprised to see her. Maybe she wasn't as good at following as she was at hiding.

Sean's belly stuck out of a stained shirt, his cheeks were ruddy, and his sandy hair was blowing in the wind. He was supposed to be the wealthiest lad in town, but he never looked it. He was two years older than Dimpna but twice as tall. She'd been following him for an hour, pleased that she was so clever and stealthy, tracking her prey like the mountain lion—another creature whose organs she'd traced and colored using her father's big anatomy book. It was just now dawning on her that Sean had known she'd been following him the entire time. That he had led her here.

"What is it?" Dimpna peered down at him from the top of the hill. A gray blanket waved from the sky, and the wind whipped her hair around her face. Her wellies were a size too big. She'd been squishing and sliding in them for so long, her calves were starting to ache.

"I found the kittens," Sean said. "I can hear them crying." He pointed somewhere in the distance.

"Liar, liar, pants on fire." They weren't anywhere near the ocean.

"I thought you were an animal lover."

"I am."

"Then you have to see this."

She knew he was lying, but she couldn't just walk away. It would haunt her. Not being able to save animals was one thing; turning away from them was another. Dimpna scooted down the hill on her backside, even though she was wearing a dress. She was eight years of age and her mother said if she got that dress dirty, she would have to wear it for ten days straight. That didn't make any sense. It seemed more of a punishment for her mammy than it was for her.

At the bottom of the hill she nearly collided with Sean. "Where?" He stuck out his arm out again, and from here she could see an old wooden outbuilding in the distance. It was weathered and leaning to one side. Something about it made her think of an old man about to slip and fall. It was bordered by thick hedges and brambles. She didn't know whose property they were on, or what the building had been used for. Perhaps someone lived there. Someone crazy and mean. "I'm not going in there."

"It's unlocked." He turned and began walking toward it. After a moment, she followed, drawing up as close as she dared. He stopped and pointed at the door. A rusty chain hung down from the lock and the door was ajar. Dimpna strained to listen for the cries of wee kittens. But all she could hear was the wind and birds. Sean put his finger over his lips. "I followed Brendan here. I followed him just like you followed me. I saw him bring a squirming sack into the shed."

He was lying. He was a liar. She was not going to fall for it. "Why didn't you tell your father? Or the guards?"

"Because. Then it will be too late to save the kittens."

"You're lying. You're a liar."

"Think what you want. Don't you want to see if they're still alive?"

No. A sack full of dead kittens would be worse than roadkill. She'd heard of such horrible things, such horrible people. Her father had explained that humans were animals too. And too many of them were rabid. Not the kind of rabies you can catch. The kind that burrows into the heart and rots the mind. Bad men. "Why aren't you helping them?"

"See for yourself," Sean urged. "I'll keep watch." He trudged toward the shed, motioning with his hand.

"I can't. I'm expected home."

"Then go home, you wuss," he said. "I just thought you'd want to save them."

"I don't hear anything."

"They're probably too weak to call for help." He was standing closer to the shed now. She nudged forward.

"I'll keep watch and you go in," she said. "Bring them to me."

"I scare kittens," Sean said. "They won't be afraid of you." She eyed the door. "I'll keep watch. Cross my heart and hope to die." He took his index finger and made a mark around his heart. The skies were gray and spitting rain. She heard a faint sound, a low whimper. She whirled around.

"You're doing that!"

He shook his head. "Did you hear them? I knew it. You have to save them."

She craned her neck out and listened again. Another low-pitched whine reached her ears. It was Sean making that noise, wasn't it? But what if it wasn't? "Keep quiet," she said.

"Hurry." She was frozen, not knowing whether or not he was messing with her. He was always messing with her. That's why she followed him. It was time somebody messed with him. "There's a storm coming. There's a leak in the roof. I suppose they'll drown."

"No!"

"They're too little to save themselves. If you're too much of a wuss, then just let them die." That did it. She ran to the shed, flung open the door, and stepped inside. It smelled moldy and it was pitch-black. The door slammed shut behind her.

"Sean!" She whirled around, pawing at the door, splinters biting into the soft flesh underneath her fingernails. "Sean?" The only sound from the other side of the door was the rain and the wind and the sound of a chain rattling. A moment later another sound was added to the mix, that of Sean O'Reilly laughing his bleeding head off. She tugged on the door again, but it wouldn't budge. He'd locked it. Her heart thudded in her chest. There were no crying kittens, just the flutter of a bird trapped in the rafters. "I can't see, I can't see!" She felt for the door handle and when she finally grasped it, she pulled and pulled and pulled, and then pushed, and pushed, and pushed. Nothing. She was trapped. She slammed her palms on the wooden door. "Sean. Please. Let me out. Sean. Please." The rain was coming harder now. Her eyes were slowly adjusting to the dark.

She heard a sound, like a lad clearing his throat. Someone else was in here. She whirled around as a dark lump in the corner slowly came into focus. Shoulders. Legs. A head. He sat on top of a pile of feed sacks. Feet swinging. "Did I scare you?" he said. "Did you think you were all alone?"

"Who are you?" Her voice sounded scared and she hated herself for it.

"I'm Paul," he said. "Paul Byrne."

"I'm Dimpna."

"You're the vet's daughter."

"How did you know that?"

"We had a dog. Your father put him to sleep." He said it matter of fact, but she knew he must be really sad.

"I'm sorry."

"He was a good dog. He had cancer."

Dimpna didn't want to talk about dogs with cancer. "Are there any kittens in here?"

"Is that what he told you?"

"Yes."

"No kittens. Just us chickens." He laughed, but it wasn't a mean laugh like Sean's.

Dimpna bit her lip so she wouldn't cry. She wanted to go home. Was he ever coming back? "Did Sean lock you in here too?"

"Yeah," Paul said.

"What did he tell you you'd find?"

"Whiskey and a cigarette."

Dimpna didn't know lads liked whiskey and cigarettes. But she was glad she wasn't the only one fooled. "Did you find them?"

"Just some butts and an empty bottle."

"He's mean."

"He's nothing but a big bully."

"I hate him," Dimpna said.

"I hate him more," Paul said. "And someday he's going to get what's coming to him."

CHAPTER 22

DIMPNA PASSED ONE LARGE TRAWLER AFTER THE OTHER UNTIL SHE came to a red sailboat wedged in between two massive ones. A recent client who walked her dog along the harbor had casually mentioned to Dimpna that Donnecha was now renting out a small red sailboat. Apparently, even being under suspicion for murder hadn't turned her little brother against boats. The minute she approached, she knew Donnecha was on board. Empty bottles of Bulmers decorated a small table on the deck along with a pack of Benson & Hedges. They might as well have been Donnecha's fingerprints. She called his number, and then listened as it rang inside the nearby cabin. Donnecha did not answer. Dimpna stepped onto the boat and sat, wondering how long it would take before her brother emerged. All day? She glanced at the pack of cigarettes. Empty. He could have more inside, but knowing her brother, he'd be popping out to the shops. No matter what else was going on, one thing was for sure. Donnecha needed to get his life together. Living like a slob. Not to mention they were in the middle of a full-blown family crisis and it had been radio silence from the youngest Wilde. Dimpna called her brother again, just to annoy him. This time, as the phone rang, she heard a distinct "Fuck!" as he hung up on her. Then she heard footsteps, and soon his voice.

"She won't stop ringing . . . I won't. I said I won't. But if I don't call her back . . ." The voice drew closer and soon the hull door opened and the top of Donnecha's head emerged. "I told you we needed to get our stories straight or she's going to have her nose up my arse—"

His head jerked up and he spotted her. "Fuck."

Dimpna smiled. "Who are you talking to?"

"What?" Donnecha tried to play dumb. She pointed to his phone.

"Nobody." He hung up and shoved his phone in his pocket.

"Lovely to see you too, little brother. It's been so nice how everyone has welcomed me back."

Donnecha reached for his pack of cigarettes then groaned when he found it empty. "I have to pop out to the shops." He headed for the dock, but she blocked his exit.

"Not a chance."

"I'm just getting a pack of cigs and I'll be right back."

"No."

"No?" He laughed. "Am I being held prisoner?"

"I'm going to see Da at hospital. And you're coming with me." Her father still hadn't been released and her mother had gone quiet. What was with this family?

"I need a pack of smokes."

"I'll go with you. Then we'll go to hospital. And after that we'll talk. And you'll explain yourself."

"Explain myself?"

"Starting with who you were just on the phone with and why you need to get your stories straight."

"You're imagining things." He did his best to look sincere, but she knew when he was lying.

"Just what the hell are you involved in?"

"Nothing." He picked up the empty bottle of Bulmers, twirled it, and set it back down with a plunk.

"I heard you were at the Dingle Inn the night of the murder with some lad. Who was it?"

"What did you hear?"

He'd lost weight. Was he using again? "For one thing, you were cleaning Johnny O'Reilly's yacht with bleach the morning they found his body."

"You know everything, do you?" He pushed past her and jumped onto the dock. "Right. I'm going to buy a new pack of fags."

"I'm coming with you."

"What are you? My child minder?"

"That fits, given you're acting like a child."

He strode away from the harbor toward the shops in town. Dimpna scrambled after him, hating the optics of the older sister hounding the younger brother. "Whatever illegal or disgusting things you're up to that you don't want me to know about, I think you should know that it really hurts." She yelled it. Not her finest moment, given there were fishermen and tourists nearby, but Donnecha had given her no choice.

He came to an abrupt stop, his face flushed. "Keep your voice down."

"Don't run away from me."

"Jesus." He pinched the bridge of his nose, then crossed his arms over his chest. Had he always been this scrawny? Was his appearance alone a cry for help. "What? What have I done to hurt you?"

She opened her arms. "I'm in town and you don't come to see me? Da is suffering from dementia and you don't even pick up the phone? Our parents are suspects in a murder inquiry and you can't be bothered?"

He clamped his lips shut. "You have no idea."

"Then tell me."

He was on the move again and this time he picked up the pace. "You have absolutely no clue as usual."

"As usual?" Now her yelling was born of rage. "What's that supposed to mean?"

"Never mind."

His vehemence came as a shock. Whatever trouble he was in, it was worse than she thought. "I need you," she said. "I need my brother."

He stopped again. "Since when?" He locked eyes with her.

"Don't do this," she said. "Don't make me feel guilty."

"You've been living your life in ignorant bliss up until the past year. And I'm sorry about that business with Niall. I really am. But most of your life you couldn't be bothered to come home. And now you want me to roll out the red carpet?"

He wasn't usually this mean. It was his defense mechanism. He was afraid of something. Someone? "That's your hangover talking, is it?"

He chortled. "Right, so. I'm still the same old screw-up you've always hated to love."

Dimpna closed the gap between them so she could lower her voice.

"Hang your self-pity on the nearest hook, because Mam and Da need us."

"I'm well aware." A couple strolled past pushing a pram. Tourists, from the grins on their faces as they took in the harbor.

"Do you know anything about Johnny O'Reilly's murder?" Dimpna's voice was a whisper. She had to ask.

He brushed his fringe back with a trembling hand. "Are you joking me?" He grabbed her arms. "I had nothing to do with that. *Nothing.*"

"Then why are you in this state?"

"I told you. The guards are crawling up me arse." He let go of her and crossed Strand Street making a beeline for the closest shop, a small market that dealt in a little bit of everything. He disappeared inside and Dimpna waited on the footpath, trying to collect her thoughts. It took her five minutes too long to realize that Donnecha was taking a long time. She went into the shop. The clerk, a twenty-something, leaned against the counter and jerked his thumb toward the back door. "That way."

Typical. That's why he'd chosen this shop, just so he could sneak out the back. *Humiliating.* "Just here for some tea," Dimpna said.

"Uh-huh."

She did her best imitation of a stroll and picked up a box of Barry's. He smirked as he took her money. "He's up to no good, if you ask me."

She hadn't, of course. "What makes you say that?"

"I hear things."

"What things?"

"Fella with a similar shop in Tralee says he buys a dozen mobile phones a month. Throwaways."

"A dozen?"

"That's what I heard."

A dozen throwaway phones a month? Even if it was a slight exaggeration, how could he be so stupid? She quickly paid for her tea and then stood on the footpath. Was he a drug dealer now? The southwest coastline had historically been a convenient drop-off point for hard drugs, namely heroin and cocaine out of Cork. Did drugs have anything to do with O'Reilly's murder? Was the O'Reilly yacht involved? Or maybe Dimpna's imagination was getting the best of her. What if Donnecha witnessed something? Maybe the killer had threatened him the same way Saoirse had been threatened. A crawling sensation up her spine prompted her to look around. She had the feeling she was being watched. Strand Street was alive with shoppers and tourists. She could almost picture Donnecha studying her from afar. He'd always been an excellent watcher. In school he knew all the gossip about everyone's mam and da just from his creeping. It wasn't something she was proud to admit, but it was the truth. Her brother liked to sneak and he liked to watch. He'd even roped her into it once.

I could teach you. You're so small, no one would ever know you're there.

And so they went to the O'Sheas'. Jack O'Shea had been a reporter, and he wore a cracking leather jacket around town that he showed off from atop his cracking motorcycle. They'd snuck into his back garden and hid behind a hedge just underneath their kitchen window. They watched him and his wife move in and out of the frame, making dinner. Once, Jack came up behind her, put his arms around her, and kissed her neck. Dimpna had never seen her parents show any kind of affection. She wondered what it would be like if Jack was her da, and his pretty wife her mam. They talked to each other as they sat at the table with their dinner, talking and laughing until their candle had burned down.

"I wish we could hear them," Donnecha said.

"Me too." They stayed until it got dark. Jack O'Shea came out to let his dog out and lit a cigarette. They were cramped up by the time he went back inside and the lights went off. When they scrambled out of their hiding nook and onto the footpath, Dimpna's dress was covered in dirt and hedge trimmings. Every time after that, whenever Dimpna saw Jack or his wife in town, she glowed with the secret. But she never did it again. She was terrified of getting caught. Not Donnecha. He thrived on the danger. And maybe he still did. But maybe this time he'd been caught. She didn't think there was anything sexual about his spying, although the feeling of being creeped on was just as violating. But why did he need throwaway mobile phones? A dark thought descended. The vial of Release. The one her father had accused Sheila of stealing. What if it had been Donnecha? Was he stealing vet meds on the side? One vial was hardly a windfall.

Donnecha had never wanted anything to do with the family business. He'd been the first to go on a middle-of-the-night call with their da. He'd come home absolutely beside himself. It had been a calving and the baby was born dead. That wasn't the part that gutted Donnecha. It was the wails of the mother. Donnecha had crawled into bed with her, his toes ice cold, snot hanging from his nose, and tears running down his cheeks. "She was crying, Dimp. She was *crying*."

"You need to focus your energy on the ones you can help," she said. But it only made him cry harder. He told Dimpna about her sad brown eyes and her wails, and he never went on another animal call again. After that he started hanging around the fishermen in the harbor. Carrying their heavy buckets, humming their shanty songs, and stinking of fish. Her mam complained about it every time she did the wash, hanging his trousers outside to dry, grumbling that she could still smell the slime. That was the start of Donnecha drifting away from them, and now it was all too clear. One of them should have reeled him back in.

CHAPTER 23

*E*AMON WILDE WAS PROPPED UP IN A HOSPITAL BED FULLY DRESSED and reading a newspaper. His luggage bag sat by the bed. "There you are," he said when Dimpna walked in. "Off to bed, Dew." He pointed to the door. Her mother rose from a chair next to her husband's bedside.

"My Dimpna," she said. "C'mere to me." She held out her arms. Dimpna rushed and embraced her, her mother's silver bracelets jingling against her back. She hadn't realized how much she'd missed her until she smelled her jasmine-scented perfume and felt her touch. Maeve Wilde still made an effort to look glamorous and it suited her.

Dimpna glanced at her father. It felt wrong to be a witness to his decline. "How is he?"

"He was given a little something to calm down," a nurse answered, stepping into the room. "He should be asleep."

"Try a horse tranquilizer," Maeve said.

Dimpna flinched. Her mother was going to have to stop being so flippant while this murder inquiry was underway. "When is he getting discharged?"

"Today," Maeve said. "After we talk to the doctor." She sighed. "That inspector has been pestering us for an interview. We need guidance."

"You also need a solicitor."

Maeve waved her hand as if brushing the thought out of the air. "We do not. We're innocent."

"Innocent people need solicitors too." Especially when they were up against the O'Reillys. "You're taking him home? And staying with him?"

"Of course. If you want to sleep in the caravan that's fine, but absolutely no animals."

"I'll stick with the upstairs flat," Dimpna said. "Where I go, my pack goes."

Maeve pursed her lips but didn't reply.

"Where's that handsome grandson of mine?" Eamon asked, looking around the room as if Ben might be hiding, ready to jump out for the big surprise.

"In Spain," Dimpna said, surprised at where his mind had gone. "With his new girlfriend."

Her father wrinkled his nose. "He has a new girlfriend? He never told me that."

"It's new. I only just found out meself."

"Ben has a half sister," her father said as if this were a delightful bit of news, as if Aisling O'Reilly had been born today and not eight years ago. "Did you know that?"

"Eamon!" Maeve's face went scarlet.

Dimpna thought of the necklace. "Has Aisling O'Reilly ever been to the clinic, Da?"

He wrinkled his nose. "What clinic?" It was then that she realized he was holding the newspaper upside down. She walked over and tried to turn it upright, but he held on to it.

Dimpna turned to her mother. "Can we talk?" Her father had suddenly fallen asleep, mouth open, snoring.

The nurse caught her eye. "Now that's exactly what he should be doing."

Dimpna pulled a chair up next to the bed across from her mother. They simply looked at each other until the nurse left the room. Dimpna's heartbeat had already ticked up a notch and she was in the midst of telling herself not to lose her temper with her mother, not here, not at the hospital. Her mother had her own ways about her and there was no changing her. A few days after Niall hung himself, Dimpna received one of her mother's postcards from Dallas, Texas: *Big problems seem small under Texas skies.*

She sent another one to Ben from Miami Beach, Florida: *Sunny days ahead. Love, Maeve.* Not Granny. Or Grandmother. *Maeve.*

"I saw Donnecha. He ran away from me," Dimpna said. It was beyond the pale.

"You have pet hair on your dress," her mother replied, handing her a tissue, as if that would do the trick.

Dimpna crumpled the tissue in her hand and looked down at her flowery green dress. "I brought a nice sheepdog back from Finbar Malone's. I've named him E.T."

"Edie? That's a strange name."

"E.T."

"I don't understand what you're saying."

"E.T. phone home?" Her mother scrunched her face. "Never mind."

"What on earth were you doing at Finbar Malone's house? Don't tell me you're sneaking around again."

Sneaking around again. As if she was a child. "No, Mammy. I was helping out a stubborn donkey." Dimpna filled her in on the call. She left out the bit about her father palming the ruby ring into her hand, and Finbar burying a mobile phone. She didn't want her parents any more involved than they already were.

Her mother's mouth twitched. "I knew Finbar's story was a fishy one," she said, laughing at her own pun. "He just happens to stop off for a smoke? Drives all that way to Clogher Strand to smoke after days gone fishing?"

Dimpna shrugged. "Do you really think a fisherman murdered Johnny O'Reilly?"

"Catch of the day," her mother mused.

"I wish you wouldn't be so flippant," Dimpna said. "What if someone hears you and takes it the wrong way?"

"What's the wrong way?"

"You're a suspect in this murder inquiry. You get that, don't you? Tell me you get that."

"If you want to speak with your brother, why don't you give him a bell?" Her mother was an expert at changing the subject whenever it didn't suit her.

"Have you even talked to Donnecha since the murder?"

Maeve chewed on her lip. "I can't recall. It's been a very busy time." Maeve examined her fingernails. They were too long for Dimpna's liking, Like sharp little knives.

"When did you get your nails done?" Dimpna leaned forward. If the answer was before the dance, then her mother couldn't be the killer. There had to have been some kind of struggle. Handling a body, placing stones on the beach. Her mother's nails would have been a wreck.

Her mother curled her nails in, like a turtle slipping into its shell. "What does that matter?"

"Was it before or after the dance?"

"Before."

"Do you have the receipt?"

Maeve frowned. "I did them myself."

Dimpna groaned. "Don't tell the detective that."

"What on earth are you on about?"

"If your nails had been that nice the evening Mr. O'Reilly was murdered, then it couldn't have been you."

Her mother examined her nails again. "That's right!"

"But you need someone else to verify that." She waited for a response. Zilch. "Did anyone at the dance compliment your nails?"

"Johnny did," Maeve said. She smiled and then abruptly stopped. "Oh."

"No one else?"

"Why? The word of a dead man isn't good enough?"

Dimpna shook her head. "Joking around when you're not a suspect is a matter of poor taste. But joking around when you are? That's a horse of a different color."

"Horse!" her father exclaimed. "He's got a scrotum the size of a football." Eyes closed, her father held both hands up as if cupping a football, or a very large horse scrotum.

Dimpna clamped her lips shut, trying not to laugh. She turned to her mother who had her head thrown back and was positively howling with laughter. When she stopped, she wiped tears out of her eyes. Her mirth was cut short by the presence of a nurse who pushed an old man in a wheelchair into the room, situating him near the empty bed. Her father's flatmate.

"Inspector O'Brien said nothing about me being a suspect," her mother said, oblivious to the fact that other people were now in the room.

A prickling sensation came over Dimpna. "You spoke with him?"

She nodded. "He came into my caravan the other day and we had a nice little chat."

"What did you tell him? I need to know every detail."

"You do not. You're not a detective."

"You shouldn't have talked to him without a solicitor."

"He said it was a normal house-to-house inquiry, and if I didn't answer his questions I would have to come into the station." Dimpna nodded, swiveling her head around. The old man was in his bed and the nurse had left the room. She turned back.

"Please, Mam. I need to know what you told him. In fact, I want to know everything about that night starting from the time Johnny O'Reilly picked you up for the dance."

"Johnny didn't pick me up that night," Maeve said. "He said he had personal business and would see me at the dance."

Interesting. "Did you tell the inspector that?"

"He had so many questions you can't expect me to remember all of them."

Dimpna took a moment to center herself. "Alright, Mam. Just tell me what you remember of the inspector's visit." Silence filled the space between them. "*Please, Mam.* I'm on your side."

Maeve sighed. "He brought the tarot card with him, the one found in Johnny's pocket, but you'll be relieved to know it wasn't my card." She frowned. "He still wants me to check my deck, so I suppose he didn't believe me."

"How do you know it wasn't your card?"

"It was brand-new. I've had that deck for ages. It's worn."

"Maybe he brought a duplicate."

Maeve shook her head. "It was in an evidence bag."

"I suppose that's a relief."

"You see. I'm in the clear."

"I'd like a solicitor to weigh in on that. What else did he want?"

Her mother leaned forward. "There was one piece of information he chomped on like a dog with a bone."

"What was that?"

"He came alive when I told him that Johnny O'Reilly didn't wear neckties. I think they found him in a necktie."

"He hated ties," Dimpna said. Dimpna hated them as well. Especially after Sean O'Reilly pretended to strangle Tommy Healy with one right in front of her.

"It seems I've given the detective a very valuable clue," Maeve said. "He should have paid me a consulting fee."

Dimpna groaned. "Tell me you didn't suggest that he pay for a reading?"

"Well, why not? I'm good, and he wanted to take up my time. He should have done so."

"I ran into Sheila Maguire," Dimpna said. "I think she's convinced Da did it." Dimpna glanced at her father, still snoring away. She'd never heard him snore. She'd rarely seen him asleep.

"Thinks your father did what?" Maeve sounded as if she didn't have a clue.

"Murdered Johnny O'Reilly," Dimpna said.

"That's ridiculous," her mother said.

"We can't ignore the bottle of Release and the syringe." Sheila was the one who notified the guards. Why didn't *he* report it missing? Who could have stolen it?"

Her mother glanced at her husband. "Your father thinks it was Sheila Maguire." Sometimes it was as if her mother could read her mind. Perhaps she did have a gift.

"Why would she do that?" If Sheila lifted it and then reported it missing—just what kind of sick game was she playing?

Her mother reached for the newspaper still on her father's lap. She folded it and put it away but not before Dimpna saw the headline: DEAD IN DINGLE. . . . "I never did trust that woman. After what she did to you?"

"That was a long time ago." Dimpna still winced whenever she remembered the betrayal. Dimpna had been days away from telling Paul she was ready to make love. She told Sheila instead. Then Sheila beat her to it, giving Paul the one thing Dimpna hadn't been ready to part with yet. And then it was taken from her anyway. Along with everything else.

"Sheila had access to the same medications your father did. What if she's the killer?" Maeve looked at Dimpna as if interested to see if her theory would fly.

"Why would Sheila murder Johnny O'Reilly?" But even as Dimpna said it out loud, she remembered how Niamh said that Sheila had been acting like she was in love, coming in late, leaving early. Dressing up for someone. Was it possible she was involved somehow? Who was the mystery man? What if it had been Johnny himself? A bit old for her, but Dimpna wouldn't put it past Sheila. Maybe Róisín O'Reilly had found out. . . .

Outside, rain began to fall, tap-dancing on hospital windows at a steady rhythm. "Was Sheila at the dance that evening?" Dimpna asked.

Her mother shrugged. "She could have been. I didn't see her, but the place was chockablock."

"Do you want to know what I think?" Dimpna rose, drawn to the windows by the sound.

"I have a feeling you're going to tell me either way, darling, and you're too old to ask for permission."

"Whoever killed Mr. O'Reilly wants you and Da to go down for it."

"Who on earth would hate us that much?"

"Róisín O'Reilly?"

Her mother crossed her arms and stared at the floor as her foot began to swing. "That thought has crossed my mind."

"If everyone else thought you and Johnny were sleeping together, surely Róisín had heard the rumors as well."

"We were just dancing! How many times must I repeat myself?"

"I believe you. That's not what I'm saying. Even if you didn't sleep with Mr. O'Reilly—"

"I didn't."

"But isn't is possible that Mrs. O'Reilly thinks you did?"

Her mother concentrated as if it were a puzzle she'd been given three seconds to solve. "I'm surprised she didn't kill one of us then."

"Maybe there's a reason she wanted him dead. And you two are the perfect scapegoats."

"Do you really think it could be Róisín?" Her mother nearly sounded excited.

"Has Róisín been into the clinic lately?" Dimpna asked. "Could she have stolen the bottle of Release?"

"She's never stepped foot in the clinic. She has people for that."

"Has Aisling O'Reilly ever been into the clinic?"

Her mother wagged a finger at Dimpna. "That's the second time you've asked that question. Now why is that?"

Her mother behaved as if she was clueless ninety percent of the time, but it was that ten percent that nailed you. One never knew when she was going to strike. Dimpna ignored the question for now. "Did Mrs. O'Reilly ever say anything to you—confront you about dancing with her husband?"

"Would you stop calling them Mr. and Mrs. O'Reilly? You're making me feel old."

"Fine. Did Róisín ever confront you?"

Maeve sighed. "I believe she sent that ranch hand after me. One-armedTommy."

"Tommy Healy?"

"That's the one."

"What do you mean she sent him after you?"

"I mean," her mother said, speaking slowly and overenunciating, "that one-armed Tommy has been stalking me."

CHAPTER 24

"*S*TALKING YOU?" SHE THOUGHT OF THE NEWSPAPER ARTICLE ABOUT Tommy in her father's folder. What part did the former jockey play in this unfolding drama? "I'm going to need some meat on the bones here, Mam."

"It was a few weeks before the murder. Every time I was in town doing my messages, I'd turn around and there he'd be."

Dimpna waited for more. Nothing was forthcoming. "Have you had any disgruntled clients lately?"

Her mother cocked her head. "How do you mean?"

"Have you given anyone terrible news, or anything like that?"

"Are you saying someone killed Johnny because I gave them a bad reading?"

"It sounds ridiculous when you put it like that."

"It is ridiculous. Pure nonsense. I tell you one-armed Tommy is following me, and you want to blame me. Typical."

"First, I don't think you should call him that. Second, I cannot believe he's still working for them."

"We're not as full of ourselves as you, Dubs. Everyone calls him one-armed Tommy. He probably calls himself that." Her mam was right. Everyone here did call him one-armed Tommy. Just like they used to call her Dimp the Imp. You just couldn't take the awful out of people.

Her mother trained her gaze on Dimpna. "When did *you* see him?"

"He was with Róisín and Sean," Dimpna explained. "They pulled up to the clinic and stood there while Róisín yelled profanities at me."

Her mother leaned in, first glancing at her husband to make sure he was still asleep. "Did she call me a whore?"

"You heard them, did you?"

"One of my clients did. Something about you being a whore just like your mother."

Dimpna felt someone staring and turned to see the old man in the bed next to her father wide-awake and listening to them open-mouthed. Her mother waved. He waved back. Dimpna stood up and smiled as she pulled his curtain closed. "You'll be wanting your privacy from us. Now," she said. She went back to her seat. "If you heard Mrs. O'Reilly call me a whore, why didn't you come out of your caravan?"

"I knew you would have it handled, darling. You're used to people insulting you."

Dimpna couldn't argue there. "Why on earth would Tommy stalk you?"

"Which Tommy is that, dear? There are so many Tommys in Dingle, don't you know? If only there was a way to quickly differentiate one from the other."

Dimpna gritted her teeth. "One-armed Tommy."

"It didn't just happen the one time. Three days in a row I look behind me in town and there he is. The post office, the bakery, SuperValu."

Dimpna tried to picture it. Was her mother being overly dramatic? "All common places to stop in town."

"Always right behind me. I tell you he was following me."

"Did you confront him?"

"I stopped and talked to him the third time. Tried to anyway. He nearly jumped out of his skin."

"Did you ask him directly if he was following you?"

"I told him he looked a little lost and asked if I could help him with anything."

"And?"

"His face went as red as a lobster. Stammered something about doing your one's messages."

"Mrs. O'Reilly." She caught the sour look on her mother's face. "Róisín."

"I assumed so."

"And that was it?"

Maeve shrugged. "That was the time I saw him hovering behind me."

"Hmmm." If anyone had reason to kill one of the O'Reillys, it was probably Tommy. He'd worked for them long enough to know all their secrets, suffer all their abuse. Then again, the O'Reillys had been the ones to give Tommy and his twin a home, and jobs. They'd stopped short of adopting them. Brendan had probably seen the O'Reillys for the ruthless family they were, but Tommy had remained. No doubt his feelings for them were complex and a mixed bag. She could make an argument for Tommy murdering Johnny, but why would he pin it on her family? Were they simply convenient scapegoats to let him get away with murder? Was it Tommy who'd been watching her from the abandoned auto body shop? "Did you tell the detective about Tommy following you?"

"No," her mother said. "Do you think it's relevant?"

"Absolutely." There were times her mother was so ditzy, Dimpna wanted to shake her.

"Dr. Wilde?" Dimpna looked up to see the nurse had returned and was speaking to her. She hadn't introduced herself as Dr. Wilde. It was that grapevine, winding its way everywhere. *Strangling.* "The doctor would like to see you in his office."

"Me?"

"I'm going too," Maeve said, rising from her chair. "I'm the wife."

"Where's me slippers?" Her father asked, suddenly sitting up and eyeing the nurse. Just as Dimpna was about to tell him that no one had his slippers, Maeve pulled a pair of slippers out of her handbag.

"Here you are," she said, tossing them to him.

"Good woman." He immediately threw them across the room, aiming for the nurse, who ducked. They sailed into the hall.

"Da! You cannot throw things at people." She turned to the nurse. "I'm so sorry."

The nurse placed a hand over her forehead, as if she had an ache. "At least he'll stop for now."

Dimpna didn't know what the nurse was on about until she turned around to find her father had once more nodded off.

"He appears to be in the mid stages of dementia," the doctor said when Maeve and Dimpna were seated across from him. His office was stately, all mahogany and important. Dimpna preferred her father's messy office.

"Appears?" Maeve asked.

"There's no one-size-fits-all test we can use to diagnose a patient. It's a multipronged approach. Usually family members help us pinpoint when the memory lapses began." He stared at them as if waiting for them to fill in those blanks. Maeve picked at her sleeves.

Dimpna felt a hot glow of shame. "I've been living in Dublin, but I'm sure we can check with his staff."

The doctor nodded. "It won't change our treatment, but it can help to establish a time line."

"To what end?" her mother asked.

"It can help determine the speed at which his illness is progressing."

"What is the treatment?" Dimpna asked when her mother did not.

"There are medications that show some signs of slowing it down, albeit not reversing any damage already incurred, but the family needs to be involved in encouraging the patient to take the meds regularly. And like all medications, there are side effects. We'll prepare some material and options for you to go over. We can also give you resources for the near future."

"What do you mean?" Maeve asked.

"There are long-term care facilities," the doctor said. "If and when it comes to that."

"It won't," Maeve said. "I'll mind him."

The doctor nodded. "For now. But if his episodes of violence begin to escalate, you're going to need outside resources to help."

"Are episodes of violence common in patients?" Dimpna was afraid of the answer, but she had to ask.

"Dementia doesn't turn people violent per se," the doctor said. "But I'm sure he's noticed the lapses in memory. This awareness can cause a great deal of anxiety. It's even more acute if the person was always in control, someone who played a prominent role in society. To suddenly lose that sense of power and respect—often those are the patients who keep their first symptoms to themselves. He may have been suffering for quite some time. Untreated stress, keeping that kind of secret, can literally eat away at a person, and it can certainly cause outbursts. It's a frustrating feeling—for example, holding a mug or a set of keys and forgetting what they're called. But when the person realizes that suddenly they do not know the function the object serves—what is it for?—well, then one's feelings morph from frustration into terror. Unfortunately, this is the stage which forces most of my patients to finally come see me."

"If he had come earlier could you have prevented this?" Dimpna asked, noticing her mother cringe beside her.

"Not the progression of the disease itself, no. But I could have helped him deal with the stress, and the inevitability of what's to come. And perhaps we could have eased his stress, and thus the outbursts."

Murder? Dimpna wanted to ask. Could dementia cause someone to murder? What if her father truly hadn't remembered that he and her mother had been living separate lives? What if he was stoked into a jealous rage over his wife and Johnny O'Reilly? Had her father killed O'Reilly? If so, why didn't he use Immobilon? It was hardly a good defense—*If my da were a killer he definitely would have used Immobilon*—but it was also the truth. Unless he didn't have any on hand. Or couldn't remember how to mix it up. . . . Dimpna vividly remembered that purple vial. Her father had warned her to never, *ever* go near it. Not that he told her where he kept it. But if she was ever to see a purple vial, she was to stay far away. She'd assumed he'd gotten rid of it somewhere along the line. Would he have grabbed Release and a syringe instead? Dimpna needed to check every nook and cranny of the vet clinic to see if her father had that Monster in a Bottle. What would it mean if it wasn't there? Would it mean he safely got rid of it, or would it mean he used it?

Should she also destroy the folder in his desk? What was happening to her? If her father was a killer, did she intend on covering it up? *Family first, Dimpna. You need to fix this.*

The doctor cleared his throat. What a pair the Wilde women must have appeared, sitting mute and wide-eyed in front of him. "What are the next steps?" Dimpna asked when her mother didn't speak.

"We'd like to run a series of cognitive tests."

"I believe he's going to need all the tests he can get," Dimpna said.

"That was the plan. So far, he has not been cooperative." From the look on the doctor's face he was underplaying her da's reaction.

"Just tell him what the average scores on the tests are, make it sound like a competition, and he'll be begging you to let him take them," Dimpna said.

The doctor jotted down her suggestion. When he looked up, he twirled his biro before speaking. "I am aware that Dr. Wilde—Dr. Eamon Wilde—is a person of inquiry in a murder probe. They may ask for medical records. Does he have a solicitor?" His tone was very measured, as if his words were agitators and the next one that tumbled out of his mouth could detonate. He flicked a nervous glance at her mam. Was he afraid of her?

Dimpna turned to her mother. "See?"

"Only guilty people need solicitors," Maeve said. "We have nothing to hide."

The doctor nodded, then jotted something down on a calling card, and slid it across the desk. "If you change your mind, please have his solicitor contact me."

When Maeve did not make a move to pick the card up, Dimpna did. "Absolutely. Thank you."

"We'll try your suggestion with the tests," the doctor said. "If we can get him to take them, we'll have a better understanding of the scope of his illness. Otherwise we'll be sending him home with some medications that can keep him calm. But I would like to stress that he cannot return to his work. He no longer has the capacity to do his job."

"Is there any way of telling when he's lucid and when he's not?" Dimpna had to ask.

"Pardon?"

"How do we know when he's confused and when he's seeing things clearly?" *How do we know he's not faking? How do I know when I can trust him and when I can't?*

"There's no clinical way to answer that question. I suppose it all depends on the context," the doctor said.

"How are we supposed keep him from his practice?" Maeve said. "He won't stand for it."

"I'll handle that," Dimpna said. Maeve shook her head, conveying she very much did not think Dimpna could handle that. "He can't put animals at risk, Mam. You know that. If he was healthy, he would be the first to agree."

Maeve took this in and then nodded slowly. "I just don't know how you're going to stop him."

The doctor waited until mother and daughter stopped speaking. "I would also suggest that once you speak with your staff and they can pinpoint dates when he appeared not to be fully himself, I suggest you go through the client records to make sure the proper treatment was given."

"Thank you. I'm already doing that," Dimpna said.

The doctor folded his hands and smiled. "Like father, like daughter, is it?"

Like father, like daughter. What would that mean if her father was a killer? Was she a killer too? Dimpna tried to smile but she knew it appeared as a grimace.

"Have the guards been around then?" Maeve asked.

"They accompanied your husband when they dropped him off," the doctor said. "I believe they intend on speaking to me again."

Dimpna groaned. It was only a matter of time before they asked this doctor if his condition could cause violent outbursts. *Doctor, could he have believed he and his wife were still living together and in love?*

Yes, that's possible.

Therefore, when he saw another man picking her up . . .

Wait a minute. Her mam said Johnny O'Reilly hadn't picked her up that evening. That might help squash the impulsive-jealousy theory. And weren't there plenty of folks who would have seen her mother at the dance? She hadn't heard an official time of death, but it had to be somewhat of a narrow window. Dimpna rose to leave, prompting the doctor to rise, but her mother remained seated.

"I'm sure you wouldn't know anything that could help those guards with their inquiry, a busy man such as yourself," Maeve said.

Dimpna snapped out of her thoughts. Her mother had a certain tone when she wanted to get her way. The same tone she was using with the doctor.

"I happened to be out to greet the ambulance when Dr. Wilde was brought in," the doctor said, taking his seat again. "It wasn't an official interview or anything like that." He looked at his watch, licked his lips. He wanted out of this room so bad, Dimpna could feel it.

"I'm sure you don't think Eamon would hurt anyone," her mother said. "You of all people."

The doctor frowned, then stood once more. "I'm afraid that's all the time I have for you today."

Dimpna took her mother's arm, coaxed her out of the chair, and headed for the door. Maeve stopped, pulled out of her grasp, and turned to the doctor. "Eamon did save that sweet girl of yours, didn't he? What was the little darling's name? Trixie, was it?"

The tips of his ears were now bright red. "Yes. Trixie." His chin trembled. He glanced at a photo on his desk, a close-up of his sweet little terrier.

"I remember that night," Maeve said. "Eamon and I had just settled in to sleep when you rang him. It was half-one in the morning, and it was lashing something horrible out there."

The doctor was visibly flustered. "Was it?" he croaked.

"The worst storm in a decade, as I recall. But my husband didn't hesitate. He didn't even get dressed. Pulled his wellies and his raincoat on over his pajamas. I knew he was going to catch his death out there, and I told him not to go, but he turned around and said that there was an animal in distress and that was more important than my fears. He was gone eight hours, because your little darling decided to eat poison, was it?"

The doctor swallowed hard. He glanced at Dimpna. "The neighbors had left poison out. A fox had been snooping around his hens. They didn't know Trixie would get into it."

"And did my husband, or did he not, single-handedly save Trixie's life that night?"

"He did." The doctor lifted a handkerchief from his pocket and wiped his brow.

"And you could have driven Trixie to our clinic, but you didn't want to drive in the storm. Am I remembering that right?"

"I was terrified Trixie was going to die. I wasn't in any shape to be driving in a storm."

"Now, my husband might not remember that, Doctor. But I remember it. And you remember it. And I expect you to remember it when that handsome detective sits across from you and asks you if you think my husband is capable of murder. Do I make myself clear?"

"I see, Mrs. Wilde. I see."

"I'm sure that detective means well. Why, he's barely out of nappies himself. From Killarney, is it?"

"I believe so," the doctor said, suddenly fascinated with a stapler on his desk, moving it from one side to the other.

"There you have it. An outsider. He's only focused on the low-hanging fruit. Isn't that always the way?"

"I do think it's a challenge to have a detective who doesn't know our ways." The doctor lowered his eyes.

"He doesn't know us," Maeve continued.

The doctor took a deep breath. "Perhaps he'll be more objective that way."

Dimpna thought about interrupting, but the truth was, she was glued to every word out of her mother's mouth and quite impressed at her ability to bend people to her will. She was a master at the game, and Dimpna was just thrilled she wasn't the only one on the receiving end of it. Maeve shook her head. "Trixie was so loyal. Wasn't she so loyal?"

The doctor had a tear in his eye. "She was the best dog I ever had."

"She was a smart little thing, wasn't she? All those tricks!"

"You remember." He lifted his chin as a look of pure pride came across his face.

"I remember everything. She was a wee dote, she was. They're like family. We know that better than anyone. She lived a long life after that night, didn't she?"

"She did." He bobbed his head in agreement. "She did, so."

"How long?"

He glanced at the photo. "Thirteen years."

"Thirteen years! Thirteen more years of the best dog of your life. Isn't that something. All because of a single decision my husband made that night. Isn't that something. At the end of the day, a person's entire life can rest on one little decision."

Dimpna was still rooted to the spot. Her mother was like a stick of live dynamite.

"All I can do is present the facts," the doctor said. But his voice sounded unsteady. Maeve had rattled him. "The facts are that your husband is suffering from dementia."

"I believe if you have no tests, that's not conclusive, and therefore not a fact."

"We are about to do the tests."

"Why don't we put those on hold? Eamon has had enough poking and prodding."

"He needs to be officially diagnosed. There are medications that can help." The doctor was desperately trying to hold his own, but he was losing his grip by the second.

"You just said yourself the medications won't reverse or stop the disease."

"They can help ease some of the symptoms."

"I know my husband. He won't take your medications. Doctors make the worst patients. Isn't that what they say?" She gave a trill of a laugh.

"There is plenty of anecdotal evidence that your husband has experienced violent outbursts." His gaze landed on Dimpna and the message in his eyes was clear: *Help me.*

"Is there any evidence—from your perspective—that he committed murder?" Maeve asked casually.

The doctor's face flushed red this time, matching the tips of his ears. "No. No. Of course not."

Maeve smiled. "And you won't allow yourself to indulge in story hour with the detective, will you?"

"Story hour?"

"'What if' this, 'Could it be' that, 'Could you ever imagine a person who' . . . All made-up scenarios."

"I wouldn't want to engage in any of that, no."

Maeve stepped forward then reached out and touched his arm. Dimpna watched her mother give it a little squeeze. "I knew we could count on you. Trixie's looking down on you from heaven, Doctor. She's so proud of you."

"I don't know about that." But the doctor's voice was softer. "But I certainly won't indulge in story hour."

"Now," Maeve said with a satisfied grin, "if you ever want to get another little Trixie, be sure and bring her in to see my daughter. She'll be open for business soon."

Dimpna perched in her bus, watching as her mam helped her da into a car she'd hired to drive them home. She was still marveling at what she'd just witnessed. Her mam was all about cards. Tarot cards, postcards, and a life built like a house of cards. She knew when to bluff, fold, or slam down a full house like she'd just done to the doc. *And the pot goes to Maeve Wilde, ladies and gentlemen. Slink off, losers. Winner takes all.* Dimpna was damned proud but also a little bit ashamed. The doctor was just doing his job. Dimpna was no better; she'd done nothing to intervene. Why? And if her father was innocent, why was her mam so worried about the doctor speaking to the inspector? She was hardly the image of a conventional, loving wife. Was it guilt? Were one or both of her parents culpable? Something was amiss. There were bigger stakes at play here, and they were palpable yet so damned slippery. Just what on God's green earth were they dealing with here? And if it was bad, was her mam ever going to confide in her? And if she did, would Dimpna go along with anything her mother might ask? There was one person she didn't have to ask. She already knew where her father stood on the issue. *Family first, Dew. Family first.*

CHAPTER 25

*T*ODAY WAS IT, THE DAY DIMPNA COULD FINALLY START ORGANIZING THE clinic for their grand reopening. Niamh had come through and put together a small work crew. They spent all day attending to the kenneled animals and making phone calls to see if they could reunite some of the strays with their owners. At least the farmer with the pair of sheep had quickly come to collect them. Dimpna was nearby when he started to give out to Niamh about how long his sheep had been missing, and she quickly put him in his place. Not only was Dr. Wilde dealing with a health crisis, the town was dealing with this murder. He should be thanking them for keeping his sheep watered and fed, and by the by, she reminded him that she had placed numerous calls to him, and it wasn't her fault if he took his time collecting them. He should be grateful they weren't charging him boarding costs. Next she reminded him how Dr. Wilde had been keeping his entire flock of sheep healthy for the past decade, not to mention his three dogs and two cats. By the time she was through reprimanding him, he had his hat in his hands and was bowing his thanks.

Another team was dedicated to cleaning the yard of the auto body shop across the street. Dimpna was never so relieved to see junk hauled away. She looked at the cleared space, trying to envision what it could look like. *One day.* Maybe they could start a garden with sweetgrass and catnip, and anything else that was good for creatures to nibble on. The interior was going to be a project unto itself, and Dimpna had gently let Niamh know that she wanted to be the first inside to check things out. What she didn't tell Niamh was that she wanted to see if there were any clues about who might have been standing there the other night staring at her. The doors were all locked, but with an establishment that had been around for a long time, who knew how many in town had keys?

A few hours into their endeavors, her mother and father showed up. "Have you come to help?" Dimpna asked her mam, feeling touched.

"I have clients," Maeve said. "But your father wants to help." Before Dimpna could argue, her mam was halfway across the field. Dimpna worried her da would get upset, or start trouble, but he seemed content to hang around the courtyard, watching the comings and goings. Every once in a while he would bark out an order to a person, or a goat. The goat listened better than the people. The rhythm of hard work soon put Dimpna into a restful state of mind. Despite all the drama, there was a comfort to being back home, and getting the clinic sorted infused her with a sense of purpose. Dimpna looked forward to driving out to farms and houses, looked forward to getting to know the villagers all over again. They just needed this murder and the suspicion of being murderers behind them.

By the time Dimpna was ready to go inside the auto body shop, it was getting to be late afternoon. Her mam and da had gone home, and the assistants and Niamh were saying their goodbyes. Dimpna felt a little silly, being so secretive about the inside of the shop, and there was little chance of finding anything at all. But she did bring her four-pack with her to explore, just in case. The shop consisted of a small office, a back storage room, and an open garage with a cement floor. Given the garage could fit at least four large vehicles at a time, it would make a nice space for animals to mingle when the weather was bad, and added extra options for kenneling. Dimpna had made a nice profit on kenneling in Dublin, and although there might be fewer folks traveling on a daily basis in Dingle, they were sure to get some customers. It felt good to focus on work for the day, and when she turned on the lights in the garage space, her pack immediately spread out, sniffing out all corners.

A quick sweep put her at ease. There were tools that needed to be boxed up and donated, and auto body paint that would have to be properly disposed of, but otherwise it was empty. She also liked the little office and storage space, where they could keep extra supplies and pet beds. Once they hired a new vet, he or she could even use some of the space. She approached the garage doors, the ones that faced her clinic. It would be lovely with glass windows, but quite an expense. Perhaps on sunny days they could throw open the doors, and if need be, have little gates set up to keep the creatures in. It would have been perfect if the yard had a stone wall just like the clinic, but that was a cost they couldn't yet afford. There were scuff marks and partial large footprints near the garage doors, but who was to say how long they'd been there?

The paint was all half-used, and dirty brushes coated with a black gloss had been dumped on the floor. Splotches of black dripped down a can and onto the cement. Maybe Dimpna should talk to Paul. They could invite kids from his group home to spend a few days or weeks painting the outside of the building and the floor. Something colorful and fun. She bet a number of them were quite artistic, and children and animals were usually a good mix. Dimpna was too tired to tackle it tonight. For once, there was no drama to the day, just work. She debated whether or not to drive to Inch Beach with the dogs. They were allowed as long as they were on a leash and all dog fouling removed. The phrase made her laugh. Just like the area around cow pats were officially called "the zone of repugnance." Fouling and repugnance. As if humans were above all that. She took her pack for a sunset walk through the field instead. This way they could be off-leash and Spike could trot alongside behind them.

She drank in the scent of honeysuckle and bluebells bursting from the hedgerows, embraced the cool sea air, and took a moment to relish the breeze on her face. E.T. got the party started, running around Pickles and Guinness until they gave chase. It was an hour well spent, and by the time they were heading back to the clinic, the sunset was a deep orange and red, oozing glory across the sky. She'd have to make a point of getting to Inch Beach soon. There was no greater magic than watching the sun set over the Atlantic with your toes in the sand.

She had just led her four-pack into the courtyard, had given them treats, and had refreshed their water bowls, when a prickling sensation came over her. *Déjà vu.* She pivoted to look at the auto body shop. One of the garage doors was halfway open. She could have sworn she'd not only closed them, she'd locked them. Or had she just imagined doing so? Sometimes when she was superbusy and focused, like today, she could swear up and down she did something, but it was only because her intent was so strong that she'd simply imagined she'd done it. That must be it. She hadn't wandered too far from home and they'd only been gone an hour.

But the prickling sensation increased as she made her way across the street. Tire marks were visible in the yard. It looked as if some-one had pulled in, then sped out in a hurry. She was grateful they'd installed bright lights around the shop just this morning, and they blinked on as she approached. She maintained a distance from the opening of the door but soon found herself on her belly, trying to peer in. It took her a moment to figure out what was different. The paint cans were gone. Every last one of them. Gone. What in the world? She picked herself up, and after making sure no one was in-side the garage she closed it from the outside, making sure it was locked, then checked every other door. They were all secured. She'd specifically told Niamh that she would arrange for the paint cans to be removed. Had Niamh gone ahead and called someone out anyway? Either way, hadn't someone done her a favor? It's not as if they had any need for automotive paint. She headed back across the street and was just passing her bus when she encoun-tered black paint slashed across its width: LIAR.

Dumbfounded, she stared at it. *Liar.* This was aimed at her. Her mind struggled to make sense of it. Was it her father? His illness striking again? Dimpna reached for her phone and had just crossed in front of her bus when the second blow struck. A post-card. Tucked into the windshield.

Was it from her mam? She picked it up, and instantly had her an-swer. Her mam had only ever sent her postcards from other coun-tries. This was a Dingle postcard. More troubling, it was an image of Clogher Stand. Dimpna felt physically ill as she took in the curved white beach, the cliff hovering in the background, the waves pound-ing the shoreline. Against the base of the cliff, someone had drawn a red X. She dropped the postcard onto the bonnet of the bus. *That's where they found the body,* a little voice whispered. *Right there.* Dimpna reached into the bus, removed a set of gloves from her glove box, put them on, and then turned the postcard over. Letters had been ripped from magazines and glued to the back: HE KNOWS.

Inspector Cormac O'Brien and Detective Sergeant Neely arrived shortly after Dimpna had called the station. She was shocked to see two more guard cars pull in after them and even more gobsmacked when they not only cordoned off the entire body shop but her bus as well. To top it all off, the inspector seemed furious. With her. He questioned her over and over about why she'd been around the body shop at all. She explained to him that Mr. Collins, who owned the shop, and still had a long lease, had given her permission to take it over. But for some reason, when it came to someone else sneaking in and hauling away the paint cans, he was suspicious. What in the world did paint cans have to do with anything? He even had them search her bus to see if there was any evidence that paint cans had been in there. It took her quite some time of going over everything she'd read about the murder to figure it out. *Polished stones.*

"Were the stones next to Johnny O'Reilly's body painted with automotive paint?"

Every guard in the vicinity swiveled his or her head to look at Dimpna. The inspector took her by the arm and pulled her away from everyone else. "You will *not* utter that suspicion to anyone else, do you hear me?" She nodded. "Say it."

"I won't say a word." She chewed on her lip as she watched the guards do their work. After all the work they'd done today, it felt like a slap in the face. She'd been looking forward to the pleased looks on clients' faces when they saw the cleared-out space. Now all they would see would be police tape. Of course she wasn't going to say anything, as promised, but it didn't take her long to figure it out, and someone else would, too. She pointed this out.

"I won't lie," he said. "You cleaning up this body shop reminds me of your brother cleaning up a boat."

"You can't be serious."

"And yet—look at my face." She did. It was a strong face. Well-defined jawline with stubble. Intense eyes with dark eyelashes. A faint scar underneath his left eye that she had a sudden urge to trace with the tip of her finger. And sadness. He had a strong, handsome, sad face.

"Do you think I painted *Liar* across my favorite ride in paint that won't wash out and wrote the postcard to myself too?"

He turned his gaze away from her. "'He knows,'" he repeated. "Who is 'he' and what does he know?"

"I haven't a clue. I swear."

"What's your best guess?" He didn't believe her.

"Maybe it was you," she said.

"Pardon?" His voice had hardened.

"You seem to think I'm a liar."

"I asked you to take a guess."

"Is that how you do your job? You just take wild guesses?"

"Why don't you try it and see?"

He knows. She'd been wondering the same thing of course. Who was "he"? Her father? Donnecha? Johnny O'Reilly? "I truly wish I could be more helpful. But I'm not a detective. And I had every right to use the space. Do you want a phone number for Mr. Collins?"

"You bet I do."

She sighed. "Follow me. I have to look it up." Nose twitching, he followed her into the clinic. Even though Niamh had transferred all their clients onto the computer, her father still had an old-fashioned Rolodex and she thumbed through it, found the contact, and jotted it down for the detective. Then she wrote the name of a local Dingle allergist.

He frowned at that one. "What's this?"

"This is the allergist I keep telling you about. See him. He can help."

He gave a half shrug but thanked her. Should she tell him about the other note? The one scribbled on the back of that horrific photo in her father's folder? *Forget everything you think you know . . .* She had no idea how long it had been there or who sent it. And the inspector was still giving off ripples of anger and suspicion. What if showing him the folder would make it worse? Convince him they were a family who covered up murders together?

"You say your parents were here earlier?" There it was. All the proof she needed. He was gunning for them. He was not on their side.

She headed for the exit. "I'll say good night."

"What?"

She held the door open for him. "I'm going to bed," she said. "Good night."

He stepped out the door, then turned to look at her. She tried not to stare directly in his eyes; there was just something so compelling about him. "We're not finished here," he said, locking eyes with her.

"I know," she said. "Good night."

CHAPTER 26

THE NEXT MORNING, DIMPNA WOKE UP WITH THE TROUBLING POST-card on her mind. *He knows.* Clogher Strand. *Such a gorgeous place to die.* Did that mean Johnny O'Reilly's murder and whoever "he" was and whatever he knew were connected? And if so, what did that have to do with Dimpna? Or was someone just messing with her? The same way he or she seemed to have been messing with her father? What if the sender was someone who knew about her mam's proclivity to send postcards? Was he or she mocking her? Or simply copying her? Her father had been near her bus all day yesterday. Was the postcard from him? If Dimpna went over to the house, would she find bits of cut-up magazines and scissors near his favorite chair? And what about *Liar* splashed across her bus in paint? Was Dimpna supposed to be the liar? Or was her father referring to himself in the third person? She needed to speak with him about everything, whether he remembered it or not. But not at the house.

Her father had always loved Dingle's beehive huts scattered about the village where the monks used to live. He needed to get out and about as much as possible while he still could. She would suggest a field trip. They could wander around the huts and have a private chat without looking suspicious. In the meantime, she had a clinic to run.

Niamh arrived-on with her hands full, and seconds later she thunked a stack of résumés on the counter. "Right, so. We have our candidates for a new vet." They spent the next few minutes chattering about the body shop being cordoned off and the break-in. Dimpna did not indulge in the details. And there was no need to explain the vandalism on her bus to anyone, for the guards had promptly towed it away. Dimpna had rented a van early this morning for the interim, and she hated it. It had been slim pickings; there were only a few that they could adjust the seat enough for her to reach the pedals, and she'd had to put it on a credit card, but given she couldn't work without one, it would fill the gap. Dimpna certainly didn't utter the words *automotive paint* while they gossiped. It was probably one of the only clues from the murder scene that hadn't been leaked to the press. A detail only the killer knew. No wonder Cormac O'Brien had been so upset; she really hadn't understood the gravity of it until this morning. Regardless—she had a job to do as well, and hiring another vet was the biggest item on their agenda for the day.

Niamh had already placed her favorite candidate on top—Patrick Kelly. "Recent graduate, fresh out of vet school. Dublin College, just like you," Niamh said.

There was a certain look in her eye. "I take it you've met him," Dimpna said.

The entire side of her neck flashed red. She nodded. "I was here the day he dropped off his CV."

"And?"

"He made quite the impression. Your pack really liked him."

"Did they now?"

She grinned. "He's a tall drink of water, don't ya know."

Dimpna laughed. "Couldn't hurt to have a tall one around."

Niamh was practically glowing. "I swear to ya, he's also kind, and funny, and smart—and look at those credentials."

"Are we hiring him or marrying him?" Niamh nearly disappeared under a red face. "I'm only messing," Dimpna said. "Farm work?"

Her head bobbed enthusiastically, sending her curls bouncing. "Yes. Small animals, large animals, and exotic animals. Australia recently and Wales."

"He does sound like a good fit."

Niamh clapped her hands. "Shall I ring him?"

"Is he local?"

"He mentioned he'd be in town a few days, just in case."

Had he heard about the murder? What if this was just a curiosity seeker? On the other hand, it would be best to have a newcomer on board, someone whose views weren't tainted by local gossip, or the Dingle Guinness-vine as her father liked to quip. "See how soon he can come in for an interview, but if it's today, it has to be before seven this evening."

Niamh looked as if she was bursting to ask about Dimpna's evening plans, but she managed to contain herself.

Paul had rung her this morning. Sheila was coming around to his place this evening along with Donnecha, and he insisted there was something urgent they needed to speak with her about. This had sent all her alarm bells ringing, and it was going to be torture to wait. Luckily, she had plenty to distract her. Patrick Kelly arrived an hour after he was called. Niamh wasn't exaggerating; he was tall, and fresh-faced, and handsome. About Niamh's age too, somewhere in his late twenties. He stood in front of the reception desk, smiling down at them.

"Where you from yourself?" Dimpna asked.

"Wicklow," he said. "But I've recently returned from a stint in Australia."

"How was that?"

"Brilliant. Once you've wrestled a few Kangas you feel invincible." He grinned.

"You're tall," she said. "And I'm not."

He nodded. "I assume you're thinking of surgeries. Since I'm not willing to chop off me legs, I'm assuming you've developed techniques."

She nodded. "I have step stools."

"Grand."

"But I do want all the shelving in here moved to lower positions."

"I could do that today." And he did. He lowered all the shelves and placed all the surgical equipment within Dimpna's reach. The last thing she needed was a vet who either pitied her, or thought it an endless source of humor, but Patrick was polite and deferential.

Her father would have liked him. Niamh, who was already out-going, laughed more often (and louder) once he showed up, and Dimpna prayed her crush wasn't going to get too out of hand. It wasn't smart to fall in love with your workmates except for the four-legged kind.

The day was filled with spays, and vaccinations, and a few infec-tions. Patrick handled them all with ease. Dimpna heard a lot of laughter in the clinic, mostly females taken with the tall new vet, but she was ever so grateful. It was six in the evening and Dimpna was ready to call it quits, when the door opened and a beautiful woman dressed to the nines walked in with a young girl. An enor-mous pink backpack was attached to the lassie and she was strain-ing to hold on to a wiggly golden retriever puppy. *Aisling O'Reilly.* Ben's half sister. Which meant the beautiful woman accompanying her was Sean's wife—definitely not a nanny. Helen O'Reilly. Dimpna suddenly realized she was holding her breath. Helen had gorgeous black hair tied back, and hazel eyes. She was slim and tall. Dimpna could picture her waving at the crowds during races, clap-ping and posing with the winners. She was everything the O'Reillys would want in a daughter-in-law, everything Dimpna Wilde was not. And yet, Dimpna instantly pitied her. What must it be like to be part of that family, stuck in their web?

"We're not open, luv," Niamh said.

"I'm sorry," Helen said. "We saw the lights on and I realized this little guy was supposed to have his second set of shots. I'm already behind; there's been so much going on. But this one is worried to death." They all glanced at Aisling, who nodded.

"I can't sleep," she said, "until he's protected."

"The other vet is overwhelmed and I heard the other Dr. Wilde was taking over. Aisling was thrilled to hear it was a female vet. Weren't you, petal?"

Aisling nodded, her eyes large and pleading. With her pained expression she looked so much like Ben that Dimpna had to grab the countertop for fear of going down to her knees. Her tor-mented thoughts changed from "Look what you've kept from him" to "Look *who* you've kept from him."

"I believe I have something here for you," Dimpna said, making every effort not to look at her too closely. Dimpna picked up the necklace from the drawer she'd stashed it in and held it up. The gold letters shimmered.

"For me?" she said, her eyes lighting up. "It spells my name." She was nearly vibrating with excitement. Dimpna was stunned. It was new to her. The necklace had obviously been dropped before someone had had a chance to give it to her. What had she just done?

"I'm sorry," Dimpna said. "I thought you'd lost it."

"No," Helen said. "I've never seen this necklace before."

"Does that mean . . . ?" Aisling asked, eyes wide with anticipation. "Can I keep it?" She shrugged her backpack off and handed the wriggling puppy to her mother. The pack landed with a loud thud. Niamh came out from the reception desk and heaved the backpack out of the way.

She groaned. "What in the world do you have in here?"

"She's been on a nature hunt," Helen said. "But I've been telling her meself that it's too heavy."

"A girl after my own heart," Dimpna said. "A nature hunt."

The puppy yelped and Dimpna took him out of Helen's arms.

"I can't believe you found a necklace that spells my name," Aisling said. A smile lit up her pretty face. "Do you know what my name means?"

Ashling. "A dream. A vision," Dimpna said. "From a genre of Irish poetry developed in the seventeenth and eighteenth centuries." She couldn't resist bopping the tip of her nose. Aisling positively beamed. She whirled around and lifted her hair. Helen clasped the necklace on her.

"I think someone must have planned on giving it to her but accidentally dropped it the last time she was in for a visit?" Dimpna peered at Helen to see if this made sense.

Helen shook her head. A strange coincidence then. Or . . . had Johnny O'Reilly dropped it during his secret visit to the clinic? Had this been the last gift a grandfather had purchased for his granddaughter? She couldn't let anyone see a panicked expression on her face. "Send them into treatment room one," Dimpna said. "It won't take long. Second set of shots, is it?"

"Yes, it is," Niamh said in a baby voice to the squirming pup. "Who's a good boy?"

Patrick, who had been nearly out the door, hesitated, his eyes lingering on the beautiful Helen O'Reilly. "Do you want me to stay?"

"Dr. Wilde can handle it," Niamh said crisply.

Dimpna tried not to laugh. She hoped once again that Niamh wouldn't fall too hard. "You're alright," Dimpna said. "See you tomorrow."

"See you tomorrow."

"Bye," Niamh called out in a singsong voice. "Bye, bye, bye, ba-bye."

"Bye. Bye, bye, ba-bye-bye." He headed out the door. Helen and Aisling started to follow. A chime sounded and Helen lifted her phone out of her designer handbag. She glanced at the screen.

"It's the funeral home," she said. "I have to call them back." She glanced at Dimpna. "I'm helping with the arrangements."

"Of course." Helen glanced at Aisling. "She can come with me," Dimpna said.

"Please, Mum."

"I'll be right in," Helen said with a nod. Dimpna gestured to Aisling to follow and they proceeded to the treatment room. "What's his name, luv?"

"Sunny."

"Perfect."

It didn't take long to give the puppy his shots, and Dimpna made sure to narrate as she went for Aisling's benefit. "There," Dimpna said. "He's all sorted."

"Why don't animals get a coffin?" Aisling's eyes were wide and serious.

"I suppose they don't want all that fuss," Dimpna said, hoping she wasn't stepping in it.

"My grandfather is going to be in a coffin."

"I'm sure it will be very grand." Johnny O'Reilly would have wanted the fuss. Dimpna stroked the puppy and was just about to lift him off the treatment table, but Aisling was running her finger along the edge of the stainless steel, and swaying to music no one else could hear.

"You shouldn't talk to strangers," Aisling said.

Dimpna cocked her head. Where had that come from? "That sounds smart," Dimpna agreed. "It's best to stick with people you know and trust."

Aisling nodded. "Even if they seem really, really nice."

Dimpna felt a squeeze. Had someone been harassing her? "Yes," Dimpna said. "Better safe than sorry."

"Animals aren't strangers, are they?"

"Most animals just want to love us. But you should never approach an animal you don't know," Dimpna said. "Some animals might lash out if they're afraid."

"Do people lash out when they're afraid?"

"Yes. Some people do." Dimpna's alarm bells were quivering.

"Is it a sin to tell a lie?"

"It's human," Dimpna said softly. She wasn't about to encourage lying, but she equally wasn't a proponent of terrifying children with the fear of God. "Some lies are very harmful. It not only harms the people you're lying to, it can be harm you to keep lies bottled up inside."

"It can give you a tummy ache," Aisling said.

Dimpna nodded. "But do you want to know the bright spot?"

"The bright spot?"

Dimpna lifted a jar off the biscuit tin and gave Sunny a treat. "Even in the darkest skies there's always a bright spot."

"Yes, I want to know the bright spot."

"It's never too late to tell the truth. Some people say it can set you free."

"Then why is my granny so afraid?"

Sunny stopped chewing and lifted his head, drool hanging from the side of his mouth. "You can always tell this guy your secrets," Dimpna said, ruffling his head. "Animals are excellent listeners. And they don't judge."

"Granny says we need to get our alibis rock solid. Is that the same as lying?"

Dimpna turned and pretended to fuss with something in the cabinet. "I'd tell Sunny if I were you, just in case." She was probably going to pay a karmic price for this, but there was no way she was going to stop this confession. The girl might be pint-sized, but what if her secret wasn't?

"My da didn't stay the night in Doolin when the bad thing happened to Grand-pappy, but we're supposed to say he did." It was jarring, hearing this young girl speak so frankly. No doubt she'd been a little sponge these past few days. "He drove us there, but then he had to turn around and go back home."

"Oh? Why is that?" Dimpna's heart was tap-dancing in her chest. She was terrified of Helen bursting in and accusing her of coaching the young girl.

"Granny went missing from awake."

Went missing from awake . . . from the wake . . .

"She was supposed to stay awake but she drank too many jars and went to pull Grand-pappy out of the dance because he was with that voodoo priestess."

Dimpna's mother—

"Granny must feel bad because she yelled at him and then he died." Her back curved in, and she sighed, then tilted her head and stared at Dimpna wide-eyed.

"You don't need to feel bad about keeping those secrets," Dimpna said. "You're too young to worry about any of that."

Talking must have been a relief for the girl, because she was eager to say more. "Tommy was supposed to pick us up the next day but the publican said he was on a mad tear and wasn't fit to drive. A friend of Mummy's picked us up, but she won't say anything because the guards don't know their arse from their elbows. I think they're very easy to tell apart."

A shadow fell on the floor and Helen stood in the doorway. Had she heard any of that?

"We're all sorted," Dimpna said, lifting Sunny and handing him to Aisling.

"Darling," Helen said. "Would you wait in the reception area for us? I need to speak with Dr. Wilde." Aisling nodded, thanked Dimpna again, then skipped off. Dimpna felt the little hairs on her arms rise. Would it do any good to tell the inspector what Aisling had just revealed? Was there any way to prove it? She'd heard talk that they'd tracked Sean driving to Doolin with his family that weekend and checking into their lodgings. Most likely they stopped there. If they kept digging, would they find that he drove back to Dingle? Was the story about Róisín dragging her husband out of the dance true? Did he die while they argued somewhere in private and she called her son for help? It had to be urgent to make him leave his wife and daughter and drive home. Or was it all a lie? Aisling was young, and no one would want to see her caught in the middle of this, not as a witness against her own family.

"I was hoping we would have a chance to say hello." Helen studied her openly.

Dimpna swallowed. "It's lovely to meet you." She knew the polite thing to say was "Sorry for your loss," but she had no idea what Helen's relationship was like with her father-in-law, not to mention Róisín, and given she wasn't sorry, she couldn't bring herself to say anything else at all. She waited for Helen to leave.

"My husband has been wanting to see you."

Dimpna didn't know what she was expecting, but it wasn't that. "I find that hard to believe."

"He's a good man now. But I know he wasn't a good lad back then."

Lads will be lads. What exactly did she know? "That's all in the past," Dimpna said.

"He's a haunted man."

"Haunted?" *Good.* Although somehow Dimpna doubted it. And she very much doubted that Sean O'Reilly had confessed to rape. Whatever sad story he'd told his wife, the truth was much worse. But that was twenty-seven years ago, she had buried it deep, and Dimpna had no desire to dig it up. "I'm not sure what you want from me."

Helen swallowed. "Maybe this isn't the best place to discuss this. Let me just say that Sean has told me all about the past."

Was she making this up as she went along? Fishing for information? "What exactly did he say?"

"He said he bullied you. Called you names. Children can be so cruel."

"They certainly can."

"Do you believe in forgiveness, Dr. Wilde?"

Was she for real? "I'm sorry. I have somewhere to be." Dimpna gestured to the door. Helen looked at her for a moment, then nodded. But she didn't put a single foot forward.

"I believe forgiveness can set people free."

"I don't." Dimpna gestured to the door again. "After you."

"Forgiveness can work miracles."

"Did he send you here?" Coward. She knew he hadn't changed a bit. She knew it.

Helen shook her head. "Heavens, no. He'd be mortified. I swear this is all me. I just . . . He's never going to find peace unless you forgive him." Dimpna moved past her and headed out the door. Helen trailed behind her, lowering her voice but still talking. "I'm not asking for him. I'm asking for my daughter. I want her to have some chance to have a relationship with her father."

Dimpna stopped and whirled around. "I heard they have a close relationship."

Helen shook her head. "She has a haunted, troubled, sad father who's never going to stop beating himself up."

"You think he's beating himself up because he bullied me in childhood?"

"I do."

"By all means, tell him his childhood bullying made me strong." She was not going to tell this woman she forgave Sean O'Reilly. In fact, if she stayed any longer, she might be in need of a little forgiveness herself. Dimpna's legs felt like rubber as she escorted Helen to the waiting room. She forced herself to say goodbye to Aisling.

"Thank you, Dr. Wilde," Aisling said. She rubbed her necklace between two fingers.

"You're welcome, luv," Dimpna said. "Take good care of Sunny." She leaned in. "And keep talking to him."

"I will."

"Thank you, Dr. Wilde," Helen said. They headed out the door. It took a few minutes for Dimpna to realize Aisling had forgotten her backpack. She picked it up, and nearly tore an arm muscle. She threw a glance at Niamh. "You weren't kidding." What in the world was in it? She was tempted to open it, but Niamh was watching. "Did you have a peek?"

"Not at all," Niamh said. "That would be like someone reading your diary."

Like someone reading your diary. Dimpna's mind flashed to the notebook from the other day: I HATE HIM. She was still dying to find out what that was all about. "What do you think is in here? Doesn't feel like books."

"School is out for the summer," Niamh said. "Helen said it was a nature project. But it feels like a ton of bricks."

Dimpna hauled it toward the door. She exited the clinic and waved in the direction of Helen's car, but she was already pulling away. They'd surely remember soon and come back for it. Niamh couldn't see Dimpna from this vantage point. She opened the backpack and stared. Niamh was wrong. It wasn't full of bricks. It was full of stones.

CHAPTER 27

*H*ELEN RETURNED MINUTES LATER, AND BEFORE DIMPNA COULD work out what to do, she'd retrieved the backpack with another smile and wave. Dimpna had a sinking feeling she'd made a giant mistake. But what choice did she have? Should she have told Helen that she was holding the backpack as evidence? She wasn't a guard. Then again, it was the inspector's job to investigate, and wouldn't he want to know that Aisling O'Reilly not only smashed her father and granny's rock-solid alibi, she also had a backpack full of them? Then again, didn't most kids shove stones in their pockets, or purses? Was it Sean who had broken into the body shop? What about Tommy Healy? He'd certainly have access to everything Sean did, including Aisling's backpack. But if one of them was the killer, why on earth were they letting Aisling haul those stones around? *Because there was nothing incriminating about a child collecting stones.* It may not be related to Johnny's death at all. Maybe it was a big fat coincidence. Dimpna hated when laymen tried to diagnose sick animals, and here she was trying to decipher a murder case. On the other hand, she didn't want to be The Keeper of Secrets. Unless they were her own.

She dialed the inspector's number, and when she reached his voice mail she relayed as much as she could, walking a tightrope between the facts and a growing sense of hysteria that the O'Reillys were not only going to get away with murder, they were going to pin it on someone in her family. She hung up feeling somewhat un-

satisfied, but at least she'd been honest. Dimpna had to pick up her
father for their visit to the huts, then drop him home and head to
Paul's. Niamh had already arranged pet sitters for her four-pack.

"Why did you want to meet here?" her father asked, the tone of
his voice an accusation. They had been walking around the stone
huts for a few minutes, and her father had been animated as he
gave her a history lesson she already knew by heart. Not that she
minded. She loved the little monuments, standing witnesses to a
time gone by. Her father seemed somewhat on point today, although had he been fully himself, they would have been talking
about the case instead of the monks from days of yore.

Her father vied a group of lads in the distance, the one in the
middle working a control, their heads craned back as a drone ca-
reened like a drunk in the sky, buzzing and dipping, barely pulling
itself up from an inevitable crash, as the lads' excited voices added
to the frenzy.

Her father lost himself in their antics for a moment and then
shook his head. "When I was a lad we were happy with wheels and
sticks."

"Wheels and sticks?" Dimpna knew the stories, but she wanted to
give him the chance to relive them. Every memory he could hang
on to was a little nugget of gold, an opportunity not to be wasted.

Her father lifted his head, a spark in his eye. "We'd take the
hoops off old barrels and roll them down hills or along the road
with a long stick. Sometimes we'd score an old bicycle tire." For a
moment he was lost in the memory. "We were trouble," he said with
a click of his teeth and a grin. "When we tired of wheels and sticks,
we'd toss pebbles at random shop windows, see if we could get the
clerk to give chase. Scarper away, leaving the slowest to get caught."
He laughed. "One time, a fella gave me a good chase, so he did, his
face red-hot as he hollered at me. I hauled arse and ran smack into
the parish priest." He grimaced. "I never tossed another pebble at
a window again. Let's just leave it at that."

Dimpna smiled. "I think I'd prefer wheels and sticks too," she
said as the drone nosedived into the field, and the boys scrambled
after it with shrieks. She gave it a moment and turned to him. "Da?"

"Yes, Dew?"

"Did you paint the side of my bus and leave a postcard on my windshield the other day?"

"You drive a bus?" He wrinkled his nose.

She laughed. "A small one. My VW bus."

"Postcard," he said. "You must have me confused with your mother."

"It's from Dingle. Clogher Stand."

Her father's face remained passive. She'd so hoped that he would be present enough to help her figure this out. "The body," he said.

"Yes," she said. "Exactly." Her father shoved his hands in his pockets and stared at his shoes. "Da," she said softly. "Niamh said that a month before he was murdered, you and Johnny O'Reilly had a private meeting in the clinic?"

"We did?" His gaze fixated on a spot in the distance.

"Do you remember giving me a man's ring? A ruby?"

He shook his head, his fist rising up to join it. "I told him no. No way!"

Dimpna stiffened. "Told who no way?"

"Who do you think?" His voice was low. His head swiveled and he met her gaze head-on.

"Johnny O'Reilly?" Her whisper was soon swallowed up by the wind.

He nodded. "I didn't realize then that it was already too late."

"What was already too late?"

Her father grasped her hands tightly. "He knows."

He knows. Had the postcard been from her father? Was it about Johnny? "Who knows what?"

"Ben," her father croaked as he released her hands. "Does Ben know about Johnny? Or does Johnny know about Ben?" He tapped his fist against his forehead as if trying to knock the answers free.

"Johnny has always known about Ben," Dimpna said, gently taking his hand away from his forehead. "And I also told Ben about the murder." *Just not the grandfather part.* Was her father reliving his other meeting with Johnny O'Reilly? Where the two patriarchs agreed never to utter a word about the baby's father, especially to the baby's father? In exchange, her father would give free veteri-

narian services to the O'Reilly horses for the rest of his life, and
Johnny O'Reilly would never press charges against Dimpna for releasing their prized thoroughbred into the dark of night just as a
horse trailer sped up the road. A deal made with the Devil. "Next
time you don't have to leave me a postcard, Da. You can just talk
to me."

"Postcard?" her father said. "I didn't leave you a postcard. It
must have been from your mother."

Sheila had just finished a guided tour and was relishing the
thought of sinking into a hot bath. Drowning in it was always an option too. But as the crowd dispersed, they revealed yet another visitor. This time it was Paul, and her heart tripped in her chest. Would
there ever be a time that she would gaze upon him without some
degree of longing? She knew he'd show up eventually. She was surprised it had taken him this long.

"I'm starving," she said. "I can't take a lecture unless I have some
food in my stomach."

"Then we'll eat," Paul said. "I'll drive."

They headed for town to a seafood restaurant they had fre-
quented as teenagers and commandeered a booth with a peekaboo
view of the harbor. Neither needed a menu; they still wanted the
fish and chips, and Sheila stuck to a Coke, but Paul ordered a pint
of Guinness. After their drinks, but before their food, while Sheila
was trying to figure out what this was all about, Paul leaned in.

"We have to tell her. Not tomorrow, or next week. Tonight."

"Tonight?" She was going to lose her fecking appetite. Why did
Paul always have to ruin things?

He nodded. "I've already invited her over. She'll arrive at seven."

"Don't you think there are people we should warn first?"

"No."

Sheila turned her gaze to the tips of the sailboats, all dressed up
with nowhere to sail. She suddenly wished she'd ordered a Guinness and a shot. "What good is telling her going to do?"

"I can't lie to her. I can't see her after all these years and just lie."

We lied to her back then. A lot. "Then tell her."

"Don't act like you're not involved."

Sheila folded her arms across her chest. "I haven't said anything to that detective."

Paul's expression belied his disgust, despite his quick attempts to hide it. She knew it. He was consumed with jealousy. She bet he thought about the detective inspector out of Killarney ad nauseam. And not just because he wanted this case. As usual, all roads led to Dimpna Wilde. She was sick to death of it. "Were you with Donnecha that Saturday night?" Paul asked.

There it was. Once a detective, always a detective. Two could play this game. Sheila wound a string of hair around her finger. "Where were *you* the night of the murder, Detective Byrne?"

He gave her a look. The waitress interrupted with their fish and chips. Paul flirted and sent her off in a cloud before turning his intense gaze back to Sheila. "I was at home. With King."

His German shepherd, the only creature who had ever been lucky enough to live with Paul Byrne. "Can anyone verify that?"

"I asked you first. And you still haven't answered."

She reached for a bottle of vinegar and drowned her fish and chips. "I was at the O'Grady wake for an hour, and then I went to the clinic. There was an emergency call—a Jack Russell hit by a car."

"What time did you finish?"

"He survived, by the way. The Jack Russell." *Thanks to me.*

"Whose dog was it?"

He was grilling her. Trying to catch her in a lie. "Oh my God. I can't believe you."

Paul took a few bites before speaking. "You've been hanging around Donnecha."

"Is that a crime?"

"I hear things. You know I hear things."

She wanted to be flattered, but he wasn't keeping tabs on her because of any romantic feelings. At least she could admit that to herself after all these years. At least she'd matured. She stabbed her chips with a fork and shoved a big piece into her gob. *Heaven.* Sheila could eat fish and chips all day long. She was easy to please, down-to-earth, *good stock.* Everything Paul needed, and at one time claimed to want. They ate in silence, a fried-food-buffer. When she was finished, she pushed her plate away and burped as loud as she could. It took Paul a moment, but he finally laughed. He shook his head like he didn't approve, but he laughed. God, he was a gorgeous man. Those dimples. Those eyes. The inspector was sexy, too. And younger. He was too short for her, but she'd definitely picked up on a chemistry between Dimpna and Cormac O'Brien. Had Paul? Knowing him, he had. It was probably driving him mental. What a waste. Pining after her all these years but not doing anything about it. She burped again, louder this time.

"Such a lady," he said.

"You didn't used to mind." She licked salt off her fingers as she maintained eye contact. He watched her with detachment. *Typical.*

"Are you telling the truth about Eamon? Do you think he's capable of murder?"

Paul Byrne was one of the only people in Dingle who called the man Eamon. He'd been the son he never had. Which did not sit well with the son Eamon did have. "Spend five minutes with him and see for yourself," she said.

"You swear he wasn't at the clinic with you the evening of the murder?"

"I wasn't working at *his* clinic. I was at O'Connell's. Dr. Wilde hasn't been practicing, remember?" Was he trying to trap her in a lie? And here she'd been giddy at the thought of sharing a meal together, even though she knew the entire reason she was sitting here across from him now was because of Dimpna Wilde. *Stupid, stupid, grown-arse woman.* When would she ever learn? She was pathetic. She'd wasted her life waiting for Paul to love her. Maybe that's why she'd been hanging around Donnecha, acting the maggot. At least it was a bit of excitement, something to take the edge off. Could she help that she was a good actress? A good con woman? She wanted a do-over. She would go to Australia or New Zealand, surround herself with hot men with accents. Somewhere far, far away.

"Do you think he did it?" Paul asked.

"Which Wilde are you referring to?"

"Any of them. All of them."

She picked up a lone chip still clinging to her plate and jabbed it at him. "If I was to play 'Pick a Murderer,' someone who hated

Johnny O'Reilly enough to want him dead, someone who was smart enough to pull it off—I would have picked you." She grinned and then stuffed the chip in her mouth.

Paul's expression remained placid. "Me? Why is that?"

"You've always blamed the O'Reillys for driving your one true love out of town." She hadn't meant to go for the jugular, but he just had to keep prodding her.

"Even if that's true. Why would I wait twenty-seven years to do it?"

"Because her husband died a year ago. You waited until she'd had a respectable amount of grieving time—and then you did the one thing you knew that would bring her back to town."

He appeared to think about it. "If I wanted to date Dimpna, I could have just showed up in Dublin."

"And leave Dingle? You're as much a part of this town as the mountains. They should name a range after you."

"You always did think you know me." He finished his pint and wiped the back of his mouth with his hand. Sheila stared at it for a moment. A man's hand. Strong. Callused. She could still feel those hands exploring her.

Sheila leaned in. "Before you tell her, you'd better think it through. You can't un-ring a bell." If she dared, she would place her hand on his cheek, run her finger down his jawline, cover his lips with hers.

"I've thought of nothing else," Paul said, oblivious to her lust. "We've already waited too long."

"Too long for what?" He stood. She raised her volume. "For her to love you?"

"Grow up." There was a hitch to his voice. She'd finally done it. Rattled him. *Good.*

"It's going to break her. Is that what you want?"

Paul threw money on the table. "Let's collect Donnecha," he said. "It's way past time for our confession."

CHAPTER 28

*T*HE DRIVE FROM THE CLINIC TO PAUL'S COTTAGE WAS NO MORE THAN thirty minutes, but in addition to nightfall sealing a dome of black overhead, the heavens had opened up and the rain was lashing down sideways, creating treacherous driving conditions. Ten minutes into the trip, and blinding lights pierced Dimpna's rearview mirror, stabbing her eyes. The offending vehicle was right up her tail. She cursed and swerved, thankful her pack wasn't with her, helplessly tossed to and fro. "Slow down," Dimpna yelled into the rearview mirror as she straightened out and funneled her anger into her horn. If the eejit tried to go around her, he or she could be smashed by an oncoming car.

She was not intimately familiar with this rental van and she would not allow some bully to force her into a dangerous speed, especially on slick, winding roads. She slowed to a crawl, just to drive the point home. The response was a jarring bump to the back of her van. She lurched forward along with the vehicle; her breasts slammed into the steering wheel. "Are you joking me?" She blinked her lights and honked her horn again. "I'm not afraid of you." The lights amplified, forcing her eyes closed as colors swam in front of her. This was no misunderstanding; someone was deliberately messing with her. Should she pull over and pray he would pass? This was not a fight she could win. Ahead, there was a fork in the road. She was supposed to take the right to head to Paul's. Should she go left instead? Would the car tail her no matter which direction she chose? She sped up; the vehicle followed suit. A psychopath. Wasn't she dealing with enough already? Dimpna aimed as if she intended on taking the left in the fork, but at the last minute she banked hard to the right. The back end of her van screeched and fishtailed, unleashing a wave of water over her windshield. *Don't panic. It's happening; go with the skid.* She straightened out just as the offending vehicle shot through the left in the fork and vanished into the dead of night. She kept driving, her heart thumping in her chest. Was it just some arsehole? Or was she in a killer's crosshairs?

Paul Byrne lived in a stone cottage wedged into the base of a hill. And even though it was set close to the road, traffic along this route was sparse, and the view of the mountains and ocean from the top was breathtaking. Not that you could see anything today. Dimpna pulled into the drive, jumped out, and made a run for Paul's front door, but she wasn't quick enough. By the time she reached his entrance, she was soaked to the bone, teeth chattering through her skull. Before she could even form a fist to knock, the door swung open. A feeling of relief washed over her as Paul filled the doorway. "Come in, come in," he said, reaching for her. "You'll catch your death."

From within a fire crackled. Dimpna stood dripping by the front door. "Someone just tried to run me off the road."

Paul looked as if he wanted to barrel out in the storm and crush them with his bare hands. "Who was it? What happened?"

She slammed the door so he wouldn't tear after her unknown assailant. "There's nothing to be done. I couldn't see a thing. Not who was driving, not the make of the vehicle, not a number plate."

He let out a sound akin to a growl. "Stand by the fire while I get you a towel." Was it wrong that his protective stance sent a little thrill racing through her? She immediately pivoted to a thought of Detective Inspector Cormac O'Brien, imagining his reaction. Equally concerned or more? *Cop on.* She was knackered and susceptible to foolish meanderings. Her life was way too messy for romance. It was just a distraction at a time of high stress. *Focus.* This was the cottage Paul had grown up in, but unlike the rest of them, the intervening years hadn't forced it to change. It opened onto a cozy sitting room with a sufficient kitchen off to the left. The thick wood floor was covered in an oval wool rug supporting a sagging olive-green sofa and scarred coffee table cluttered with newspapers and empty coffee mugs. A tall bookshelf crammed with offerings towered over a slim desk by the window, topped with an enormous pair of binoculars.

"Dimpna," a familiar voice said. She whirled around to find Sheila huddled by the cooker in the small kitchen. She stepped aside and behind her lurked Donnecha. Sheila lifted a glass sloshing with gold liquid. Whiskey. Sheila arched an eyebrow. "Want one?"

"Please." Dimpna edged forward. Her plans to tear into her brother came to an abrupt halt. He had dark circles under his eyes, and they were rimmed in red. He was holding a glass of water and his hand was shaking. Big-sister-love cracked open inside her.

"Donnecha," she said. "C'mere to me." He plunked the water down and rushed for her. Her arms encircled his trembling body.

"I'm sorry, Dimp. I'm really, really, really sorry." Sobs tore from him. What nightmare had created this? She pulled back. "Are you sick?"

"Just with worry." He sniffed, then wiped his nose with his sleeve.

Her hands curled into fists at her side, her nails digging into her palms. "What on earth is going on?"

"We'll get to that," Paul said. He'd returned with a towel, and a T-shirt, and a blanket. "This is all I have, but it should fit you like a dress. Change first, horse the whiskey into ya, and then we'll have a proper talk." He pointed to a bathroom off the kitchen. Silence fell as she left the room to change. He was right; the T-shirt was like a long dress on her. She hung her wet clothes over his shower, then hugging the blanket around her, she returned to the kitchen and downed her whiskey. Outside the wind shrieked and rattled the windows as the rain drummed steady on.

"Typical," Sheila said. "It's always stormy with the three of us." For a second her joke was greeted by silence and then Donnecha began to laugh. Soon the rest joined in. Trad music played softly on a nearby radio. For a second Dimpna had an urge to play her fiddle, and allowed herself to imagine they were just here for the craic. No problems, no unsolved murders, no awkward memories, or sibling rivalries. Just old friends on a stormy night. Paul refilled her whiskey. Her sense of dread returned. One uneasy-old-friend was bad enough. Three was downright Biblical. Add in the storm, and Dimpna wondered if this was her last night on Earth. If so, she should have brought the four-pack.

Paul was the first to speak. "Let's sit." He gestured to the sofa, so she settled into one end and Donnecha retreated to the other. Her brother was having difficulty looking her in the eye. Sheila too for that matter, which was completely out of character. She never had been able to stand silence, always filled it with sordid gossip, or salty jokes, and when she ran out of those, farts and belches. Sheila and Paul each lowered themselves into facing armchairs. Down the hall nails clicked on the hardwood floors and seconds later an old German shepherd appeared.

"This is King," Paul said.

"Well, hello there, gorgeous." Dimpna leaned forward and held out her hands. King trotted over and sniffed, then licked her palms. She scratched him behind the ear, cooing. "What a good boy."

Satisfied with the newcomer, King heaved down near the fire with a groan.

"Who died?" Dimpna finally said, raising her voice over the beating rain. "Besides O'Reilly," she added. Not even a smirk. This was a serious crowd. Or a guilty one.

"Have you heard from Ben?" Donnecha asked.

The question felt jarring, as if it belonged in another dimension. It was dawning on her that her family felt closer to Ben than she had ever realized. "He's grand," she said. "In Spain with his new girlfriend."

"When did you last have a chat with him?" Paul joined in.

Her family asking her about Ben was one thing. Paul's curiosity elevated this conversation to a bizarre new universe. She jumped up. "You'd better not be telling me that something has happened to my son." If something had happened, they wouldn't have heard about it first. Would they?

"Nothing like that," Sheila said. "I swear. He's *fine*."

Dimpna's head swiveled to Sheila. "Hope to die?" Dimpna knew she sounded childish, but she was at her wit's end.

"Cross my heart, hope to die," Sheila said, making the motions.

"Sorry," Paul said. "Please. Sit. Let's start over."

This time Dimpna perched on the edge of the sofa. She felt coiled up, and if they were lying, if Ben wasn't okay, there was a chance she was going to get violent. "What's going on?"

Donnecha cleared his throat. "Does Ben know about the murder?"

"I told him a prominent man was murdered in Dingle." She nearly spit out that he didn't know the man was his grandfather when she realized that *they* didn't know the man was his grandfather either. "Why?"

"But you did speak with him since the murder," Sheila said. "And you're sure it was Ben?"

What a question. It was so ridiculous that Dimpna laughed. "I think I'd know me own son."

"Of course," Sheila said. "But people's voices often sound alike on the phone."

"We video chatted," Dimpna said. "But I would still recognize my own son's voice."

"Ben called me," Donnecha said. "And I should have told you, but he asked me not to."

Dimpna turned to her brother. "He did?"

Donnecha nodded. "He had a lot of questions."

Dimpna almost did it again. Outed herself. She was surprised Ben had called her brother, but so what? Donnecha didn't know anything. "That's why you have been avoiding me? Because my son called you?"

He swallowed and glanced at Paul. "Because you always know when I'm lying," he said quietly.

"That doesn't sound good." She looked at Paul. He was staring into the fire. She looked at Sheila. She was staring at King. None of them would look her in the eye.

"You're all sitting in front of me like a firing squad because Ben called his uncle?" She made eye contact with them one by one. "Jesus. And I thought Finbar Malone burying a mobile phone was awkward."

Donnecha shot up from his seat. "What?"

Dimpna relayed the story, wondering if any of them would make a "phone home" joke. They didn't. The inspector had understood her joke right away. Was that why she was thinking of him? Is that all it took—someone who got you?

"Where is that phone now?" Sheila said, coming to her feet as well.

Dimpna glanced at Paul. His arms were folded across his chest and he was staring at a spot in front of him, a look she knew well. He was listening intently. "That's what got your attention? A fisherman's phone?" Her brother and Sheila exchanged a panicked look. "Donnecha? Sheila?"

"It's nothing," Sheila said. "That's not what we're here to discuss." She shot Donnecha a glare and they sat back down.

"I thought we were here to discuss the murder?" Dimpna could hear the fear in her own voice. Donnecha covered his face with his hands. Paul leaned in, staring at Dimpna with an expression close to pity. "You guys are really scaring me." Actually, they were churning her into a homicidal rage, but she managed to swallow the thought.

"Did your husband leave a suicide note?" Paul asked.

"What?" How was that any of his business and why was he even asking it? What the hell was going on? "No," she said. "Niall didn't leave a note." It had bothered her greatly. It wasn't like him. Communication had been a pillar of their relationship.

"What if we told you he did," Paul said quietly. "In fact, he left two notes."

"Two?" She shook her head. "I'd say someone is messing with you." When no one replied, she rose to her feet again. "Why on earth are we talking about Niall? Didn't you hear what I said? Someone is trying to frame my parents, not to mention you," she said to Donnecha. "For *murder.*" She turned to Donnecha. "I heard they brought you into the station."

"They did," he said. "But I swear. I didn't tell them everything."

"Why the hell not?"

Paul jerked his head toward Donnecha. "Show her the notes."

Donnecha reached into his pocket and pulled out two folded-up pieces of paper. The brilliant white of the paper instantly conjured up Niall's fancy company letterhead. "You're going to be really mad at me. At all of us. But none of us knew what to do." He held out the notes. "One is for you, and the other was to Ben."

"This is insane," Dimpna said. She snatched the notes out of Donnecha's hand. One had her name written across the fold. *Dimpna*. The other, *Ben*. Sharp black ink. Slanted *D*'s. Loops at the bottom of the *p*'s. No question the handwriting belonged to Niall. She felt the room tilt. "Why do you have these?" *Open them.* Her hands remained still.

"You know that I was living on Johnny's boat," Donnecha said.

"Where did you get these notes?" Dimpna demanded.

"Don't worry," Donnecha said. "I haven't told the guards."

"Why would the guards care about my husband's suicide notes?"

"Johnny O'Reilly told me he had a special guest that evening," Donnecha said. "And that I was to leave the boat in the afternoon and return in the morning to clean it." Dimpna clutched the notes and crossed her arms against her chest. "And that's what I planned on doing. But I also wanted to know who this special guest was. I was staying at the Dingle Inn so I could pop over and have a look-see. But I wasn't there alone."

Dimpna had it with the hemming and hawing. A flock of sheep in the road at rush hour was less maddening than this lot. "Is this your coming-out declaration?" She wanted to read Niall's notes but not in front of them. Not a chance. Had *they* read them? How was this even possible?

"I'm straight," Donnecha said. "But this isn't about me." Donnecha looked as if he was about to cry. "Why didn't you tell us what that bastard did to you?"

Dimpna's body reacted immediately. Her face heated up. She couldn't form words. She shook her head. How did they know? She could feel Paul and Sheila looking at her too, but she couldn't meet their eyes.

"It makes sense now," Sheila said. "Why you never forgave me. I was your best friend. I should have been there for you."

"Why didn't anyone tell the guards?" Paul said. "Why didn't your father go to the guards?"

"Shut up. All of you, just shut up. You don't know anything. How could you?" She followed her gaze down to the notes in her hand. One for her. One for Ben. Niall was the only other person who

knew about Sean O'Reilly. What he had done to her. "Oh my God."
She moved to the fire with what she now knew were evil little notes
and she thought about throwing them in. Burning them. Burning
her husband's last words. What had he done? What had Niall
done?

"Ben came to Dingle after Niall died," Donnecha said. "After he
read the notes."

"No," Dimpna said. "No."

"He spent eight months here, but he never said a word about
Sean." Donnecha hung his head. "If he'd only said something,
maybe we could have helped."

Dimpna whirled around. "My son was here for eight months and
you didn't tell me?"

Donnecha's face was stricken. "He begged me. His father had
just committed suicide. I knew you two were still somewhat talking—so I stayed out of it. I thought I was helping."

"What does any of this have to do with anything?" Dimpna was
nearly shouting. She was going to lose it. There was only so much
stress a person could take. "Where did you even get those notes?"

"Ben must have left them behind. They were in one of my
overnight bags. I hadn't been using it, so I only just found them."

"And you read them even though they're clearly not addressed
to you." Dimpna wasn't ready for this. She wasn't.

"We can point fingers later," Paul said. "Ben knows about Sean."

"What?" She heard what he said. She just couldn't process it.

Paul gestured to her hands. "It's there in the note."

He knows. She turned on Paul. "Did you leave a postcard on the
window of my bus?"

"What?" Paul's shock sounded genuine. "What postcard?"

"Never mind." She started to pace. A thought stopped her cold.
"Does . . . does Sean know about Ben?"

Paul stood up. "He must."

Dimpna felt ice-cold. "Are you just guessing?"

"Ben was Johnny O'Reilly's VIP guest on the boat that evening,"
Donnecha said.

"No," Dimpna said. "Stop talking!" King struggled to his feet and
barked.

"I saw it with my own eyes," Donnecha said. "Ben had been staying at the inn with me, but when I returned that afternoon, he was gone. I went to the harbor. And I saw Ben get on that boat."

"I said stop talking."

"Tommy Healy was there to meet him," Donnecha said. "Healy was dressed in all black, like it was some kind of a spy game. Or maybe he just knew something bad was going down and he didn't want to be recognized. But I stayed. And I watched. Tommy Healy came off the boat. Ben stayed. He was waiting for Johnny O'Reilly."

"No," Dimpna said. "No."

Donnecha stepped forward. "Mam saw him the day of the dance. She was worried about him. She gave him something to ward him off temptations."

Devil days. The tarot card. Words, like vicious, hungry little sharks, circled her. Blood in the water. Niall *did* leave a suicide note. Two of them. Ben was the one who found Niall hanging from the carport. Ben found the suicide notes. He kept them from her. Her son had kept her husband's last words from her. *Like mother, like son . . .* Then he disappeared for eight months. He was secretly meeting with her father. With her brother. Her mam. All behind her back. And now, the most damning revelation of all: Ben had been on that boat the night Johnny O'Reilly was murdered. A VIP guest. She saw the black paint splashed across her bus: *Liar.* The note in the windshield: *He knows.* Was that awful message a reference to Ben? Or were the awful messages *from* Ben? She sank onto the sofa with a low moan and buried her head in her hands. King trotted over and pushed his wet nose through her web of fingers. The ruby ring . . . Was it meant for Ben?

"Ben even bought a necklace for Aisling," Sheila said. "I think he was excited that he had a sister."

The gold necklace in the dirt. Sheila so casually talking about it. *Everyone knew.* Her secrets had blown wide open and she'd been clueless. The lingering looks Sean had given her that day when he and his mam pulled up to the clinic. Ben chatting with her on the phone, asking her questions—he'd been testing her. And she'd failed. "Do Ben and Sean . . ." She could barely form the words. "Do they like each other?"

"I think they do," Donnecha said. "But there was one person who wasn't having it."

Johnny O'Reilly.

"Ben had been to the clinic on several occasions," Sheila said. "Talking to your father." *That's why her father kept bringing up Ben.* "I haven't told the guards, I swear," Sheila continued. "But I saw Ben at the clinic. The morning the vial of Release went missing, Ben was there."

Dimpna was making a concerted effort not to lash out. She wanted to grab Sheila by the hair and drag her to the floor. She wanted her to finally admit the part she played in that awful evening. And here Sheila was calling her son a murderer? "Did you ever tell Paul?" she said. "About that *other* evening?"

Paul stepped forward, his face half in shadows, the other half bathed in the red of the fire. Sheila wilted before her eyes, guilty tears pouring down her cheeks. "For God's sakes, Dimpna, I was just a girl."

"Even after all these years," Dimpna said, "you can't admit what you did."

"What's done is done."

"Tell me," Paul said. "Everything."

CHAPTER 29

Then

DIMPNA WILDE WAS READY. PAUL HAD BEEN RESPECTFUL AND TAKING things slow, but lately she'd been flooded with all these feelings, her body was singing with desire, and she'd found herself fantasizing about making love. Paul would be such a great lover, and they'd come so close, but every time, she'd held back. "There's no hurry," he'd say. She knew of lads who pressured girls into sex. Cajoled, flattered, and downright lied all in the pursuit of a ride. A few resorted to convincing their loves that their balls would fall off if they didn't get any release. They couldn't pull that one off on Dimpna who knew from experience it took a lot more than that for balls to fall off.

But Paul Byrne wasn't one of those guys. She wanted him to be her first. And if she was honest, her last. It had always been Paul. She'd be off to university soon, and Paul was a homebody. But they could make it work. Dublin wasn't a world away, and she would come home on weekends, and he could visit her. They could make it work. She knew the exact night too. The night before the big race. With Tommy Healy as his jockey, Last Dance was sure to win. Dimpna had been avoiding Tommy ever since that awful strangling prank a week earlier, and he seemed equally keen to stay clear of her, not to mention the press. Rumors were flying that Healy was no longer training. All flirtations between them had evaporated.

Not that anything had ever really happened, but there had been shy smiles, a few moments of prolonged eye contact, and once an accidental touch of their hands that sent a spark through her. After his hateful prank with Sean, she was beyond grateful it had never gone farther. Sean O'Reilly had completely pulled him into his dark orbit.

But none of that was on her mind at the beginning of that evening. She was all about her secret rendezvous. She wanted to surprise Paul, wanted to seduce him. And as odd as it may have seemed to anyone else, she also knew the perfect place. The leaning shed where they had first met, where Sean O'Reilly had trapped them like prisoners. She was going to decorate it with white lights, and candles, and place soft bedding on top of hay. Their own little sanctuary. Taking back her power, although she didn't think of it in those terms back then. She was excited beyond belief as she headed to Inch Beach to meet Sheila. She couldn't wait to tell her best friend all about her plans.

Sheila was on board. She helped Dimpna decorate the little hideaway. Everything was perfect. Time to surprise Paul. She'd made up an excuse, asking Paul to meet her at the shed at half-six. Dimpna's father was headed out to a call at six. But just as she was leaving, Dimpna was waylaid by a dog with an infected leg. She couldn't get ahold of Paul to tell him she'd be late, so she'd begged Sheila to go and give him the message. An hour later, Dimpnna raced to the shed. She could hear noises as she approached, moans in the night. She threw open the door. Sheila and Paul were naked and wrapped around each other, the candles casting their sweaty bodies in a flattering glow. It was an image Dimpna would see for the rest of her life.

Now

"What did you think was going to happen?" Sheila said. "You were an hour late. We were in this shed with candles, and bedding, and lights—and one thing just led to the other."

"You told me Dimpna was in love with Tommy," Paul said. "That she was going to break it off with me."

"Wow," Dimpna said. "And you believed her?"

He closed his eyes briefly. "You had been flirty with him. And he was running that big race."

Sheila stepped forward. "Is this even the part that matters? Isn't it what happened after the part we need to work through? Do you blame us for what happened next?"

Dimpna got hammered. She showed up at the O'Reilly barn. She headed for Last Dance; she wanted to touch him, feel his face. She didn't hear Sean come up behind her until the weight of him crushed her, until his breath and sweat were on her neck, until his grunt rang in her ears. He pinned her against the stall. The rigid boards cut into her sternum as his fingers found the snaps on her denims. "No." No, no, no, no, no. Her scream was lost in the wind. It was blowing fierce that night, rattling the siding on the barn, setting all the horses on edge. Her pants slid down along with her knickers. How strong the smells. Rain. Pungent earth and animal droppings, and hay. He was inside her so quickly, a sharp pain, a tearing sensation, her head still spinning from drink. His breath on her neck. Wetness all down her thighs.

Dimpna slapped her hands over her ears. "Stop it. I don't want to talk about it. I have to find my son." She turned to Donnecha. "When is the last time you heard from him?"

"The day of the murder. He hasn't answered a single text or voice mail from any of us since."

"Shit." What happened that evening, and where was Ben now? The three of them tried to stop Dimpna from leaving, but she wasn't having it. She hurried back into her clothes, still damp from the storm and clinging to her. If she didn't get ahold of Ben and figure out what was going on, she was going to have a mental breakdown. She flung herself out the door. Paul barrelled after her. "Dimpna, *please.* I'm sorry. About everything. I wasn't there for you back then, but I'm here now. I'm here now. For you. For all of you. For us."

"There is no us."

"Give me a chance. *Please.*"

There was a time his plea would have rung like bells in her head. Now there was only a dull thud. "I've nothing to give you."

"I'll help. Whatever Ben has done, I'll help."

Dimpna whirled around. "He hasn't done anything. Don't you see that? It's us. We're the ones who keep on doing things."

"Sean will pay for what he's done. As I live and breathe, he's going to pay for this."

Dimpna barged up to Paul, standing so close she could feel his thumping heart. "This is my fight. Not yours. Do. Not. Interfere." She moved away just as swiftly and jumped into the van, letting the door slam between them. She peeled out and pushed the pedal as far as she dared. This time there was no psychopath on her tail, but she wished there was. The rain had eased, but despite slick roads and the dark, dark sky, she made good time. She picked up her pack from the clinic, stopping to kiss and squeeze every single one of them, and then piled them into the van and drove straight to her parents' home. They were both asleep in the living room, her father snoring in a reclining chair, her mother cocooned on the sofa.

Dimpna slid open the doors separating the sitting room from the kitchen and camped out at the center table. She poured a generous swig of whiskey and dialed Ben over and over. She didn't care if he was asleep, or if she made him hate her. She had to speak with him. Was there really a girlfriend? He wasn't in Spain and she'd never met or spoken with this Angelina. She had never seen her on video, never heard her voice. Ben had made her up. *Lied.* Like mother, like son.

She swiped through family photos on her phone, grasping for happier memories, searching for her missteps. Was Ben the one who painted "Liar" across her bus? He certainly wasn't the one who had tried to run her off the road, and he wouldn't have set her parents up for murder. And the tie . . . The killer had mocked Johnny O'Reilly by placing that tie on him. That's not a detail Ben would have zoned in on, was it? It was Tommy Healy who sat across from her, grinning. *The tie was my idea.* She called Ben again. He must have turned his phone off, this time it didn't even ring. She sent a text.

I have Niall's notes. I'm so, so sorry. We need to talk. Let me help you.

She laid Niall's final betraying words out on the table and took another swig of whiskey. It burned all the way down. She did it again. She knew she had to watch it; she was still a working vet, and she could not perform surgeries if she was too hungover. The last time she had been blind-drunk was that awful night. Ben had been the one good thing to come out of it. Ben had been everything. Dimpna Wilde believed in a woman's right to choose, and she never could have imagined wanting to keep a baby that was the product of a rape, but the minute she found out she had a baby growing inside her, he was wanted. *She* wanted him. Sean was the one at fault. Not the baby. And not her. She knew she would love the baby, but she also knew she had to keep her child away from the poison that permeated the O'Reilly family tree.

Telling her parents had been the hardest thing she'd ever done. She couldn't bring herself to tell them everything, so she just called it a terrible mistake. The blowback from letting Last Dance hurtle to his eternal finish line had nearly destroyed her. She told herself she deserved it; she deserved every horrible thing and then some. Her baby did not. Her baby deserved a chance. She would not start a war with the O'Reillys by accusing their only son of being a rapist. She just wanted to get far, far away. All these years she'd wondered if she'd gone too far. But now she'd realized the truth. She hadn't gone far enough.

But right now, she needed her wits about her. She needed to help her son. She needed a plan.

She opened the letter to her first. A single paragraph stared back at her in Niall's orderly black ink.

> *Dear Dimpna,*
>
> *I'm sorry. I know that sounds trite after all I've done, but I am. I am deeply sorry. You probably hate me, and I don't blame you. I have an awful feeling that despite the letter I am sending to the media, no one will believe that you and Ben had no inkling of my unlawful activities. You do not deserve this, and I did not deserve you. If I may be so bold as to offer a bit of ad-*

vice—the truth shall set you free. I hope one day you'll see that
and forgive me.
   Niall

Her hands shook, anger rumbling deep within her as she opened the letter to Ben.

Dear Ben,
   I've always loved you like a son. And your mother had her
reasons for keeping your father a secret. He was not a jockey
who passed away unexpectedly before you were born. His name
is Sean O'Reilly and he lives in Dingle. Your grandpa Eamon
Wilde and your paternal grandfather, Johnny O'Reilly, made a
pact that your biological father would remain a secret. From
what I am aware—even Sean doesn't know that you're his son.
He comes from wealth and greed—ironically my downfall in
the end as well. In those days it was too shameful to say words
like rape, *but that is the circumstance under which you were*
conceived, and the reason your mother did not ever want you to
know. I sense the anger in you, and it's my firm belief that
knowing where you come from might set you free. Your mother
will not be happy with my decision, but it's also for her sake
that I'm telling you. Take it from me, secrets are too heavy a
burden to carry. I'm sorry I failed you. I'm proud of you.
   Niall

"Dew?" Her father materialized in the doorway.

"Da," she said, turning the letters over, her heart thudding in her chest. Her father glanced at the upturned notes, but then was distracted by the whiskey bottle. He pulled out a chair and sat across from her. "How are you feeling?" she asked gently. She hoped he wouldn't ask her the same thing. She was gutted. A non-person. She no longer knew who she was or what she was going to do.

"Fair to middling," he said with a soft smile. A sob escaped her. She didn't want to cry in front of him, but it was too much. His hand came across the table and he placed it on top of hers. "Is he okay?"

Her head jerked up. She stared him in the eyes. "Have you been faking it?"

He frowned. "Faking what?"

"You asked me if 'he' was okay. Who did you mean?"

"Ben."

"You have to tell me everything you know about Ben."

"He came to visit." He rubbed his face. "Or do I have that wrong?"

"You're right, Da. I need to know what happened when he came to visit."

"He was angry." Her father scrunched his face. "He was so angry."

Dimpna found herself repeating a phrase, even the fact that she was having the thought had shocked her. *My son is not a killer, my son is not a killer, my son is not a killer.* "What did he say? What did he do?"

"What time is it?" Her mother stood in the doorway, rubbing her eyes.

"Look who's home," her father said, pointing to Dimpna with a grin. "We need to feed her."

Her mother eyed Dimpna, then the whiskey, and finally the notes. Her eyes widened with understanding; her mouth dropped open. "How could you keep this from me?" Dimpna pleaded.

Maeve sighed, then fetched another glass from the press and poured herself a whiskey. "Everything happened at once," she said. "Ben came to visit and at first we were thrilled. Then your father started having his memory problems, and then Ben showed us those awful notes. He made it clear that he planned on confronting the O'Reillys."

"You should have called me. You should have called me that minute."

"He was on a warpath, and that wouldn't have calmed him down."

"Then what? Why hasn't Sean confronted me? What did Ben do?"

"What he planned on doing and what he did are two different things," Maeve said. "One minute he said he was going to see to it that Sean O'Reilly rotted in jail for the rest of his miserable life, the next thing I knew, the pair of them seemed as thick as thieves."

"Seemed?"

"I think it was an act," Maeve said. "Ben is definitely a Wilde."

"What?" Dimpna rose from the table. "What?"

"He was very convincing," her mother said. "They got on like a house on fire."

"Johnny wasn't happy," her father said. "He threatened me."

Dimpna knelt by her father. "Is that what the secret meeting at the clinic was all about? Did Johnny O'Reilly drop his ruby ring?"

"Sean bought that ring for Ben," her father said. "Johnny said, 'Over my dead body.' He didn't drop it—Sean gave it to me. To give to Ben. I can't find it."

"You gave it to me," Dimpna said.

"Did I?" He was tired.

"Yes, you did." She paused. "Then what were you looking for in the clinic?" But she already knew. With a growing sense of dread, she knew. He'd been looking for a monster. A Monster in a Bottle. Her father had been looking for Immobolin. That was *after* O'Reilly was found dead on that beach. Which meant her father wanted to make sure someone—*Ben*—hadn't taken it. And from the way he'd torn apart the clinic, the answer was clear. The deadly vial was missing. But if someone had killed Johnny O'Reilly with Immobolin, why was there a vial of Release and a syringe at the scene when one drop of the Monster would have done the trick, not to mention it wouldn't have left a mark. There would have been no reason for a detective, let alone a pathologist, to suspect murder . . . Unless it was a set-up. Unless the killer wanted the guards to nab her parents for this murder.

Her mother swiped an envelope from the table then stood over the rubbish bin, furiously ripping it to shreds and letting the pieces fall like snowflakes.

"What's that?" Dimpna asked. "What else are you hiding from me?"

"For God's sake, Dimpna, everything is not about you."

"Then what is it?"

"Morton's Funeral Home!" her mother said.

"Again?" her father asked. "Is it addressed to me or you?"

Her mother waved her hand like it didn't matter. "Every single day they send us notices. Do we want to pick out coffins? Headstones? Plan our funerals. I have half a mind to kill them, but first give them a minute to plan *theirs.*" She sighed, then returned to the table. "If Ben and Sean are thick as thieves, why didn't Sean give the ruby ring to Ben himself?"

"They had a falling-out," her father said. "Ben wanted to meet his sister. Things got too real for Sean O'Reilly. He said he wasn't ready for that."

"What were you looking for at the clinic, Da? Why did you tear the room up? Tell me."

"When?" Her father frowned. "What are you doing here? You don't live here."

"I told you he's not faking it," Maeve said.

"Where is my son?" Dimpna said out loud. "Where is he?"

Maeve shrugged. "I hope he's far away by now."

"Are you calmly sitting there and inferring that Ben killed Johnny O'Reilly?"

"He helped Aisling gather rocks from the beach," Maeve said. "I told him not to approach her—Sean was livid."

Dimpna began to pace as Aisling's face rose before her. *You shouldn't talk to strangers . . . even if they seem really, really nice . . .* Ben. She'd been talking about Ben. "I can't believe this. I can't believe any of this."

"Ben didn't tell Aisling they were related, but Sean was still angry. He warned him that his father was going to reign terror down on all of them."

Reign terror down on all of them. "Did you or did you not give Ben a Devil card?"

"You can't think I had any idea what he was going to do with it," Maeve said. "I was trying to stop him—"

"My son is not a killer. He's not a killer."

Maeve rose from the table and approached Dimpna. "Listen to

me. It's going to be alright. Sean is covering for Ben. He's acting like a father should. He's protecting him."

Like hell he was. "How do you figure that?"

"He hasn't said a word about Ben to anyone—not the guards, I'm assuming not to his mam—not even to you."

Was it Sean who'd been standing at the auto body shop and staring at her? Or Ben? They were both the same height—so eerily similar. Wouldn't she have recognized her son's own voice? Why hadn't Sean said anything? Why hadn't Ben?

Even Helen hadn't mentioned Ben. Who knew about him and who didn't? And how long before the detective inspector knew? And what would happen when he did?

"Did you see Ben the day of the murder?" Dimpna asked. "Was he at the dance?"

"I saw him that morning. He said he was finally going to meet his grandfather. The other one. I tried to stop him. I gave him the Devil card."

There had always been a darkness in Ben. A longing she couldn't satisfy. It was as if he always knew. As if being conceived in that horrible moment had brought with it some kind of kinetic trauma that had grown right along with the embryo.

Twenty-seven years of protecting this lie and it had all been for nothing. For nothing! She had to think this through. Step by step. Ben wouldn't have collected a mountain of stones to write out the words *Last Dance* by O'Reilly's body. The horse meant nothing to him. Donnecha saw Ben enter the boat, but that was in the early evening. Ben must have dropped the tarot card while he was on board. That's how the killer got it. Donnecha couldn't say for sure whether or not Ben actually stayed on that boat. He could have left way before the killer got on. Tommy Healy had been at the boat. Tommy Healy was always around. Stalking. Would there be CCTV footage of Ben exiting the boat long before it pulled out of the harbor? And what about Saoirse Griffin? What or whom had she seen? What had she told the guards? Dimpna needed to talk to the girl. A part of her wanted to talk to the inspector. He was smart. She wanted to trust him. He gave off the vibe that he wasn't going to be swayed by local politics or the prestige of the O'Reilly family. But was that the truth? Or was it all an act?

"Why did Johnny O'Reilly keep Tommy Healy employed all these years?" Dimpna said. "He didn't turn out to be some esteemed jockey, winning them millions. The O'Reillys aren't sentimental. So why did they keep him on?"

"Do we have a call?" Her father stood. "I'll grab my bag."

"There's no call, Da. Go back to sleep."

"Why don't you stay the night?" Maeve said. "You're not going to solve anything tonight. It's late."

"It's not Ben," Dimpna said. "He wouldn't write *Last Dance*, he doesn't know how to drive a boat—and even more so—he wouldn't care about Johnny's aversion to ties." The more she talked, the more she knew she was right. The killer knew Johnny O'Reilly intimately. Her son did not.

"Unless Sean told him," Maeve said. "I told you they've seen quite a bit of each other."

Dimpna grabbed the back of a chair so she wouldn't go to the ground. Like it or not, and she most certainly *did not*, she couldn't afford to alienate Sean right now. She needed his support. Devil days. These were certainly Devil days. "Tommy Healy," she said. "Remember that prank he and Sean pulled?"

"How could I forget?" Maeve said. "You were in hysterics. Convinced one-armed Tommy had been murdered."

"Tommy was thrilled when we showed up with the guards. Grinning like a maniac—and do you remember what he said?" Maeve shook her head. "'The tie was my idea.' He was very proud of it. What if he was poised to inherit from the O'Reilly estate? But here comes Ben. Another blood relative. Maybe he was worried that he was going to lose out on his share. So what does he do? He murders Johnny O'Reilly and sets us up for it."

Maeve frowned. "But no one has said a word about Ben."

"Fine. Maybe the motive is slightly different—for all we know, Johnny has been cheating Tommy all these years. Or maybe Tommy had been skimming from the O'Reillys and Johnny confronted him. There could be a million reasons why. Are the guards even looking into it? Last Dance. The stalking. The tie. It all points to Tommy Healy."

"That's true," Maeve said. "But it's not us you need to convince. And theories won't do the trick. We're going to need hard evidence."

"We?"

"We're family," Maeve said. "We're in this together." Dimpna stood still, but suddenly her mother was there, reaching for her. "My girl. My sweet, sweet girl." Dimpna allowed her mother to comfort her, pull her into a hug.

"Is that why you were dancing with Johnny O'Reilly?" Dimpna asked. "To gauge how he was feeling about Ben?"

"I had to calm him down," Maeve said. "Johnny was livid that Ben was trying to insert himself into the family. Not to mention the wedge it was driving between Johnny and Sean. He'd kept his son from him all those years." *I did the same thing,* Dimpna thought. *Oh, the tangled web we weave . . .* "I was trying to keep him calm," her mother said. "I did me best."

Dimpna nodded. It had been her mother's version of a selfless act. She turned to her father. "Da." He looked at her. "I found a folder in your desk."

"Stay out of my desk, Dew."

"It was about Last Dance. Someone scribbled a note on the back of a photo. It was a photo from that night, just after Last Dance had been struck down. It said *Forget everything you think you know.*"

"That's a mouthful," her mother said.

"Agree," Dimpna said. "But not the point. Da?"

Her father shook his head. "I'm sorry, Dew. My mind is such a mess. I keep forgetting things."

"It's okay, Da. Do you know who wrote you that note?"

"I think . . . I think . . . there was a call . . . That's right. I went to the stall. There was a lameness call. A horse with an infected hoof. The note and a photograph of Last Dance—someone slipped it into me vet bag."

"He's remembering that correctly," Maeve said. "There was definitely an emergency call about a horse with an infected hoof."

"Was the call at the O'Reillys?"

"That's right." He lit up. "That's right, Dew!"

Tommy Healy. He was the one who made the calls when they needed veterinarians out to the estate. She'd check the records. Then she'd go to the estates and snoop around a bit. See if she could rattle Tommy. Talk to the other foremen, see what any of them knew. She'd bring Patrick Kelly in case they had to deal with Róisín. She hugged her father. He was stiff at first, and then she felt his hands on her back. "I hope you never go through this," he said. "I wouldn't wish it on my worst enemy." He pushed her back a little and stared into her eyes. His grip tightened; he was almost hurting her. "I wouldn't even wish it on Johnny O'Reilly."

CHAPTER 30

CORMAC FINALLY HAD THE NECKTIE IN HIS POSSESSION, BUT SO FAR all he'd learned was the maker. It was a Patrick Francis tie and they were sold in numerous outlets in Ireland and online. It felt and looked brand-new; Johnny O'Reilly had been the first and last man to ever wear this tie. Cormac stood in the Garda Station and held it in front of him, eliciting a few chuckles from nearby guards. "Can I buy one in town?"

"Trying to class up your act?" one quipped.

"Can't hurt to try."

The garda suggested a few shops in town that might have something similar.

Cormac snapped a photograph of the tie; it would be less sensational than flashing an evidence bag around the shop. He headed out to town, hopping on the bicycle he'd rented for the duration of his stay. He could hoof it easy enough, but went for the bicycle in case he needed to return to the station in a hurry. As he rode, enjoying the wind in his face, that sharp ocean tang, and the irrefutable beauty that blessed the Dingle Peninsula, he chewed on the case. Noticeably absent from Johnny O'Reilly's pockets: a mobile phone, keys, and a wallet. Cormac knew this murder wasn't the result of a random thief. Why take his wallet and mobile phone? *Evidence.* Something incriminating on the phone or in the wallet? Something that would lead to his killer? What keys would O'Reilly have had on him? Had the murderer kept them? Needed to open something? Or had the killer tossed them into the raging ocean? When it came to solving murders, the Atlantic was not their friend.

Another thread he had dangling was information on Brendan Healy. So far, the private investigator he'd hired to nose into it hadn't come up with a thing. Was he still in America? Alive or dead?

Dimpna Wilde had left him a voice mail about Aisling, that she purportedly blew up her father's and granny's alibis and had a backpack full of stones. It wasn't that he didn't believe Dimpna—she hadn't lied to him yet, as far as he knew—but when it came to the O'Reillys, he had to tread carefully, even more so when it involved a child. He was set to interview the widow and son this evening, and he would see if the young girl was around and find a sly way to have a chat with her.

Róisín O'Reilly had come through quickly with one request, giving them access to monitor Johnny O'Reilly's credit card and bank activity, with the warning that she and Sean also used the same cards. But so far, zilch outside of charges made by the other family members. If the murderer wasn't family, and kept those cards, he or she hadn't used them. Cormac would have been shocked if someone had, especially someone as sophisticated as the killer. They still had to monitor them. Everything had to be done by the book. At its worst, detecting work was a constant loop of tedious dead ends, akin to banging one's head repeatedly against a stone wall.

Cormac had also filed a request for Johnny O'Reilly's phone records. The request had been granted, but it was a waiting game. That reminded him of another set of mobile phone records they were waiting on—the fisherman's. Was Finbar a drug user? Cormac hadn't heard anyone say he was, but who knew what men did to cope when they were out at sea for long periods of time? If he was worried about incriminating evidence, it was odd that the fisherman didn't just toss the phone into the ocean. Cormac had a theory. Finbar hadn't stopped at Clogher Strand just for a smoke that morning. He'd stopped because he was supposed to meet someone there, or he was waiting for a call and wanted somewhere secluded, somewhere no one would overhear him. Something so private, he drove all the way out to that strand early in the morning . . . But then . . . he saw Johnny's body. After that, he'd had a total freak-out and, sensical or not, decided to bury the phone on his property. *Had he been lured out to Clogher Strand?* What if the killer wanted the body found as soon as possible? Cormac was definitely going to have to pay another visit to the fisherman, but first he had loose ends to tie up. Given he was all alone, his "tie" pun was lost in the wind, but he got a chuckle out of it nonetheless.

Colorful shops and restaurants lined the streets of downtown Dingle. Cormac soon found himself at a clothing shop that sold fine menswear. He leaned his bicycle against the shop wall, partially curious to test his theory that despite the recent murder, Dingle was a safe place to reside. Or maybe there was a tiny part of him who would welcome an adrenaline-filled chase if any hooligan tried to nick his ride. The shop fit Cormac's definition for overpriced and haughty, with bells dinging as he entered, classical music playing in the background—perhaps embedded with hypnotic suggestions to upgrade the old wardrobe—and a tailor standing at the ready, wielding his measuring tape.

The shopkeeper was pinched but polite, insisting the store had never carried that particular tie, but admiring it nonetheless, and then trying to sell Cormac something, anything, that might make him look and feel like a better man. Cormac led him on a bit before politely declining and asked after similar shops in town. The shopkeeper reluctantly gave him two other possibilities. Cormac headed for the second shop where he received a quick answer— *No.* The shop was more touristy, the ties with shamrocks and leprechauns and all that shite. Cormac asked a follow-up question: Had anyone come in in the past month inquiring about ties? *No.* He made his way to the third and final shop that carried men's ties. This one was less ritzy than the first and less touristy than the second. Cormac laid eyes on the clerk. Perhaps Goldilocks would get her porridge after all. He was a bald man with red-framed glasses. He wore a light gray suit, white shirt, and a tie very similar to the one found on their victim, only his had polka dots instead of stripes. Cormac quickly turned into a customer and seconds later was a proud owner of his own Patrick Francis red tie. He flashed the photo of the tie found on O'Reilly. Before he could pose his questions, the clerk spoke.

"I didn't think you'd actually follow up on it," he said. "Your hands full with murder and all."

Cormac felt that prickly sensation at the base of his neck. "Here I am," he said. "Following up on it." He had no idea what "it" was, but he was keen to find out.

"Did you catch someone?" The clerk cocked his head and waited for an answer.

"I need to go over the incident again."

"How is it you have a picture of it? Did you catch the little . . ." He stopped speaking then silently mouthed *thieving bastard*. Or something like it.

"Let's just go over the incident again, shall we?"

The clerk nodded. "He came in Friday morning to purchase it. For the fundraiser. You heard about the poor woman who died of cancer, did ya?"

"I did." Cormac had to regulate his breathing; he could feel the adrenaline pumping.

"He said he needed a tie to attend the fundraiser. Only, he didn't have enough money. Thirty euro short. I says to him, how on earth are you going to donate to the fundraiser if you spend your last bob on a tie? I offered him other ties; he said it had to be this one. Which was odd in itself—"

"Why was it odd?"

"Someone special-ordered this tie about a month ago and then when it arrived, they called back and said they'd already found it somewhere else."

"Who made that call?"

"I haven't the faintest notion."

"You didn't get a name?"

The clerk shook his head. "Only that it was a special order and he would pick it up."

"Didn't he give you a call-back number?"

"He said his number was changing but promised to come into the shop the next month to pick it up."

"I would think you would have required a credit card."

He pursed his lips. No one liked being criticized. "I don't usually get scammed. Call me old-fashioned. I still think a man's word should mean something." He shook his head sadly.

"You're saying that the person who actually came to get this tie was not the person who actually ordered the tie?" Cormac felt like he was being wrapped in a knot.

"It sat here for six weeks. I had no choice but to find another customer."

Six weeks. Premeditated indeed. "And do you have any idea who this customer was?"

"Of course, I do. He owes me thirty euro. When I said I couldn't give him a discount and no, he couldn't have the tie until he paid up, the (*thieving bastard*) yanked it straight out of the box and did a runner." He'd mouthed the curse words again.

Cormac nodded sympathetically. "And you called the Gardaí?"

"Right as rain I did. It's still stealing even if he paid fifty euro, isn't it?"

"Of course."

"A guard took down my info, and I've been waiting ever since. I assumed with the murder and all I'd never hear back—" He stopped mid-sentence and gasped. "Does this have anything to do with the murder?"

"Absolutely not," Cormac said. "Not a thing."

The man cocked his head. "You're a detective inspector, are you not?"

Cormac grinned. "And you're a respected shopkeeper who not only wants to keep his reputation intact, he wouldn't want to say anything, and I mean anything, to anyone about my inquiries. Heaven forbid they might think you had something to do with it?"

"Me?" His eyes widened. "Apologies for being nosy. I won't say a word." His accompanying wink did nothing to convince Cormac.

"Who was the 'thieving bastard'?" Cormac said, enunciating the words clearly. "Do you know?"

"Would you like to see for yourself, Detective Inspector? I have him on CCTV."

"I'm definitely going to want to take the CCTV footage, but given I'm new in town, and I'd like a name—"

"Donnecha Wilde," the clerk said. "Donnecha Wilde is the *(thieving bastard)* who stole that tie."

The minute Cormac arrived back at the station, a guard poked his head out the door. He was grinning.

"Lay it on me," Cormac said.

"The Technical Bureau successfully hacked into Finbar Malone's phone." The guard pumped his fist. "We've just received the readout, and it's waiting for you." Cormac whooped. "They said there are deleted photos they haven't retrieved yet—so far, just the text."

Cormac double-timed it to the incident room. D.S. Neely was perched on the edge of a table. "I want Donnecha Wilde hauled in here," he said. Neely caught the eye of a guard standing by the door. "Did you hear that?"

"Yes, D.S. Neely. Inspector." He nodded and headed out the door. Neely handed Cormac the transcript and soon everyone in the vicinity was gathered around to read it.

Did you get the photo? :)
You bastard
What would the wife think?
I'll kill you, you little maggot
Three thousand euro or we send it to the missus

"Blackmail of some sort," Cormac said. "Let's hope the tech team is able to get us that photo."

"Finbar Malone is on his way in as we speak," Neely said.

"Brilliant." He glanced at his watch. "Donnecha Wilde bought the green tie at a shop in Dingle on Friday morning."

"Jaysus," she said. "Speaking of Donnecha Wilde—I just got a call from the Dingle Inn. They have the CCTV footage ready. I figured I would go and have a look."

"Please," he said. "After we have a little chat with Finbar Malone and Donnecha Wilde. I have that meeting at the O'Reillys."

She nodded, then flashed a grin. "I'd say we're sucking diesel now, Inspector."

He grinned back. "Indeed."

Another guard poked his head in. "State pathologist is on the phone for you, Inspector."

When it rained, it poured. "I'll take it in my office." He hurried to his cramped space, and they transferred the call.

"Inspector O'Brien."

After exchanging pleasantries, she got right to the point. "I pulled some strings and headquarters rushed the toxicology. Release was detected in the bloods but not at high enough levels to kill our victim."

"Tell me you have a cause of death?"

"I'm afraid that's the bad news. In addition to Release, we ran our standard toxicology screening and nothing turned up." She paused. "I can run additional tests, but of course I'll need specific suggestions of what we might be looking for."

"What about . . ." What was it called? Monster in a Bottle. "Hold on." He rummaged through his notes and returned to the call. "There used to be a euthanasia medicine that vets whipped up on the sly. Immobolin. It's a combination of acepromazine and etorphine."

"You're right, you're right. A single drop of it would do the trick." She paused. "But they wouldn't have had to inject him—and we did find an injection mark on the neck as well as Release in the body. I'll run the test, but it's a puzzler why someone would use both substances when the one would have done—no need even for a syringe."

"I believe Release was a red herring." *To frame Eamon Wilde.*

"Interesting. Okay, I'll run another report for acepromazine and etorphine. But I can't promise they'll be able to rush this one."

"I understand. Please order the report." He felt a buzzing in his skull as he hung up. Things were clicking in place, but what did they all mean? Donnecha had been living on the boat. It might suggest he was estranged from his parents? Saoirse said she saw a man all in black exit the boat that evening. That could have been Donnecha. They only had his word for it that he went to the Dingle Inn. They'd have to see what the CCTV yielded. Donnecha would have had access to vet meds, and the tarot card. Cormac wasn't sure how he fit in with Last Dance. Perhaps that was a red herring as well. Given the auto body shop was across from the clinic, Donnecha could have broken in and nicked automotive paint for the stones. They were still waiting on a judge's order to enter the auto body shop. He'd have to amp up the pressure now that more evidence was coming in. The waiting game was maddening. But he was getting closer. He'd let his fascination—let's face it, his infatuation—with Dimpna Wilde cloud his judgment. Being perpetually single was becoming a job hazard. He needed a social life. Play a little trad music, throw back a few jars, meet a nice woman. One whose family wasn't the subject of his murder probe. Keep his wits about him. No more fantasizing about the enigmatic doc. He'd been scripting a story about her, about them, telling himself they had a connection, a chemistry, marveling over the thrill that shuddered through him whenever he locked eyes with her. He'd been thinking about her nonstop. Unprofessional! *Cop on.* He needed a clear head. Perhaps she had been playing him. Perhaps one of the Wildes was their cunning killer after all.

CHAPTER 31

FINBAR MALONE WAS HAVING A HARD TIME SITTING STILL. CORMAC wanted to grab his bouncing knee and put him in a wrestling hold, but given they were in an interview room at the Garda Station, it probably wasn't wise.

"Do you need to see the texts again?" Cormac asked.

Finbar turned his face away. "No."

Cormac leaned in. "What's going on here?"

"Blackmail."

"Who's blackmailing you?"

"Dunno."

Cormac sighed. "You must know something, otherwise it's not a very effective blackmail scheme, now is it?"

"Huh?"

Neely leaned in. "Finbar. Work with us here. What do you know?"

"Some colleen gets me drunk, you know? Chats me up in the pub. Next thing I know, she wants to take me to her fancy boat for a nightcap."

"What fancy boat?"

"At the harbor. I should have known it was the O'Reillys' boat."

Cormac snapped to attention. "Johnny's boat?"

"Who else?"

"Was he there?"

"No." Finbar's eyes shifted to a spot over their heads. "I have no idea why he was letting that hooligan let out his boat."

Donnecha Wilde. "Was Donnecha on the boat?" Cormac asked.

Finbar shook his head. "I didn't see him. But I know the boat. Everyone knew Donnecha was living on it and none of us could figure out why. The Wildes and O'Reillys hate each other."

Cormac gave it a beat. "Who was the woman?"

Finbar rubbed his chin. "Said her name was Candy. I have my doubts."

You think? "Then what?" Cormac pressed.

Finbar shook his head. "She wants to give me a tour. Next thing I know I'm down in the cabin. She fixes me a drink. Then I wake up on the pier. Couldn't remember a thing. Get myself home and next thing I know she sends me a photo."

Cormac leaned in. Now they were getting somewhere. "Do you still have this photo?"

Finbar squirmed in his seat. "It's not what it looks like."

"Let me see it and maybe I make your little problems with the Gardaí go away." Cormac leaned back and folded his hands across his stomach, wanting to convey this was just a friendly chat, and they could help each other out.

Finbar narrowed his eyes. "Didn't realize I got problems with ye."

Cormac focused on his breath. Neely took over. "You lied to a detective inspector during a murder inquiry. You'd better believe that's a problem."

He shifted in his seat, glanced at Cormac. "Sorry. Didn't realize you cared that much about me mobile phone."

"Let's see the photo," Cormac said, leaving the lukewarm apology sitting in the air.

"I deleted it. But then they sent me this." He reached in his pocket and slid a printed photo across the table. Cormac picked it up. Finbar Malone was reposed on the built-in seating in the cabin of the yacht. His head was back and his eyes were open but he looked absolutely blotto. In between his legs, you could make out the back of a woman's head. She had wavy black hair. You could see feminine shoulders and a brief profile of a lipsticked mouth. It looked like Finbar was getting a blow job.

Finbar rubbed his beard. "My first thought was pity that I didn't remember it."

Neely piped up. "They sent this photo to you, then asked for three thousand euro or else they'd send this to your wife?"

Finbar bobbed his head. "That's exactly right."

"Where were you supposed to deliver the money?" Cormac kept his voice measured, despite the adrenaline pumping through him.

"You're the inspector. You haven't figured that out yet?"

Clogher Strand. Early Sunday morning. Fuck. Why didn't Cormac have Finbar's truck searched? He'd been too obsessed with the scene on the beach. "You had the three thousand euro with you that morning?"

"Are you joking me? I don't have that kind of bob. I had a crowbar with me." Neely shook her head slightly. "Not that I planned on using it on a person, or anything like that."

"Did you see anyone there at all?" Cormac needed answers. He needed more.

"Just Mr. O'Reilly. Dead as a doornail."

"Do you have reason to believe that Donnecha Wilde was behind this?" Neely shot Cormac a look as if she didn't approve of the question. She was right; it was somewhat leading, but this wasn't a court of law. It was his interrogation and he was going to use every tool at his disposal. And no doubt, the man sitting in front of him was a bit of a tool.

"I dunno," Finbar said.

"What do you know?" Cormac quipped.

"I know one thing. Yer one was wearing a wig." Finbar wiggled his eyebrows as his head bobbed between Cormac and Neely.

"This woman?" Cormac studied the photo. Now that Finbar mentioned it, the hair was a bit skewed. It could be a piece, alright.

"That's right." Finbar sunk into his chair. "I'm starting to think I didn't even get a blow job."

Cormac turned his laugh into a cough. "Dollar to doughnuts? I'd say you're spot-on."

"Am I in trouble? When I didn't even get a blow job?"

"Did you pay her for sex?" Neely asked.

"Hell, no." The fisherman's cheeks blazed red.

"Then you're grand," Neely said.

"Am I free to leave? Are you going to tell my wife?"

"I don't see why we'd have to do that," Cormac said. "But we can't stop gossip, as you know. You might want to tell her yourself."

Finbar shook his head. "I won't be doing that, now." Cormac and Neely stood, and Finbar followed suit. He headed for the door.

"Just one more question," Cormac said when the fisherman was nearly gone. "Why were you trying to bury your mobile phone?"

"Bury my mobile?" He shook his head. "Must have fallen in while I was digging the hole. I was burying a wild rabbit. Thought the woman vet would have told you that."

Later that afternoon, Neely handed Cormac the department iPad loaded up with CCTV footage from the Dingle Inn. It was from Saturday, the day of the murder. The time in the corner read 5 P.M. Cormac watched as Donnecha Wilde entered the lobby, nodded at the clerk, and headed to an elevator bank. The footage then switched to Donnecha getting off on the third floor.

"What time does he leave the inn?"

"Not until Sunday morning."

"Are you sure?"

"Positive." That was a solid alibi. He wasn't their killer. "I can switch to Sunday morning, to show you when he leaves the room again, but there's something else." She fast-forwarded to 9 P.M. A man exited the room Donnecha had entered. He was dressed in denims, a long plaid shirt, and a cap. He kept his head down, never once lifting his face to the cameras.

"Do you think that could be a woman?" Cormac asked.

Neely replayed the footage. "It's grainy, the clothes are baggy, and the person never looks at the camera. I wouldn't have thought woman, but I suppose it's possible."

"How do we know that's not Donnecha?"

She fast-forwarded again. "Because of this." Eleven P.M. A delivery boy carrying a sack knocked on Donnecha's door. Donnecha stuck his head out the door, then stepped out to pay. It was clearly him.

"Then who the hell is the other man?" Cormac's pulse ticked up.

Neely replayed the footage. "That's what we'll need to find out."

"This is maddening."

"I agree."

Cormac talked through the time line. "Saoirse Griffin saw a man dressed in all-black leaving the boat at approximately 10:45 P.M." He looked again at the stranger in the footage. "Plaid and denims. Does this rule him out as the man Saoirse witnessed?"

Neely cocked her head. "Maybe he changed on the boat?"

"Is there any footage of anyone even getting on the boat?"

Neely sighed. "The harbormaster said high winds interfered with the cameras that weekend. And by the time the boat leaves, the harbor is congested with people."

"Someone had been counting on that." *Someone local.* His phone buzzed. He glanced at it. "We've got Donnecha Wilde and Sheila Maguire here."

"Sheila Maguire?" D.S. Neely couldn't hide her surprise.

"Finbar said the woman who scammed him was wearing a wig. There was something familiar about her. I believe it's Sheila Maguire."

Neely tilted her head. "You can tell that from her shoulder?"

"What can I say? I'm observant." He grinned.

"Sheila Maguire is a hot mess," Neely said. "But maybe that's your type?"

"I'm investigating a case, not swiping through dating profiles," Cormac said. "And a little bird told me that Sheila Maguire's behavior patterns had changed recently."

"What do you mean?"

"Apparently, when she was still working at the Wilde Clinic, she started dressing up and going out. This little bird thought she had a secret boyfriend. I think she had herself a little blackmailing scheme."

Neely groaned. "Niamh Dowd is your eyes and ears at the Wilde Clinic?"

Cormac shrugged. "I'll never tell."

"Be careful. That one gets crushes like kids get snotty noses."

"Are you saying I'm irresistible?" He grinned.

"To a twenty-something receptionist who's never been off the peninsula? I'd say you're a regular Prince Fecking Charming." Neely was rarely cheeky. When he recovered from his shock, Cormac laughed. Were they bonding? It felt like they were bonding.

"She's a good kid," Cormac said. "I didn't turn on the old charm. I just asked her for an old-fashioned favor."

"Dimpna Wilde isn't going to be happy when she finds out you're using her staff to spy on her."

He looked away, feeling his face grow hot. "It's not my job to please Dimpna Wilde." *But boyo, I would like nothing better.* Enough. *Jaysus.* What was happening to him? Even his mam had said something about how often he'd been mentioning her name. Was he compromised? Should he be on this case? No. More. Roaming. Thoughts.

Neely perched on a nearby desk and folded her arms. "I see the way you look at her."

"Same way I look at everyone."

Neely scoffed and gave him a look. "I'd stay away from her as well."

"Are you warning me off all women, or just those three?"

Neely laughed. "Once this case is over, you're free to woo whomever you'd like."

He laughed. "Wooing," he said. "Not really my style."

"Sheila Maguire did have access to those vet meds," Neely said. "I suppose it's within the realm of possibility that she's involved." Neely chewed on her lip. "But to what end?"

Cormac picked up his case files and headed for the door. "Hopefully we're about to find out."

Donnecha Wilde and Sheila Maguire were brought in together then led to separate interrogation rooms. Cormac went back and forth on which subject he should speak with first. Finally he decided on Donnecha. If Sheila was involved, he'd bet she was the brains behind whatever operation the duo had going. D.S. Neely took her seat first. Cormac thumped a file down on the table, making Donnecha jump. He set Finbar Malone's burner phone on top of it. Donnecha eyed it then glanced away.

"Recognize it?" Cormac said, holding it up.

"Should I?" The pitch of Donnecha's voice raised as he slouched in the hard chair.

Neely kept her gaze on the folder in front of her as she spoke. "According to the clerk at the shop, you've been buying a lot of burner phones."

Donnecha waited to see if she would make eye contact, and when she didn't, he shifted in his seat, making it squeak. "Is that a crime?"

"What are you doing with the phones?" Cormac asked.

Donnecha shrugged. "I have a lot of friends."

"Is that what you call them?" Cormac turned to Neely. "Want to read me the text exchange that Donnecha had with one of his many friends?"

"I'd love to, so I would." Neely cleared her throat. "'Did you get the photo? Smiley-face emoji. You bastard. What would the wife think? I'll kill you, you little maggot. Three thousand euro or we send it to the missus.'"

Donnecha folded his arms and hung his head. "That must not be my phone. I don't recognize that exchange."

"We have your phone at the counter now," Detective O'Brien said.

"You can't look in my phone," Donnecha said. "That's illegal."

"I think a judge would be intrigued enough to let me have a look," Cormac said.

"Judge is awful friendly lately, isn't he?" Neely said. "Especially when there's a high-profile murder inquiry underway."

"I wonder if Sheila Maguire will have anything to add to the conversation," Cormac said. "I believe whoever talks first gets the better deal."

"That's always the way, isn't it?" Neely said. "Early bird gets the worm."

Cormac leaned forward. "And just so we're clear. The worm gets to stay out of jail."

"We know this is you, or Sheila, on this text exchange, and we know this was sent to Finbar Malone," Neely said.

"Chatty fella, Malone, isn't he?" Cormac said.

"Ah, he is, so." Neely smiled and nodded. "Regular chin-wagger that one." Donnecha's face was passive, but Cormac could feel the heat radiating off of him.

"Were you working on behalf of Johnny O'Reilly?" Cormac asked Donnecha.

Donnecha looked away. "No."

"I'm going to have Garda Neely read you that text exchange again."

"It's not necessary."

"Let's take it from the top, Garda."

Neely started again. "'Did you get the photo?'"

"Is there a photo?" Donnecha interrupted. He was trying to sound cool, but Cormac could see he was sweating.

"What do you think, Mr. Wilde?" Cormac asked. "Care to explain the photo?"

Donnecha folded his arms across his chest. "I'd like to see it first."

"Seems like you'd remember a photo like that," Neely said.

"You're right about one thing," Cormac said. "I don't think his wife would like it." He removed the photo Finbar had given them from the pocket of his blazer and slid it across the table. Donnecha stared at it and swallowed.

"The wife would definitely not like it," D.S. Neely agreed. "Who would?"

"I'm not in that photo," Donnecha said. "You can't prove I had anything to do with it."

"It took place on Johnny O'Reilly's boat," Cormac said. "You were the caretaker. I guess we'll have to let Sean and Róisín O'Reilly know that you let strangers onto their yacht."

"Fine. It was a job," Donnecha said. "Is that what you want to hear?"

Cormac shook his head. "I think you're going to have to keep talking."

"Johnny O'Reilly said I could live on his boat if I helped him collect on a few debts."

"What kind of debts?"

"They weren't for Johnny, per se."

"Who were they for? Per se?" Cormac asked.

"One-armed Tommy."

"You were collecting debts for Tommy Healy?" D.S. Neely said.

Donnecha nodded. "He's a mad poker player, and gambler. People think he cheats, and they've stopped paying him. Johnny had a whole list, mostly fishermen, who owed Tommy money. O'Reilly was sick of hearing about it, that and he was sick of Tommy always getting into fisticuffs trying to get his money back. He said if I collected the debts, I could keep twenty-five percent and live on the boat."

Cormac shook his head. "You're threatening an entire bastion of fishermen?"

"One at a time." Donnecha grinned. It soon faded as Cormac continued to stare at him. "Not exactly threatening them," he added.

"Tell me about the photo."

Donnecha squirmed. "She wasn't really doing it, you see? We got them drunk, waited until they passed out, and then all she had to do was make it look like she was doing it."

"To be clear," D.S. Neely said. "When you say 'she,' you're referring to whom?"

"Sheila Maguire," Donnecha said.

Cormac mentally pumped his fist in the air. "Do you have a matching photo on your mobile? Otherwise we're going to see everything on your phone whether it relates to this case or not."

"If you'd kindly retrieve me phone, I'll show you."

Cormac was hoping he'd say that. He removed Donnecha's mobile from his pocket and slid it across the table. This would be way faster than waiting for a warrant. Donnecha typed in a password then swiped through the phone. He then slid it back to them. Cormac picked it up. It was the exact same photo of Finbar Malone seated in the cabin. His head was thrown back, mouth open, eyes closed. *Passed out*—but you wouldn't know that from looking at the photo. The gesture could be one of a man in the heat of the moment. "Was Finbar Malone drugged?"

"No," Donnecha said. "Just passed out from the drink. I swear. And we certainly didn't have to pour it down his gob."

"Why would Sheila Maguire involve herself in this sordid mess?" Neely said, a note of sadness in her voice. "She's a hardworking vet tech. Does volunteer tours around Dingle. I was hoping you were wrong about her involvement." She gave Cormac a look. "Good instincts, Inspector. Well played."

Donnecha looked stricken. "You mean you were just guessing?"

"You sit tight," Cormac said pushing back from the table. "You need anything?"

"Can I smoke?"

"No."

"Can I leave?"

"No."

"What if I want a solicitor?"

"You can ask. But I'm not going to give you any credit for helping us."

"I've answered enough of your questions."

"You haven't answered hardly any yet," Cormac said. "But I'm hoping that's about to change."

"I'm not actually giving him any pleasure," Sheila said, pushing the photo back across the table. "His pants aren't even down."

Cormac shook his head. "Let me see if I have this straight. You get these men drunk—"

"They get themselves drunk—"

"You pretend you're performing fellatio on them, then snap a photo and use it to blackmail them?"

Sheila shrugged and looked at her nails. They were bitten to the quick. The tough woman exterior was just an act. "Is it really blackmail if they owe the money anyway?"

"Yes," Cormac said. "Believe me, I have plenty of evidence to charge you and Donnecha with blackmail."

She shifted her eyes to Neely, then back to him. "Then why haven't you?"

"Because I'd rather solve a murder probe. And given this little scam involved Johnny O'Reilly and Tommy Healy, I'm wondering if you didn't just piss off the wrong man."

Sheila frowned. "You think someone killed Johnny O'Reilly over this?"

"Is it possible?"

She shook her head. "So far, everyone has paid but Finbar." She stopped. "Oh my God. He found the body. Do you think it's him?"

"Where were these victims supposed to meet you to pay up?" Cormac asked.

She chewed on her lip. "Clogher Strand."

Cormac pounded the table. She jumped. "You didn't think it was relevant to come to me with this?"

"I truly thought it was just a coincidence. Honestly. It was a bit of a laugh. If there's anything more to it, it's Tommy Healy you should be grilling."

"Why do you say that?" Cormac crossed his arms and waited.

"Tommy is the one who was owed the money. He's the one who always showed up to collect. He said he liked seeing the look of horror on their faces." She exhaled. "He's one sick puppy."

"And what are you?" Neely asked sharply. "A bed of roses?"

Sheila glowered and pressed her lips together.

Cormac leaned in. "Are you telling me Tommy Healy was at Clogher Strand the morning the body was discovered?"

"I'm saying he was supposed to be. Whether he was or not, only he can say."

"Have you had any communication with Tommy Healy about that matter?" Cormac was tired of her nonchalance.

"What?"

"Did you ask him?" Neely said. Her tone was cross.

"No." She twirled a strand of red hair around her finger. "I figured with the discovery of the body, the pickup was botched. Otherwise I assume Tommy would have reached out to us. That's how it worked. He'd collect from one and call us to set up another. There have been no calls since the murder."

Cormac jotted down a note. "Where were you the night of the murder?"

"At O'Connell's."

"The other vet in town?" he asked.

She nodded. "You can check with him."

"I will." He paused. "And Donnecha? Where was he?"

"All I know is that he wasn't on the boat."

"And how do you know that?"

"Donnecha said he'd received a message from Tommy Healy. Johnny would be at the dance until late and he wanted the boat."

"Blackmail is a serious charge," Cormac said, and Neely nodded in agreement.

Sheila chewed on her lip. "It was only a bit of fun. It got out of hand."

"A bit of fun?" Neely said. "Why would you do this, Sheila? You've got a good head on your shoulders, or at least I thought so. A decent job. You're an attractive woman. I can't make sense of it."

Sheila crossed her arms and slid down in her seat. "Sometimes life is just so . . . mundane. Don't ye think? I mean, don't you ever feel like you're going mad? I never have been one for the drink, or drugs. But I always liked a little mischief. I wasn't trying to hurt anyone. We were just collecting debts. And having a little fun."

"Have you ever heard of yoga?" Neely said.

"Are you having any fun now?" Cormac asked. "Because you're in a heap of trouble."

Sheila straightened out. "What if I helped you out a little more?"

Cormac tapped his biro on the folder. "We're listening."

Sheila's eyes shifted between them as if trying to figure out which one was the weakest link. "I'll need something in writing."

Cormac shook his head. "I can't do that unless I know what you're on about."

She looked to Neely who only nodded. Sheila took a deep breath, sat up straight, and folded her hands on the table in front of her. "Did Donnecha Wilde mention that eight months ago a stranger came to town?"

CHAPTER 32

*T*HE VIDEO CALL CAME AFTER EIGHT EXCRUCIATING HOURS. DIMPNA was in the courtyard and answered immediately. Ben appeared on the screen, a plain white wall behind him. His sandy hair was mussed up and his eyes were red. She fought back the urge to lecture. *Are you eating? Are you sleeping? Are you drinking too much? Do you hate me?* Despite looking rough today, he was so handsome. He'd been through so much in the last few years. Pain she hadn't been able to soothe. Her son. Her beautiful son.

"Are you okay?" She had been willing herself not to cry, but her voice wobbled. She wanted him with her. She wanted to shake him and then hug him. She wanted to sit for hours and listen to the details of his trip. She wanted her happy lad back. She'd done this to him. "I didn't tell you because I couldn't," she said. "I didn't want him to win."

His jaw set. "I had a right to know."

"We need to have a long discussion. In person. But I am so, so sorry."

"Sorry because you've been lying to me my entire life or sorry because you got caught?"

The image of her bus rose in front of her: *Liar.* "Because I got caught," she said.

"That's my mam. When she decides to be honest it's the brutal variety."

"It's too difficult to lie. Too much to keep track of."

He leaned in. "You know I would never hurt anyone, don't you?"

"Of course."

"I wasn't on that boat."

She held up her hand and glanced around. The old Lab by the door lifted his head. "Don't say anything more over the phone. Are you safe?"

"Yes."

"Do you need money?"

He shook his head. "I know what happened back then was awful. But . . . I think he's changed. He's been good to me."

Sean. Ben's voice sounded stilted. *Rehearsed.* Was someone there with him? Listening? "Does Sean know where you are?"

There was a slight hesitation and she watched her son wrestle with whether or not he was going to lie to his mammy. Again. "Yes."

She closed her eyes briefly. Ben did not react well to anger. If she got angry, he would get defensive and probably hang up. "I don't think you should tell Sean where you are. Can you go somewhere else? If Róisín finds out—"

"He hasn't even told his wife," Ben said. "He wouldn't betray me."

"You can't tell Sean that I know that he knows." She couldn't believe the sentence was coming out of her mouth. But Dimpna had been giving this a lot of thought. Sean hadn't confronted her about Ben because somehow he planned on using it to his advantage. She didn't know exactly how, or what his endgame was, but he'd always been a master at playing games. Ben wrinkled his brow. "You're not listening. He's on our side."

"I hope that's true." *Not a chance.* "But you need to stay away until they catch the killer." *Tommy Healy.* It all fit. It had to be him. "And no one can know where you are."

"No one does except for Sean."

That stung. But there was no time for self-pity or games. And if Ben stopped talking to Sean, he might get suspicious. Dimpna had to be so careful how she handled this. So, so careful. She had to understand exactly what she was dealing with first. There had been a thought-out plan, one misstep and everything would be gone. Her son. Her parents. Not just their reputations, but them. Once a person had killed, they were probably comfortable doing it

again. The first time, he or she might wrestle with his or her con-
science, but after that . . . wouldn't it be smooth sailing? She needed
to understand every aspect of the killer's plan or she would be out-
played. At least that's what her little voice was screaming at her. And
little voices didn't usually scream, or they'd be called big voices. But
it was screaming at her now. This was a three-alarm fire, and she
was going to listen.

"You have to stay safe until the murderer is behind bars." *The tie
was my idea.* It had to be Tommy. He checked all the boxes.

"Were you ever going to tell me?"

The truth, Dimpna. Your son is asking for the truth. "No." She thought
of Niall. Did she feel set free? She didn't think so. Maybe it wasn't
automatic. Like everything in life, she supposed. Maybe *one day* this
would set her free. Today was not going to be that day.

"I don't know what to say to that."

"I know. We're going to have to work through it."

"What if I just come to Dingle? Tell the truth?"

"No."

"You're such a hypocrite. You say it all the time—that you have to
tell people the truth no matter how hard it is. You do it day in and
day out for animals. Animals! But lying to your son his entire life
about who his da is—that's perfectly fine!" He was yelling now, that
old anger coursing through his veins.

"I'm so sorry," she said. "You're my world. And I know you don't
understand it—but he is not a good man."

"*Was* not a good man. Was he even a man then?"

"He was twenty years of age."

"That's barely a man."

"He raped me." She held eye contact. "I know that's a horrible
thing for you to deal with. I didn't wish it on you. But now that you
know—I will not sit here and listen to you minimize what he did. I
swallowed it for twenty-seven years. I didn't press charges. I didn't
ask for a dime of their filthy money. I did the right thing by you. I
get that you're angry. But your father was not and is not a good
man. And you will not sanitize the worst thing that ever happened
to me for his benefit. You will not."

Ben reached toward her, then the screen disconnected. He'd

hung up. Oh, God. Did she just say worst thing that ever happened
to her? He knew she wasn't including him in that, didn't he? Of
course, he knew. Her son was not stupid. But he was angry, and
maybe he wasn't listening properly. Maybe he did think she was including him in that statement. What the hell was wrong with her?
Dimpna bit her lip, wishing she could reach out and bring him
back, equally wishing she could push Sean O'Reilly off the edge of
a cliff and watch him fall to his death. If he thought he was going to
take her son away from her, or manipulate him in any way, he had
another think coming. If anything, Sean O'Reilly had just made his
biggest mistake. For the first time in . . . ever? She wasn't afraid of
him. It was he who should be frightened. Of her. No one, and that
went double for him, messed with her son.

Cormac headed for his car with one eye on the dark clouds gath-
ering above him. It was time at last, time to sit down with the
O'Reillys and see what he could squeeze out of them. Sheila
Maguire's alibi for the night of the murder checked out and so did
Donnecha Wilde's. That was something. That was progress. The
real bombshell had been dropped by Sheila Maguire. Ben Wilde.
Dimpna's son. He had been in town the night of the murder. In
fact, he'd been in Dingle for eight months prior without Dimpna's
knowledge. That was jarring enough. Cormac hadn't seen the second punch coming. Ben Wilde was Sean O'Reilly's son, apparently,
something that had only came to light recently through Niall Flor's
suicide note. Why was it every time he turned around, another
Wilde was implicated? Sheila insisted that Dimpna had only just
found out that her son knew about his father and had come to Dingle. Would she tell him? Or would she cover for her son even if he
was a murderer? Cormac wasn't sure he wanted to know the answer, wasn't sure he was ready to see her fall from the pedestal he'd
put her on. But he would have to figure all that out later. Right
now, he had a single mission. He had parked near the harbor so
that he could get a little exercise. Walking helped him think. He
was about to hop into his Toyota when he heard someone shouting
his name. He turned to see D.S. Neely striding toward him with
purpose. She knew he was off to the O'Reilly estate so this must be
important.

"Hey," he said, gesturing to his car. "I'm about to head off." She glanced at the watch on her wrist, tapping it several times. "You could have just rung me."

She finally looked up from her gadget and started marching in place. "I need the steps. I'm only a few hundred away from fireworks."

He grinned. "I figured you had one of those yokes."

"Winner winner chicken dinner."

He grinned. "What's the story?"

"Did you hire a private investigator to dig into Brendan Healy?"

"I did." How did she find out? And why did it piss her off?

"Your man left a message with the station. Said there's no trace of him, and if you want him to keep looking it's going to cost extra."

Shit. "I'll handle it."

"Care to tell me why you're poking into Brendan Healy? He's been gone for ages."

"It's just a loose end," Cormac said. "I was curious."

"Curiosity killed the cat."

"Guess it's good I'm allergic," he quipped. He waited for a laugh. No laugh.

"You can pull on any thread you like, Inspector. But you kept it to yourself, and that's out of bounds."

He sighed. She was right. He still didn't want to be reprimanded. "I was waiting to see if anything came of it."

"Like what?"

"I don't know. The O'Reillys have a lot of money. Money is always a motive in murder. Maybe he felt cheated."

"And crawled out of the woodwork nearly three decades later to kill Johnny O'Reilly?"

He gave it a beat. She was making him dizzy with all that marching in space. "Maybe to blackmail him. And when that didn't work . . ." She held up a finger and tapped at her watch.

"Fireworks. I'm done." She stopped marching and removed an enormous phone from her pocket.

"Fancy." He'd never carry that giant thing around. He was going to keep his flip phone until it disintegrated in his hands.

"It's the latest and greatest," Neely said, letting out a breath and blowing a strand of her fringe straight up. "I bet if I took a photo of the moon you could see the craters." She turned it off, then stuck it back in her pocket. "Now."

"Did you just turn your phone off?"

She looked around. "Better safe than sorry."

"I'm listening."

"Did you know me father was a detective sergeant?"

"I did not."

"He was around just before Brendan Healy vanished."

"Vanished?" Cormac shifted his weight. "I thought he took off for America."

She tilted her head. "That was the story."

"I take it your father had another story?"

"Those Healy lads had a rough start to life. Parents left them on the side of the road at five years of age and drove off into the sunset."

"Jesus."

"They bounced around from home to home, but Brendan kept landing himself in juvie."

"I had no idea."

She shook her head. "That's why it's me you should have come to and not some private dick out of Killarney."

"My deepest apologies."

"Me father had a nickname for the lads. He called them The Good Twin and The Bad Twin. If you haven't guessed, Tommy was The Good Twin."

"Tommy probably liked that one better," Cormac said.

"About a week after Brendan vanished, and Last Dance was killed, Tommy Healy went away for a while."

"Okay."

"Rumor was he was in a psych ward."

"I don't know much about horse racing, but it sounds like he was traumatized."

"Me father was in the station at the time. He was also at the station when he was called out to a farmhouse to listen to a much younger Dimpna Wilde, teary-eyed and panicked, swearing up and down that Sean O'Reilly had just strangled Tommy Healy."

"You've mentioned this prank before." He stopped. "The tie," he said.

"There's that." Neely nodded. "Something you said got me thinking. Creaturely habits. Johnny O'Reilly never did anything that didn't serve him. So you tell me why he's kept Tommy Healy on all these years, even after he stopped racing."

"You have a thought on that?"

"Brendan Healy was a scrapper. The O'Reillys were wealthy and fawning all over his twin. I can't imagine he liked that. Me father said Brendan Healy was a little psychopath." She crossed herself. "You think a lad like that would just up and leave? Without trying to get a piece?"

"Maybe the O'Reillys paid him to leave?" Cormac suggested.

She mulled it over. "Or maybe Dimpna Wilde actually witnessed a murder. She certainly believed it. My da was certain of that."

He edged in. "And what? Brendan Healy has been pretending to be his twin, Tommy, for the past twenty-seven years?"

"It sounds even crazier when you say it out loud."

"Tommy Healy was born without an arm," Cormac said, thinking it through.

"Correct." Neely bit down on her lip and waited.

"Are you saying Brendan Healy had his arm cut off just so he could pretend to be his twin?" It was ludicrous, but he had to think it through.

"He did go away for quite some time," Neely said. "Maybe it wasn't a psych ward. Maybe it was a proper hospital. Somewhere far enough from Dingle that no one would ask questions."

Cormac mulled it over. "The guards were immediately called out to the O'Reillys' when Dimpna accused Sean of murdering Tommy," he said. "Even if Brendan was pretending to be him, there's no way his arm had been severed that quickly."

"True," Neely said. "But how hard would it be to keep your arm by your side with your sleeve hanging down for a spell?"

She had a point there. "I'm sure he could pull that off," Cormac conceded.

Neely's cheeks flushed with satisfaction. "And it's not as if anyone was suspicious that Tommy wasn't Tommy—Gardaí were checking on whether he was alive or dead," she said. "And I'm sure Dimpna's shock at seeing him alive had knocked everything else out of her poor head."

"And it would explain why 'Tommy' never rode a horse again," Cormac added.

"Spot-on," Neely said.

In order for any of this to be true it would mean that Brendan Healy either knew and helped plan, or stood aside while his twin was murdered and then helped the murderer get off by eventually cutting off his own arm and pretending to be his brother for the rest of his life. That would make him a psychopath, alright. Was he? "How the hell could we prove any of this?"

"I don't see how we can." She reached into her pocket again, pulled out something wrapped in plastic, and thrust it at him. "Best lemon tart in town."

"Thought you were browned off with me."

She eyed it like a lover. "If I eat it, I'll have to march for two hours." She started off. "Good luck with Widow O'Reilly."

"Hey." She stopped. Waited. "If your crazy theory is right—why now? Why would Brendan Healy kill Johnny O'Reilly now?"

"I'm not convinced he did," Neely said. "It's just a possible part of a much larger picture." She smiled, then headed off again.

"Has anyone ever told you that you can be maddening?" Cormac yelled after her.

"Me husband," she said. "Nearly every fecking day."

CHAPTER 33

*T*HE SUN WAS STARTING TO SINK INTO THE HORIZON WHEN CORMAC finally set off for the O'Reilly estate, coating the skies in three shades of pink. The massive estate and racing barns were situated a short drive outside of Dingle town at the base of Mount Brandon, one of ten highest mountain peaks in Ireland. Cormac had hiked the ridge numerous times in his twenties, alone and with lovers, and friends, and then alone again. And as the mountains came into view, he felt a stirring to do it yet again. There was something powerful about walking in the footsteps of thousands of others. Named after Saint Brendan, Mount Brandon was at the center of the Brandon Group, a ridge of seven peaks, and a popular destination for hill walkers and pilgrimages. The mountain was made of red sandstone, which gave the range its purplish-reddish color. Green slopes on one side, juxtaposed with sharp cliffs and craggy rocks on the other. It was known for the best ridge walks in the country.

Upon approach, Cormac felt a rare twinge of jealousy. The O'Reilly estate was in a sweet spot, granting them outstanding views not only of Mount Brandon, but of The Three Sisters mountain peaks, an iconic and adorable sighting, and of course the ever-churning, wild Atlantic Ocean. They could keep their fancy cars, and fancy clothes, and elite club memberships, but Cormac was a sucker for a stunning view. As he pulled up the winding drive leading to the estate, he was struck how a collection of sleek white barns, rectangular in shape, contrasted with a stately three-story manor house made of limestone. They were at odds yet somehow blended seamlessly. Perhaps it was due to the matching ruby trim that had been painted around the doorways and window frames of every building on the property. (Cormac assumed this was done after Ruby's big win). The manor house and three large barns were so far apart that if one wanted a cohesive photo, one would need to take them from the sky.

It wasn't until Cormac was pulling closer to the estate and was waved on by employees with white-gloved hands that the chasm between the O'Reillys and well, basically everyone else he ever fucking met, crystalized. He was a bit shocked they'd even given him this case in the first place, and he was starting to suspect he was like a piece of meat his superiors were throwing to the wolves. If Cormac wanted to adopt a brighter outlook, perhaps he was chosen because he wasn't a man swayed by money. He didn't believe one could draw a line between a person's bank account and their worth. The Three Sisters mountains aside, money, greed, and power were the triple peaks the O'Reillys operated under.

Cormac parked the car in a spot that no less than six gloved men guided him toward. He thought of his intelligent and humble mam, already rehearsing the details with which to regale her with this evening. As she'd often stated, true happiness came from day-to-day experiences—listening to big band on the radio while rain drummed on the roof, reading a book of poetry by a crackling fire, savoring each line, or simply clutching a mug of hot tea and watching the steam rise from the surface. True beauty was sown in the fertile land and embedded deep within the raging sea. Give him jaw-dropping sunrises and sunsets over fancy estates. Give him rainbows after a lashing and stars that sparked up the night. Greed was a never-ending beast. And the motive for most murders. The Good Twin/Bad Twin angle was intriguing, but Cormac didn't quite know how it fit in. The beach scene was staged to a tee. Who stood the most to gain from Johnny O'Reilly's death? Even if Brendan was the one hanging around the O'Reilly estate—he must have had it good, because he'd been here a hell of a long time. Had O'Reilly suddenly decided to cut him off? Or was Cormac getting distracted? Was the widow better off with her husband dead? Was an insurance payout her game all along? Cormac exited his vehicle and tossed the key to the nearest white-gloved-hand. "Careful not to scratch it," he said with a wink. "She's only two decades old."

He maneuvered to the entrance through a tripped-out rose garden and trickling fountain. Rising from the middle, reared back, was a statue of a female horse, and by her side: a gleaming black colt: He leaned in to read the raised print on a plaque at the base: *RUBY AND LAST DANCE. RIDING THROUGH THE GATES OF HEAVEN.*

The shade of black on the colt was a match to the painted stones on the beach. He felt a buzz as he snapped a photo.

Seeing the statue reminded him that he'd forgotten to stop and have a look at the spot in the road where Last Dance had been struck by a trailer. Not that there would be anything to see after all this time, but the tragic incident seemed to be the glue that bound the Wildes and the O'Reillys, and he needed to know more. An irresistible itch begging to be scratched.

Speaking of itch, Cormac had taken Dimpna's advice and gone for the allergy meds, and she was right, they were a game changer. But he had his inhaler with him just in case. He approached the entrance to the manor and was greeted by an ornate wooden door with a racehorse as a knocker. He was poised to use it when the door opened and Róisín and Sean stepped out, dressed as if they were attending a high-society function. The gloved men all disappeared into a massive stone garage to the side. From the size of it there was room for at least a half a dozen vehicles.

"Hello, Detective," Róisín said. Her mouth curled up like a snarl and Cormac nearly laughed when he realized it was her approximation of a smile.

"Mrs. O'Reilly, Mr. O'Reilly."

"Please," Sean said. "Call me Sean."

"We're on a tight schedule," Róisín said. "I'm afraid there won't be time for a tour today."

"With the exception of the barns?" Cormac asked.

"The barns?" Róisín said. "Are you a racing fan?"

"The biggest," Cormac said, threatening himself with bodily harm if he scratched his nose. "Huge fan."

"We'll let Tommy Healy handle the tour when you've finished at the house," Sean said.

"I'll be wanting to speak to each of you alone," Cormac said.

Róisín O'Reilly pivoted, and as if by magic, the door swung open. A butler stood in the soft light of the foyer, created by candle sconces flickering against a lavishly wallpapered background: teal blue with abstract white flowers. A chandelier above them mimicked the white abstract flowers, and for a moment Cormac allowed himself to admit that living in a place like this wouldn't entirely suck. The butler gave a slight bow as they entered, and Cormac followed his gaze to the green marbled floors. "It's Connemara marble," Róisín pointed out.

"That's very patriotic of you," Cormac quipped. He felt an ounce of satisfaction when she frowned. Past the foyer, massive ceilings were decorated with ornate tiles and wood, topped by another glittery chandelier poised over a winding staircase. The banister, curved and polished to a high shine, was downright sexy. Cormac was going to have to find an old Irish pub this evening, have a few pints of the black stuff, and play the squeezebox just to scrub off all this wealth. To the left and right, open parlor rooms beckoned. A hallway lined with paintings began at the edge of the stairwell. The butler gestured to the room on the right, and Róisín headed for one of the creamy sofas, so lush and soft looking, that if he hadn't known better, Cormac would have thought they'd stolen them right out from underneath an angel's arse.

"I'll be in my study," Sean said.

The butler bowed in response. Cormac was already regretting the suit and tie. He should have rolled in in denims and flannel. He would take an old Irish whitewashed cottage by the sea any day. He took a seat in a matching plush sofa across from the Widow O'Reilly and couldn't help but gawk at the view out of the floor-to-ceiling windows. Land as far as the eye could see, and in the distance a peekaboo view of cliffs and the ocean. It seemed wrong somehow that the poor horses did all the running, and the O'Reillys did all the taking. He set a recording device on the table in front of him, noting how Róisín winced. The butler hurried over. "May I?" Before Cormac could respond, he slid a marble coaster under the device. It was an old-fashioned recorder, but Cormac loved how nervous it made people.

"Tea and sandwiches, madam?" the butler said.

"No, thank you," Róisín said. Her smirk didn't get past Cormac. It was as if they'd rehearsed this. He didn't need her fancy finger sandwiches anyway.

He took a moment to study Róisín. She was in another suit, this time in royal blue with a white ruffled blouse. Cormac was no fashion designer, but even he could tell the outfit probably cost more than his monthly rent. He wouldn't be surprised if it was three or four months' worth. The room had an elaborate fireplace and mantel, another impressive chandelier, imported rugs, and not only landscape paintings on the wall, but even the vases and sculptures sported lush renderings of the Irish countryside.

"I was expecting a wall of winning medals and trophies," he said. The only horse-specific items that he spotted in the room was a miniature replica of the fountain statue, a black colt, rearing up, above it a large photograph of the horse that had been the O'Reillys' first big winner: Ruby. Cormac, having never been around horses, could see something special in this one, an energy that radiated from it like waves. Perhaps this racehorse business wasn't all about money, but he wasn't here to peer underneath anyone's souls.

"We have other rooms for all those medals and trophies, Detective. But I'm afraid my son was right. We are under a tight schedule. We have to meet with the funeral home in precisely one hour."

"I understand. I'll be attending the service tomorrow," he said.

"It's an invitation-only affair, Inspector," Róisín said. "Did you get an invitation?"

He was expecting this and he was prepared. "I would advise against that," he said. "I understand that you want a private affair. But the old trope is true—murderers can't resist attending such affairs. I want to see who shows up. I want to have Gardaí there to observe everyone. If anyone dares be disrespectful, I can assure you they will be removed immediately."

Róisín pursed her lips. "And if I say no . . . I assume you'll think I'm trying to hide something or someone. Is that your game, Detective?"

"My job is to find your husband's killer. Please. Let me do my job."

"I've already told you who murdered my husband. The Wildes. I assure you, are not on the guest list."

"I'd rather fancy tea and sandwiches," Cormac said. He hadn't expected to say that, but he had to admit, he rather enjoyed watching her mouth twitch. She flicked a hand and the butler bowed.

"Right away, madam."

Cormac leaned back. "Tell me about the days leading up to the murder."

"What do you want to know?"

"I want to know your husband's movements. His frame of mind. And anything that seemed out of the ordinary."

Róisín looked up and to the right. "We weren't attached at the hip. We could go for days without much interaction, especially when Johnny had meetings."

"Meetings?"

She nodded. "We own some of our racehorses privately. But others are in partnerships, clubs, and corporations. Johnny always had meetings. Trainers, agents, other owners, breeders. If he wasn't in meetings he was out in the barns."

"Or dancing?" He waited to see if jealousy flared.

"Yes, Detective. My husband was a fabulous dancer."

"You didn't share this activity with him?"

"I have my own interests. It's the secret to a happy marriage."

"You had a happy marriage then?"

He saw it then, the first flicker of irritation. "Digging for drama, are we?"

"It's a simple question."

"This year would have been our forty-sixth wedding anniversary."

"I'm sorry." It didn't mean those forty-six years were happy, but a little credit was due to any couple who made it last that long.

Róisín reached for a folder on a small table next to her. Cormac silently reprimanded himself for not noticing it. She offered it up and he accepted it. "What is this?"

"Answers to every question I assume you're going to ask. I've written down everything I remember about the week up until the murder. Johnny's schedule is in there—not that he followed it like glue, by any means—but it's everything that was on his calendar."

"I truly appreciate this and I will read it like a treasured bedtime story."

Róisín stood. "Shall I send Sean in to speak with you?"

Cormac set the folder down. "I need to hear it from you, in your own words, what you remember about the few days leading up to the murder." Róisín glanced behind her, as if calculating how many steps led to freedom. "I especially need you to walk me through your day on that Friday leading up to Sunday morning."

Róisín sighed. "This is very upsetting."

"I apologize. I assure you, it's necessary."

"I'm not any good at giving speeches. Ask me questions and I'll answer." She folded her arms across her chest.

"Please. Sit."

"I'd rather stand."

Cormac was starting to wonder if there was something in the local drinking water. Why was everyone so obstinate? "Did you notice anything strange or different about your husband in the days leading up to the dance on Saturday?"

"No."

He waited for her to say more. She did not. Had she been coached by a solicitor? "Give me a brief run-through of the week leading up to the murder."

"We had breakfast together. He went to his meetings. All of which I've carefully outlined for you. I went about my day. I'm on several charity boards, and I was busy planning the fundraising memorial for Deborah O'Grady."

The woman whose fundraiser was being held the night of the murder. Cormac nodded. "That's very noble."

"Little did I know I'd be planning my own husband's funeral a week later."

"Did you meet up with your husband on the Saturday night of the wake and the dance?"

"No."

"So if someone saw you pull him out of the dance and have an argument with him . . . ?"

"He or she would be lying."

"And if this witness also said that you called your son, Sean, later that evening, and whatever it was must have been urgent, for Sean left Doolin and drove back to Dingle."

"Preposterous." Her eyes flashed with anger. "I have a pub full of witnesses, and my son not only has his wife and daughter to back him up, they have witnesses in Doolin as well."

He was dying to say it. Say she was calling her own grand-daughter a liar. Then again, children misunderstood things all the time. It was possible that some of the details were true, and others were misshapen. The murder had been planned for a long time. It wasn't caused by a spur-of-the-moment fight or phone call. He actually hadn't planned on saying anything of the sort to Mrs. O'Reilly, but her stoic demeanor had grated on him so much that he couldn't help himself. He wanted to see if anything could rattle her. So far, she was the top cucumber. He pulled a plastic bag out of his suit jacket. "As you're aware we've had to hold on to your husband's effects while the inquiry is underway." He laid the ruby ring on the table.

"Thank you," she said. "That ring was very dear to him." She picked it up and rubbed her fingers along the ruby through the plastic.

"Are you going to bury him with it?"

"Nonsense," she said. "He won't need it where he's going."

Interesting. Cormac nodded as if that were an entirely appropriate thing to say about one's husband of forty-six years. "Is there another ring like this?"

She lifted a carefully drawn eyebrow. "Another one?"

"Maybe your son has one?"

"No" she said. "But Tommy has one."

"Tommy Healy?"

She nodded. "Johnny gave it to him as a good luck charm before he was to ride Last Dance." She frowned at the memory. "When Tommy dropped out of the race, I told my husband to take the ring back. For some reason, he refused. I never understood Johnny's affection for that lad. He treated him better than his own son." A haunted look came over her. "I don't think Sean ever forgave him for that—but we all have our wounds to carry, don't we?"

CHAPTER 34

Then

*D*IMPNA WAS KNACKERED—THEY'D BEEN AT IT SINCE HALF-SIX IN THE morning—and she was dying to go home, put her feet up, and watch telly with supper. But she had one more call to make; the O'Reillys had a horse with an infected hoof they had treated days earlier, and she needed to make sure he was on the mend. It was exciting to be around the estate; all talk was on Tommy Healy and Last Dance. He was going to win; she could feel it. Her father was on an emergency call, and now that she was nearly eighteen, she could drive out to farms herself. She'd be going off to university soon, most likely Trinity for her undergrad work before applying to vet schools. She was at ease at the O'Reilly stables now, as long as she stayed away from the Wicked Witch, and she was friendly with most of the staff and trainers. The visit didn't take long. The horse was healing wonderfully, and after putting on some new cream and changing the bandage, she was winding her way through the barn toward the exit. She was nearly to the door when she heard voices raised in anger. Sean and Tommy. She couldn't remember what they were saying to each other, but she knew from their tones it was bad. She hadn't intended on sneaking up on them, but as she approached, they were so engrossed in their row, that neither of them noticed her. Wanting to keep it that way, she quickly slipped into an empty stall across from them, crouched down, and peeked out between the slats.

They were dressed in navy suits with crisp white shirts. They must have come from a publicity event; everywhere you turned these days there was a picture of Tommy Healy atop Last Dance. Sean was grasping a green tie in his hand and his face was red with anger. Dimpna can't remember exactly what happened, but the next thing she knew, Sean was suddenly behind Tommy, the green tie wrapped tightly around his neck. Tommy struggled and clawed at the tie, his eyes bulging.

"Hey!" Dimpna darted out from the stall. "Stop. Stop. Stop." It seemed like forever before Sean made eye contact with her. Tommy's face was beet red, and when Sean released him, he slumped to the floor. Dimpna screamed again, but before she could run to Tommy's side, someone else was there. Johnny O'Reilly, towering over her, his breath smelling of whiskey and uncomfortably close.

"Lads acting the maggot," he said. "I'll deal with them."

"We need to call an ambulance." Tommy was still on the floor. Sean was dragging a large black tarp over to him. Dimpna tried to peer around Mr. O'Reilly to see what he was doing. Was he wrapping him up?

"Go home."

"Tommy," she shouted. "Tommy get up."

"Go," Johnny said, then pushed her forward.

"I'm calling the guards," she yelled. And then she ran. And ran. And ran. Her da's truck was parked all the way at the end of the drive. She reached it. The rest was a blur. The bumpy ride down the street, which had since been paved smooth, but at the time it was filled with dirt, and rocks, and little dips that jolted the bonnet of the car every time she dipped down. The car was old, and shook when she tried to speed up. By the time she reached the nearest house, she tumbled out of the car and hurled herself at the front door, babbling that an ambulance was needed at the O'Reillys'.

An hour later Dimpna sat in one of the grand dining rooms in the O'Reilly estate, the first time she had ever set foot inside the enormous building. Her father sat next to her, and two guards stood behind her. Across the table was a grinning Sean O'Reilly and a somber Tommy Healy. Angry red lines were visible on his neck. It was so good to see he was alright, but he wouldn't meet her eyes. "We knew she was there," Sean said. "It was a prank."

"It wasn't," Dimpna said. "You were yelling at each other."

"We waited until she walked by, and then pretended to have a row," Sean said. "We were only messing."

We were only messing.

"Tommy," Dimpna said, desperately trying to get him to look her in the eye. "He tried to kill you. Tell them."

Tommy stared at her for a moment, one arm on the table, a long empty sleeve hanging down. "We were only messing," he said. "The tie was my idea." He held her gaze for a few seconds, and then winked. It was so unlike him, it made the hairs on her arms stand at attention. Moments ticked by as Dimpna tried to convince the guards that she saw what she saw. Tommy strangled. She saw his face go red. She saw him slump to the barn floor. She saw Sean dragging a large black tarp over to where he lay. Yet here he was, planted across from her next to Sean, the pair of them grinning like eejits. Her father stood. "Let's go, Dew." She didn't move. He gently took her arm and pulled her up.

"Tell them," she yelled at Tommy. "Tell them what he did."

"You're clueless," Sean said, shaking his head. "You're too gullible."

"We'll see ourselves out," her father said, but not before treating the pair of lads to a searing look that made their sloppy grins disappear. It wasn't until they were standing near their vehicle, that Dimpna tried to plead with her father.

"Tommy's lying," she said. "Why is he lying?"

"Get in the car," her father said. The first few minutes they rode in silence, tears running down Dimpna's face. She'd always thought of Tommy as her friend. A week before the biggest race of his life and he's nothing better to do than play pranks on her? What had she ever done to him? It was her size, no one took her serious, and she was sick of it. Sick of being treated differently. Sick of being called an imp, an elf, a wee girl, a *victim.* How dare they. She didn't know *what,* but she was going to do something about it. She had to do something.

"In the rainforests of Brazil, there's a small wild cat," her father said. "The ocelot." Dimpna leaned her forehead against the cold glass as rain started to fall. "It relies on a prank to get its supper. It's quite good at it. It mimics the call of a baby monkey. When it knows the monkeys are nearby it lets out a high-pitched squeal, just like their babies. The adult monkeys run toward the ocelot to save their babies. And that's when it attacks. And they become dinner." He sighed. "Monkeys are very curious, Dew. They fall for it every time."

"Are you calling me a monkey, Da?" Dimpna said.

He shrugged, losing himself for a moment in the windshield wipers. "There's nothing wrong with being curious, Dew," he said. "Just don't be dinner."

Now

It was raining out of the heavens, and rain had a funny effect on the vet business. It was either dead to the world or drowning with creatures in need. Just when Dimpna had been fully prepared to seek out Sean O'Reilly, and have it all out, they were slammed. Thank God for Patrick Kelly; he was excellent at spays and neuters, and stitches, and shots. It was all routine until the early afternoon when an emergency call came in. Instead of taking the message and relaying it Dimpna, this time Niamh had her get on the phone. The caller was none other than Tommy Healy. "We have an emergency with one of our expecting mares. She's in great pain and nothing is happening. Please."

"Do the O'Reillys know that it will be me, Dimpna Wilde, coming out to their property?" She kept her voice steady despite her tripping heart.

"They do." He cleared this throat. "We've tried three other vets. Please. We can't lose either the mama or the foal."

"I'll be right there." She grabbed her emergency bag and summoned Patrick. He was confident he could handle the rest of the animals crowded in reception, but Dimpna needed him. "Call Sheila," she said to Niamh. "Whatever you have to do to get her here, do it. Otherwise, we're going to have to reschedule the lot." Niamh nodded, keeping her cool under pressure. Dimpna and

Patrick gathered all the supplies they might need and jumped in her bus, which had finally been released and re-painted. She played the radio loud as she took the wet roads. Patrick cheerfully pattered on about the cases from the morning, and although Dimpna was happy for the distraction, she did more nodding than talking.

When she pulled into the start of the long and so familiar drive up to the O'Reillys' sprawling estate, she felt her stomach clench. She couldn't let past memories prevent her from doing her job. Tommy, in his usual black shirt, denims, and white cowboy hat, stood with a torch waiting to escort them. He eyed Patrick through the rain. "I thought you were alone."

"This is Dr. Patrick Kelly. He's just joined our clinic."

"I didn't expect him." Tommy looked on the verge of panic. Had she missed something? Was there another reason Tommy had lured her out here, and the horse was just an excuse? Did she just ruin an ulterior motive?

"I assure you, you're in good hands."

Horses whinnied and pawed the ground as they made their way to the back barn and Healy filled in the details. Striker was a sixteen-hand gorgeous black thoroughbred. The ribbons hanging near her stall conveyed what Tommy had already reported; the mama was one of few fillies who'd successfully competed against stallions. A winner. She was also in great pain, her nostrils were flared, her eyes glazed and rolling back in her head as she stomped and swayed in the stall, her head drooping.

Dimpna and Patrick washed their hands in a bucket of sudsy water that Tommy had prepared, before putting on gloves and boiler suits. Next, Dimpna slipped a harness over Striker's head, designed to keep her still, while Patrick stood on the ready and Tommy detailed how long Striker had been in pain. Dimpna lubed her right glove and had just inserted her hand into the horse's vaginal opening, feeling for the foal, when a crack of thunder pealed outside and Striker reared up with a whinny. "Easy, girl." Just as her front legs settled back on the ground, she suddenly kicked with her back leg. The hoof caught Dimpna on the chin, sending her teeth crashing together, throwing her head back as pain soared through her. A rookie mistake.

"Oh my God," Patrick said. "What can I do?"

Dimpna tasted blood in her mouth. "Birthing ropes." It hurt to talk.

"On it." Patrick pulled a hood over his head and hurried out of the barn. The rain was torrential, beating atop the roof. Tommy Healy waited until Patrick was out of sight then quickly came up behind her.

"Are you hurt?"

Dimpna shook it off; she didn't know whether her injuries were serious or not, but she still had a job to do. She felt around with her tongue to make sure she still had all her teeth. "I'm fine," she said through a clenched jaw.

"Don't look at me," he said. "Pretend I'm not talking."

"You shouldn't be talking," she said. "I need to concentrate." She needed to reach into the mama again, but it was foolish to do it without backup. She removed the first pair of gloves, sanitized her hands, and started the process over—washing up, new gloves, and more lube. The more time that passed, the more danger the foal was in. The mama was agitated now. "Dystocia," she said, forgetting for a moment that Patrick was gone. Dystocia was a familiar term for a difficult birth, reasons ranging from an abnormal fetus size to an awkward positioning. In this case, the foal was completely turned around. His hind feet and legs were wanting to come out first, and that would not work. She would need to try to turn him, and it would involve herself and Patrick pulling with ropes.

Dimpna spoke to the mama. "Let's get your little one turned around. Hang in there, Mama. Just a little longer." If they didn't get the foal out quickly, it would die. And if she couldn't get the baby turned around, the only other option was a Caesarean. Not her preferred route on a stormy day on the floor of a horse barn.

Tommy stepped up behind her, uncomfortably close. "You're in danger," he said.

"I know what I'm doing." He had two seconds and she was going to yell at him to back up.

"I'm not talking about the horse. You think our staff has never helped deliver a breach?" She turned to look at him. His pupils were enlarged, his eyes like a pair of black stones. "You still don't get it, do you? After all these years?" He shook his head.

"Unless you want this foal to die, whatever this is has to wait."
Patrick had returned, lowering his hood, shaking the rain off, and
setting down equipment. He approached the stall and Tommy took
a step back. Dimpna guided her hand into the mama again and
soon felt a hind leg and a hoof. "Clamps and rope?" Patrick
stepped forward with the equipment.

"Is she going to be okay?" A child's voice piped up from somewhere behind her. Dimpna whirled around to find Aisling O'Reilly
staring into the stall. She wasn't wearing a raincoat; her wet clothing and hair were plastered to her shivering body.

"Hey there," Patrick said. "You look like you need a towel." He
glanced at Tommy.

"Does your father and granny know you're in here?" Tommy
asked.

"I'm not leaving," she said.

"Would you get her a towel or a blanket?" Dimpna said. Tommy
glared at her, but turned and left, presumably to fetch something
for the shivering girl.

"A puppy and a foal," Dimpna said. "You're a lucky girl."

"Please don't let my horses die."

"If you're going to stand there, I need you to stand back behind
Dr. Kelly," Dimpna said calmly. "If you like, you can hold the
torch." Patrick handed her the torch and she obediently stepped
back. "You're tall," she heard Aisling say.

Patrick laughed. "I am, so. I probably look like a giant to you,
do I?"

"Have you thought of a name?" Dimpna asked, welcoming the
distraction. Dimpna had slim hands so it was easy to fit inside the
horse, guiding in the clamp and the rope, but turning around a
breached foal took more than access; it took muscle and sweat, and
all her concentration. Weirdly, Dimpna often concentrated better
with distractions. She had nearly turned the foal, half-aware that
everyone watching was also witnessing her struggle, when a tall figure entered the barn, speaking in a deep voice.

"Aisling, you can't just disappear without a word to me or your
granny."

Sean. Dimpna nearly lost her grip.

"Save the lecture for later," Dimpna had no choice but to say. She finished getting the goal into position. "Now," she said, "we're ready to pull."

"Ropes?" Aisling cried out.

Sean knelt beside her. "It will help them get a better grip." Patrick stepped up beside Dimpna, and together they maneuvered the rope into position and tugged. *Please,* Dimpna thought. She didn't want this child to see a dead foal. There was a hitch, and then an adjustment. "Pull again." This time, the rope slid between their fingers, and the front feet came out, followed by a nose, and then the rest of the baby was born. Slick with fluids, the foal had yet to take a breath. Dimpna quickly administered a suction cup around its mouth and nose. "Come on, little one, you're here now. What's all the fuss?" Soon the suction cup was doing its job, the passageways were cleared, and the foal was breathing. "It's a boy," Dimpna said. "A colt."

Tommy returned with a blanket for Aisling that he handed to Sean. He wrapped it around his daughter. "Your laces are untied." He knelt and tied them for her. Seeing the fatherly gesture out of her periphery sent Dimpna's insides pinging with fear. Was he a good father or just trying to show her that he was?

"A colt," Patrick repeated as he stepped in to clean him up. "What a handsome lad. Good work, Dr. Wilde. I'm proud to be a witness to your mad skills."

"Thank you, Dr. Kelly. You were spot-on as well." Dimpna took a minute to watch the miracle that never got old, then stood up, dripping with fluids as she and Sean made eye contact. She felt numb, like she'd been dipped in an ice bath but had yet to feel the burning cold.

"Thank you," Sean said, his voice husky. Tommy stood behind him trying to catch her eye. When he finally did, he mouthed something. *Ben.* Was that what he said? Or was it *Help?* She frowned. Was he trying to warn her that Sean knew about Ben? If so, was he honestly attempting to help or was he up to his old tricks? Or was he asking for help? What help did he need?

"I'm due to speak with the inspector," Sean said.

"You're going out in this?" Dimpna couldn't help but ask.

Sean shook his head. "The inspector is here."

"Here?" Dimpna and Tommy said in stereo. She couldn't tell if Tommy seemed upset or relieved.

Sean gave Tommy a curious look, then focused on Dimpna. "Dr. Wilde, will you please come up to the house when you're finished?"

What did he want? Was he furious? Did he want to get her alone, confront her about Ben? Was Ben here? She had to find out. "I'll be there as soon as I've cleaned up."

"Thank you, thank you, thank you," Aisling said, kneeling close to the colt.

"Time to get cleaned up for supper," Sean said to his daughter, his voice still thick. "You'll have plenty of time with your horses tomorrow."

"But I want to stay with him now."

As if summoned by his desires, a young woman appeared at the door to the barn. Sean turned. "Please see to it she gets back and out of these wet clothes?"

"Yes, Mr. O'Reilly. I'm sorry she snuck past me."

"Not a bother. She got to see the miracle of birth. But this storm is here to stay. I want you inside until morning, petal."

Aisling and the young woman exited the barn hand in hand. Sean gave a nod of thanks, then disappeared into a sheet of rain. Tommy watched him go, a strange look on his face. He jerked his head slightly to the left as he looked at Dimpna. She stepped closer.

"I don't know you very well," he said. "But I need you to trust me."

She frowned. "I've known you since we were young," she said.

"You haven't," he said. "Not really."

"What's the story?"

"You're in danger." That was the second time he said it. Patrick edged up, clueless as to the tension, and grinning.

"That never gets old," Patrick said, glancing back at the mother and colt. Sean had returned and was framed in the door of the barn.

"Talk later, will we?" Tommy said quickly, then disappeared down the long hall that led to the bathrooms. Patrick had prepared buckets of soap and water, and Dimpna soaked her arms in one as he washed his hands in the other. "They have showers here," she said, nodding to the hallway that Tommy had just traversed. Sean was no longer in the doorway. The rain was still coming down in sheets. "Separate shower rooms for mna and fir if you would believe that."

"You've convinced me," he said.

"You'll love it. And you wouldn't want to sit next to me on the drive home if I didn't partake."

"With this rain, not sure we'll be driving anywhere soon," Patrick said. "It's not often you get to take a hot shower in a barn in the middle of a storm."

"Never said anything about hot," Dimpna said. "But everything else is spot-on." For a moment they stood by the open door of the barn watching the fierce rain and wind. Slow-rolling thunder made the ground shake beneath their feet and a bolt of lightning cracked open the sky. The smell of hay and wet earth amplified in the electric air. Horses whinnied throughout the barn as they pawed the floors in protest. A cat wound its way sharklike between their legs before darting into an empty stall and hiding behind a bale of hay. The newborn colt snuggled up to its mother, shivering as his mama licked him with a ginormous pink tongue.

Dimpna grabbed her bag with her towel and change of clothes.

"I didn't come prepared," Patrick said. "But I didn't get as dirty as you either."

Dimpna laughed. "You'll remember next time." She headed down the hall, looking forward to scrubbing up. She entered the female showers and quickly undressed, leaving her dirty scrubs in a heap on a nearby bench, and tossing her towel over the shower door before stepping in and blasting the water. It was freezing, which she had been prepared for, but it still gave her a shock. She nearly wished she could be a fly on the wall when Patrick felt the ice-cold water. It was like a Christmas polar bear swim. Body soap and shampoo were attached to the wall in fancy plastic bottles although they were positioned so high up that Dimpna almost couldn't reach the nozzles, even on her tippy toes. For a second she wondered if Sean or Tommy had moved them out of reach, another prank on her, perhaps they did it the minute they called her out to the farm. She finally managed to get a squirt from the bottle and lathered up, aware that she was being super paranoid. For them, twenty-seven years had passed since all those shenanigans. But the minute Dimpna had entered Dingle again, she felt as if she'd been sucked back into the past; there was no need for a time machine where her imagination would do. Was she holding Sean and Tommy prisoner for mistakes they'd made in their youth? Should she let it go, let those resentments slide off her body like the suds now trailing down her legs and winding into the drain?

She skipped shampooing her hair, rinsed, and reached for her towel. She did a quick dry, wrapped it around her body, and stepped out. She wasn't alone. A man was lying on the floor, faceup. Tommy Healy. She let out a startled scream, her heartbeat echoing in her ears, fear hammering at her brain. "Jesus," she said. "You put the heart in me crossways. Get up!" *Get out.* He didn't move. "You are seriously messed up. I'm not falling for this again, Tommy. I'm not." Unlike the first time he'd played dead, his eyes were closed. Her attention was drawn to the fogged-up mirrors above the sinks. A word started to form in the mist: *Ben.* She screamed again, whipped off her towel, and attacked the mirror, rubbing and rubbing until the word was gone. That's when she saw another note, this one made of paper and tucked into the corner. She held her towel against her, fighting the panic welling up from deep within her, the voice that was telling her this wasn't a prank this time, he was really and truly dead. She made herself look at him. His mouth was open, foam pooled at the corner of his blue-tinged lips. "No, no, no." There was an object on the floor by his left hip. A purple vial. She'd only seen a vial like that one other time. In her da's office. It was a vial of Immobolin. There, by a truly dead Tommy Healy, was the Monster in a Bottle.

CHAPTER 35

*T*OMMY HEALY'S BODY WAS SITUATED A FEW METERS AWAY FROM THE door. Dimpna yanked on her clean clothes and boots, and was grateful to find plastic gloves shoved among them that she hadn't used. Not that she intended on touching anything, but she'd learned to be deathly afraid around that vial. If any was spilled on the floor, it could kill whomever touched it. She left her bag on the bench and the towel over the shower door as she swung as far left of the body as she could, stepping carefully but quickly before opening the door and running down the hall. "Help," she yelled. "Somebody, help."

She came to a screeching halt at the end of the hall shocked to find Róisín O'Reilly standing just inside the barn, bone-dry underneath an enormous black umbrella. Behind her, the rain continued its unrelenting assault. By her side, dripping wet, was the inspector. He took one look at her face and stepped closer. "What's wrong?"

Dimpna pointed down the hall toward the shower, her teeth chattering. "Tommy Healy," she said. "He's on the floor of the women's bathroom."

"Is he ill?" the inspector asked.

"I hope you're not accusing him of being a peeper," Róisín said. "I hardly think there'd be anything of your tiny body to see."

"Mrs. O'Reilly," the inspector said loudly. "That is unacceptable."

Róisín's mouth dropped open. She'd probably never been spoken to like that in years. No doubt she'd be on the phone as soon as she could, complaining about the rude inspector.

"He's dead," Dimpna said. "Poisoned."

"Poisoned?" the inspector and Róisín said in stereo.

"There's a purple vial next to his body." She gulped. "Me father used to keep Immobolin in a purple vial. He has foam at the corner of his mouth." She swallowed again as she thought of the word in the mirror. *Ben.* The note; she'd meant to take the note. But in her panic she'd forgotten. Whatever Tommy had to say would be there for everyone to read. Would it be filled with lies about Ben? Why hadn't she taken the note?

"Stay here," the inspector said, making his way down the hall.

"Dr. Kelly is down there," she said. "He's in the men's." He didn't hear her so she hurried after him, defying his orders. He stood with the door to the women's room thrown open.

"Cormac," she said sharply.

He whirled around. "Stay back."

"You stay back. That vial?" She squeezed in behind him and pointed. "Don't touch it. Don't touch anywhere around it. If it makes contact with your skin—even a drop—there's going to be another body on the floor."

He looked at her, his eyes trailing down to her hands. "Why are you wearing those gloves?"

"Because I saw the vial. They were in my bag with my change of clothes. I told you. You don't want to take any chances with that stuff." He nodded. "There's a note," she said, hoping to get back in his good graces. She pointed it out.

The detective ushered Dimpna back into the hall as he pulled out his mobile. He looked to her. "How do we handle it?" he asked.

"Gloves are usually good enough," she said. "But we can't be sure it hasn't spilled, so anyone who enters should be covered head-to-toe in protective gear. Everyone needs to know how deadly it is."

"Is there an antidote?"

She nodded. "Revivon. We'll have to ask the staff if there's any on hand. It's too late for Tommy; it would have had to be delivered immediately. But if anyone else accidentally comes into contact with it, we absolutely should have Revivon on hand."

He swore and shut off his phone. "I still can't get a signal."

"I think we're going to have to wait it out." She handed him the gloves. "They're one size so they should fit."

"How long were you in the shower?"

"Less than ten minutes, Inspector."

"Enough of Inspector, Doc. Cormac works just fine."

"Then call me Dimpna."

"I kind of like calling you Doc."

The door to the men's bathroom opened and Patrick stepped out whistling. "Man," he said. "That was freezing. You got me." He stopped short when he saw their faces.

"Did I take too long?" he said. "I took too long, didn't I?"

"I'm going in for the note," Cormac said. "Someone needs to find Sean and Aisling, and anyone else who's either in the barns or in the house. We need to get everyone in the same space." He jerked his head to Patrick. "I need you to exit this area."

"I missed something, didn't I?" Patrick said. "I always miss something."

Dimpna paced the barns, staying away from the others as much as she could. They were at the mercy of the storm now. Help wasn't going to come until their mobile signals were restored. She was stuck here. This was supposed to have been an emergency call; she should have been home by now. Had she known she'd be stuck back here, the place of her worst memories, she would have tried to send Patrick with someone else, anyone else. To make matters worse, this was the barn where it had happened. Where Sean raped her and where she had purportedly stumbled over to Last Dance's stall afterward to set him free. Her memories of that evening were like patched-over holes, the gaps filled in with shame. And now, the only other witness of that evening, Tommy Healy, was dead. Earlier he'd been trying to talk to her, tell her something. She'd heard Cormac refer to the note tucked into the mirror of the bathroom as Tommy's suicide note. Why would he tell her they needed to talk and then kill himself? Why did she have that same dreaded feeling as she'd had that awful, awful night?

Against her little voice telling her not to, Dimpna gravitated to the stall where Sean had violated her. She stood in the exact spot, allowing the memories to flood in. Mostly she remembered how she felt just after it was over. Her desperate, clawing need to get away from him. She'd pulled up her knickers wet with blood and fluids. She hurried back into her denims, her adrenaline pumping, her brain fully on flight mode. Sean was pulling up his own trousers, watching her with a lazy smirk. "Don't be like that," he said. "You liked it." Where had Tommy been that whole time? Hiding? Watching?

Her next memory isn't letting Last Dance out of his stall. It's running full-out across the field, arms and legs pumping in the dark. Ahead, headlights glared in the road, and she thought it was a sign, a beacon. "Help," she said. "Stop." She kept running and screaming and running, and it took her forever to reach the road. There was no need to yell at the vehicle to stop. The trailer was dead still. Jerked sideways on the road, the front cab plunged into a ditch. She'd started to babble, she remembered that. *Oh my God, hello, hello, hello. Is anyone there? Is anyone there?* The engine was crooning out a high-pitched mechanical whine. The front headlights blared into a patch of trees. The back wheels were spinning, stuck and going nowhere, like a turtle flipped on its back. She drew closer, and that's when she saw him. Last Dance. First, his legs, those sinewy gorgeous legs, instead of upright and running like he'd been born to do. A one-in-a-million racehorse, the smartest, sweetest, most naturally talented specimen she had ever met, the first horse she had helped birth, was lying still on his side. In the middle of the road. In a pool of blood.

Dimpna screamed, the sound ringing in her ears. She'd pleaded with his dead body. *Come back, come back, come back to me. Please, please, please. No, no, no.* Not Last Dance. She'd do anything. She told God she'd do *anything* if he would just bring him back. And then . . . someone was there. A figure standing over her. Talking to her. Tommy Healy. What was he saying? She remembered his hands on her shoulder, gently trying to pull her to her feet. But when the guards arrived, she was still clinging to Last Dance. It took three grown men to finally hoist her up—

"Dimpna?"

Startled, she whirled around. Sean stood in front of her holding a steaming mug. "Are you alright?"

She nodded. "Fine."

"Coffee?"

She took it. Half of her was still back on that road. It hadn't been a real memory at all. She must have made it up. Her mind either protecting her or playing tricks. Because if Tommy Healy had been there, it wouldn't have been *hands* she felt on her shoulders. It would have been *a hand*. Was she just filling in the gaps? Had he been there at all? Was he the one who took the photo she'd found in her father's desk drawer?

"Why don't you join us?" Sean said. He gestured to the group huddled near a space heater. "Did you hear about the note?"

"I saw a note tucked in the mirror," Dimpna said. "I didn't touch it."

"He left another one in my office," Sean said.

"It doesn't make sense. I was just talking to him. He said there was something he wanted to talk to me about. In private."

"That makes sense," Sean said.

"What about that makes sense?"

"It's in his note," Sean said. "Believe me. You're going to want to read it."

Cormac stood near Dimpna Wilde as the guards swarmed in. It had been two hours since they'd discovered the body. When the skies finally cleared and his mobile signal was restored, he didn't even have to make a call. His super reached him first. Tommy Healy had left more than the note on the mirror. He'd sent one straight to headquarters. It was delivered by messenger around the same time that he was presumably opening the little vial of death. A third note had been given to Sean O'Reilly. He'd found it on the desk in his office. *Overkill.* Some people didn't leave a note at all; this guy left them everywhere and to everyone. Why?

Cormac had no power to keep it under wraps. By now everyone

had read it over and over. No doubt it would be splashed over all the newspapers in the morning. *One-armed jockey turned murderer.* Or, *One-armed jockey takes his own life but not before making a series of startling confessions* . . . Cormac couldn't help but continuously pick over the shocking revelations. The note was handwritten and signed. Tommy admitted to murdering Johnny O'Reilly. He said he'd nicked the stones from Aisling's nature project. Painted them with gloss from the auto body shop across from the Wilde Clinic. Found the Devil card lying on the floor of the yacht. He didn't know how it got there, but to him it was a sign that his plan was a just one. He instructed Donnecha Wilde to buy the tie, told him Johnny wanted the boat for a VIP guest that evening, and stole the vial of Immobolin from an 'old vet who was losing his mind.' He said he didn't realize there was a young girl on the yacht, but he didn't harm her. He said all of that, but he did not answer Cormac's most pressing question: *Why?* Why did he murder Johnny O'Reilly? And why did he kill himself? Why now? There was one last confession. One that no one had been expecting. Cormac read it again, holding the note up to the light of the barn and reading it through the clear evidence bag:

> *Dimpna Wilde didn't let Last Dance out of his stall that evening. I did. Then I blamed her for it. I'm sorry. I loved her. I loved Dimpna Wilde. When I saw her and Sean making love in the barn—I lost it. I was going to ride away on Last Dance, just the two of us escaping the big bad world. But something spooked him the minute I opened the gate. There was a trailer passing by—and it backfired. Last Dance took off, throwing me off of him and into the field. I collected myself as quickly as possible and ran after him. But it was too late. He ran directly in front of the trailer. He was dead. Dimpna heard the commotion—and in a panic I decided to tell her I'd seen her open his gate. She was drunk and easy to convince. My biggest regret is letting her carry that guilt—my guilt—for twenty-seven years. I'm sorry, Dimpna Wilde. Dr. Dimpna Wilde. I hope you forgive me. I hope God forgives me. But most of all, I hope my horse forgives me. I hope when I get up to heaven, he'll be the first to greet me, racing through those pearly gates.*

CHAPTER 36

*T*he morning of Johnny O'Reilly's funeral the skies were a surly shade of gray. That didn't stop the elite, the racing community, family and friends, and the gawpers from spilling into the church and filling up the streets. Cars were pulled over to the side of the road, and folks flanked Slea Head Drive for miles to pay their respects. Many wore the O'Reilly racing colors, others held signs with photos of Ruby, and Last Dance, or homemade signs that read: THE DANCING MAN. They held flowered wreaths and ribbons aloft, nodding their respect to the mourners as the line of silent black cars glided by. Bagpipers were among those standing in the streets, crooning out a rich and somber goodbye. Dimpna sat in the back of a limousine, Ben beside her, his hand in hers. Sean, Helen, and Aisling O'Reilly perched across from them, no doubt forced out of their comfort zone by the presence of Dimpna and Ben.

Aisling was continuously sneaking looks at her older brother and proffering a shy smile that Ben returned twofold. Dimpna could only imagine how *that* conversation had gone down. If she hadn't recovered from the shock, she assumed Helen hadn't either. The only person making her objection clear was Róisín O'Reilly. She had refused to ride with them and had pulled out all stops to get Sean to change his mind, but Sean wouldn't budge. Dimpna felt hollowed out and numb. Sean had shown up at the clinic the morning following Tommy's suicide. He had knocked on her door, and when she threw it open, she saw Ben standing there. She embraced him, her face wet with tears. And behind him stood Sean.

"I want you at my father's funeral tomorrow," he said. "Along with your family. And, of course, our son."

Our son. Sean and Dimpna locked eyes. His were defiant. Dimpna fully intended on using her mouth to form the word *no.*

Sean pulled her aside. "I forgive you. It's time for a fresh start."

You forgive me? You forgive me? He hadn't changed at all. He stepped closer and lowered his voice. "I saved your life," he said. "And Ben's." Memories shifted inside her like puzzle pieces locking together, nearly forming a picture.

Ben stepped up.

"Mam. Look at me." It took her a moment, but she did. Her son looked as handsome as ever, a younger version of his father. At times Ben had been troubled, his darkness had always turned inward; he had never been a bully. In fact, standing before her, taking control, he seemed different somehow, more mature. Perhaps the trauma of the last few years had forced him to grow up. She found herself wishing there was an Angelina, hoping he'd meet a love soon. "We all have a lot to discuss. I know that. You know that. Sean knows that. But this is not the time nor the place, and I want you to hear him out."

"Ben," she said, her voice pleading. "Pet." She'd always had a hard time saying no to her son.

He leaned in. "Trust me," he whispered quickly as he kissed the side of her cheek.

And so she had. What Sean had to say was convincing and here they were. Her parents, joined by Donnecha, Sheila, and Paul, followed behind them in yet another limo. Róisín, of course, was situated in the lead car, and the image of her on her own in the expansive back seat was striking: the cold, lone widow. Dimpna could only imagine what her father was thinking and feeling at this moment. He'd started on a medication that calmed him down, but it also muted him and that made Dimpna sad. She hadn't had time to process anything; she seemed stuck on replaying Sean's words. "There's only one way to prove to the people of this town that your family has been cleared of all blame, and that's if you accompany us to the funeral. That will do the trick."

"And Ben?" she asked.

"I want people to know he's my son. I want him to know my side of the family."

She looked at her son. He held her gaze, then leaned in. "Trust me," he whispered again. What was he up to? They would speak privately, he assured her. They would. Everything else aside, Sean was right. Even though the guards had legally cleared her parents, and her brother, suspicion was like a vapor that hung in the air, unseen, ever-clinging, and able to slip through the smallest of cracks. Many folks would have simply thought they got away with murder, and those whispers would have rippled through town. Yes, many had stood with them throughout the entire ordeal, but not all of them. But now, everyone would see. They would see Sean and his family walking side by side with hers. They would see him embracing his son. And that was something. Wasn't it?

"Ashes to ashes, dust to dust." Dimpna loathed having a front-row view of the casket lowering into the ground. After spending twenty-seven years trying to keep Ben cocooned from the O'Reillys, here they were shoulder to shoulder. And she couldn't stop thinking about the case. Cormac O'Brien was here, standing at the back of the crowd. She'd caught his eye a few times. Despite getting accolades in all the papers and press conferences, his expression was more aligned with Dimpna's. Was he having doubts? Did it even matter? It was obvious the officials were thrilled to close this case. Dimpna would bet half of them, maybe more, wouldn't even care if justice had been served. Ironically, the same money that propped Johnny O'Reilly up his entire life had now conspired to prevent a thorough investigation. Another clump of guards was in attendance, and Dimpna could hear them talking among themselves, whispering about the one-armed jockey turned murderer. One minute he'd been there, alive and talking to her, the next he was dead on the floor. With a note explaining everything but the most nagging of questions: *Why?*

There had to be a reason that he killed Johnny O'Reilly *now* and not years ago. And whether or not she wanted to face it, the very last word he'd mouthed to her had been *Ben*. And it was there again, in the steam of the bathroom mirror. That could only mean one thing.

Healy had been the one leaving them messages. He'd been trying to *warn* them. First, he'd tried to warn her father. And Eamon
Wilde might have figured this out if it weren't for his illness. *Forget
everything you think you know . . .*

He'd been following her mother. He left the postcard on
Dimpna's bus: *He knows.* Every chance he could slip away, he'd
been trying to warn them.

He knew Ben was in town. He knew Sean wanted a relationship
with his son. And he knew Johnny O'Reilly had not been thrilled.

Dimpna had also heard talk that Tommy Healy's body would be
off to a crematorium as soon as it was released from the morgue.
There was a sense of relief in town. Justice had been done. A killer
who could not kill again. But it didn't fit. It didn't fit and she knew
it. Just like Cormac O'Brien knew it. Sean's words were swimming
in her brain. *I saved your life. And Ben's.* Had it been mere hours ago
that he'd whispered it to her? How did he save her life? *When?*

The family was tossing red roses into the grave now, coming up
one by one to pay their last respects to The Dancing Man. Sean had
seemed unnaturally calm, even pleasant. Was he happy Tommy was
dead? He'd always been so jealous. Especially when his father gave
Tommy a ruby ring the night before he was to ride Last Dance. . . .

Tommy's face flashed in front of Dimpna. But it wasn't a recent
memory. It was from that long-ago prank. Sean behind Tommy,
strangling him with a green tie. Tommy's body, slumping to the
floor of the barn. Tommy had changed after that. She'd always assumed he changed after Last Dance was killed, but that wasn't the
truth, was it? He changed after that prank. Never looked at her the
same sweet way again. Never rode a horse again. What if her memory was correct? What if he *had* come up behind her when Last
Dance was killed? Tried to pull her off. *With both hands.*

Tommy standing next to her in the barn moments before he was
dead: *You don't know me . . . Not really . . .*

Sean. *I saved your life . . .*

When had he saved her life?

When she witnessed a murder. Immediately after Tommy's body
had slumped to the ground, she'd turned to run. And literally
slammed into Johnny O'Reilly. What would he have done to pre-

vent his only son from being arrested for murder? From the vet's daughter being a witness against him? From the stain of his son's crimes crumpling his empire?

Anything.

I saved your life.

Sean murdered Tommy in a jealous rage. It wasn't a prank. He didn't know Dimpna was there. Until he did. *I saved your life* . . . No murder. No witness.

A prank. He was known for them. And Dimpna was known to fall for them. But he couldn't do it alone. He needed help. *Brendan Healy.*

She could only imagine what it had taken to convince Brendan to pretend to be his dead, one-armed twin. Money, no doubt. Lots of it. It was Brendan who smirked at her across the dining room table hours later in front of the guards. It was Brendan who had hauled her to her feet with both hands. And it was Brendan who leaned into her recently and told her she didn't know him. *Not really.* He must have eventually had his own arm cut off. Who knew when and how? Probably an "accident" with farm equipment. Had they reported an incident, pretended it was one of the farmhands? Or had it all been done in absolute secrecy? She could only imagine what the O'Reillys had offered him to do such a thing. However, at the time he hauled her up in the street, he still had both arms. Tommy had been *born* with only one arm. If Dimpna was correct, and Brendan Healy had severed his to become Tommy, his body would tell the tale. And that body would soon be on the way to the crematorium. Once Healy was ashes, the killer who'd gotten away with it nearly three decades ago, would get away with it again. *Sean.* The preacher was finishing his sermon.

Ben was suddenly at her side, leaning into her. "Mam."

She turned. They hadn't had a moment to speak privately. "Niall Flor is my father," he whispered. "I just need Sean to think I'm falling for his good-guy routine."

Before she could reply, Sean was on the other side of him. She felt her insides twist. Ben was planning on exacting revenge for what Sean had done to her. He was more like his biological father than she cared to admit. She could not let him go up against Sean O'Reilly.

"In the name of the Father, the Son, and the Holy Ghost. Amen."

"Sorry I'm late," Cormac said. "I was officially being given the boot."

Dimpna and Cormac stood outside in the rain, on the beach at Clogher Strand. "I knew you'd come." Dimpna reached into her pocket and handed Cormac the photo of her in the road with Last Dance, as well as the note that had been left on the windshield of her bus. Cormac studied them both. He turned the photo over without her even having to ask. *Forget everything you think you know . . .*

Then he looked at the other one.

He knows.

He frowned, and she had an urge to smooth out his eyebrows with her fingertips. "What is all this?"

"I found the photo in a folder in my father's desk. It was labeled LAST DANCE. It contained all the newspaper articles of the time. And that photo with the message scrawled on the back."

"It's a disturbing photo." He turned it over again. "'Forget everything you think you know.'" He studied her. "Do you have a guess as to what it means?"

Dimpna nodded. "The photo had to have been taken by Healy. He was the one who found me like that."

"Brendan," Cormac said, almost to himself.

Dimpna was gobsmacked. "Yes," she said. "Brendan Healy." She stepped closer. "How did you know?"

"Early in this investigation I tried to track him down. But there was no trace of where he went after he supposedly left Dingle. I contacted a private investigator. He's the best I know. He couldn't find him. *Poof. Gone.*" He stared at the waves, hungrily lapping the shore. "D.S. Neely's father was also a detective sergeant. He remembered Brendan Healy. Called him The Bad Twin. A psychopath. Neely wanted to know why Johnny O'Reilly would remain close to Tommy Healy all these years."

Dimpna nodded. "Because he could ruin them," Dimpna said. "He knew Sean had murdered his twin. Mutually assured destruction."

They held eye contact and she felt a light-headed buzzing go through her. Cormac held up the other note: *He knows.* "And this? What does this mean?"

"I thought it was a note about my son. That's why I didn't tell you about it."

"I don't understand."

"I had only just learned Ben was in town. I kept that from you. I didn't know how to process it."

Cormac nodded. "You also didn't know whether or not he was involved in Johnny's death."

Dimpna swallowed. "It had me worried when I learned my mam gave Ben the Devil card the day of the murder. To ward off temptations, mind you. Temptations like wanting to get to know his father. But I knew my son wasn't capable of murdering his own grandfather. But involved? I knew somehow his appearance in Dingle had triggered a series of events. And now I know that he's only trying to get close to Sean to exact some kind of revenge for what Sean did to me. But he has no idea who he's up against." She could only imagine Sean's rage when he found out the son he's been embracing, the one he killed *his* own father for, to welcome into the fold, was playing him for a fool. Maybe he couldn't help it. Maybe it was in his blood.

Dimpna took a deep breath. "Remember when I told you there was a part of Tommy's suicide note that was a lie?"

Cormac nodded. "The bit about you and Sean making love," he said softly.

She had to bite her lip. "Yes. The night that Last Dance was killed, that wasn't the only horrible thing that happened." He waited. She took a deep breath. "Sean raped me. In the barn." Cormac didn't look surprised. Empathetic, and full of concern. But not surprised. "You knew."

He nodded. "I learned about it during an interview."

Sheila. "I was drunk at the time."

"It's still rape."

"I know. At least I know that now. But it is the reason I thought maybe Healy was right, maybe I did let Last Dance out of the gate."

"Do you still think you did?"

"No. Once Tommy was murdered, Brendan didn't have the skills to even ride a horse, let alone participate in a big race. They needed an explanation as to why 'he' couldn't ride. That's why they killed him. They killed my beloved horse to cover up a murder." She was shaking. The truth was even more horrible than she'd imagined, except this time she knew the truth. It wasn't her fault. It wasn't her fault.

"You never returned to Dingle," Cormac said. "And Sean O'Reilly never knew he had a son." He paused to look at the base of the cliff where they had found The Dancing Man's body. "A secret that his own father had kept from him for twenty-seven years."

Dimpna felt the repercussions of that decision in her bones. It had been a mistake. That did not forgive Sean's actions, but keeping Ben from him had been a mistake. Dimpna would never be able to move on without acknowledging that. Had she told Sean, and Ben for that matter, the truth, that his father was Sean O'Reilly, and he had been conceived from a rape, had she told the guards the truth, maybe Sean would have gone to jail, or maybe his wealth would have shielded him, but either way, there would have been no secrets leaking poison into all of them for all of these years. In the end, Niall had been right. The truth would set her free. "It's not over," she said. "Sean is still a threat. Not just to me, but to Ben, and Saoirse. To everyone."

"The scene," Cormac said, starting to pace. "You think he was targeting all of you?"

"I think he was trying to draw me back to Dingle."

"And here you are." She nodded. "Your son, Ben. He and Sean look like they've grown close."

Dimpna felt a lump in her throat. "Ben and I haven't had much time to talk. But from what he whispered to me at the funeral, I think Ben is playing Sean, trying to find a way to punish him for what he did to me." She stepped forward. "I cannot let that happen. I will not let Sean O'Reilly drive my son to a decision he can never take back." She could not let history repeat itself. This vicious cycle needed to end now.

Cormac turned to her. "I know Sean is our killer. I even sent Aisling into the barn with her shoe untied. It came back in a triple knot. The same knot Sean used to tie the dinghy back up. But I can't crack this case with a shoelace. I need you just as much as you need me. So tell me. What do you need?"

"I know Sean. I know he's not finished."

Cormac held open his arms. "I'm here. I'm on Team Dimpna."

She took a moment to process that. Then nodded. "The pathologist needs to check Healy's arm. Tommy was born without one. If our theory is correct and Brendan severed his—"

Cormac nodded. "I wondered why there was a rush to the crematorium." He held up his mobile. "I need to call the state pathologist. Maybe we'll get lucky and she still has the body." He walked away, his shoulders hunched against the summer wind. Waves crashed on shore. She thought of Saoirse Griffin swimming to shore in these treacherous waters. In the dark. While Sean O'Reilly was dragging his father's body to the beach . . . She wasn't the only one in danger. Saoirse was a loose end. And Sean O'Reilly was not the type to overlook loose ends.

Cormac was making his way back to her. He saw the look on her face. "What's wrong?"

"Saoirse Griffin," she said. "She's not safe."

Cormac glanced at the waves as if he too was imagining the girl swimming to shore. "The body is en route to the funeral home. It just left the morgue."

"Which funeral home?"

He raised an eyebrow. "Morton's?"

Dimpna nearly laughed. "I know who else's help we're going to need."

"You do?"

She nodded. "We're going to distract them with a customer they've been wooing for quite some time apparently." She headed for the car park as she took out her phone to dial her mam. "Your ride or mine?"

She pressed the gas pedal nearly as far as it would go, slowing only when other cars were nearby. Cormac had been worried that if anyone saw his red Toyota headed to the funeral home that it would set off more alarms than Dimpna's vehicle. After all, she might be racing to an emergency animal call. "My mam is calling them right now, and if I know her, she'll be able to stall them with enough questions."

"Even if we stop the cremation in time and confirm that the deceased is Brendan Healy, they're just going to claim Brendan is the murderer," Cormac said.

"I know," Dimpna said. "We need a full confession from Sean O'Reilly."

"If you have a plan, now's the time to share it," Cormac said.

"It's not just your help I'm going to need," Dimpna said. "We need Saoirse Griffin to tell us everything that happened the night she snuck onto the yacht."

"Good luck with that," Cormac said. "Paul Byrne ruined my attempts to speak with her."

"I know," Dimpna said. "That's why he's my next call."

"Are you going to enlist the entire town?" Cormac said off the cuff.

"If I'm going to pull this off," she said, "I'm going to need a fair number of them." Not the O'Reillys or anyone in their orbit. Not the politicians. Not the guards. But the regular, everyday folk. This was Dingle. They would help. Because the killer, and his poisonous family, was an outlier. Dingle was made of far greater folks. And there was no one group she trusted more in a crisis than her friends and neighbors.

"There it is," Cormac said, pointing to an ambulance pulling into the funeral home. "I'm going to need a little help of my own." He took out his mobile and dialed. "Neely," he said. "It's Cormac. I need a favor."

CHAPTER 37

Sean emerged from his truck and gave a half wave to Dimpna. It was early and the Valley of the Mad had yet to be taken over by hikers. Sean glanced around, uneasy. "Where's Ben?"

"He's on his way." Dimpna kept her voice upbeat. She didn't want him sensing danger.

His eyes flicked to her bus. "No dogs?"

"Just us." Sean looked around as if he didn't believe her. "Ben will be here in thirty minutes. I wanted a chance to speak with you privately." The Valley of the Mad. Where, based on Sean's order, Healy had tracked Saoirse down and terrified her into silence. It was sickening what money could buy.

"Why are we meeting here?" He was definitely on edge. It wasn't easy, pulling pranks on people. People always had their guard up.

"It's private. I don't want the eyes of the town on us."

"It's a little late for that, isn't it?"

She laughed. "I like it here. I've missed this valley."

He shrugged. "I don't have long." He didn't trust her.

She walked farther into the valley, her wellies sinking into the muck, made even softer by the recent storms. She wanted her pack with her, but Sean would have felt vulnerable. She needed to soften him up as much as possible.

"I know you must be very angry with me." It was easier to talk as they walked; she didn't have to see the rage in his eyes.

"The mother of my *son.*" There it was. The fury. "Do you know how that feels? Can you even imagine? To find out you have a son? And that you've missed the first twenty-seven years of his life?"

"You raped me."

"That's not true."

She whirled around, forcing him to come to an abrupt stop. "You know it is, Sean. You know."

He sighed. Kicked a rock. "That was a long time ago." He shook his head. "Is that the story you told Ben?" *Story.* She hated him. "I saved your parents. And Donnecha. I gave them their lives back."

"I know that. Why do you think I'm here? I want us to bury this. For good. All of it."

"That doesn't sound like the Dimpna Wilde I know."

"That's because you don't know me as a mother. But trust me. I'd do anything for Ben. Anything."

She started walking again. This was it. He would either follow her, or he would turn and go. If he left now, he'd be a free man. Her heart thudded in her chest as she waited.

"What exactly do you have in mind?" Sean asked after a moment, striding right behind her.

"I want to repay the favor."

"What favor?"

They reached the area where Dimpna had seen Saoirse peeking out from behind a hill. She'd come here to hide, but the man with one arm had found her. A loyal soldier following orders from Sean. Only, this time he had been playing both sides, and in the end, he had tried to warn them. And that was something. She stopped. This was it. The big lie. The prank. Would it work? "You said you saved my life."

He shook his head. "I didn't mean it literally."

"You did. I know exactly what you meant."

He ran his hand through his hair and looked around before crossing his arms. "You think?"

"Do you know that inspector is trying to stop Healy from being cremated."

He dropped his arms. "What are you on about?"

"He wants to see his arm."

"That's sick."

"Tommy Healy was born without an arm."

"I know that."

"Brendan Healy on the other hand was born with both arms. If he now has only one, a state pathologist would be able to tell whether he was born without one, or whether it was severed later in life."

"There's no autopsy. It was ruled a suicide."

"Until the inspector tried to reopen it."

"You brought me all the way out here, when that business is going on?"

"Relax. I only said he *tried*. He's off the case. Everyone is calling him a nutter."

Sean exhaled. "I have to get back." He took a few steps away.

"That is Brendan's body they're about to cremate, isn't it?"

He whirled around. "Shut. Your. Gob."

"I'm trying to help. I go everywhere. Hear and see everything. You know that. People overlook me."

"Nobody overlooks Dr. Dimpna Wilde." Sarcasm dripped from his voice.

"You did. Once. When you were standing behind Tommy Healy, strangling him to death with a tie."

He covered the space between them in one swift move. "You're up to something." His big hands were all over her, trying to pat her down. She wanted to kick him in the shins, but she couldn't let him find the vial on her. If she did, it was all over. She held up her hands.

"Stop. I'm trying to prove that I'm on your side. For Ben." He stopped just short of finding the vial in the small satchel underneath her shirt.

"You think what? I murdered Tommy Healy, and then got his twin to pretend to be him for the past twenty-seven years? Even convinced him to cut off his own arm?"

"Didn't you?"

His eyes narrowed into slits. "Sounds crazy to me."

"It was crazy enough to save my life."

He shrugged. A faint, but noticeable, shrug. Sean never could resist taking credit. "That wasn't the only time you saved my life," Dimpna said.

"Say again?"

"Remember the stowaway who was on the boat the night your father was killed?"

"Saoirse Griffin," he said. "I heard about it, alright."

"It wasn't her," Dimpna said. "It was me."

He drew close once more. "What the fuck are you on about?"

"I was on the yacht looking for my brother."

"You weren't even in town."

"I was. I found out Ben had been lying to me. That he was in Dingle with my brother."

"I would have known."

"I told you. I can be overlooked when I want to be."

"It was Saoirse Griffin."

"I heard someone come in. I hid in the small closet behind the bench on the right-hand side. I knocked over cleaning supplies." Paul had come through and talked to Saoirse. Dimpna could only pray she was getting the details correct. The Devil, after all, was in them. Sean's head was tilted. He was listening intently, comparing her story to his memories. "Your father came on the yacht first. He picked up the tarot card from the floor. Ben had been in there earlier to meet with you and dropped it. Your father was standing there, holding the card in his hand, trying to figure out where it came from, what it meant. That's when you came in."

"Is that so?"

"You actually saved me a third time."

His hands curled into fists. His eyes darted around. "What do you mean?"

"He saw me. There's a little gap in the door. He must have caught me peeking through. He had just taken a step toward me when you came in." When Saoirse had relayed this part, it had given Dimpna goose bumps. How close she'd come to being another one of their victims.

"No."

"You came up from behind. Wearing gloves. The purple vial was in your left hand. I almost gasped when I saw it. Gave myself away. You dabbed a Q-tip into the vial of Immobolin." Sean clamped his lips together. "Your father jerked around. Looked at you. Slapped his hand over his neck where he felt the wetness."

"Shut up."

"He said a single word."

"I said stop."

"'Why'. He just wanted to know why." Sean closed his eyes. "Silly of him to ask, wasn't it? He knew it was about Ben. When Ben came to town, Brendan felt threatened, didn't he?"

"He told my father if we recognized Ben into the family that he would go the guards and tell them I murdered Tommy. He didn't care if he went down too. I thought he was bluffing, but my father was freaking out. He said we had to do something. I couldn't take the chance that he would hurt Ben." He stared at her, his pupils large, his lips curled in a snarl. "Because that's what fathers do, Dimpna. Fathers protect their sons."

"I'm proud of you," Dimpna said. "I know you're a good father."

"Bullshit."

"I know it now. I've seen how you are with Aisling. And you saved Ben. You don't think I get that?"

"You've known all this time and you . . . what? Didn't tell the police? That doesn't make any sense."

"I didn't do it for you. I did it for Ben." She forced herself to touch his arm. "He wants to get to know you."

He stepped away from her, covered his mouth with his hands, and began to pace. "I feel like you're messing with me. It was Saoirse Griffin on that yacht."

"After he was on the floor, you started the yacht. I didn't have time to run."

"Shut up." He began to pace, running his hands through his thick hair.

"You had the tarp waiting in the back room along with the stones, and the board that you used as a ramp."

"Why did the guards think it was Saoirse Griffin?"

"She was at the harbor that night and she didn't come home. They found small prints on the hillside at Clogher Strand. But she never got on that yacht. It was just bad luck that she had a history of breaking into boats and ran away that night."

"Why would she do that?"

"Because it was her birthday. And her mam thought it was an unlucky number. Thirteen." Ironically, it had turned out to be an unlucky night for the girl. "I saw you taking your father's body to shore in the dinghy. He was in a black body bag. The kind you use for horses."

"You brought me out to the middle of nowhere to confront me about killing my own father?" He came closer to her, towering over her. "That's the dumbest thing I've ever heard of someone doing. And you, Dr. Wilde, are not dumb."

"Then what am I doing here?"

"It would be very easy to kill you. I don't need a tie. Or Immobolin. I would just use my hands." He held his hands out, as if to show her. Scare her.

"There's no need to kill me. I'm on your side. Team Sean." She forced enthusiasm into her voice.

"I want to believe you, Dimp. I do." He shook his head. "You're not going to throw another bag of shite at me, are ya?"

"That was you?"

"Guilty." He pawed the ground with his boot. "I wasn't trying to scare you—I was just trying to get up the nerve to talk to you. I'm tired of the past. I wanted to start fresh."

"You painted 'Liar' across my bus."

He looked away. "That was impulsive. And you deserved it."

She bit her lip. "Your father lied to you as well. I can only imagine how that felt."

"No, *Doc,* you cannot."

"It enraged you."

"You're twisting things. I didn't kill my father out of some kind of impulsive rage."

"It was a measured act."

"The minute Ben came into town, my father was in a state. He went from defensive, to sorry, to worried, to downright manic."

"I don't understand. Ben knew nothing about Tommy Healy. Why was your father so worried?"

"Because of Brendan. You have no idea what it feels like when the great Johnny O'Reilly is no longer enamored with you. Brendan heard my father and I talking—he realized Ben was my son. I admit—this next part is my fault. I told my father in no uncertain terms that Ben would be recognized as a full heir of the O'Reilly estate. I even took the ruby ring off Brendan. Told him it belonged to my son. I shouldn't have done that. He started blackmailing us, saying that if Ben was welcomed into the fold, that he would tell. And then do you know what he did? The man I called my father? The one who kept my son secret for twenty-seven years?"

"No," Dimpna said. "What did he do?"

"He took Brendan's side. Wanted nothing to do with Ben." He gave a wry laugh. "I was never good enough. And then—his own grandson wasn't good enough."

"Where did you get the Immobilon?"

Sean laughed. "Now that's a funny story."

"You have my attention."

"Your father gave it to my father. He was in one of his paranoid moods. Said Sheila Maguire was stealing his meds and he didn't want it in the wrong hands. It was your father who took the Release, the syringe, and that purple vial of death and gave it to my father." Sean squeezed his eyes shut for a moment and shook his head. "Terrible, terrible thing, to lose your mind. My father knew what Immobolin was, of course. He'd grown up during the times vets used to whip it up. He knew how dangerous it could be. He brought it to me. Showed me the purple vial. That's when I knew. What had to be done. What *I* had to do."

Genuine tears filled her eyes and her throat constricted. "You tried to frame my parents."

He laughed then, a genuine laugh which made it all that much creepier. "No," he said. "I framed your parents, to bring *you* back home. I knew it had to be something big to get you here." He opened his arms. "And here you are."

Dimpna reached into her handbag and brought out a set of plastic gloves.

He frowned. "What are those for?"

She put on the gloves and removed the purple vial from her satchel. She uncorked it as he watched. This was the one part of the plan she'd kept from Cormac. The one part that was all hers. And it had been a long time coming. She splashed it on Sean's face.

"What the fuck?" He slapped his hand over the wetness. "What have you done?"

She removed the last piece in her plan, a vial of Revivon and a syringe. She held it up. "This is the antidote. We're talking a matter of seconds."

He eyed the purple vial, discarded on the ground. "The police have that vial."

"My father kept two of everything."

"What do you want?" His voice cracked. "Please. Dimpna. I have a *daughter.* She's only eight years of age."

"Say it."

"Say what? I killed Tommy? You already guessed. You're right, okay?"

"He sat right across from me at your dining room table shortly afterward, smirking. How did I not notice he had both arms?"

Sean shook his head as if she was a foolish girl. "I taped it to his side. He really got into the spirit of it."

"He does all that for you, and you end up killing Brendan anyway." Dimpna hoped the disdain in her voice would rattle him even further.

"He didn't do it for me. He did it for money. And because that's just the kind of lad Brendan Healy was." She'd hit her mark, the panic in his voice was ratcheting up, Sean O'Reilly was unraveling. He reached for the Revivon, his hand shaking violently.

Dimpna squelched a nibble of pity and held the precious vial at bay. "Lunge for it again and I'll spill it," she threatened. "Then you're dead."

"What more do you want?" His voice was desperate, clawing.

"Say it."

Sean's face contorted with impatience and rage. "Say what?"

"You murdered Brendan."

Sean's eyes were glued to the vial of Revivon and sweat trickled down his face. "I murdered Brendan." He reached for it again, his hand shaking.

"Who else did you murder?"

His head jerked around. "Are they watching?" He took a step toward her, his hands outstretched as if he was going to wrap them around her neck and squeeze.

"If you kill me, I won't be able to deliver the antidote, and you only have seconds."

"I killed my father."

"And?"

"Fuck!"

"And?"

"I raped you."

"Again."

"I raped you. But you fucking deserved it." There it was, the hateful, evil Sean.

"Sean O'Reilly, you're under arrest." Cormac came out from behind the remains of the stone house, flanked by D.S. Neely and a whole posse of guards.

"Give me the antidote!" Sean screamed. "Give me the antidote, you fucking bitch."

Dimpna knelt, picked up the purple vial, and drank from it as Sean stared at her, wild-eyed and terrified. "It's only water," she said. "Just not the holy kind."

CHAPTER 38

One month later

THE CLINIC WAS CHOCKABLOCK. THEY HAD A DUCK WITH A SPLINTED-UP leg, a calf on intravenous fluids, and a dog under anesthesia for a tooth extraction. Her father was shadowing her, every once in a while offering advice or corrections, but often soothing the animals with his calm voice. Niamh's laughter and chatter rang through the crowded waiting room as she kept the clients and their pets in as good of spirits as possible. Patrick was really settling into his groove, still a favorite among the ladies. Dimpna was looking forward to the end of her shift, dinner with Ben. He was leaving Dingle; he'd been accepted to university in Galway. He was ditching finance and going to study animation. It had taken him awhile to have a proper sit-down where they'd attempted to hash out their shared trauma. It wasn't perfection, but it was progress. And then there was Cormac.

They were going to meet up again tonight for a session. He'd been offered a position at the Garda Station in Dingle, and he'd accepted it. Nothing romantic had transpired between them, but she could no longer deny the attraction, and she knew he felt it too. They were both so busy. Demanding jobs, and parents. His mam had ALS and she would be living with him. Dimpna was currently in the family home as well, helping to keep an eye on her da. But she and Cormac had been playing a regular session together in Tralee, and for now they were funneling their attraction through their music. Listening, adapting, riffing, mingling notes together. They had their favorites: "Galway Girl"; "Dirty Old Town"; "Irish Rover"; "The Rocky Road to Dublin"; "Black Velvet Band" . . . Dimpna loved getting lost in the music, allowing it to lift her up, up and away. Dingle felt vibrant again—colorful, upbeat, and ever-singing.

Before heading out, she stopped at the reception desk. "Niamh?" Today there was a bright orange flower in her hair and her nails were electric blue.

"Yes, Dr. Wilde?"

"I'm not trying to be nosy."

"Go on."

"I saw something you'd written in your notebook and—I have to admit I'm curious."

"Yikes." From Niamh's expression it was clear that she feared whatever was coming out of Dimpna's gob next.

"In big red letters you wrote 'I hate him.'"

Niamh looked stunned for a moment and threw her head back in laugh. "Right, so," she said. "I remember that."

"Was it my father?"

"It was the inspector."

Dimpna hadn't expected this. "Inspector O'Brien?"

Niamh nodded. "I suppose you might give me the boot for telling you this, but early on he came in here and charmed me into keeping an eye on what went on in the clinic."

"I see."

"I'm so, so sorry. Am I sacked?"

"No. I'm glad you keep an eye on things around here. But just out of curiosity—how did he charm you?"

She waggled her finger at Dimpna. Dimpna came around and Niamh sheepishly opened a drawer. It overflowed with chocolates. "It's basically a lifetime supply," she said. "How could I say no?"

"Indeed."

The bell dinged, the door burst open, and a young man flew in. "Doc, Doc, you gotta help."

"What's the story?"

"I just hit a fox. He's hurt real bad. I can't kill him, and I can't stand to see him suffer. Can you help? Do you have experience with wild animals?"

Niamh stood. "Does she have experience with wild animals?" Niamh handed Dimpna a chocolate from her drawer, like a mammy soothing a toddler before bad news. "Of course, she does, pet," Niamh said. "She's Dr. Wilde, isn't she?"

ACKNOWLEDGMENTS

Thank you to my editor, John Scognamiglio, my publicist, Larissa Ackerman, and my agent, Evan Marshall. Thank you to Corinna Galvin. Thank you to all the veterinarians who write memoirs and work so hard for animals, but especially a big thank-you to Irish veterinarian Austin Donnelly, author of *Whiskers, Feathers & Fur: Veterinary Tales,* which I highly recommend giving a read. Austin, your input was invaluable for this book. Finally, a shout-out to my Irish friends I originally visited Dingle with—James and Annmarie Sheedy, Eileen Collins, and Kevin Collins.